CREAT...

Liz's guests were waiting for Alan Longchase.

Of all her artists, he had that indefinable star quality, a magnetic appeal that drew people into his orbit. When he walked into a room, the occupants always seemed to sense his presence before they saw him. Good looks made him a head-turner. Charisma made him memorable. Talent made him a giant.

Unless Alan arrived soon, the opening was going to be the biggest failure in the gallery's history. The thousands of dollars spent on invitations, advertising, airfare and hotel rooms for out-of-town artists, to say nothing of the caterer, the food, the cases of champagne, the wining and dining of prospective buyers, would be a total loss. Considering the half a million Liz had just borrowed, she couldn't afford a loss tonight. In fact, it was going to take record profits to keep the gallery out of the red this season.

But the risk, the sleepless nights of planning and worry, would not be in vain if Alan arrived – no, she silently amended, when he arrived and she announced her plans. She could hardly wait to see the look on his face when she told her guests she would be opening a Manhattan gallery devoted exclusively to Alan's work. The idea had come to her during the sleepless night's she'd spent wondering how to bridge the chasm created by their quarrel.

ALEXANDRA THORNE

Creative URGES

NEW ENGLISH LIBRARY
Hodder and Stoughton

First published in Great Britain in 1991
by New English Library Paperbacks

*A New English Library paperback
original*

Printed and bound in Great Britain for
Hodder and Stoughton Paperbacks, a
division of Hodder and Stoughton Ltd.,
Mill Road, Dunton Green, Sevenoaks,
Kent TN13 2YA. (Editorial Office: 47
Bedford Square, London, WC1B 3DP)
by Clays Ltd, St Ives plc. Typeset by
Hewer Text Composition Services,
Edinburgh.

British Library C.I.P.
Thorne, Alexandra
  Creative urges.
  I. Title
  813 [F]

ISBN 0-450-51335-1

Creative
URGES

1

OCTOBER 16, 1988

Liz Kant dressed for the coming evening as carefully as a gladiator girding for combat. Hooking a garter belt over her slender hips, she pulled on a pair of gossamer stockings, stepped into a teddy and smoothed the fabric over her breasts, unaware of the innate sensuality of her actions. Her mind was on more important matters.

Slipping into high-heeled sandals, she moved to her dressing table, sat down and surveyed herself dispassionately in the mirror. Liz was a knockout, knew it and used it without having any conceit about it. The credit belonged to her gene pool. She had never permitted her startling beauty to define who she was. Just past forty, most people thought she was five years younger. But this evening, tiny lines around her mouth betrayed the strain of the last few weeks. Worry clouded her blue-green eyes and she was exceptionally pale. With good reason.

Her carefully constructed existence was in jeopardy. Although she would be hosting the Kant Gallery's tenth anniversary exhibition tonight, there was more at stake than the success or failure of a single Scottsdale art show. She had triumphed over her past. Now she was gambling her future, her hard-won financial security, and the only love she'd ever known, on this evening's outcome. A single throw of the dice – winner take all.

Liz Kant intended to win.

Five hours earlier, with the show ready for viewing and

customers arriving for highly-coveted, by-appointment-only previews that labelled them important collectors, she realized there was nothing more she could do to assure the opening's success. She would be better served by going home and trying to rest, leaving the gallery in the capable care of her assistant, Rick Mason.

"I don't care who's still here at five," she told him on her way out. "Invite them to come back to have some champagne with us this evening, and close up. The caterer needs a couple of hours to get ready. You know what a prima donna Henri can be."

"Sure thing. I'll see you back here at seven," Rick had replied, giving her his best dimpled smile before heading toward a newly-arrived female customer.

The woman was slender and well-dressed, Liz noted, but she had a pinched, anxious look – a look that said she didn't trust her own taste when it came to purchasing a work of art that cost five figures. Liz had trained her entire staff to watch out for that look, and now she paused in the gallery's bevelled-glass doors to scrutinize the results of that training.

The customer circled the first of the gallery's seven rooms warily, her humming-bird glance darting here and there. When she finally came to a halt in front of a painting, Rick appeared by her side, his timing impeccable. "You have a very discerning eye," he said, moving in to make his preliminary pitch. "That's the best oil in the show. I'd be happy to answer any questions you may have about the artist."

So far, so good, Liz thought.

The customer turned away from the painting long enough to take in Rick's blond, well-tanned, all-American good looks. An approving smile blossomed on her face. "Who is the painter?" she asked.

"Alan Longchase, *the* Alan Longchase," Rick replied, lowering his tone as if he were speaking of something holy.

2

"Oh, I've heard about him. He's the famous Apache artist, isn't he . . . ?" the woman's voice trailed off.

Liz made her exit before Rick responded. An approving smile curving her full lips as she crossed the sun-burnished Arizona sidewalk to her Rolls. Rick had learned his lessons well. He was the best "street man" in Scottsdale's half a hundred art emporiums, almost as important to her gallery's continuing success as any of the artists she represented.

But no one was more important to the gallery – or to her – than Alan Longchase. The fact that the buyer had recognized Alan's name was a given. Thanks to Liz's carefully calculated ten-year publicity campaign, Alan was as visible a figure on the landscape of contemporary south-western art as Georgia O'Keefe had been in her lifetime. Alan had an exceptional gift. He painted with his soul and, although he usually portrayed native Americans, his canvasses spoke volumes about the universality of the human condition.

He has, Liz thought . . . no, she silently amended . . . *we have* a glorious future.

Scottsdale Road was a bumper-to-bumper mass of cars when she turned onto it from Main Street. Other locals might curse the traffic jams that occurred with predictable regularity in mid October. She welcomed them. They signalled the returning horde of wealthy winter visitors. Arriving from colder climes, boasting addresses such as Sutton Place, Cold Spring Harbor, Deer Park and Beacon Hill, they opened their second homes and their bulging wallets, indulging themselves in an orgy of vacation spending.

So Liz happily ignored the honking horns, the muted growl of straining engines, and thought only of the coming evening, anticipating a standing-room-only crowd and a sold-out show. She arrived at her Camelback Mountain estate twenty minutes later, with plenty of time for a long soak before Dante arrived to do her hair.

3

Like all great craftsmen, Dante had a talent for simplicity. He had done his usual masterful job. Now, glancing at her bedroom's mirrored walls, she approvingly surveyed the mane of deep auburn hair that fell in an uncomplicated sweep to the top of her shoulders. No matter how vigorously she shook her head, the perfection of the cut assured that each hair would ultimately return to its proper place. Dante was a genius with scissors and a blow-dryer, worth every penny of his exorbitant fees. And, if the gallery's sales were as large tonight as they had been in the past, there would be no question about her ability to go on paying those fees, despite the fact that she had just mortgaged her gallery to the hilt.

She applied a last expert stroke of mascara to the thick lashes fringing her eyes and glossed her lips. Then she rose and walked to the closet where a new Karl Lagerfeld gown hung on a padded satin hanger. The dress, a blue-green beaded mousseline, was a perfect foil for the turquoise and diamond necklace Alan Longchase had given her six weeks before.

Alan. He was so much a part of her that she felt the pain of their recent quarrel with every breath. He couldn't go on ignoring her existence after she told him what she had done, the risk she was prepared to take for him. A half-million-dollar risk.

Suddenly, Liz's eyes filled. Damn. She mustn't cry and ruin her make-up. She had wept for hours eleven weeks ago and it hadn't made her feel better. If only she'd told Alan the truth about her past long ago. But she hadn't been able to muster up the courage, and now she didn't know if she ever would. Instead of truth, she would offer the realization of a long-held dream as balm to heal the wounds they had inflicted on each other. The peace offering had to work. Alan had to come back to her. She couldn't imagine going on without him.

Taking the dress from the closet, Liz shook it as if to dispel the unhappy thoughts that crowded her mind. She

4

pulled the delicate fabric over her head, careful not to upset her make-up, and returned to the closet to retrieve the necklace from the wall safe. She could still remember the empty feeling she had when she put it there the morning after she and Alan argued.

Then her hand stopped in mid air. *Argue*. What a feeble word to describe what had actually happened. She and Alan had wounded each other as cruelly as Aztec priests violating living victims.

They hadn't spoken since.

How many times in the intervening weeks had she been on the verge of telephoning him to beg his forgiveness? But pride had stopped her. Humility wasn't her style. Any more than it was Alan's. He was as fiercely proud as any of his warrior ancestors.

Clasping his gift around the slender column of her neck, she walked to her bedroom door and opened it, calling out, "Rosita, I need help with my zipper."

"Coming," Rosita replied from somewhere nearby. Rosita's domain, the kitchen, was in another wing. Liz knew the housekeeper must have been waiting near the master suite hallway in anticipation of being summoned.

Rosita hurried through the bedroom door seconds later, her large brown eyes widening in appreciation as she looked at Liz. "*¡Qué bonita! Muy hermosa*," she said, lapsing into Spanish as she did when emotion overcame her.

"Do you really like the dress?"

Rosita Vasquez was as close to family as Liz had in Arizona. The housekeeper was small-boned, short and whipcord thin, her face lined by fifty years exposure to the Grand Chimeca's unforgiving sunshine. But her eyes were merry, set deep in laugh lines. She had come to work for Liz a decade earlier. Their unlikely friendship was based on mutual respect. Despite their cultural differences, they shared a common bond. Both their characters had been tempered in the forge of hardship.

Now Rosita nodded her head so emphatically that the tiny gold crosses dangling from her earlobes swayed wildly. "The dress is beautiful, but not as beautiful as you." Carefully slidding the zipper that ran up the back of Liz's dress, Rosita added, "Ramon's out front. Ay, ay, that one thinks he's the king of the road when he drives the limousine." She paused, a frown deepening the grooves on either side of her mouth. "Will Señor Alan be at the gallery tonight?"

Rosita was the only person who knew about the argument. She couldn't have helped overhearing its fury. Eleven weeks before, after Alan slammed out of the house, Rosita had knocked on Liz's door, asking, "Are you all right?"

When Liz hadn't answered, Rosita had slipped into the room. Seeing Liz's stricken face, she had rushed to the kitchen to brew a pot of herbal tea whose efficacy she guaranteed as a panacea for troubled souls.

"Of course he'll be there," Liz responded, comforted by the certainty of Alan's professionalism. He wouldn't let a lover's quarrel interfere with his career, she reassured herself.

From the first time he had walked into the gallery almost ten years before, they had been in daily contact. As his master dealer, she had been in charge of every facet of Alan's career. He'd come to her a total unknown, and now he was one of the most famous artists in the country.

Considering all they meant to each other, she still had trouble dealing with the fact that he had shipped his paintings to the gallery for the tenth anniversary show, rather than delivering them in person as was his custom. Hadn't he realized how much that would hurt her? Didn't he care?

The questions continued to reverberate through Liz's mind as she left her home. Would Alan really show up tonight? She wished she could be sure. All she knew for certain was that his absence could prove disastrous.

*

An hour after Liz Kant opened the gallery's bevelled glass doors, she was still stationed there greeting new arrivals. Her employees bustled around supervising the caterer's staff, making sure all the guests were kept liberally supplied with champagne and hors d'oeuvres.

Out-of-town collectors, critics, society columnists, artists and a few bonafide celebrities mingled in the crowded rooms. Twenty feet away, Archer Harrison was discussing one of her sculptures with a cluster of admirers. Archer was the rarest of breeds, an independently wealthy woman consumed by a passionate desire to excel as an artist. Although Archer always looked every inch the well-bred aristocrat, she had a wonderful way of talking to people on their own level without seeming condescending or pretentious. Poised, intelligent, and always gracious, she was a real asset to the gallery.

Making a quarter turn, Liz glanced through a vaulted arch into an adjacent room where Maryann Van Kamp was hugging a wall as if she hoped it would swallow her up. Looking a little too artsy-craftsy in a floor-length peasant skirt and a handwoven shawl, Maryann had a glass of champagne in her hand and a smile frozen on her face. She was chain-smoking and maintained a white-knuckled clutch on an ashtray. Of all Liz's current stable of artists, Maryann Van Kamp had the slimmest reputation and the least professional training when Liz had taken her on. She was virtually a self-taught painter.

But Liz had never required her artists to have a Bachelor of Arts degree or a diploma from a place like Pratt or the Chicago Art Institute. The only thing Liz insisted on, the single trait all her artists must share, was a burning desire to be the best.

Lawrence Lee, who had arrived promptly at seven, had that quality in abundance. With his shoulder-length mop of silver hair and his flowing beard, he looked a personality to be reckoned with. His advent, with his equally talented wife, Mary Wyant, on his arm, had created a brief stir.

7

As had the entrance of the famous Yaqui lithographer, Amado Pena, fifteen minutes later. But the excitement had quickly dissipated.

Liz's guests were waiting for Alan Longchase.

Of all her artists, he had that indefinable star quality, a magnetic appeal that drew people into his orbit. When he walked into a room, the occupants always seemed to sense his presence before they saw him. Good looks made him a head-turner. Charisma made him memorable. Talent made him a giant.

His absence was upsetting the opening's fragile chemistry, the delicate blend of art and haut monde that could produce a smashing chef d'oeuvre, or fall as flat as an ill-timed soufflé. Liz glanced anxiously at her watch, uncomfortably aware that tonight was turning out to be the soufflé.

Instead of the usual boisterous shouts of greeting as the art world's movers and shakers met, there was a subdued drone of conversation. Worse still, Liz's couturier-gowned, black-tie-garbed guests weren't buying. They moved from art work to art work, never settling in front of any one piece long enough to give Liz's staff a chance to react.

Even Rick seemed anxious as he approached her. "From the looks of things," he said under his breath, "I think it's time we started spiking the champagne. I haven't been able to close a single big sale."

"It's early."

"It's eight o'clock! This time last year, I'd made three hundred thousand dollars in sales." A frown marred his even features.

"Instead of bothering me, why don't you get back to work and try harder," Liz snapped back.

Rick retreated into the crowd, but not before she saw the wounded look in his eyes. She hadn't meant to take it out on him. The lack of sales wasn't his fault. He was doing his best.

8

Unless Alan arrived soon, the opening was going to be the biggest failure in the gallery's history. The thousands of dollars spent on invitations, advertising, airfare and hotel rooms for out-of-town artists, to say nothing of the caterer, the food, the cases of champagne, the wining and dining of prospective buyers, would be a total loss. Considering the half a million Liz had just borrowed, she couldn't afford a loss tonight. In fact, it was going to take record profits to keep the gallery out of the red this season.

But the risk, the sleepless nights of planning and worry, would not be in vain if Alan arrived – no, she silently amended, when he arrived and she announced her plans. She could hardly wait to see the look on his face when she told her guests she would be opening a Manhattan gallery devoted exclusively to Alan's work. The idea had come to her during the sleepless nights she'd spent wondering how to bridge the chasm created by their quarrel.

She was reluctant to move away from the vicinity of the front doors until he arrived. But she felt conspicuous waiting by them once the flow of new arrivals slowed to a trickle. Seeing the Lundgrens, major collectors from New York, eyeing one of Alan's paintings, she headed for them. Howard Lundgren, having made millions in sanitary landfills, liked to boast that he was turning dross, the refuse he buried, into gold, the art he so avidly collected.

"It's so nice to see you again," Liz said. "I hope you had a pleasant trip."

Howard was a short, beefy man with hot, acquisitive eyes. He had an impressive Dunn and Bradstreet rating, and his wife, Skip, dressed to show it. Tonight she was wearing a pouff-skirted Krizia that would have looked divine on a younger, more slender woman. A fur draped her shoulders in spite of the room's warmth.

"Skip, darling, you look fabulous, as always," Liz enthused, before turning her attention to Howard. "How like you it is to zero in on the best painting in the

9

entire show." To her credit, she made the line sound fresh.

"It's damn good. But I've already got three Longchases at home. I'm not sure I should buy another one. Besides, you know how I operate. I like to talk to an artist, get his personal view of a specific painting before I take out my cheque book." Howard stopped to scan the room. "So where the hell is Longchase? When I called from New York, you told me he'd be here."

"I'm expecting him any minute." Liz's pulse fluttered in her throat and her mouth felt dry.

"That Apache's got a *je ne sais quoi*, a . . ." Skip seemed to be searching for the right word.

"Great buns, isn't that what you're always telling me he's got?" Howard glared at her. "I swear, the only reason you come to Scottsdale is to see Longchase."

"Howie, you're embarrassing me," Skip reprimanded.

As was his custom, Howard ignored his wife. "If you'll excuse us, Liz, we haven't had dinner yet."

Liz barely kept from giving them an astonished blink. The Lundgrens flew in from New York once or twice a year to attend her openings, and Howard liked to get his money's worth. As long as Dom Perignon flowed and caviar was on hand, so were he and Skip. They never left early – and never without making a five- or six-figure purchase.

Forcing herself to smile, she replied, "Why don't you come back after you eat. I'm sure Alan will be here then, and I know he'll be devastated if he misses you."

"We'll see," Howard equivocated.

Liz walked them to the door and they were gone with a final flutter of Skip's false eyelashes and genuine Russian sables.

Feeling as if the walls of the gallery were closing in on her, Liz stepped outside. Would Alan never get there? Her emotions see-sawed between anticipatory excitement and dashed hopes. Taking a deep breath of cool night air, she walked to the curb and glanced up at the sky. The cold white light of the stars failed to soothe her. They were so remote, so uncaring; never once had they granted the wishes she made on them. There was no point in wishing on them now.

Although she tried to resist the impulse, she glanced up and down Main Street, hoping against hope to see Alan's familiar figure striding toward her. The avenue was crowded with slow-moving traffic, the diagonal parking spaces were full. A steady stream of pedestrians strolled along the sidewalk, peering through the gallery's large show windows at the well-dressed throng inside.

From their vantage point, the opening probably looked like an unqualified success. But Liz could feel failure hovering over her shoulder like a carrion-eating bird waiting its turn at a kill. Taking a last deep breath, she turned to go back inside the building.

And then she saw him.

Relief melted the chunk of ice in her stomach, and she began to plan what she would say when they were face to face. He was half a block away, walking towards the gallery with the unconscious grace that marked his every movement, his shoulder-length ebony hair swept back from his face by the breeze of his rapid stride. Fortunately, he hadn't seen her yet. She couldn't let him catch her outside, looking like a lovelorn teenager hoping to run into the star quarterback coming out of the men's locker room.

Play it casual, she cautioned herself, hurrying for the door although her thundering heart urged her to run down the sidewalk and throw herself into his arms.

Once she was safely back inside, she took a glass of champagne from a passing waiter and downed half of it without pausing. Then, determined to appear busy and totally unconcerned over Alan's tardy arrival, she threaded her way through the crowd to the desk in the far corner of the room, put down her glass, picked up an

11

order pad and began to study the empty pages as though they were full of hastily written sales.

Thirty seconds more and Alan would reach the gallery. When her mental count-down reached zero, she returned the pad to the desk and glanced over her shoulder. Her timing was perfect. At that very moment, he walked through the doors.

Without realizing it, she swayed toward him. Formal attire made the perfect foil for his bronze-skinned, exotic good looks. The scarlet warrior's band circling his forehead added a hint of latent savagery to his otherwise urbane appearance.

Not surprisingly, the crowd surged toward him and he was quickly enveloped by well-wishers. Alan was not a man to suffer fools gladly, but she had taught him to be gracious to collectors. Normally, he would have taken time to exchange greetings, shake hands, sign autographs.

Not tonight. He pushed through the throng like a hot knife through butter. An excited buzz filled the vacuum he left in his wake. The crowd seemed to sense that something was about to happen and, although Liz kept her eyes lowered, she could feel their inquisitive stares.

Putting the order pad down with exquisite care, she turned and prepared to greet him.

Alan had stopped just three feet away. She smelled his scent, felt the heat radiating from his body. When she looked up at his face, her words of greeting froze in her throat. His sensually carved lips were tautened into a cruel thin line. And his eyes. Dear God. She would never forget the look in them. Bleak. Empty. Incredibly hostile.

The room was enveloped in an expectant hush, and the ensuing quiet moments felt like an eternity. Alan continued to stare at her wordlessly. He seemed to be fighting an internal battle.

She longed to put her arms around him, but the expression in his eyes held her at bay. Instead, she pasted a brave smile on her face. "Good evening, Alan," she

12

said. "As you can see, everyone has been waiting for you."

The muscles in the lower half of his face contracted and for a second, she thought he was going to return her smile. Then, an almost imperceptible shudder ran through him.

Into the pregnant silence, he said, "I'm sorry, Liz. It isn't going to work. It's over."

2

JULY 23, 1988

Main Street was hibernating. Half the galleries, boutiques, and antique shops lining the broad avenue had closed for the summer. Their empty windows stared blankly. An errant piece of paper, caught in a heat-buoyed dust devil, skittered down the softening asphalt, passing a legion of empty parking spaces before it flew aloft to lodge at the top of a palm whose wilting fronds seemed to shrink from the sky.

Sun licked the sidewalk hungrily. Thermometers peaked at one hundred and fifteen degrees. The only sound was the deep-bellied rumble of air-conditioning units working non-stop in the few businesses that stayed open throughout the long, punishing season.

The heat began at the end of April, as softly as the pianissimo strains of a distant song. By the end of July its fortissimo cascaded from the sun's molten orb, reverberating off every exposed surface – walls, rooftops, even lawns and swimming pools – driving everyone indoors.

Cocooned by her gallery's temperature-controlled environment, Liz Kant sat at the desk in her private office, so absorbed by the tasks at hand that she was able to close her mind to the summer doldrums enveloping the rest of Scottsdale.

The visible trappings of success surrounded her and the man who was with her. A museum-quality Navajo rug, in the soft pastel shades favoured by Burnt Water weavers,

14

covered the room's bleached oak floor. A Mies Van Der Rohe sofa and two Barcelona chairs created an elegant conversational grouping by the window overlooking the sculpture garden. The best of Liz's personal art collection, Schnabel, Rothko, Warhol, Gorman, Scholder, Lee, and several Longchases – pictures acquired at bargain prices during her years as a dealer – were artfully hung and perfectly lit on the creamy white walls.

But Liz was oblivious to the beauty of her surroundings. Nothing was going right. Had she believed in signs and portents, she might have forseen the disaster looming seven weeks ahead.

"Damn, look at this," she said disgustedly, skimming a thick, triple-folded square of vellum across her desk. It was an engraved invitation whose colour pictures featured the best paintings and sculptures the gallery would be exhibiting at the season's opening show, the tenth anniversary gala.

Rick Mason, sitting opposite her and looking poised and cool in a trendy summer-weight Armani suit, caught the invitation before it could fall to the floor.

She watched while his eyes widened in disbelief and he suppressed a smile.

"This is a little more than your average typo," he said, handing the vellum back.

She scanned the frontispiece again, still unwilling to believe what she read.

LIZ KUNT
proudly invites you to
a gala tenth anniversary exhibition . . .

it began.

"I suppose a few of my competitors have used that term to describe me, but I've never seen it spelled quite that way before, let alone three thousand times. That's how many invitations are sitting in those boxes in the corner." Her eyes flicked to the pristine white cartons the printer had delivered just an hour before, and she groaned. "I can't believe no one caught the error before now. I certainly didn't see it on the printer's proof."

"People do make mistakes, Liz. Obviously, you won't have to pay for this one. And the printer will certainly redo the order. Why are you so upset?"

"You don't know this business the way I do. Gossip and innuendo are its lifeblood. The story about those damn invitations is probably already making the rounds in Scottsdale. By this evening, they'll be repeating it in Manhattan." She paused thoughtfully, realizing the impossibility of making Rick understand how she felt.

From her sophomore year in college when she chose to major in art history, she had dreamed of becoming one of the country's leading art dealers. She had scrimped and saved during the ten years she worked for another dealer, until she had enough money to open on her own. She had willingly worked seventy and eighty hour weeks to insure success for herself and the artists she represented.

Liz revelled in bringing beauty to a world grown increasingly ugly – a world where watching the nightly news, replete with murders and rapes and needless poverty, constituted an outrageous assault on the senses. The tenth anniversary show was intended to crown her unremitting effort – to be a major coup, a succès d'estime that would be duly noted in all the important art magazines.

Conceived in the womb of her ambition and nurtured by her hunger for success, her business had grown to splendid maturity. In the art world, where buyers were accustomed to making high ticket purchases in New York, London or Paris, she had achieved the impossible – making the mountain of collectors come to her Mohammed of a resort-town gallery.

"We need to get the invitations in the mail," she said through clenched teeth, "before our clients get other invitations for the same date. I believe in beating the competition to the punch, getting there first with the most."

16

"Tell the printer to put a rush on the reprint if he wants to continue doing business with the gallery," Rick offered.

Liz shook her head. "That isn't the only thing that's gone wrong. Take a look at the advance copy of our October full-page ads in *Southwest Art* and *Art News*." She shuffled through the jumble of papers on her normally well-ordered desk, singled out two glossy pages, and passed them to Rick. Along with the ad-copy, they featured photographs of four of Alan Longchase's most recent canvasses.

Rick scanned the pages quickly. "They seem all right to me."

"Look again. The colours are muddy," she declared hotly. "Alan's paintings are never *muddy*! And it's too late to ask the magazines to do new new colour separations. They're already printing their October issues."

Rick shrugged. "Demand a refund."

"If you plan to make selling art your life's work, you better realize there are some problems money can't solve. The ads don't begin to do justice to Alan's work. I can't have collectors — to say nothing of museums and other gallery owners — get the idea that he's slipping." She paused long enough to take a cigarette from an open pack on her desk. She was smoking more instead of cutting back the way she planned.

But then, nothing was going the way she had planned.

Rick retrieved a lighter from his pocket, leaned across the desk and lit her cigarette, his hand brushing hers as he did so, his eyes seeking hers out. It was a strangely intimate moment, considering their employer-employee relationship.

"Look, you know I'll do whatever I can to help," he said. "I'll take the invitations back to the printer this afternoon myself. As for the ads, I didn't notice the colour being off, and I don't think anyone else will either. Besides, I've seen the new work coming in for the show. Our artists have outdone themselves. I guarantee

17

buyers will be standing in line on October 16. So please try to stop worrying." Concern warmed his eyes.

She sighed heavily. Rick puzzled her. One minute he acted as if the only thing in the world that mattered was money, and the next he was so considerate that it forced her to see him in a new light. But how she felt about him personally didn't matter, she reminded herself; the way her clients perceived Rick was far more important. And they seemed to trust him implicitly. His outstanding sales record spoke for itself.

"You're right," she said. "I probably am over-reacting. Thanks for letting me use you as a sounding board."

"My pleasure." Rick nodded, rose and crossed the room to the boxed invitations. "If that's all, I'd better be getting these back." He picked the heavy cartons up easily, his shoulder muscles straining at the fabric of his jacket as he balanced the boxes in one hand while opening the door with the other.

"That's it for now." Liz hurried to help him. "And Rick, thank you," she said before shutting the door behind him.

Returning to her desk, she sat down and closed her eyes, thinking about her brief awareness of Rick's masculine charm. He was an undeniably considerate, hard-working, and very attractive man. But he didn't compare to Alan Longchase.

No one did.

While Liz meditated in her elegant office, Maryann Van Kamp was trying to paint in a studio that was, by necessity, monastically stark. Maryann was attempting a feat that had forced other artists to starve in garrets, run off to places like Tahiti, or even lop off their ears in moments of deep despair. For the last three years, she'd been struggling to get by on what she earned as an artist.

Her rented home in a run-down, thirty-year-old housing tract west of Phoenix, reflected her precarious financial condition. When she moved in, she managed to convince herself that suffering and hardship would elevate her art. Now she knew that was a crock. It was hard to concentrate on painting when she was worried about how she would pay her bills and put food on her table.

Maryann stood opposite a blank canvas, rocking back and forth in an ancient pair of sneakers. An hour earlier, filled with resolve, she'd placed the canvas on the easel in the tiny bedroom she had converted to use as a studio. She'd been staring at it ever since. Its virginal surface seemed to taunt her, to challenge her to create a masterpiece. Squinting fiercely, she tried to compel inspiration.

Three years ago, when she moved to Phoenix and began painting south-western landscapes, she had been more familiar with the interiors of bars than with saguaro-covered mesas or red-rock canyons. So she copied pictures she saw in Arizona Highways magazine. Then, one afternoon when she was trying to sell her work in an amateur art show at one of the malls, someone told her that those photographs were copyrighted. Copying them was against the law.

It had given her a terrible scare. The last thing she wanted was an unexpected encounter with the boys in blue. So, although it put an additional strain on her limited budget, she began spending one weekend each month travelling around Arizona. She'd come home after two days of riding buses, her mind roiling with visions of things she had seen. Normally, all she had to do to begin a new painting was close her eyes and summon up one of those visions.

But not today.

She had been living in mortal terror of inspiration failing her. And now, to her horror, it was actually happening. Squeezing her wide blue eyes shut, wrinkling her turned-up nose, and pressing her full lips together, she battled with her muse. Hell and damnation! Her mind

19

was as empty as the banks of the Rio Grande after the immigration boys made a sweep. Panic welled up her throat. What if she never had another idea for a painting?

"Screw it," she said out loud, her breathy voice echoing in the unfurnished room.

Turning abruptly, she headed for the hall bath and splashed the lower half of her face with water, careful not to wet her false eyelashes. Then she ran a comb through her unruly cap of platinum blond curls. The improbable hair colour could be found on the heads of infants, but hers came from a bottle. Six years ago, when she bleached her pubic hair with the same product, the experiment led to an embarrassing, painful, and expensive visit to her gynaecologist. He treated her kindly, but she was sure he'd been thinking, "only her gynaecologist knows for sure". The memory still made her cringe.

Now, retrieving her bag from her bedroom, she hurried from the house. Twenty minutes later she was driving through north Phoenix, her car windows open to a blast-furnace wind that sucked her skin dry. The Datsun's air-conditioning didn't work any more. In fact, the auto-mobile seemed on the verge of a complete break-down. But Maryann didn't allow herself to think about that possibility. She firmly believed that imagining disaster invited it to happen.

There were lots of potential disasters she didn't permit herself to fantasize these days; little ones like getting a run in her last pair of pantyhose or spending an entire evening paying for her own drinks in a singles bar, and middle-sized ones like owning a terminally ill car she couldn't afford to replace or not selling a painting all month. Worst of all was the disaster looming on her personal horizon like the iceberg that sank the Titanic.

She had just turned thirty-six and her biological clock was ticking away with complete disregard for the fact that she didn't have a man in her life. She wanted kids, a guy to call her own, but those things had never seemed more out of reach. Somehow, no matter how good a job she did of refusing to contemplate any calamity – large or small – she could feel all of them hemming-in her life and its possibilities.

She repressed a familiar twinge of envy as she reached her destination, Archer Harrison's stately home. Being best friends with a woman who had everything – inherited millions, a good-looking husband, and a successful career as a sculptress – didn't always come easy.

Turning off the ignition, Maryann slid from the driver's seat as the car's ailing engine dieseled to a halt. A wall of heat enveloped her diminutive form as she walked up the path to the Harrison's front door and rang the bell.

While Maryann had been losing the battle with her muse, Archer Harrison was in her studio, winning the fight with hers. Becoming an artist had been a long, often frustrating endeavour. It was a solitary occupation. When Archer failed, she had no co-workers or boss to blame. There was only herself. Too often, the forty-four year old sculptress's artistic reach far exceeded her grasp. She imagined sublime works and produced what she considered to be run of the mill pieces.

But today, Archer was enjoying one of those exhilarating times when her hands and heart, her skill and her creativity worked in perfect harmony. The results, she admitted, stepping back to survey a three feet tall sculpture of a Navajo woman, were more than acceptable.

Archer was a tall, slender woman, whose seeming delicacy concealed a wiry strength. Born into the Philadelphia aristocracy, she had an oval face, serious grey eyes, and the even features and perfect white teeth that good nutrition and good genes produce in America's élite. But being born with the proverbial silver spoon in her mouth hadn't spoiled Archer. She'd been too involved in her personal lifelong struggle to feel that having money made her better than anyone else. Talent was the yardstick by which Archer judged herself and others. And, on that scale, she often found herself wanting.

Moving closer to the sculpture on the hip-high work-table, Archer took a moment to study the face. Were the cheekbones pronounced enough? Perhaps not, she decided, pinching off a tiny piece of clay from a twenty-five-pound block and adding it to the area in question, using her fingertips with skilled precision.

A couple of dozen tools were scattered on the table, but Archer preferred using her hands, her nails, the curve of her thumb, her palm, whenever she could. Tactile contact with the clay reinforced her intimacy with each sculpture.

She worked with feverish intensity for the next half hour and then she stepped back again, sighing with satisfaction while her eyes roamed the new piece from top to bottom. It was finished. She knew she couldn't improve on it if she spent the next week trying. Wiping her hand on the apron that circled her waist, she was preparing to cover the sculpture when the intercom buzzed.

Walking to it, she spoke into the mouthpiece. "Who's there?"

"It's me," came Maryann's disembodied voice.

"Hello, me. I'm in the studio. Come to the side-gate and I'll let you in."

Maryann walked past the house's imposing Spanish façade to an antique gate set in a stuccoed wall. The sound of a buzzer signalled that the gate could be opened. She pushed it wide and entered the oasis of the Harrison's half-acre grounds. Tall trees, velvety green grass, the sound of water falling into a deep blue pool, gave an illusion of coolness although Maryann could feel sweat trickling down her deep cleavage.

Archer was waiting in her studio's over-sized door-way.

22

"I hope you don't mind me coming over without calling," Maryann said, the broad vowels and nasal twang of west Texas evident in her voice.

"You couldn't have come at a better time," Archer replied, smoothing a strand of ash-blond hair into the pony tail she always wore when she sculpted. Somehow she managed to look like a former débutante, even in clay-grimed jeans and an old work shirt. "I just finished a sculpture," she continued, leading Maryann inside to a pair of high stools next to a large work table.

"What do you think?" Archer indicated a large clay sculpture of a Navajo woman portrayed in mid-stride, her full skirts flaring around her legs.

The clay was still wet, making the piece look uncannily alive. "It's terrific, as usual," Maryann replied, wondering how come Archer never seemed to run out of ideas for her work.

"Thanks. It's for my November show at the Santa Fe Museum of Art and I want each sculpture in the exhibit to be my very best. Give me a minute to cover it and clean up a bit, and I'll fix us both something cold."

Archer worked with swift, economical movements, wrapping the piece in plastic, sweeping the table free of bits of clay, and putting her tools in a large container, while Maryann glanced around the room.

It was an ideal work space, high-ceilinged and flooded with light. Shelves filled with twenty-five-pound bags of clay, powdered glazes, a variety of armatures, and two dozen sculptures in various stages of completion, lined two walls. A well-stocked kitchenette took up another, and a bank of windows the fourth.

"Now, that's done," Archer said, wiping her hands. "How about that drink?"

"I'd like a double bourbon on the rocks."

Archer went to the kitchenette, quickly pouring a Jack Daniels for Maryann and an iced tea for herself.

"I can see something's bothering you," she said, joining Maryann at the work table. "Want to talk about it?"

"Sugah, I've got painter's block." Maryann's brow knit up in a scowl. "I still owe Liz two canvasses for the tenth anniversary show, and I'm as tapped out of ideas as a beer keg after a barbecue. I don't know what ever made me think I could paint."

"You don't mean that."

"Like hell I don't! I gave myself three years to make it as an artist, and those three years are just about over. I'm still struggling to pay my bills and, if I don't sell something soon, I'm not sure I'll have enough to cover next month's rent."

"I'd be happy to lend you . . ."

"I know you mean well," Maryann interrupted, "but I hate being made to feel like a poor relative." She took a long pull on her drink.

Archer's eyes brimmed with sympathy. "I wish you'd let me help. It would mean a great deal to me. I'd much rather invest in you and your talent than in some blue chip stock."

"It's more than just being broke all the time." Maryann fumbled in her over-stuffed bag, found a crushed pack of cigarettes, took one out and lit it. "It's the whole art scene. Who am I kidding? I don't belong. I never even went to an art show until I went to one of my own. Hell. There weren't any galleries in Del Rio when I was growing up. Remember the first time we talked art? I thought impasto and gouache were things to eat until you set me straight." Maryann took another belt of bourbon. She'd already told Archer so much about herself, from her illegitimate birth and her failure to finish high school to her lousy marriage to a man who used her for a punching bag. She'd bared her soul. *Almost.*

But she had never dared talk about the time in Vegas when she'd worked as a bar girl. That was how she put together the stake that made her move to Phoenix

24

possible. On days like today, with poverty licking at her heels, she was tempted to return to that life. But when her paintings sold and she had some money, she was scared stiff she'd run into one of the high rollers she'd bedded.

Now, hating her own past – and fearing its attractions even more – she forced herself to concentrate on the present. "If I don't come up with a couple of terrific paintings before October 16, I'm going to be on Liz's shit list. I bet she's wondering why in the world she agreed to represent me."

Archer shook her head in vigorous denial. "Don't be silly. Liz believes in you."

"I wish I did."

"How can you say that when you've told me you wanted to be an artist all your life?"

Maryann flung her arms out in a gesture of utter hope-lessness. How could she make someone like Archer, some-one with supreme self-confidence who never failed at anything, understand what it was like living on the edge of a total wash out. "I've made up my mind. If things don't get better soon, I'm calling it quits; I'll get a . . . a day job. Believe me, there are worse things than waiting tables."

Archer didn't reply. She got up, walked over to her desk, took out a bank book and quickly wrote out a cheque. When she pressed it into Maryann's hand, Maryann saw it was for two thousand dollars.

"Don't even think about refusing," Archer admonished. "Now listen to me. How many times have you lectured me about visualizing what you want? Why don't you start visualizing lots of sold stickers next to your paintings on October 16."

Archer smiled as she stood in her driveway, waving good-bye as Maryann's Datsun sputtered around a corner. Solving Maryann's immediate financial problems had been easy and gratifying. Too bad she couldn't solve her own marital problems as effortlessly, Archer thought. She and Louis had been through some rough times in their twenty-four years together, but the last year had been the worst.

Now, glancing at her watch, she realized she would have to hurry if she wanted to be bathed and dressed by the time he got home from work. Spending the evening together, sharing a meal, was becoming an increasingly rare treat. She wanted to make the most of the coming evening.

She heard Louis bounding up the stairs as she sat at her dressing table, wrapped in a bath sheet, dabbing perfume between her breasts.

His colour was high and his hazel eyes sparkled when he hurried into the master suite. Leaning over and folding her still damp body in his arms, he murmured, "Mmm, you smell good."

She studied him in the mirror over the dressing table. A short man, he compensated for his lack of height by wearing power clothes. Today, a custom-tailored suit hid the extra ten pounds that thickened his waistline. His light brown hair, silvering at the temples, was perfectly cut in the accepted corporate style. Ordinarily, he came home tired and irritable, but this evening he looked more like a triumphant warrior than an over-worked, fifty-one year old executive.

"I've got the most wonderful news!" he said.

"You can tell me about it while I dress." She walked over to the chest that held her underclothes and made her selections.

"Steve Carpenter had a heart attack today!" Louis exulted.

Archer's eyes widened with shock. Carpenter was the CEO of World Business Electronics and according to Louis, one of his closest friends and associates. "That's what's making you so happy? I thought you liked Steve."

"I do."Louis practically danced his way across their spacious bedroom, shrugging out of his jacket and undoing his tie. "Look, honey, Carpenter's a tough old bird. It was a mild coronary and he's going to be fine. But meanwhile the company needs an acting CEO." He paused, letting the brief silence punctuate his next statement. "I got the job."

Louis had spent the last twenty-five years on a slow, steady climb up the corporate ladder. Becoming the chief executive officer of a large firm had been his goal from the day he earned a master's degree in management from Temple University. Archer wanted to share his current euphoria, although she suspected that hidden in his "good news" would be a price she would be expected to pay. Each one of his past promotions had its penalties – new obligations, often a move to a new town, the forced withdrawal from old friends who suddenly became Louis's underlings.

Even worse, her husband's upward mobility had crippled her career as a sculptress. How many times had she established a local following for her work, only to be forced to leave it behind when a promotion and transfer loomed on Louis's professional horizon? Their current stay in Scottsdale had been the longest of their entire marriage, and she'd made giant strides as an artist during the precious period of relative stability.

"Aren't you going to congratulate me?" he asked.

She forced a smile. "Of course. Congratulations, darling. I know how much this means to you. But I can't help wondering what it's going to mean to me."

Louis's brow furrowed. "Any other wife would be thrilled for her husband. A substantial raise goes with the job, to say nothing of stock options, and an incredible bonus at the end of the year."

Turning her back, she slipped into her bra. If they were going to get into a full-blown disagreement she'd be damned if she'd do it naked.

Apparently, he interpreted her action as a rejection. "Pardon me all to hell," he continued, "for talking about money. You'd think after all this time I'd realize it isn't very important to you. But then, I didn't have a rich daddy. I've always worked for a living."

She took a slow calming breath, refusing to rise to his bait. Lately, he'd been rehashing problems she thought they'd settled years ago. It wasn't her fault she'd been born into a wealthy family, or that he was their housekeeper's son. She'd married Louis despite her family's objections. That should have proven for all time how little she cared about money or status.

But somehow, Louis had never managed to forgive her the sin of being born on the right side of the tracks. "Instead of getting upset with each other," she said, "let's concentrate on celebrating your promotion. We could even go somewhere special for dinner if you like."

Anger fled his face as suddenly as it had appeared. "I'm sorry but in the excitement I forgot to tell you I don't have time for dinner. I've got a lot of catching up to do, stepping into Carpenter's shoes. I'm due back in the office in half an hour. I just came home to freshen up, give you the news and tell you to pack your bags."

"What are you talking about?"

"Carpenter was leaving for Hong Kong on October 17. We're shutting down our factories there."

"But why? I thought they were so profitable?"

"The cost of labour has risen to more than fifteen dollars a day in Hong Kong. We can get the same job done in Mexico for two. It's a matter of dollars and cents."

"How long will the trip take?" Pulling her slip over her head, she sat down at her make-up table, wishing her creams and powders contained a magical ingredient to smooth away the lines of worry and frustration she saw when she looked at herself in the mirror.

Standing by the armoire, Louis put on a fresh shirt. "Six months, give or take a few weeks. I'll spend three months in Hong Kong closing things down, and then three more in Guadalajara and Juárez getting our new factories going.

Considering how much you love to travel, it should be a ball."

"More likely a ball-buster. But I can't possibly go. You know I'm supposed to do a show at the Santa Fe Museum of Art in November. Most artists would sell their souls for a chance like that. Surely you don't expect me to cancel it?" She raised her palms in an unconscious gesture of supplication.

"What about me? What the hell am I supposed to do? Stay home and pass up the opportunity of a lifetime?"

"Of course not. I'm just asking for a little consideration. I've stood on the sidelines, cheering you on, for twenty-four years. Don't I ever get equal time?" Archer bit her lower lip. An hour ago, she'd been fighting for Maryann's artistic life, never realizing she'd soon have to fight for her own.

"Damn it, Archer, what's six months out of your life?"

"Artists have to be reliable or galleries won't represent them. If I leave town, if I disappoint Liz and the museum and the other galleries that are counting on getting my work on a regular basis, I won't be able to start over again in six months. By then, no one will take me seriously."

"It's not like you need the money." His tone was decidedly accusatory.

"You're right. I'd sculpt even if no one bought my work. It isn't something I want to do. It's something I *have* to do. My life is more than half over, and I've spent it doing things for other people – my parents . . . you . . . our sons. Just once, I'd like a chance to do something for myself."

His voice rose. "I thought you loved being a wife and mother."

"I do." She trembled with frustration and the sheer impossibility of making him see things through her eyes. "But I love being an artist too! I want to see how far I can go. You of all people, should be able to understand how I feel."

He walked across the room, pulled her to her feet and

gazed into her eyes. "I really want us to make this trip together. You're my wife. I need you by my side."

For a wordless moment she studied his familiar features, surprised by the anxiety she saw on them.

His grip on her shoulders tightened. "Please, honey. It would mean so much to me."

She struggled against the familiar tug of obligation and duty. "If you asked me six months ago, I wouldn't have hesitated. I'd have gone with you gladly. But no artist in their right mind reneges on a museum show, especially with an important artist like Roman De Silva."

"I guess that's it, then," Louis capitulated abruptly.

She hated disappointing him. "It isn't the end of the world."

"Yeah, sure. Of course it isn't," he replied, turning away from her.

"I've gone on these jaunts with you before, and you never have any free time anyway."

He picked up his suit jacket and folded it over his arm, carefully avoiding her eyes like a chastened child. "I'll tell my secretary she only needs to book one plane ticket."

Archer could feel her resolve cracking. "The least we can do is crack a bottle of champagne and toast your promotion before you go back to work."

"There isn't time." Unexpectedly, he smiled. "Maybe we can do it later tonight."

"I'll wait up for you," she said.

"I guess I was being a little melodramatic. Hell, it's just a few months. And I'll be home for a couple of weeks at Christmas." His voice had a hopeful, almost youthful timbre she hadn't heard in a long time.

"You do know I love you? And I am happy for you." Returning his smile, she got up and went to hug him. He smelled of the cologne he'd just splashed on, something new, she thought, as the musky scent filled her nostrils – new and very sexy. Brushing her lips against his, she found herself wishing they had more time.

30

He held her close, sexual heat and remembered tenderness vibrating between them before he let her go. "Sorry, Hon, but I'm running late."

Before she had a chance to respond, he was gone.

Returning to her make-up table, she gazed into her own bewildered eyes. The future that had seemed so secure and predictable when she got up that morning, was suddenly up for grabs. She felt off balance, as if her world had suddenly gone tilt, like a man-handled pinball machine.

3

AUGUST 1, 1988

Growing up on the San Carlos Apache Reservation, Alan Longchase never dared dream of a day like the one he'd just spent. He'd risen at dawn and ridden Odii, his beloved Apaloosa mare, in the foothills surrounding Pinnacle Peak, before going to work in a studio that was the envy of all but his most successful peers. While painting, he'd lost all track of time as ideas leapt from his mind, through his brush-wielding hand and onto the canvas, so effortlessly that, although he worked non-stop for eight hours, he left the studio more energized than when he'd entered it. And now he sat across a dinner table in one of Phoenix's finest restaurants, the sort of place that wouldn't have let him through the front door fifteen years ago, with the most beautiful woman he had ever known.

Such a day would have seemed totally out of reach during his boyhood, when poverty limited his vision of the future. He'd been perennially hungry and cold, a have-not surrounded by a white world of haves. The reservation's rocky soil had been more hospitable to tumble weeds and scorpions than fantasies of success. Had anyone told him then that he would someday be one of America's pre-eminent artists and a millionaire in his own right, Alan would have laughed out loud.

Now, members of his tribe held him up as a rôle model for young Apaches. But deep down, Alan couldn't help wondering if the boy who had matured in the desolation of the reservation would ever be completely accepted in the world of wealth and privilege his talent had earned the man.

Tonight, he intended to find out.

"You're awfully quiet," Liz said, folding her napkin, "and you didn't eat very much. Didn't you enjoy your meal?"

"It was delicious." He'd made reservations at Vincent's because he wanted dinner to be memorable. And Vincent Gutierez hadn't disappointed him. The food and wine had been ambrosial, the service unobtrusively excellent, the country French ambiance elegant without being pretentious. And their secluded table afforded them privacy. Alan couldn't have asked for more. But he still felt as scared as an untried youth faced with choosing a female partner at his first squaw dance.

Earlier in the evening, Liz's mood had almost mirrored his own. She had been so keyed-up when he arrived at the gallery at five that he had contemplated postponing any serious discussion. But now he could see serenity in the line of her body, the easy way she relaxed into her chair's upholstery. How magnificent she looked; how magnificent she was. He had tried to capture her spirit and fire on canvas many times, and yet the essence of her beauty continued to elude him.

She embodied the eternal female mystery – unknowable, unfathomable, and utterly desirable. Tonight she wore a simple black sheath, suspended from her shoulders by narrow straps he had been aching to lower all through dinner. An urgent heat suffused his groin as he imagined her breasts fully exposed, her sweet nipples waiting for his touch.

Liz's colouring made her a painter's dream. She had flawless ivory skin and shoulder length, coppery hair framing a face whose perfection still startled him even though ten years had passed since he first saw it. The chiselled planes of her high cheekbones and narrow, slightly

33

aquiline nose offered a fascinating contrast to full, sensual lips that blushed coral without the benefit of make-up. Her eyes were her finest feature. Set beneath well-arched brows and fringed with naturally jet-black lashes, they were the same astonishing shade of blue as Bisbee turquoise.

"I want to make love to you," he blurted.

"Here?" Mischief sparked in her eyes. "What am I? Dessert?"

"I'll make a fool of myself if we stay here much longer." Reaching for his wallet, he put three fifty-dollar bills on the table. In his haste, he almost knocked his chair over as he got to his feet.

Liz smiled, but her speed matched his as they hurried from the restaurant.

Ten minutes later, Alan turned his Blazer onto the steep road that lead to Liz's mansion halfway up the flank of Camelback Mountain. He drove automatically, pulled up in front of the house and walked Liz to the door, while mentally rehearsing what he intended to say later in the evening.

"I want to tell Rosita I'm home, and check for messages," Liz said, as he shut the front door behind them. "How about getting a bottle of champagne and meeting me in my bedroom?"

"Now that's an offer I can't refuse," he replied. Although he took time to return to his car and retrieve a jeweller's box from the glove compartment, Alan arrived in Liz's bedroom before she did. He set a silver tray bearing a chilled bottle of Perrier-Jouet and two Waterford flutes on the table in front of the fireplace. Then he removed the box from his khaki safari-jacket and placed it on the table as well.

Six months ago he'd commissioned his friend, Ted Charveze, the internationally-acclaimed Isleta Pueblo gemologist, to make something special for Liz. Charveze had spent weeks finding exactly the right Bisbee turquoise, flawless stones with depth and *zat*. "Good diamonds are a hell of a lot easier to come by these days than top-notch turquoise," Charveze had explained, "especially when you insist the stones match Liz's eyes."

The results had been worth waiting for. Charveze, who designed for Cartier, had outdone himself, producing a golden, jewel-inlaid collar that took the form of *Avanyu*, the sacred life-giving serpent. Now, Alan opened the box one last time, adjusting the masterwork in its satin-lined lair. Although money meant little to him personally, he enjoyed being able to give Liz beautiful things. Tonight, he wanted to envelop her in his love. The excellent meal and the gift were only a small part of the pleasure he planned.

Years ago, when he and Liz became lovers, he quickly realized how little she knew of passion. The first time he bedded her she had faked her orgasm – and not very well at that. Back then he'd still been a bit in awe of her success, the ease with which she moved through the glitzy world of high-priced art. But that night he pitied her. To be a stranger to her own body, a body so perfectly crafted for sensual delight, seemed a tragedy. It still astonished him that Anglos, despite their cultural preoccupation with sex, could be so untutored in the ways of a man and a woman.

Liz had taught him how to get along in the white world, how to dress, to make small-talk, to order in the five-star restaurants she liked to frequent – where being seen at the right table with the right people was more important than filling an empty stomach. In return he brought her, slowly and patiently, to the full realization of her womanhood. Now he was as comfortable dealing with a *sommelier* as if he'd been to the manor born, and she revelled in the pleasures of the bedroom like the most knowledgeable Apache female. It was, he thought, a fair exchange.

Taking off his jacket, he sat in one of the large armchairs

that flanked the fireplace. Liz's bedroom was almost as familiar to him as his own, but he never felt quite as ease in it. His own home was built of adobe and furnished in a rough, masculine fashion, with antiques from Santa Fe, Chimayo rugs, and artifacts from the numerous Indian cultures of the Grand Chimeca. By contrast, Liz's room was ostentatiously, sensually feminine. The walls were mirrored, the floor covered with a thick white Australian wool carpet. The furniture was white too, pickled-oak custom-made to Liz's specifications. A quilted, white silk spread covered her oversized four poster bed.

The room had been designed as a backdrop for the painting which hung over the fireplace, a four by eight feet portrait of Liz, nude, lying on her bed as if she waited for a lover. As Alan studied the painting, satisfaction warmed his eyes. The portrait, finished six years earlier, had held up well. It was still one of his best works. He'd come very close to doing Liz justice, even though it had been distracting as hell to paint her like that. Grinning, he recalled how much faster he would have completed the canvas if he hadn't stopped so many times to make love.

He had wanted Liz from the day he walked into her gallery. Then, his reaction had been immediate, visceral – a triumph of desire over reason. He had never expected to have her, to love and be loved by her. As an impoverished Apache artist, he'd known the Liz Kant's of the world were out of his reach, no matter how beautiful or desirable he might think they were.

He'd grown up well-schooled in hatred and distrust of all whites. His tribal elders had taught that white men had taken everything from the Apaches, their ancestral hunting grounds, their culture, their freedom – even their lives in the bloody, desperate battles of the late eighteen-hundreds when government policy had insisted that the only good Indian is a dead Indian. The warrior's death roll – Mangas Colorado, Victorio, Geronimo, as well as

Alan's own ancestors, Cochise and Nachez – was still repeated around countless campfires.

In accordance with his earliest training, Alan had expected to fall in love with a woman of his own people, a girl whose character and fortitude had been tested in the ceremony of the White-Painted Woman, to marry her and have many children as his brothers and sisters had, and to raise them as true Apaches.

Then he'd met Liz and his expectations had changed irrevocably.

"You look a million miles away," she said, walking into the room and closing the doors behind her. "Is something wrong?"

"I was thinking about us." He paused. This was a momentous evening, and he wanted to do things properly. "I want to talk about our future. But first, I have something for you." Taking the case from the table, he placed it in her hands.

Her matchless eyes widened as she opened it. "It's beautiful, Alan," she said throatily, lifting the necklace and clasping it around her neck.

Although he longed to take her in his arms, he poured two glasses of champagne and placed one in her hand. "I've been waiting to talk to you all night. Why don't we sit down?"

Liz put her glass down, and moved so close to him that her breasts brushed his chest. "I want to thank you properly first."

Seeing his eyes heavy with desire, she stood on tiptoe to meet his lips. Returning his first kiss eagerly, she opened her mouth in welcome while he probed and explored, caressing her inner, liquid softness. Then he took her tongue between his teeth, nipping gently, drinking deeply of her sweetness as if it could nourish him. A hot, urgent warmth blossomed deep within her body and she pressed her pelvis against him, feeling his hardness, surrendering to the fire racing through her blood, wanting him inside her.

Unexpectedly, he broke their embrace and stepped back. "Not so fast. We have all night."

While her breath caught in her throat and she fought to slow the frantic beating of her heart, he unbuttoned his shirt. She watched intently as he slowly revealed his upper torso, as perfectly muscled as Michelangelo's David. His skin was deeply bronzed, his chest hairless. At first his lack of body hair had surprised her. Now, she couldn't bear the thought of touching a pale, heavily-thatched male body. Reaching forward, never taking her eyes from his, she caressed his firm pectorals, teasing his nipples with her fingers until she felt them harden.

"It's my turn," he said. Slipping her dress's narrow straps from her shoulders, he traced the long line of her neck, feathering her collarbone with fingers that left fire in their wake before they drifted down to the valley between her breasts.

How could so soft a touch create such pangs of longing? Moving close enough to feel his erection against her stomach, she reached behind herself and undid the zipper that held her dress closed.

It slithered to the floor unheeded. Underneath, she wore only lacy, black bikini panties, a garter belt and black stockings. She had chosen her undergarments carefully, knowing the effect they would have on him, and now his harsh groan was her reward for having chosen well.

"You're so beautiful," he said, as he cupped the weight of her breasts in his hands, squeezing gently before tracing circles around them with his fingertips. She shivered with anticipation as the circles grew ever smaller and he finally reached the place she longed to have him touch. Her wide-aureoled nipples hardened instantly, thrusting upward as he alternately pinched and rubbed.

"You're driving me crazy," she whispered.

"Lady, the feeling is mutual," he replied before lowering his head and sucking, pulling hard. She felt a spasm deep in her body as he took one nipple between his teeth while continuing to pinch and pull on the other. The sight of his bronze cheek burrowed into the white globe of her breast initiated another spasm and she felt her panties dampen. God, she was so ready for him. "Bite me harder."

His teeth closed on one sensitive nub, sending an exquisite message of pleasure that was almost pain. When he finished paying homage to one breast he turned to the other, working it until both her nipples were red-hard. At last, he paused to admire what he had done.

Liz looked at Alan, seeing his manhood tenting his trousers. "You'd better get out of those clothes," she said, placing her hands on her own breasts, knowing what that would do to him.

Watching her caress herself was incredibly erotic, he thought, repressing a groan. He stepped out of his trousers and briefs, freeing an erection that was so hard it hurt. He wanted her desperately, could have thrown her to the floor and taken her then and there. But he knew the greatest pleasure came from delaying pleasure, so for the time being he ignored the aching need in his loins.

"Do you have any idea how exciting that is?" he asked, watching her toy with her own body.

"Are you ready to make love yet?" Her eyes glinted, a smile tugged at the corners of her mouth.

"Not quite. You're still not undressed."

"It will only take a second." She reached for her stockings, but he stopped her.

"Leave them on," he said, "and the garter belt. Just take off your underwear."

When she had done as he instructed, he backed away to study the results. The gossamer black stockings and lacy garter belt accentuated the creamy whiteness of her thighs, drawing attention to the gentle curve of her belly and the deep crater of her navel. Inexorably, his eyes were drawn to the copper curls between her legs. Not until he looked his fill did he pick her up and carry her to the bed. Lying down beside her, he began to explore the places his eyes had lingered on, using his lips, tongue and hands.

Her nipples were incredibly swollen. He brushed them lightly with his palms and she responded instantly, reaching for his penis. Her touch sent an urgent, liquescent fire roaring through him. Not yet, he thought, gritting his teeth. Tonight he wanted to pleasure her, to make her come again and again. Taking her hand in his, he gently made her release him.

He could see the surprise in her eyes as instead, he placed her palm against the mound of her own femininity. Her legs were slack with desire, her thighs open. "I'm going to put one of my fingers inside you," he said, "and I want you to put one of your fingers next to mine. I want you to feel what I feel." Parting the soft, moist lips of her sex, he guided her into the heart of her own womanhood. She was gloriously wet, slick with desire, and so close to orgasm that he sensed her body's anticipatory tension. "Do you want more?"

"Yes, damn you, yes!"

Now, he took two of her fingers between two of his own and thrust firmly, watching with fascination as one white hand and one dark opened her wider and entered deeper. He schooled her to an easy rhythm at first, withdrawing almost completely and then re-entering lazily, slowly, stretching each stroke to the ultimate. When the sound of her breathing grew harsh and the movement of her hips more insistent, he accelerated the pace.

Propped on her pillows, Liz watched as intently as Alan, feeling herself hurtling toward fulfillment. The muscles deep in her loins began to spasm as her body flooded their twined fingers with moisture, contracting and releasing against their insistent probing. Closing her eyes and crying out Alan's name, she spiralled into that moment of eternity when the giver and the receiver are one.

After she finished, he took her hand and sucked the fingers that had been inside her just moments before. And then, moving down on the bed, he began to tongue her secret places. Incredibly, she could feel the glorious aching tension gathering again.

Alan lay against the pillows, completely spent, sweat evaporating on his body while passion's musky odour permeated the bedroom. He didn't find the scent of the life-force unpleasant, although normally he would have got up to bathe. Tonight he lacked the energy and, from the slack way Liz's body moulded to his, he suspected she did too. After all he had done to her and with her, it wasn't surprising.

Now, the time for pleasure had ended. The time had come for talk – serious talk. He had anticipated this moment for years. There was power in its arrival. "Are you awake?" he asked.

She stirred and turned toward him. "Just barely. You certainly know how to make sure a lady needs her beauty sleep."

"Would you mind sitting up? There are things that must be said between us."

She groaned. "Can't it wait until morning? I'm exhausted, thanks to you."

"No, it can't."

Burrowing into her pillows, she muttered, "Don't be unreasonable, Darling. It's after three."

"It's important, Liz."

Sighing, she sat up. Then, stretching lazily, she put her arms behind her head, in a gesture that tautened her breasts so that her swollen nipples became an open invitation. "Maybe I'm not so sleepy after all," she murmured huskily.

He couldn't prevent the instant response in his groin, but refusing to be distracted, he pulled the sheet up to her collarbones.

"Mmmm," she said, "you must be serious."

"I am." He had rehearsed this speech a hundred times. Now, all the romantic declarations he'd expected to make seemed locked in some forbidden corner of his mind. "I ought to have a dozen horses waiting outside," he burst out.

An astonished grin parted Liz's lips. "I would think you'd ridden enough for one night."

"I'm not talking about lovemaking." He paused. "When an Apache wants a wife, he offers his finest horses as a bride-price. And this Apache wants a wife. I want you, Liz." He waited for her to respond, but the only sound in the room was his own harsh, in-drawn breath. "I love you. I thought you loved me."

Wide awake now, Liz sat up straighter. "Of course I love you. I adore you!" she declared. "But we've never talked about marriage before. I just assumed you were happy with the status uo."

"I have been. But now I want more. I want everyone to know you're mine."

She hesitated, as if she needed to measure her every word. "I don't think that would be wise. We agreed, a long time ago, to keep our private lives private. I've worked damn hard to make you into a superstar in the art world. Do you want the critics to think I did it because we were lovers? Don't you see what a mistake marriage would be, for both of us?"

He felt the beginnings of concern prickle his mind. "I don't agree. And I don't care what anyone says, not the critics, not the collectors. The only thing that matters is how we feel about each other."

"I'm yours. You know that. We've been so happy. Why tempt fate."

Alan's jaw clenched. "Pretty words, Liz – pretty and utterly meaningless."

She lowered her arms, snugging the covers around herself protectively. "Is this sudden desire to get married some macho male thing, a need to produce a carbon copy of yourself? Have you forgotten that I'm too old to start a family? Besides, we already have one. The gallery artists are our family, and your paintings are a more magnificent heritage than the children most men leave behind."

"More empty words," he muttered.

"Please, Alan, don't force the issue."

Knowing she was a consummate actress, he distrusted the pain he heard in her voice. "You owe me an explanation."

"It's a long story." Her mind raced dizzyingly. She would have to reveal part of her history. But not all. She couldn't risk it, couldn't expose who she was. The habit of deception was too deeply ingrained to be abandoned. She had created herself as surely as Alan created a painting. Her entire life had been built on a lie. How could she tell that to a man who despised liars?

Inhaling deeply, she launched into an expurgated version of her history. "I've always been grateful you never asked about my past. People assume I grew up with money. I didn't. Most days, my parents were lucky if they could put food on the table. My father was an intellectual of sorts, a perpetual student, content to exist on handouts. I made up my mind to be a success, to do whatever it took. Love and marriage weren't part of the blueprint." She met his eyes, pleading for understanding. "The gallery was everything to me until you came into my life. You've fulfilled me in ways I never thought possible. I love being with you, I love sharing my life with you."

"Don't you see, Liz, the past doesn't interest me. The future does. As far as I'm concerned, our lives began the day we met. I want to spend the rest of mine with you."

"We can do that without being married. There are important business complications, legal ramifications that we have to think about."

"I've already considered that. If you want a prenuptial

43

agreement, I'm perfectly willing to have our lawyers draw one up."

"You've thought about everything, haven't you?"

There was a hint of anger in her voice that he more than matched as he answered. "I tried to. I wanted to ask you to be my wife years ago, but I waited until I could come to you with the world in the palm of my hand." He held his fist up, clenching it so tightly that the muscles in his arm corded. "I have that world in my grasp now. It's yours for the taking." He knew his words of love were harshly spoken, but their conversation had tumbled down a dark, dizzying path he hadn't anticipated.

"Darling, you know the crazy demands the gallery makes on my time. I'm just not good marriage material," she paused, her voice huskily seductive as she added, "but you must admit I'm a wonderful lover."

Damn her. Her excuses sickened him. Rising from the bed, he began to pace barefoot across the carpet, oblivious to his nudity. "I don't understand. You say you love me. Has it been a lie all these years?"

Her eyes blazed in the shadowed room. "Of course not. Why won't you leave well enough alone? Does wanting to get married after all these years have something to do with your pride?"

He stood motionless and stared at her, feeling as if he was seeing her for the first time. "And does not wanting to marry me have something to do with yours? What's the matter, Liz? Isn't an Apache good enough for you?"

She blanched and turned away, hating the pain she was inflicting, but even more terrified of telling the truth.

"That's it, isn't it?" His voice rose, filling the room's quiet corners. He was losing control but he didn't care. The memory of a thousand hurts, the mindless, cruel prejudice that had plagued his youth surged in his mind, and his throat filled with bile.

"How dare you say that to me, let alone think it?" she protested. "There are things you don't know—"

44

"I know everything I need to know," he interrupted. "The great Liz Kant thinks too much of herself to marry an Indian. I should have realized you're no different from any other white woman. What a fool I've been." At that moment, he hated himself for having been taken in by her.

She threw the covers aside and ran to his side, but he pushed her away so roughly that she staggered against the edge of the bed. "For the love of heaven, Alan, don't do this to us."

He reached the chair where he'd so carefully tossed his clothes a few hours ago and began pulling them on. "There is no us, only a foolish dream. But I'm wide awake now."

Disbelief contorted her features into an ugly mask. "Come back to bed," she begged, her arms reaching for him. "We're both upset. You'll feel differently in the morning. For God's sake, Alan, it doesn't have to be like this."

"This is the only way it can be between us from now on." Shrugging into his shirt, he noticed the discarded jeweller's box on the table. "Keep the necklace. It cost a great deal, but women like you always do – one way or another."

Snatching up his jacket, he headed for the door, stopping as he reached it to take one last look at her. She clung to one of the bedposts, her nude body shivering uncontrollably. The echo of desire tugged at his loins as he saw her breasts trembling with each ragged breath. But he forced his eyes away and left.

The dream was dead.

Liz sobbed out loud when she heard the front door slam. Collapsing on the bed, she pulled Alan's pillow against her body, cradling it as she began to rock back and forth. She and Alan had argued before, but never like this. God, if only she'd been able to explain. But she couldn't. He believed in honesty. It was the corner stone of his character. And her entire life was a lie, a façade, a carefully orchestrated scenario.

If only she'd told him the truth years ago, before they became lovers. God knows, she considered the idea, but she had discarded it out of hand. Back then he had needed her strength, needed to believe in the myth of Liz Kant almost as much as she now needed to believe that he loved her wholly, completely – that he would come back to her.

She ignored the tears streaking down her cheeks, ignored the growing chill. Her mind had room for only one thing. Alan was gone. She struggled to comprehend the enormity of her loss. Her body still bore the marks of his passion, her nipples still ached from his hunger. His scent clung to her and his warm seed oozed from between her thighs. He should have been in bed beside her, sleeping. She rocked compulsively, her body automatically seeking childhood's succour while his name reverberated through her brain.

Alan. Alan.

She had hurt him tonight, but she had to believe his pain would lessen. Tomorrow or the day after, he would remember how much they meant to one another, how deeply woven were the skeins of their lives, and he would come back. They would go on together.

They had to.

4

OCTOBER 15, 1988

Alan Longchase took a last swallow of coffee, pushed his chair back and stared out at the muted colours of the landscape bordering his patio. Loving the desert, he'd refused to tame the grounds around his ranch with lawns and flowerbeds the way Anglos did. A sandy, rock-strewn vista of cactus, mesquite and palo verde filled his eyes, reaching from the terrace to a range of nearby hills.

"Have you decided what you're going to do about the tenth anniversary show tomorrow night?" Hank Begay's deep voice rumbled in the still morning air.

Alan looked across the patio table to where Hank sprawled in a chair, thinking how like a mother hen the big Navajo sounded.

"You have as much right to be at that opening as any one," Hank declared in a basso profundo that came from deep in his barrelled chest.

He was an enormous man, over six foot five inches tall. A sheath of fat enveloped his heavy torso, concealing the long, sinewy muscles that were characteristic of Navajos. His brown eyes squinted above a flat, broad-cheeked face bisected by a knife-sharp nose. Hank was one of the most menacing-looking men Alan had ever seen – and one of the gentlest. Their friendship began years ago when Hank Begay had been his art teacher at the Phoenix Indian School. They'd been student and mentor then – and close friends ever since.

Alan shrugged. "I'm not sure I'm ready to see Liz yet."

"I know it hurt like hell, having her turn down your marriage proposal. Frankly, I've never been able to understand that woman – or any woman for that matter. But tomorrow, you won't just be representing Alan Longchase. You'll be representing your people. From what you've said, the place will be crawling with media. Damn it. You can't pull a no-show."

Alan rose and walked to the edge of the patio, turning his face up to the sun and letting its blessing wash over him. "I don't think I can go on working with Liz," he murmured, as if he were talking to himself.

A mixture of surprise and dismay played across Hank's features, making the huge Navajo look even more intimidating. "You can't mean that! Liz has been your master dealer from day one. She knows more about the business end of what you do than you do."

Alan sighed heavily. Hank was right, but that didn't make the thought of working with Liz any easier. He had been avoiding her for weeks, had even paid a shipping company to crate and deliver his paintings for the tenth anniversary exhibition so he wouldn't have to face her. But he couldn't avoid a confrontation for ever.

The sound of Hank's chair grating on the patio roused Alan from his reverie. "I'm going into town to buy some groceries," Hank said. "Can I get you anything?"

"No, thanks. I'm going to stay here for a while. I need to think." Alan felt Hank's huge hand thump his back in a rough gesture of sympathy.

"Later," Hank said, by way of goodbye.

The sound of his footsteps receded as Alan returned to the table, sat down, and poured a fresh cup of coffee. Liz. Damn it. He hadn't been able to think of much else for weeks. Part of him never wanted to see her again. The other part kept on remembering the enormous debt he owed her, a debt that could only be paid in full if he

48

maintained their business relationship, no matter how painful that might be personally.

The fame, success, and wealth he now enjoyed all began on that long ago afternoon when he walked into the Kant Gallery as an unknown artist, hoping for a big break. He'd shown Liz his portfolio, and her face had come alive. "You and I are going to have a long talk," she'd said.

He remembered struggling to keep his expression impassive although he longed to shout in triumph. He'd been going from one gallery to another for months, trying to get a Scottsdale dealer to talk to him. He knew his work was good, far better than the things most of the dealers already exhibited. But half of them wouldn't even look at his paintings once they'd taken a good look at his frayed jeans, worn boots, and the colour of his skin.

The bastards just shrugged and said they didn't have room for another artist. What they meant was they didn't want to represent an *Indian* artist unless he was already a success. Alan thought he was tough – anyone who'd survived a childhood on the San Carlos Reservation had to be – but the unending rejection had got to him. Maybe the dealers were right. Maybe he'd been kidding himself for years.

He wouldn't be the first guy to return from Nam suffering from a delusion or two. Without Hank Begay's steadying presence, Alan knew he would have given up – stopped making the rounds of the art emporiums. It was Hank who urged Alan to give the Kant Gallery a try, even though Liz Kant, despite her newness on the Scottsdale art scene, already enjoyed a reputation for being merciless when it came to rejecting artists who didn't meet her high standards.

Alan hadn't expected her to give him the time of day, let alone ask him back to her private office. He'd been stunned by her beauty when he first saw her at her desk and had stood in the doorway like a tongue-tied idiot, thinking he'd give his soul to paint her. Five minutes

49

later, following in her wake as she led the way through the gallery, he tried to guess her age. She could be twenty-five, thirty-five. Hell, he didn't have a clue. The women on his reservation reached a lush peak at fifteen. By twenty they had two or three children hanging on their skirts, an extra thirty pounds padding their waistlines and hips, and lines of worry etched on their faces.

He was doing his level best to ignore the tantalizing movement of her buttocks when she stopped short and turned to face him. He almost bumped into her but stepped back quickly, painfully aware that most white women recoiled from the touch – even the inadvertent touch – of an Indian male.

"How do you like the gallery so far?" she asked.

"It's all right," he replied stolidly, backing off even further.

"Just all right?" she frowned. "I mortgaged my soul to redo this building. When I first saw it the place was a disaster. The floors were covered with worn linoleum and the ceilings were badly water-stained. It was ghastly, but I wanted a big space and the price was right. So I repeat, what do you think of it now?"

A sweeping gesture of her hand indicated white rough-textured walls, ten-foot-high ceilings finished with traditional *latillas* supported by hand-hewn *vigas*, and Mexican paved floors waxed to a satiny sheen.

Alan's eyes tracked her gestures. "It looks like money," he answered truthfully.

"Money!" Liz exploded. "You think it looks like money. It's supposed to be authentic Indian décor!"

He didn't even attempt to control his instant hostility. "What the hell do you know about authentic Indian décor? Have you ever been inside a house on a reservation?"

"Don't be ridiculous. I don't know anyone who lives on a reservation."

"You do now, Lady. A lot of Apache houses have

no electricity, no running water, and the walls sure as hell aren't white. A family with four or five children is lucky to have two beds and a few lousy chairs. That's authentic Indian décor, and this," his eyes swept the elegant showroom, "isn't even close!"

"Are you always this charming?" she asked, her voice edged with steel.

Alan knew he'd blown it, blown the only chance anyone in this sanctimonious Anglo town seemed likely to give him. But he was sick and tired of people who used Indians and their culture for financial gain, without giving a damn about the way Indians really lived. "You asked me, Miss Kant," he replied, inwardly cursing himself for a fool, "so I told you."

He expected to be shown the door but she surprised him. "Oh for God's sake," she said, "since we may be working together, call me Liz."

Moments later she turned into a corridor and paused in front of a door before flinging it open dramatically, revealing a room that looked as if it had been torn from the pages of *Architectural Digest*. Alan judged it to be twenty feet square. Natural light streamed in through a series of skylights, illuminating a group of paintings that would have been perfectly at home in the Guggenheim, the Hirschhorn, or the Museum of Modern Art. For the second time that afternoon he felt awed. When he had first seen Liz her beauty had stunned him. Now her obvious wealth and exquisite taste intimidated him as well. She crossed the room and sat down behind her desk, indicating that he was to sit opposite her.

"Are you with any other galleries?" she began.

"No, although I've talked to every dealer in town."

"Why did you leave me for last?" Her eyes locked with his, direct and challenging. God! What a colour they were.

"I heard you only handled established artists. I didn't think you'd give me the time of day."

"You thought wrong, Alan Longchase. I've been looking for someone like you for a long time." She paused to light a cigarette. "It's perfectly obvious you know everything you need to know about how and what to paint. But what do you actually know about art as a business?"

Her question took him by surprise. Although he'd been painting all his life, he hadn't given much thought to art as a commercial enterprise. Of course there were people, a lucky few, who managed to make a fortune painting. But so far he'd hardly dared dream of joining their ranks.

She inhaled deeply, expelling smoke in a thin stream. "It takes more than talent to be a success in the art world. And by success I mean getting international recognition for your work, shows in New York, Paris or Tokyo. You're going to have to want it more than you've ever wanted anything in your life. First of all, you'll have to paint all day, every day. You won't be able to wait for inspiration. Steady production is the foundation of a successful career."

Alan blinked in surprise. International recognition, steady production! Liz's ambition surpassed anything he'd imagined for himself. His goal had been to paint truthfully, honourably, to give his people – the Mescalero Apaches – a reason to be proud of him. He hadn't concerned himself with critical acclaim or financial reward.

"I've been painting every day for years," he said, deliberately choosing not to tell her that, as an Apache, he considered his talent to be a *power*, one that imposed serious obligations. "As long as I can afford paint and canvas, I work."

"Then you're off to a good start. But discipline and talent don't sell paintings. It takes an enormous publicity campaign and a great deal of money to launch a career. I'm not going to risk mine unless I stand to benefit by it. If I'm going to represent you, I'll want you to sign a five-year contract naming me as your master dealer."

"What does that mean?"

"It means that, aside from forty per cent of the retail price the gallery collects for everything we sell here, I'll get ten per cent on every dollar you make no matter where your work sells or who sells it."

"And what will you do in return?"

"In return, I'm going to make you famous, Alan Longchase," Liz said with utter conviction.

Neither of them could have predicted how fast success would come. His first one-man show opened four months after he walked into the Kant Gallery and it sold out in a week. Within a year Liz had placed his work in prestigious galleries in Santa Fe, Houston, Palm Springs and New York. Critics acclaimed his talent. Women flocked to his shows to get a glimpse of the new and gorgeous phenomenon in the art world. Their husbands invested in his paintings, gloating over their rapid appreciation. Alan's prices doubled, tripled, then tripled again as demand for his work outstripped his ability to produce it.

But it all began with Liz. He owed her his career. More than that, he owed her his sense of himself as a man. He'd had other lovers – but she was his only love. He'd admired her so much when they first met; her strength had called to something deep inside him. He'd seen only her virtues and been blind to her faults.

But he could no longer ignore the fact that she'd used him and his talent to further her own goals. She might part her legs for him, but she would never let him put a wedding ring on her finger. It was that simple and that painful.

An Apache, born and raised in a shack on the San Carlos Reservation, would never be good enough for the very social Liz Kant.

The massive cliff soared into the cobalt night sky. Two thirds of the way down its face, a large cave gaped wide like a giant eye in a stony brow. In the depths of that open orb stood an ancient, three-storey Indian ruin. Liz stared at the spectral view and a tremor ran through her body. It was the loneliest place she'd ever seen. The stark vision absorbed her, transfixed her. Her skin prickled as she felt a cold that seemed to emanate from those empty, thousand-year-old rooms. Piled atop one another like children's blocks, they were protected and preserved by the enormous stone overhang. Although she couldn't see the moon, the canyon was bathed in a crystalline light that transformed the red sandstone walls into a silvered grey.

Peering into the shadowed ground in front of the cliff-dwelling she saw the rounded form of a sacred kiva and, for one soul-wrenching moment, the ghostly chant of the long dead priests who worshipped there reverberated in her mind. Drawn by the eerie, echoing silence she stepped forward boldly, her hand reaching out. As she touched the painting's surface the spell was broken.

No one's work had the power to reach her the way Alan's did. This particular canvas, so real that she'd been pulled into its depths, made her ache for him. Did it mean what she hoped? Was Alan trying to tell her he felt lost without her?

A masculine voice brought her musings to a halt. "From the expression on your face, you must like the way I hung the show." Rick Mason's lips parted in a disarming grin. "How about a pat on the back for yours truly?"

Liz turned to face him. The cut of his jacket emphasized his broad shoulders. His thick, sandy blond hair was perfectly trimmed and his enviably long lashes cast feathery shadows on his cheeks. Thirty-two-year-old Rick Mason was an extraordinarily attractive man, but she was immune to his considerable charms.

"You'll get that pat on the back when I'm certain you deserve it," she said crisply, taking a moment to study the front room, her critical gaze looking for flaws in the exhibition's presentation.

There had been a time before the Kant Gallery became

a fashionable, haut-monde favourite, when she'd hung all the shows herself, struggling with giant canvasses and heavy sculptures. Now she had a staff of eight, but none more capable than Rick. Wooing him away from the investment firm where he'd been a valued employee had been a real coup. Although he'd readily confessed to knowing damn little about art, he had other qualities – a quick mind, ever-ready charm, to say nothing of an Ivy League business degree that made him a valuable addition to the gallery.

She'd been searching for a street-man when she met Rick at a charity gala. She needed someone capable of soliciting major accounts outside the gallery, someone capable of impressing the important decorators and art consultants who purchased art for banks, hotels, hospitals, resorts, department stores, and other corporate accounts.

Rick more than filled the bill. In the months he'd been with her, he exceeded all of her expectations. He was the quintessential yuppie, aggressive in a well-bred way, always impeccably dressed, his eyes shielded from Arizona's blazing sunlight by Cartier glasses, a chunky Rolex on his wrist. In the art business, where style is often more important than substance, Rick wore all the right labels with casual panache.

Teaching him to mount a show had been surprisingly easy. He quickly grasped the elements of balance and flow needed to create a unified exhibit from the disparate work of a dozen different artists. Today he could do the job as well as she – perhaps even better. He had wisely chosen to feature the Longchase painting on the gallery's *power* wall, opposite the entrance. She was pleased to see its title, "Mysterious Traveler", and its $75,000 price clearly displayed on a card at the viewer's eye level on the right hand side of the painting.

A lot of dealers didn't post prices, in the mistaken belief that clients who were concerned with cost probably couldn't afford to buy anything. Liz knew better. No one was *more* concerned with money than people who had a great deal of it.

"Don't keep me in suspense. What do you think?" Rick's voice returned her to the present.

"So far, so good. How about walking me through the rest of the gallery?"

She took her time, stopping in each of the seven rooms. Archer Harrison's new sculptures ought to have collectors standing in line, Maryann Van Kamp's paintings sang with colour, R.C. Gorman's and Amado Pena's stone-pulled lithographs were powerful, Lawrence Lee's acrylics were evocative. But no one's work surpassed Alan's. He remained the unequalled master of the south-western idiom.

Reaching the last room, Liz turned to Rick, her voice deepening with appreciation. "You've done a beautiful job."

"Thanks. I really worked at it. But I had a very good teacher." He paused, searching her eyes as if he expected her to say more. When she didn't, he turned on his heel and headed in the direction of his own small office next to the storerooms at the back of the gallery.

Liz had already dismissed Rick from her mind as she opened her office door, pausing to check her Patek Phillipe watch. How puzzled Alan had been years ago when she paid a small fortune for it. "I don't understand why the thinnest watch is the most expensive," he'd said.

"In some cases, less is more," she explained.

He'd simply shaken his head, as if to say the ways of the white world were unfathomable.

Alan. He was never far from her thoughts. Had the past eleven weeks been as hard on him as they had on her? Did he wake in the middle of the night whispering her name, reaching for her? She closed the office door and leaned against the unyielding wood. Damn it all! Why couldn't things be as uncomplicated as they'd been on that long ago April afternoon when she and Alan first met?

It had been half an hour before the gallery was due to close, and she sat at the desk in the front room, tallying the day's sales. Open a few months, the Kant Gallery was already making inroads in the Scottsdale art market – no small achievement in a city where fine art was big business. The mortgage, which seemed disproportionately huge when she opened her doors, was assuming a more manageable size as her profits grew. But she wasn't satisfied. She'd set her sights on becoming one of the best-known dealers in the world.

A moment passed before she realized the figure of a man, haloed by the late afternoon sun, stood poised in the gallery's entrance. Shifting from one foot to the other, he seemed to be struggling with a decision. He's probably wondering what happened to the drugstore that used to be in this building, she decided before returning to a careful accounting of the day's receipts.

She stopped working when a shadow crossed her desk, blocking the light. The man had obviously reached his decision because now he stood directly in front of her. Looking up, she saw an Indian in his late twenties or early thirties. He wore faded jeans and a threadbare khaki shirt. Dusty, sweaty, and obviously apprehensive, he still made an indelible impression. In one quick survey she took in his slender, well-muscled body, shoulder-length blue-black hair, unblemished bronze skin, and exotic high cheekbones. She barely managed to suppress a gasp. He was the best-looking man she'd ever seen, of any age or any race. His eyes were a velvety brown with golden flecks smouldering in their depths. What would it take to ignite the fire she sensed in his glance? A woman? Money? Success?

They stared at each other for what seemed an eternity before he looked away. She followed his glance down to the artist's portfolio under his arm. Please God, she thought, not another would-be artist. Let this one be able to paint, *really* paint.

While renovating the building she had approached a number of well-known south-western artists asking to handle their work, only quickly to learn how difficult it was to deal with established artists and the people who represented them. If she wanted to make a name as a visionary dealer, to rise above her competition, she had to ferret out new talent herself.

She dreamed of discovering someone she could promote, develop and control without having to worry about interference from other dealers. But genius was a rare, precious commodity that didn't just wander in through the front door. From the day the gallery opened, she'd been besieged by a series of no-talent, aspiring artists. Few of them met her exacting standards, and she doubted this rag-tag Indian would either.

She waited for him to speak. After the silence had grown uncomfortably long, she said, "I assume you want to show me what's in that portfolio under your arm."

He hesitated a moment before placing the cheap cardboard container on her desk, untying the string that held it shut.

The contents spilled out in a triumphant blaze of colour. She forced herself not to smile although she felt like letting out a great whoop of joy. A quick glance assured her that the sketches and paintings spread on her desk were glorious, masterful, created with a fresh interior vision and a forceful technique.

Then she took the time to study them more carefully. She couldn't put them into any category that came readily to mind. They weren't expressionistic, impressionistic, or realistic, although they combined elements of all three styles. The Indian had done what every truly great artist must do; he'd coined his own unique idiom.

"Do you speak English?" she asked the silent figure.

"Of course." He paused. "Believe it or not, most Indians do."

There had been a sharp edge to his reply that she

58

liked. Despite his obvious poverty, he had spirit. Well, she thought, making an instant decision, he was going to need it to get where she hoped to take him in the art world.

"What's your name?" she asked, continuing to stare at the paintings on her desk.

"Alan Longchase. I'm an Apache," he added, his voice colouring with a curious mixture of defiance and pride.

"Alan Longchase, did you paint these?" she asked, placing both her hands on the edge of the desk and leaning towards him.

"They're my work." He hesitated briefly. "Are you interested in representing me?"

She let out an unrestrained peal of laughter. Most artists bored her with a long recitation of their credits – their training, the awards they'd won, the major shows they'd been in – before displaying their portfolios and slides. It usually took an hour before they worked up the courage to ask if she'd carry their work.

Not this man. He marched through her door looking like he'd just come off a cattle drive, plopped his portfolio down on her desk, gave her three minutes to study it, and then asked if she'd represent him. Obviously, he didn't believe in wasting time.

Neither did she.

"Yes, I'm interested," she said firmly. Gathering up the pictures, she closed the portfolio, tied it shut, and handed it back. "You and I are going to have a talk – a long talk."

Now, as she stood in her office remembering the past and preparing for another critical meeting with Alan Longchase, she could only hope it would go as well as that first one years before.

5

OCTOBER 16, 1988

"So you've decided to go to the gallery after all." Hank Begay looked up with an approving smile as Alan, dressed in formal attire, entered the living room. "If it means anything, I think you've made a wise choice."

Alan grimaced. "I hope you're right."

Checking his watch, Hank asked, "Don't Liz's openings start at seven? You're an hour late."

"Let Liz sweat." Alan made no effort to hide the bitterness in his voice. "I'm not doing this for her. The only reason I'm going at all is in the hope that some poor Indian kid will catch my picture in the Phoenix papers tomorrow and see that sometimes impossible dreams do come true."

Hank shrugged and the Tony Hillerman mystery he'd been reading fell off his lap. "I guess it would be pointless to tell you to have a good time."

Alan nodded. He couldn't remember looking forward to an evening less. Not trusting himself to say another word, he picked up his keys from the table near the door and headed out into the night.

The cool evening air didn't lower his emotional temperature. How the hell was he going to handle seeing Liz when the memory of her rejection still churned in his gut? Pausing in the drive, he glanced up at the star-strewn sky, seeking his old friend, the constellation the whites call Orion. The great hunter soared in his accustomed place above the horizon to the south. But Alan found no peace in contemplation of the heavens.

The dilemma that had plagued him for eleven weeks continued to weigh heavily on his mind and heart. He drove the twenty miles to downtown Scottsdale automatically, fighting an internal battle all the way. Somehow, he would have to find a way to treat Liz as if she were just another art dealer.

Main Street was crowded when he turned onto it from Scottsdale Road. Costly foreign cars lined the kerb. Expensive restaurants, boutiques, an auction house, antique shops, and galleries all vied for the patronage of the fashionably-dressed strollers who moved down the sidewalk with the confident walk that wealth seems to breed into the bones. It had been an alien, intimidating world the first time he walked its broad avenues, he recalled. Now, familiarity bred contempt.

He finally found a parking space three blocks from his destination. Oblivious to the curious stares invoked by his passage, he strode towards the Kant Gallery like a warrior preparing to meet the enemy.

Alan did not know how formidable he looked when he walked into the gallery. He was barely aware of the people surging towards him as he paused in the entrance, his eyes seeking Liz.

She stood at the desk in the far corner of the room, her back to him. And then she turned, revealing the pure beauty of her profile, the womanly swell of her breasts and hips. His determination to establish a purely business relationship with her fled as his body betrayed him by remembering the things he'd been struggling to forget – the honeyed taste of her welcoming mouth, the sensuous silk of her stomach and thighs, the slick, tight cage of her womanhood.

In that instant, he knew it would never work. He couldn't play the casual acquaintance, pretending they shared nothing but a mutually beneficial commercial arrangement. *He could not go on working with Liz Kant.*

His momentum carried him across the room and, as he closed the distance between them, he saw the Avanyu necklace, the symbol of his rejection, around her throat. Rage ballooned in his chest. So be it. He would inflict hurt for hurt and pain for pain.

"Good evening, Alan," she said coolly when he was three feet away. "As you can see," a nod of her head indicated the quietly expectant crowd, "everyone has been waiting for you."

He fought to control the anger bubbling up his throat. When he felt certain his voice would be steady, he replied, "I'm sorry, Liz. It isn't going to work. It's over."

Not giving her a chance to reply, he turned and made his way toward the door, shutting it softly behind him.

Liz tried to laugh into the excited chatter that accompanied Alan's departure, but the sound she produced was as brittle as glass. She felt impaled by curious stares and the need to say something – anything – compelled her to speak.

"Well, ladies and gentlemen, now you know what we dealers mean when we talk about artistic temperament," she said brightly.

When Danny Medina, the gossip columnist for *Art News*, hurried to her side, she prepared to do battle for her gallery. Squaring her shoulders, she gave him a composed glance. "Somehow I knew you'd want to talk to me."

"Now, now, Liz. We go back a long way. What the hell got into Alan? That was quite a scene."

"You're exaggerating."

"Darling, this is Danny you're talking to. What did Longchase mean when he said, it's over?"

Stalling for time, Liz picked up the half empty champagne glass she'd left on the desk and sipped daintily. "It's really quite simple. I'm afraid that was Alan's rather dramatic way of turning down a major commission. We've been arguing about it for days."

Danny began to remove a notepad from his jacket pocket, but Liz stayed his hand. "This is off the record," she said sternly. "I wouldn't tell you at all if you weren't such an old friend. Unfortunately, after Alan signed the contract, the buyer insisted the painting be done in certain colours. Alan doesn't do decorator art, but the collector is an old and valued client, so I asked Alan to give it his best effort." She shrugged. "It's really a tempest in a teapot. But I'm afraid the whole affair has upset him."

From the expression on Danny's face, Liz knew her explanation wasn't satisfactory. But it was the best she could do. "As much as I love talking to you," she said, "I have to spend time with the paying customers. But let's do lunch sometime next week."

She headed toward the back of the gallery a few minutes later, wishing she could closet herself in her office and forget all about what was obviously a doomed evening. But hiding was out of the question. Instead, she began to make the rounds, chatting gaily as if nothing untoward had occurred.

An hour later, with the rooms half empty and her artists standing around talking to each other rather than to collectors, Rick walked up with a stranger in tow. For the first time that night, Rick's perpetual grin seemed genuine.

"I'd like to introduce you to someone," he said, indicating the tall, thin man at his side. "Liz Kant, this is Reginald Quincy."

"It's a great pleasure to meet you at last," the newcomer said.

"Mr Quincy just purchased a Harrison and three Van Kamps," Rick explained.

Quincy? Liz thought frantically. Where had she heard the name before?

"You have a magnificent gallery." Quincy spoke with

a cultivated eastern accent. "Friends back east recommended it and I must say, the place exceeds my highest expectations. I intend to become a regular. You see, I collect women artists and, from what I've seen, you represent some of the south-west's finest."

Suddenly, Liz recalled where she'd seen his name. A Reginald Quincy had paid a record price for a Mary Cassatt at a recent Sotheby auction. This had to be the same man. Perhaps the evening wasn't a total loss after all. "It's an honour to meet a collector of your stature, Mr Quincy," she said.

Maryann Van Kamp lit another cigarette before checking her watch. She despised openings – and this one was dragging more than most.

"You can't leave yet," Archer said, walking up behind Maryann.

"I know Liz wants us to stay and talk to clients till the bitter end, but there aren't very many left to talk to." Maryann indicated the sparsely-populated room with a nod of her platinum curls. "I was going to try and sneak out early."

"It has been a disappointing evening," Archer agreed. "Nobody seems to be in the mood to buy."

Maryann shrugged. "It's funny. Once a few sold stickers go up, everybody plays follow the leader."

"It's the psychology of crowds," Archer commented.

"Nobody wanted to talk about art tonight. They were too busy speculating about Alan Longchase's behaviour." Maryann sighed heavily, and was about to explain that she wouldn't be able to repay Archer's loan for a while, when Liz and a man Maryann had never seen before joined them. Not a bad looking man either, Maryann thought, giving him a side-long glance.

"Here *she* is," Liz said to the man. "I told you she hadn't left. Maryann, I'd like you to meet an admirer."

"I can always use one of those," Maryann replied, while

giving the newcomer a second look. He was tall – well over six foot – slender, probably in his late forties, and very pale, like most newly-arrived easterners. A long nose and thin lips, punctuated by a narrow slash of a moustache, echoed his body type. Back in Texas, he'd be described as a long drink of water. Not unattractive, she thought, feeling her mood brighten. The stranger was elegantly dressed and obviously well-off.

"Reginald Quincy, I'd like you to meet one of the finest painters I represent, and my personal discovery," proprietary pride coloured Liz's voice, "Maryann Van Kamp."

"It's an honour," Reginald Quincy said, his long, narrow features softened by a warm smile.

"And this is Archer Harrison," Liz continued. "Now, if you don't mind, I should be getting back to my other guests."

Quincy nodded politely without taking his eyes from Maryann.

"I can't tell you what a pleasure it is to meet someone with your talent," he said after Liz had gone. "Miss Kant failed to mention that I just bought three of your paintings." He turned his gaze on Archer and added, as if it were an afterthought, "and one of your pieces too. You see, I collect the work of women artists."

Maryann's breath caught in her throat. Three paintings. Good Lord, even after the gallery's fifty per cent cut, she would be able to pay Archer back and still put a tidy sum in the bank. "Which ones did you buy?"

"I'd be delighted to show you," Quincy replied, placing her hand in the crook of his elbow. "And you too, of course, Miss Harrison."

"It's Mrs," Archer corrected him. "Perhaps some other time, Mr Quincy. I promised to discuss a commission with someone else, and it's getting late."

Maryann silently blessed Archer's tact as the sculptress took her leave. Maryann didn't want to share her new male

65

collector with anyone, not even her best friend. Talk about the power of positive thinking. She'd been conjuring up visions of herself on the arm of a tall, handsome, stranger. And here he was!

"Well, Mr Quincy," she said, smiling up at him, "how about showing me those paintings."

Liz had never known an opening to drag like this one. It was nine thirty. *Only nine thirty.* The Mariachi band she'd hired for the evening still played gay, foot-tapping tunes in front of the gallery. But the tinselled sound served as an unfortunate counterpoint to the restrained murmur of the few people who lingered in the show rooms. That so few clients were still present was unthinkable, an unparalleled disaster. Although the invitations to her shows clearly said seven to ten, she'd never before been able to bid her last guests good night until eleven or later.

It was said that the Scottsdale season didn't begin until Liz Kant held her annual anniversary show. But this opening had the feel of a wake – a funeral. Hers! The evening's one bright spot had been Rick's large sale to Reginald Quincy. She'd never seen Rick look handsomer, be more charming, sell harder. Too bad he wasn't an artist instead of a salesman; she could make him into a superstar.

But even Rick's above-and-beyond-the-call-of-duty effort hadn't succeeded in turning the tide. Collectors who, at previous shows, had drunk and drunk and bought and bought, had only stayed long enough for a single glass of champagne. They talked about Alan's peculiar behaviour, and she repeated the story about the botched commission so often that she almost believed it herself. Most clients, after taking a quick look around the quiet rooms, left to seek livelier entertainment elsewhere.

She had attended openings that failed to catch fire at other galleries, dismal affairs where the artists and the sales people outnumbered the guests. The way a show was put together, the chemistry of a crowd could spell failure. But it had never happened to her before. She knew what, or rather who, was responsible for tonight's disaster. If Alan made the mistake of walking through the door this minute, she'd take great pleasure in killing him – slowly and painfully.

"Smile," Rick warned, materializing at her side.

Nodding, she managed to paste a brittle grimace on her lips. She'd been very close to going over the edge, revealing her inner distress, exposing her vulnerability. Shivering, she unconsciously moved closer to the warmth of Rick's body. His arm slipped around her waist and she welcomed his steadying strength as, together, they said good night to the last guests.

Fifteen minutes later the gallery was empty except for the staff.

"Thank God that's finally over. Lock up for me, Rick," she said. It was a duty she usually performed herself, one which signalled an evening's official end. But tonight it felt good to relegate the job, to pass the reins and the responsibility to someone else.

When he had finished, Rick returned to her side, leaving the rest of the staff to scurry about, following a routine they'd learned at dozens of openings; cleaning the débris of used glasses, dirty ashtrays, paper napkins, half-eaten hors d'oeuvres. Even the most sophisticated people could be pigs when the food and drink were free, Liz thought bitterly, watching her employees bring order from the chaotic remnants of the last three hours.

"Are you all right?" Rick asked, concern evident in his tone.

"Of course."

"I thought it went fairly well."

"It was a complete disaster!" she replied through clenched teeth.

"Come on, Liz. It wasn't that bad. Lots of collectors showed up. They just didn't buy."

She didn't bother to respond. Rick didn't understand the agony of her shattered expectations. He hadn't been with her through the early years, when every sale felt like a triumph, and every collector who left without making a purchase served to remind her of the financial risk she'd taken to open the gallery. Tonight, she was in no better shape financially, than she had been ten years ago. The thought of the half a million she'd borrowed to open a New York gallery for Alan . . .

"I have a feeling Reginald Quincy is going to be one of our best customers," Rick's voice brought her back to the moment, as he put his arm around her waist. "He told me he just purchased an estate in Paradise Valley, and he wants to build a major collection of south-western art."

She could feel the warmth of Rick's hand through the thin silk of her gown. Suddenly, she realized how much she needed that warmth; needed to be touched, held, made love to. She couldn't face being alone. Not tonight.

"Rick, come home with me," she said impulsively.

His eyes widened. During the year he'd been in her employ, he'd deliberately made a habit of touching her, putting his arm around her shoulder or her waist, leaning so close when they looked at a new piece of art together that his breath stirred her hair. Although she'd never responded to his physical presence, Rick hadn't accepted the fact that she didn't find him attractive. He'd wanted her the first time he laid eyes on her at one of the charity balls that festoon the Scottsdale holiday season – and *laid* was the operative word. A man would have to be six feet under not to desire a woman like Liz Kant. Heat flooded his groin as he responded to the need in her voice.

"Look at me, Liz," he commanded, "and ask me again."

Her eyes, deep drowning pools of the most incredible shade of blue, met his. "Come home with me," she repeated, her voice husky with need.

"There's nothing I'd rather do," he responded. He prided himself on being a man of action, adept at thinking on his feet. Now, he didn't give her a chance to change her mind. Still holding her close, he led her through the gallery's seven rooms, stopped briefly in her office to get her purse and her fur, and then gently propelled her out of the back door to his Porsche.

The Turbo Carrera was his pride and joy. He lavished the same loving care on it that other men give their women, or their families. Rick hadn't been part of a family for a couple of decades, not since his father, Beverly Hills' most renowned plastic surgeon left home and hearth for a twenty-year-old, torpedo-titted starlet. Rick had been twelve then, just old enough to realize that the privileged life he'd been leading behind the gates of a Bel Air estate was about to come to a screeching halt. It had all been snatched away in the blink of an eye, that special place in the world that was reserved for the very rich – for people like Liz and her clients.

He opened the Porsche's passenger door and helped her inside, his manners impeccable although her detached attitude disturbed him. Reaching Scottsdale Road, he took a moment to study her profile. She was very lovely. Her features were in repose, and yet he sensed tension in the way she held her body. Obviously, the evening had upset her deeply. And yet Rick couldn't help a silent thankful prayer to the gods of art for the opening's failure. Without it, he wouldn't be headed for a night in Liz's bed.

There was no casual conversation on the drive to her house, no small talk to smooth the rough edges of being alone together for the first time outside the gallery. She seemed to have nothing to say and, for once in his life, his glib tongue deserted him. The silence didn't end until, pointing to a road that climbed the steep flank of Camelback Mountain, she said, "You turn right up ahead."

He knew she lived at the edge of the Phoenix Mountain Preserve, but he'd never been invited to her house before. As he drove, the car's headlights outlined scattered mansions clinging to the mountain's rocky slopes. While negotiating the steep turns, there were times when the halogen beams reached out into the nothingness of a sheer void and the dazzling display of the city was illuminated below. Reaching the end of the blacktop, he pulled into a spacious parking area that had been bulldozed into the mountainside, and cut the engine.

Liz continued to stare straight ahead. One incautious word, he thought, and the mood would be broken; she'd send him packing. He opened the driver side door and stepped out into the flawless, moon-lit night, absent-mindedly caressing the Porsche's fender. Liz sat immobile until he opened her door. Then she took his arm and permitted him to escort her to the front door.

Her mind was filled with a mixture of apprehension, curiosity, and defiance as she cast a sidelong glance at Rick. His behaviour, under what had to be unsettling circumstances for him as well as for her, couldn't be faulted. There was no doubt that he was desirable, the picture of urbane virility in his perfectly-cut tuxedo. And yet, she wasn't sure she could go through with it – give him what he had every right to expect.

She took a key from her bag and handed it to him. He inserted it in the lock and the house sprang to life as lights suddenly illuminated the interior.

"I hate walking into dark rooms," she explained, seeing him start, "so I had a sensor installed to turn the lights on when I unlock the door."

The interior was even more lavish than her office. Rough-hewn beams vaulted high overhead. A tiled floor echoed under their heels as Rick followed Liz across the entry and into the living room. It was immense. A far wall of glass revealed the city below in all its night-lit, fairytale splendour. The furniture, custom-made and quietly expensive, was a tribute to the inimitable design sense of Brunschwig & Fils. A fortune in art decorated the walls.

"This place is stunning," Rick said, looking around appreciatively. Then he paused, his eyes probing Liz's. "Look, I know you're upset. I care about you too much to take advantage of the situation."

Liz hesitated for a fraction of a second. If she was going to back out, this was the time. But her anger with Alan urged her onward. "There's some Dom Perignon in the kitchen refrigerator," she said softly. "You'll find glasses in the pantry. My bedroom's down the hall. I'll be waiting."

Hank was sitting in front of the television in the den, snoring gently, when Alan returned from his aborted foray to the gallery. The sound of the front door closing with a thud woke Hank. "I'm here," he called out.

Alan's shoulders were slumped when he walked into the room. He sank wearily into the well-worn leather couch opposite Hank's chair.

Hank rubbed his eyes, stretched and straightened his spine. He could see trouble clearly written on Alan's face. "You're home early," Hank said cautiously.

"There wasn't much point in staying out."

"Do you want to talk?"

Alan rose, turned off the television, and went to the sideboard. "How about a drink?"

Hank nodded yes. So something had gone wrong at the gallery, very wrong, he thought from the size of the drink Alan poured for himself.

Handing over one of the amber filled tumblers, Alan returned to his seat. "I made a damn fool of myself tonight," he said, his voice tight and controlled. And then he told Hank what had happened and why.

Hank sat quietly throughout Alan's recital, nodding from time to time, knowing the other man had to speak his piece without interruption. When Alan finally finished, Hank got up and poured them both another drink. "Where do you go from here?" he asked, putting the refilled tumbler in Alan's hand.

"The hell of it is, I don't know." Alan's eyes had the same haunted look Hank had seen in them when Alan came back from Vietnam.

"We've been friends a long time," Hank said. "You know I think of you as a son. So I'm going to try and give you a father's advice. From what you've told me, nothing is settled as far as you and Liz are concerned. You're going to have to have it out sooner or later. And you know me. I believe sooner is better."

Alan nodded his agreement. "You're right. Things can't go on the way they have the last eleven weeks. But that's no excuse for the grandstand play I made tonight."

Hank checked his watch. "The opening ought to be winding down. Why don't you go back to the gallery right now. By the time you get there, Liz should be free. Talk things over. I'm sure the two of you can come to some kind of an agreement."

Alan finished his drink, got up and returned the empty glass to the sideboard. "I'll give it a try," he said.

His voice was firm but he had a hollow feeling in the pit of his stomach. His heart told him to follow Hank's suggestion, but his mind argued that it would be a mistake. If he returned to the gallery, Liz might take it as a sign of weakness. She was the toughest, most aggressive and ambitious human being he'd ever known. In the early days of their affair he'd admired those traits. He'd even made the mistake of thinking they made her more like an Apache – fierce in battle, loyal unto death. But now he was convinced that Liz lacked the inner softness which balanced an Apache's raw courage.

"We can talk again after you get back," Hank said.

For the first time that night, Alan smiled. Hank would have made a terrific father. "I'd appreciate it."

72

Alan drove to the gallery faster than he had earlier that night. The traffic was lighter, and he was filled with purpose. Before this night ended, he intended to have settled things with Liz once and for all. Perhaps there was a way to continue his association with the gallery. Perhaps some third party, one of her staff or even Hank, could act as a buffer between them. That way Alan could continue repaying his debt to Liz without having to see her constantly.

He checked the dashboard clock before turning onto Main Street. The small hand had just moved past eleven. Coming to a halt in front of the gallery, he was surprised to find a quiet, empty boulevard. Liz always hired a band to play out front during an opening, but now the sidewalk was deserted. The gallery, which he'd expected to find blazing with light and crowded with merry-makers, was quiet and uninhabited.

He slid from the Blazer's high seat and walked to the doors. Where the hell was everybody? Peering through one of the large show windows, he waited for his eyes to adjust to the darkness. His paintings were in the front room, lonely sentinels in the gathering gloom. Obviously, Liz had closed earlier than usual. Perhaps it was for the best. What they had to say to each other would be better said in total privacy.

Fifteen minutes driving brought him to the Camelback Mountain turnoff. He looked to his right, up the side of the brooding, boulder-strewn peak, and saw lights blazing near its peak. So Liz was home.

Rick walked into Liz's cavernous kitchen. You could prepare a goddamn banquet in here, he thought. Overhead a series of copper-bottomed pots were suspended from a wrought-iron rack. To his right an eight-burner stove with a gas grill big enough to barbecue a side of beef took up most of one wall. A huge refrigerator-freezer bulked in the corner. Opening one side, he saw several bottles of

Dom Perignon tucked amid cartons of milk and sixpacks of flavoured seltzer.

He selected a bottle of wine, put it down on the counter and, walking through an arch which he thought might lead to the pantry, found himself in a space bigger than the bedroom of his rented apartment. He'd guessed right. This particular pantry bulged with Rosenthal china, Waterford and Lalique crystal, and Sheffield silver. Rick selected two long-stemmed glasses from one of the shelves, returned to the kitchen and expertly popped the cork on the champagne, not wasting a drop.

With the wine and glasses in hand, he headed toward the long hall where he'd last seen Liz, not quite sure what her mood would be. Pushing a pair of double doors open, he found himself on the threshold of a spacious room. A king-size bed dominated one wall. The opposite one held a fireplace. Above it hung a life-sized painting of a nude woman. Her flesh had the delicate gleam of living ivory. One arm was flung back above her tousled hair; her legs were slightly parted. It was a portrait of Liz and Rick recognized the artist's work at once. Longchase! An unreasoning jealousy coursed through him. Forcing his eyes away from the painting, Rick saw Liz standing in the middle of the room, still in the gown she'd worn for the opening, a desirable red-haired flame of a woman in the all-white room.

"I see you found the champagne," she said, her tone giving no clue to her state of mind. He was accustomed to feeling confident when he was with a woman. Somehow, this particular woman managed to unsettle and arouse him at the same time. The feeling engaged his combative nature, his urge to emerge the victor in their encounter.

He filled their glasses and handed one to her. "To us – and new beginnings."

Liz drank thirstily. The aching void that had engulfed her when Alan walked out was receding, banished by the wine she'd consumed and the admiration she saw in Rick's

74

eyes. There'd been few men in her life before Alan – and none since. She'd locked desire away the night he walked out of this room, content to wait for his return.

How stupid she had been. Now she knew, beyond question or doubt, that she and Alan were finished. She had to put their relationship behind her, no matter how much it hurt. Rick was the perfect antidote to her aching sense of loss. She could feel her pulse beating in her throat.

"Like I said before," Rick's voice intruded on her musing, "I don't want to take advantage of the situation tonight. I don't want you to do something you'll regret."

The only thing she regretted, she thought bitterly, was devoting almost ten years of her life to Alan Longchase. "Actually," she replied, "I've been wondering why we haven't done this before." She finished her wine in one resolute swallow. "And now, Rick, I'd like you to do me a favour."

"Whatever you say, Liz."

"Undress for me. I want to see if you look as good with your clothes off as you do in that tuxedo."

She walked to her bed and sat down facing him. I don't need you, Alan Longchase, she told herself, swallowing the huge lump in her throat and vowing not to think of him again that evening.

Rick slipped from his jacket, undid the jet studs that closed his ruffled dress shirt and pulled it off. Kicking free of his Bally evening shoes and unzipping his fly, he resisted the urge to roll his pelvis and really put on a show. Liz's eyes were exploring his body, arousing him. Fully erect, he stepped out of his French briefs and stood still, giving her time to take a good long look. He'd lost count of the women he'd bedded, women who raved about his body. A great physique was the one inheritance his father hadn't been able to deny him and, knowing the value of such an asset, Rick worked at staying in shape.

At that moment, Liz almost ran out of the room. But

the image of Alan, looking at her with hate-filled eyes, saying "it's over," made her stay. She rose from the bed and stepped into Rick's arms.

"God, I want you," he said, pulling her close. Tilting her face up, he began to explore it with soft kisses that caressed the fullness of her lips, the corner of her mouth, his tongue barely brushing hers before he broke the contact, bending to kiss her neck while his hands explored her body.

"Your turn," he commanded, ending their embrace and nodding toward the painting above the fireplace. "Let's see if you look as good as that portrait."

Liz hesitated. Although Rick was an undeniably skilled lover, capable of arousing her body, she didn't love him. Then a bitter chuckle escaped her lips. Love? What a joke that was. From here on, she would concern herself with pleasure. Opening her eyes, she smiled at Rick and shed her dress.

Rick knew the dress must have set her back at least $5,000, but she kicked it out of her way as casually as if she'd purchased it at Penney's. Damn, she's a hell of a woman, he thought. Her gossamer teddy and hose barely impeded his view but he couldn't wait until they too fell to the floor.

Longchase had been one hundred per cent accurate when he painted her, Rick realized, except Liz was even more stunning in living, breathing flesh. Her arms and legs were long and supple, surprisingly athletic. Obviously, she was paying her dues in a gym because nobody over sixteen looked that good without working at it.

She was slender, almost delicately built, but her breasts were much larger than he would have imagined, and tipped with large, blushed nipples that invited his mouth. His glance held on them before moving downward. Surprised by what he saw, he put his champagne glass down so quickly that it tipped over. She was a natural redhead. The curls covering her pubis were the same coppery shade as the hair on her head. He reached for her and fell to his knees, kissing that unexpected thatch of red in tribute.

She still wore her turquoise and diamond jewellery when he lifted her to the bed and began exploring her body. He wanted to know all of her, completely and at once; her mouth, the hollow of her neck, the swell of her breasts, the deep indent of her navel, the honeyed wet of her cunt. Parting her legs, he knelt between them.

Alan parked in Liz's drive, exited his Blazer in one lithe movement, and headed up the path to the front door, not noticing the black Porsche parked in the shadow. He knocked and, to his surprise, the door yielded under his hand, swinging wide on silent hinges. Pausing in the entry, he called Liz's name. When no one answered, he headed toward the wing which held the kitchen, thinking Liz might be having a cup of tea with Rosita as was her custom when she needed to unwind.

Although he and Liz had overseen the house's construction together, had chosen the furniture and accessories, Alan felt like an interloper. He had no idea how Liz would react if she found him, unannounced and uninvited, but he was determined to talk to her. As he slipped down the hall with the unconscious stealth of his Apache ancestors, the house seemed to exude a charged atmosphere which tugged at the superstitious beliefs of his childhood. His mother would say *chindi* infested this place, he thought.

The lights were on in the kitchen, and a champagne cork had been left on one of the counters, but there was no sign of either Liz or her housekeeper. For the first time, Alan felt a nasty twinge of concern as he considered the possibilities. The front door had been unlocked. Several unpleasant what-ifs raced through his mind.

His concern for Liz grew as he returned to the hall. Now, rather than calling Liz's name, he moved with increasing stealth and caution, checking the rest of the rooms in the house's western wing. Back in the entry once more, he turned toward Liz's suite and for the first time he heard muffled voices. Not conversation; it sounded more like a series of low groans. The hair on the back of his neck rose and every sense came alert as adrenaline pumped through his body. He sensed trouble lurking behind her chamber's partially-closed doors.

Opening them, he paused in the entry. At the far end of the room, sprawled on the bed, lay Liz. Her skin glowed in the soft light, her hair tumbled across a pillow. A man knelt between her parted legs, a rapt look of pleasure on his face.

Steadying himself against the door, Alan choked back a curse. The bitch. No wonder she'd closed the gallery early. Liz and her fucking assistant couldn't wait to get each other in bed. Alan stood frozen as Rick rose on his knees, holding his engorged penis, preparing for penetration. With a deep groan of pleasure, he plunged deep into Liz's waiting body.

Alan saw the gleam of the Avanyu necklace on her throat before he turned as silently as he had come, ran down the hall and out of the house.

6

OCTOBER 17, 1988

Maryann was in the middle of her favourite recurring dream, the one where a man gave her everything she longed for, from unquestioning love and total commitment to fantastic sex and financial security. Her phantom lover, whose face she had never been able to remember even though her dreams were incredibly vivid, always took her to beautiful places – fabulous hotels where they occupied the best suites, elegant restaurants where they ate ambrosial meals that miraculously never added inches to her waistline or cellulite to her thighs. Afterward they would go someplace and dance until dawn, floating across the floor like Fred and Ginger at their best. Then they'd watch the sun rise, toast each other with champagne, and slowly, sensuously, remove one another's clothing.

Beneath closed lids her eyes moved rapidly as she experienced the thrill of lovemaking. She had just parted her legs for an ardent cock when a distant phone sounded. "Let the maid answer it, honey," she mumbled sleepily.

But there was no maid and by the third ring she'd been jerked from the warm, wonderful dream into the reality of her bedroom's fading wallpaper and cheap modern furniture. Rubbing her eyes, she struggled free of the bedclothes and staggered toward the living room to answer the insistent summons. Damn. Her caller was certainly persistent. Six ringy-dingies. Then seven. Someone sure wanted to talk to her. She snatched the receiver from its

79

black plastic cradle and said, "Hello," to the dial tone.

Shaking her head, she hung up, stretched and looked around. The thirty-year-old tract home was broodingly quiet. She filled the silence by turning on the television. A gorgeous female newscaster was grinning into the camera, displaying a set of dazzling uppers and lowers as she reported a fire that killed three children. The silly bitch would probably smile while announcing the end of the world, Maryann fumed, heading for the bathroom. Standing over the sink, she inspected herself in the mirror. Not a pretty sight, she decided.

She'd been too lazy to take her make-up off before going to bed after the opening last night. Now, smudged mascara rimmed her eyes, adding ten years to her appearance.

Not having to worry about the way she looked in the morning was one of the few benefits of being single. But she no longer believed the benefits offset the disadvantages; the loneliness, the feeling of life passing her by – to say nothing of the sexual deprivation that had turned her vibrator into her best friend.

Splashing water on her face, she forced the sense of dissatisfaction away. She'd been thinking too many dark thoughts lately and in the gospel according to Van Kamp, that was inviting trouble. She inspected her gums, thanked God they hadn't started receding, and brushed her teeth vigorously.

She had just positioned herself on the toilet with an old issue of *Cosmopolitan* for company when the phone rang again. "Nuts!" she muttered. Who in the world would call her this early? Her few friends knew she was a confirmed late-riser.

Predictably, the ringing stopped before she reached the phone. Just what she needed, she thought angrily, a determined bill collector calling morning, noon and night. She was easing her bottom into a pair of faded, too tight jeans when the ringing began again. This time she sprinted to the living room.

"Good morning, you'all," she said with determined cheerfulness.

"It is a good morning, isn't it?" a strange male voice responded.

Who the hell can it be? she stewed, wishing she'd had time for a cup of coffee. She was never at her best in the a.m.

"I hope I didn't waken you, Miss Van Kamp."

At least it wasn't a bill collector. They were never that polite. "Of course you didn't, Sugah," she answered, desperately searching for the name that went with the distinctively thin, cultivated voice. And then it came to her. The opening last night – the angel of an art collector who bought three of her paintings. Please, Lord, let him be single, she prayed as she drawled, "Why, Reginald Quincy, I've been in my studio for hours, painting. Having you acquire my canvasses has been a genuine inspiration."

She knew she was laying the southern belle bit on with a trowel, but there was something about the man that made her defensive. Probably his obvious wealth and breeding, and her own feeling that just plain poor folks like her were intrinsically inferior.

"How kind of you to say that. I'd love to see your studio, perhaps even have the privilege of watching you paint. As I mentioned last night, I particularly admire the work of women artists." He paused. "Aside from your own marvellous oil, I have a number of fine things by other ladies, including a Bonheur, an absolutely glorious Cassatt, several O'Keefes and a Nevelson wall sculpture."

Maryann gulped. Anyone who owned work of that calibre had to be a major collector as well as a very rich one. She'd have to add his name to her CV under the *In the collection of* column. "I'd love to see them someday," she replied with spontaneous exuberance.

"I was hoping you'd feel that way. In fact, I called to see

if you might join me for dinner tonight? I could pick you up and see your studio before we went out." He sounded eager.

She looked around her living room, trying to see its virtues and vices through a stranger's eyes. Her couch and easy chairs were presentable and she had made her own coffee and end-tables from glass bricks and slabs of sand-stone. Her paintings hung on the walls and one of Archer's larger sculptures stood in a corner. She had painted the room's interior at her own expense a few months after moving in, and convinced her landlord to replace the shabby drapes with vertical blinds from Sears.

But, in the end, her attempts at decorating merely served to point up the house's shortcomings, the thread-bare carpet, the out of date appliances and plumbing, and the cheap construction. An uptown guy like Reginald wouldn't be impressed. Even worse, the neighbourhood was a disaster area of run-down homes and rattle-trap cars that oozed end-of-the-line hopelessness. He'll see this house over my dead body, she concluded.

"I'd love to have dinner with you," she replied. "Since I have an appointment in Scottsdale late this afternoon, why don't we meet in front of the Kant Gallery at five?"

"Of course. Whatever's best for you. I guess I can see your studio some other time. *A bientôt, Chérie,*" Reginald concluded.

His French farewell tugged at her memory. Damn! She'd have to resuscitate her two-years-in-Del-Rio-High knowledge of the language since he sprinkled his conver-sation with it. Then she grinned as a word popped into her memory bank. "*Merde* – shit." It wasn't much, but it was a beginning.

Whistling "I Love Paris", she walked across the room and through the doorway into the kitchen. It had been a long dry spell between dates. But Reginald seemed like he was worth waiting for.

*

The day's mail, including an envelope from the Guggenheim Museum, sat unopened on Liz's desk the morning after the tenth anniversary show. Normally a letter from a world-famous museum would have taken precedence over everything else, but she was too angry with herself to think about business. How could she have compounded her current problems by inviting Rick into her bed last night?

Rick had exhibited extraordinary sensitivity by leaving before dawn. She had pretended to be asleep when he got up and dressed, lightly kissing her cheek before tiptoeing from the room. Obviously he'd sensed their new intimacy wouldn't stand the test of facing one another over a breakfast table. She needed Rick last night and he had been there for her. The question was, did she still need, or even want him in the morning's cold light?

Leaning back, she closed her eyes and rubbed her temples. First things first, she reminded herself. Any decision about Rick's place in her life would have to wait until she'd decided how to handle Alan. She had no intention of permitting him to ruin his career or hers by leaving the gallery. There had to be a way to prevent it, but the solution eluded her.

Sitting up and squaring her shoulders, Liz reached for the stack of mail and opened the letter from the Guggenheim. Before she could scan its contents, she heard a soft knock on her office door. "Come in," she called out.

The door opened to reveal Archer Harrison. The sculptress was handsomely attired in a St John knit, her make-up flawlessly done and her hair perfectly coiffed. Yet she had a harried, unsettled look. "Liz, I hope you don't mind my stopping by without an appointment."

Liz gave her a distracted smile. "It's not a very good time."

"I only need a few minutes."

"All right," Liz relented. "Have a seat."

Archer took a chair opposite the desk. "There's something I need to discuss."

"I hope it isn't something to do with the Santa Fe show. Exhibiting with Roman De Silva is the opportunity of a lifetime. You do realize he insisted the museum include your work?"

"Yes. And I'm very grateful to him. In a way, that's why I'm here. To make a long story short, my husband is leaving tonight on a six-month business trip. I refused to go with him but ever since . . . well, I've been wondering if I'm doing the right thing. I'm not sure I have enough talent to warrant disappointing my husband, let alone risking my marriage."

"And you want me to reassure you?"

"No. I want you to be honest."

Liz took time to frame her answer carefully. She couldn't afford to lose another artist. Not after last night. "Are you seriously considering going with him?"

Archer nodded.

Liz's eyebrows rose. "You realize I have a vested interest in your decision?"

"I know." Archer was nervously clasping and unclasping her alligator handbag. "But I trust your judgement."

Liz stared off in the distance. She was hardly qualified to give anyone advice about their personal life. Not after the mess she had made of her own. But she was an expert on the subject of ambition, the personal sacrifices ambition imposed. Suddenly, she felt an almost irresistible urge to tell Archer about her own life, to unburden her heart and soul to another woman. But she stifled the desire. Archer had come to her for help – not True Confessions.

"You have a great deal of talent," Liz began. "But do you have staying power? As I see it, there are three kinds of artists in the world – local talents with a home-town following, regional artists who show their work in a five- or six-state area, and people with national and international reputations whose work is auctionable at places like Christie's or Sotheby's. I'll represent an artist on any level if he or she has talent. But, if they can't or won't

84

make the commitment to take the next step, if they're lacking ambition, they don't belong in my gallery."

"Where do I fit into that picture?"

"I think you already know the answer. You're on the brink of breaking through on the national scene. How far you go is up to you and, to a lesser extent, to me."

"I thought it was up to the public, the collectors and the critics."

"Don't be naïve. There are no limits for a zealous artist with a powerful mentor. I don't know what's right for you when it comes to your personal life." Liz knew she needed to hang on to Archer. "If it will help, I'll tell you about the decision I made a long time ago."

Nodding, Archer settled in her chair.

Liz gazed across the room, thinking back. "There was a time when I wanted to be an artist."

Archer's eyebrows rose. "I didn't know."

"Not many people do," Liz laughed dryly. "Unfortunately, by my sophomore year in college, I knew my work was mediocre. I had a good eye even then, 'a dealer's eye', my professors called it. I decided to capitalize on it. From that day forward, I dedicated myself to the business of art rather than its creative aspects." There was so much more she could have said about the years of deprivation, of scrimping and saving to open her own place.

"Didn't you ever want to get married, have children?"

"I didn't have the time. Success demands commitment," Liz replied, explaining her life with the three words that served as her credo. "You can have an unlimited future, Archer. The show in Santa Fe is just the first step. I can't tell you if you made the right choice in terms of your marriage. But know this. I expect from you what I demand from myself – dedication and hard work." She paused briefly. "Well, Archer, what's it going to be?"

The Impeccable Pig was jammed with the usual luncheon crowd, and the hum of a dozen lively conversations rose

85

above the clink of silver and the clatter of dishes. Archer and Maryann had dined with an eye to calorie intake, and now they dawdled over black coffee.

"Are you sure the belt and scarf will jazz up my blue dress enough?" Maryann asked. "I want to make a good impression tonight."

"Mr Quincy is expecting to go out with an artist," Archer replied, "not a fashion model. You'll look just fine."

They had spent the morning going through half a dozen stores in the exclusive Borgata shopping complex nestled among the luxurious resorts on north Scottsdale Road. The Borgata, built in the style of a medieval Italian walled town, was a mecca for the monied. Maryann had been especially enthralled with Capriccio's, an exclusive boutique, and it had taken all of Archer's persuasive powers to successfully steer Maryann away from buying a designer dress which she couldn't afford.

"So give," Maryann said, adding another packet of sweetener to her cup. "Tell me about your meeting with Liz."

"There's not much to tell. I woke up thinking I was making a tragic mistake by staying here instead of going with Louis. After talking to Liz I realize I'd be making an even bigger one if I left. The problem is," Archer confessed, "I still feel like hell."

Maryann nodded her understanding. "I know the feeling – damned if you do and damned if you don't. If it's any consolation, I think you're doing the right thing. How's Louis taking it?"

Archer leaned back and crossed her legs. "I'm not sure. He's been so busy ever since Steve Carpenter's heart attack that we haven't had a chance to talk. Not really." She paused. "Look, I'm sick of thinking about my problems. Why don't you tell me about your date tonight. This Quincy is giving you quite a rush."

"I guess he's lonely. He's new in town." A sudden

smile lit Maryann's face. "You know, I think he really likes me."

"Why shouldn't he?" Archer replied indignantly, wishing she could find some way to counteract Maryann's perpetual inferiority complex.

Maryann ignored the question. "How did he strike you?"

"What I think doesn't matter." Archer couldn't bring herself to tell Maryann that something about Quincy made her edgy. Perhaps it wasn't Quincy at all, she rationalized, but just a reflection of her own dark mood. "What do *you* think?"

"He's sure different from the guys I've met in bars. They're either married and looking for a one-night-stand, or single and queer. Reginald has class. And his taste in art is fantastic." Maryann chortled happily. "After all, he bought three of my paintings."

They chatted easily for fifteen more minutes before the bill arrived. Later, driving back home, Archer couldn't help thinking how their rôles had reversed. Seven weeks ago, Maryann had been broke and desperately lonely. Now, she was going off to spend the evening with a new man in her life, while Archer was steeling herself to say goodbye to the man in hers.

Alan had been driving steadily eastward for six hours. Gazing through the windshield, he saw the peaks of the Animas Mountains pushing against the sky forty miles away. They marked the continent's spine, the place where the waters divide to flow east or west. The place names on his highway map – Mescal, Texas Canyon, Apache Pass, Dos Cabesas and Pedregosas – lifted his spirits. The very name, Arizona, came from the Indian word, Arizonac, meaning "little spring". Here his ancestors had roamed free. It was a hard, unforgiving land, and he loved it.

Just west of Wilcox he turned the Blazer south on Route 666's narrow asphalt. The Dragoon Mountains, journey's

87

end, loomed on his right, leaping from the desert like the bony, armoured crest of a dinosaur's back. In his hurry to reach them his foot settled more firmly on the accelerator and the Blazer surged eagerly forward. He checked his rear view mirror, saw the horse trailer swaying and, not wanting to jar Odii, slowed again. Twenty miles to go. He'd be there soon enough.

After spending the small hours of the night driving around aimlessly, tormented by what he'd seen in Liz's bedroom, he had gathered his camping gear in the pre-dawn, hitched up the horse trailer and loaded Odii. The Apaloosa had looked like a *spirit horse* in the moonlight, her white spotted hide a ghostly shimmer as she walked up the ramp. The mare had whinnied plaintively when he went into the house to change his clothes and talk to Hank. Odii was anxious to leave, but nowhere near as anxious as Alan himself. When he finished dressing in jeans, a chamois shirt, and a sheepskin vest, he went into Hank's bedroom and shook his old friend awake.

"What's the matter?" Hank said, rubbing sleep from his eyes.

"We need to talk," Alan replied hoarsely.

Hank got out of bed with surprising agility for a man his age and size, and retrieved a robe from the closet. "What time is it?"

"Four."

"In the morning?"

Alan nodded.

"Sorry I didn't wait up last night. When you weren't home by two, I figured . . ."

Realizing Hank must have concluded that he and Liz were spending the night together, Alan laughed acidly. "You couldn't be more wrong."

For the first time, Hank seemed to notice how Alan was dressed. "Are you going someplace?"

"That's one of the things we need to talk about. I made coffee," he said, leading the way to the kitchen.

He busied himself pouring them each a cup, black and hot the way they both liked it. When they were settled at the breakfast table, Alan said, "I'm leaving town for a while. Camping in the Stronghold. I need a favour."

"You've got it," Hank replied confidently.

"I want you to take over as my master dealer and pull my work out of the Kant Gallery." Alan could see Hank's confidence evaporate.

"That's a hell of a favour," the older man replied.

"I wouldn't ask if I had any other choice." Alan couldn't bring himself to tell Hank why he wanted out of Liz's gallery and her life.

"Don't you have a contract with Liz?" Worry made Hank look fierce.

"It ran out five years ago. We didn't think we needed . . ." Alan's voice trailed off. Five years ago he and Liz had been so much in love that the thought of signing a new legal agreement hadn't occurred to either of them.

Hank blew on his coffee and then swallowed deeply. "Hell. I don't know a damn thing about the art business. Isn't there someone else?"

Alan shook his head. "I don't trust anyone else."

"If I do what you want, I'll probably screw up royally. It could cost you money."

"I don't care about the money. Call Liz later today and tell her what I've decided. I don't want to have to see her when I get back."

Reluctantly, Hank agreed. A few minutes later, he followed Alan out to the Blazer, caught him in a rough embrace, and wished him well.

Now Alan drove with fierce concentration. He felt sick, dirty inside, the way he'd felt after crawling through the mud of Vietnam and killing men who were closer to him, racially, than his own white officers. No Apache took a life easily. Alan believed the spirit of a dead enemy was more dangerous to him than a living, fully-armed opponent.

He also believed that killing was a sickness, a fever

89

in the blood. He'd felt it in Nam and again last night, the need to maim, to hurt, to destroy. He'd been one incautious moment away from bursting into Liz's bedroom, pulling Rick from her body and beating the life out of them both.

The rage was a madness. As an Apache he believed he'd fallen out of harmony with the natural world – and only the natural world could make him well again. In the old days a *dijn* would have prescribed an *edota*, a curing ceremony. But there were few practising medicine men in twentieth-century Arizona. Leaving Scottsdale seemed Alan's only sane alternative.

As he negotiated the final stretch of dirt road leading to the Stronghold, his thoughts turned to Cochise, the Apache leader who, in the second half of the nineteenth century, had tried to make peace with the whites, to live with them in harmony. Of course, it hadn't worked. The whites had taken, TAKEN, *TAKEN*. It never stops, he thought bitterly as the memory of Liz knotted in his chest. *She had taken his soul.*

His jaws clenched as he reached the Stronghold's narrow entrance. Anglos had made the sacred place into a campground. In the summer they desecrated it with beer cans and liquor bottles that would foul the land forever. Music from their transistor radios echoed from the canyon walls, drowning out the song of the wind. Now, thank God, the chill autumn nights would keep all but the hardiest souls away. Pulling into the parking area, he saw he had the place to himself. But he didn't intend to stay so near the canyon's entrance. He intended to ride up through the Stronghold, retracing the ancient path the *People* had used when General Crook forced them to flee their homeland.

A half hour's work saw Odii unloaded and saddled. The horse curvetted, tossing her head and flaring her nostrils to better breath the intoxicatingly fresh air. Winding her reins around a sapling, he began to pack. He bundled his clothing in his bed roll and tied it behind the saddle. An old blue enamel coffee pot, a frying pan, small sacks of dried beans, coffee, flour, salt and sugar were tucked in his saddle bags along with a supply of jerky and a slab of salt pork. Then he threaded the scabbard of his hunting knife through his belt. Last, he tucked an old bolt action twenty-two into the boot under the saddle's girth.

What he hadn't brought he would take from the land. Pinon nuts were plentiful in the fall and *nopals*, juicy young cactus leaves, could be found at the lower elevations. He smiled, remembering the richness of the countryside. Fifty years from now how many Apaches would still know that the newly green buds of prickly pear tasted like asparagus when they were sun-dried and simmered with wild onions – or that the ripening seed-pods of mesquite were as tender and crunchy as raw snap-peas? The high desert, so ugly and forbidding to most Anglos, was as sweet as a loving woman to Alan, and as nourishing to his body and soul. The Dragoons covered 250 square miles of wilderness, rich in game. He wouldn't go hungry, physically or spiritually, no matter how long he stayed.

His packing done, he locked the Blazer, pocketed the keys, took a last look around the campground and, mounting Odii, reined her toward the trail that led into the heart of the Stronghold. A freshening breeze blew from the peaks and the Apaloosa danced with delight, her steel-shod hoofs ringing against an occasional rocky outcropping on the dirt trail. The mesquite, greasewood and palo verde of the lower elevations soon gave way to pinon and juniper. Clumps of cacti bristled from green grasses that had been nurtured by late summer rains. The air was so still that he could hear the busy hum of insects as if the sounds had been amplified. A steady thunk, thunk, told him a woodpecker was nearby, chiselling at pine bark in search of grubs. The air looked different, smelled different. He felt better already.

Overhead, a red-tailed hawk circled the sky, calling

to its mate with a high, faint scream. Alan looked up, admiring its effortless flight in the brilliant turquoise sky – a sky the colour of Liz's eyes. And then the anguish of remembrance struck him. God, would he never be free of her?

"Liz." The tormented cry burst from his mouth and caromed off the canyon walls. He spurred his horse forward, in a desperate attempt to escape even the echo of Liz's name.

Hank postponed calling Liz all morning. Instead, he went grocery shopping and stopped at the feed store. Then he decided to clean the house although the maid had been in three days earlier. He washed the kitchen floor, vacuumed the den, and was just starting on the living room when he admitted the futility of his actions. Sooner or later, he was going to have to make that damned phone call.

Contemplating it made his stomach grumble. His large frame required vast amounts of food, and he was never at his best when he was hungry. A few minutes later he stood over the kitchen sink, finishing a bagel laden with cream cheese, belly lox, and slices of Maui onion and tomato. Life should be simple, he thought, licking a crumb from the corner of his mouth before rinsing his plate – good food, good friends, a sound roof over your head, and enough money to go on enjoying them. Somehow, Liz and Alan had a talent for complications.

Feeling marginally better, Hank returned to the living room and picked up the telephone.

An hour later, freshly showered and shaved, wearing his best western shirt and slacks, a pair of Tony Lama snakeskin boots, and a concho-banded black Stetson, he parked in front of the restaurant where he and Liz had agreed to meet. His shoulder-length hair was knotted into the traditional bun called a *chongo*, and a thick necklace of Spider Web Turquoise nuggets hung down his massive chest.

The Glass Door, just a couple of blocks down Main Street from the Kant Gallery, was one of Scottsdale's most elegant eateries. It was to the restaurant's credit that the maître d' didn't blink an eye when Hank, looking like an apparition straight out of a Louis L'Amour novel, asked for Liz Kant's table.

Hank arrived early on purpose, wanting to scout the terrain before confronting the enemy. The restaurant's art deco décor and muted mauve colouring soothed his eyes, while the deep carpeting and plush upholstery wrapped him in luxury. He drew a deep breath, settling himself in the booth before setting his mind to the task ahead. Wresting Alan's work from Liz's control wouldn't be easy. Damn those two! They're still in love, Hank thought, even if neither one was willing to admit it.

His own experiences with love had been far less painful. As a young man he'd been too engrossed with getting an education and becoming a good teacher to have time for marriage. And face it, he'd been so damn ugly that the girls hadn't exactly stood in line. Now there was Eleanor Tsosie, a plump, stately Navajo nurse up at Window Rock, who he hoped to marry one of these days – when and if Alan got his life straightened away and no longer needed him.

Alan had always been the son of his heart, Hank thought with a quick burst of pride, if not of his loins. He'd never forgotten his first meeting with the defiant Apache some thirty years ago when Alan had been nine and Hank a twenty-five year old art teacher at the Phoenix Indian School. Even then there had been something special about the boy, a proud, angry light in his eyes that Hank rarely saw on Indian faces anymore.

"Will you help me leave this place?" Alan asked at the conclusion of his first art class, making it sound more like a demand than a request. "My mother needs me at home."

"I'm sorry," Hank replied, "but the Bureau of Indian

Affairs says you're to have an education. There are no schools on your reservation."

In those days, Hank spent a great deal of time every September consoling students who were so homesick for their distant families that they couldn't eat or sleep, let alone study. But Alan hadn't been like that. He'd been defiant and angry at the way the white world dealt with the red. Part of that anger lingered deep inside him even now, refuelled by Liz's rejection. Seeing her approach across the almost empty restaurant, Hank wondered if he would ever know why she had said no to Alan's proposal.

She looked even more beautiful than he remembered. Liz was one of those fortunate females who grow lovelier with each passing year. Rising to greet her, Hank studied her carefully as she slid into the booth. Others, Alan included, described her as a true patrician. But Hank saw something in the narrow, slightly aquiline arch of her nose, the deep-set intensity of her eyes, the breadth of her cheekbones, that reminded him more of an Eastern Odalisque than an Anglo aristocrat. He saw in her looks something tribal – but what tribe? Who is this woman? he mused as he had so many times in the past, and where does she come from?

"Good afternoon, Hank," Liz said, settling herself against the upholstery.

A nod of her head brought a hurrying waiter. After ordering drinks, she turned her full attention to Hank. "Why did you want to see me?"

Might as well get on with it, Hank thought. "Alan has asked me to be his master dealer. He wants me to withdraw his work from your gallery as soon as possible."

Liz paled, but she didn't flinch. Hank had to admire her courage. "The fact that you taught Alan how to paint doesn't qualify you to run a multi-million-dollar enterprise," she said. "And that's what Alan is today. You could ruin everything I've worked so hard to help him achieve."

94

"You know how I feel about Alan," Hank grudgingly replied. Damn her. She wasn't making it easy. But he hadn't expected her to. "I wouldn't do anything to hurt him, or his career."

"Having you take over as his master dealer could be a disaster," she said quietly.

"Look Liz, I don't want to get into anything personal here. That's between you and Alan. But his instructions were clear. He wants out."

"Do you realize how complex his affairs are?" She didn't give him a chance to reply. "The images he creates are being reproduced as limited edition prints, posters, wearable art, greeting cards, stationery . . . the list goes on and on, and each item involves contractual relations with other firms. Just last week, I had an inquiry from a major soft drink company, wanting to know if Alan would be interested in designing promotional drinking cups for them. The minister of culture in Beijing has written, asking if Alan would like to be the first native American painter to exhibit in the Palace of Art. And I'm in the middle of negotiating his retrospective with the Guggenheim. Given the proper guidance, Alan can be the next Picasso."

"You've made your point, Liz. But Alan's the boss. I have to do what he wants."

"No you don't," Liz replied emphatically. "Do you understand your duties as Alan's master dealer?"

"In general."

"You must be aware that a master dealer has total control over an artist's career." Liz stared at him resolutely. "I can't believe you'd willingly damage Alan's future by doing the wrong thing now."

"I'll do my best to see that doesn't happen."

"Your best isn't going to be good enough. From here on you're going to have to choose which galleries exhibit Alan's work. It isn't as easy as it sounds. I get dozens of letters every year from dealers wanting to represent him.

Alan can afford to be associated with one bad gallery – but put him in three or four and the critics will start wondering what's going on. They're like piranhas when they scent blood. Are you ready for that responsibility?"

Hank didn't respond. He knew his shortcomings even better than Liz.

"There have been times when Alan accused me of a lack of loyalty. That seems rather ironic now." She pulled a pack of cigarettes from her purse and took one herself before offering them to Hank.

"No thanks," he said, taking her lighter from her hand. He pretended to ignore her slight tremor as he lit her cigarette. Despite her outward calm, he realized she was under an enormous emotional strain. But her face and manner didn't betray her.

"I have a proposition for you," she said, exhaling a thin stream of smoke, "one I hope you'll accept, because it's in your best interests and mine. And Alan's, though I doubt he'd admit it."

"Go on."

She stared straight into his eyes. "Hank, I would like to train you to handle Alan's affairs. I don't want him hurt by this change in management, and I can't think of any other way to avoid it."

"What do you want in return?"

Her eyes flashed. "I'm willing to give you two mornings a week until you're comfortable with your duties, to be available to you at all times should problems arise you can't handle."

He didn't trust her. "I repeat, what do you want in return?"

"I want you to sign a five-year contract in Alan's name, guaranteeing that he will continue to do a major show with me every year, and that I will go on getting first choice of his canvasses."

"That sounds like blackmail," Hank said. "I don't think Alan would agree to your deal."

"You're missing the point." She leaned towards him. "When Alan asked you to be his master dealer, he gave you the authority to control his career."

Hank was damn glad he'd never played poker with Liz. There was no doubt in his mind that she'd win every pot. "Supposing I go along with you. How do I explain my decision to Alan."

"That's up to you."

"It will help if I tell him you've offered to teach me the art business."

"You can't," Liz said flatly.

"Why?"

"That's none of your business either," Liz replied, the harshness of her response softened by her obvious anxiety.

Hank picked up his empty glass and stared into its depths. It didn't take him long to decide that Alan's future was more important than any other consideration. Hell. The next Picasso? Hank didn't intend to stand in the way of that happening.

"You said I was supposed to choose which galleries carry Alan's work, didn't you?" he asked.

"Yes."

"In that case," Hank paused, knowing he was in for a major battle as soon as Alan came home, "you've got a deal."

7

OCTOBER 17, 1988

Twelve weeks earlier, when Archer had chosen to stay in Phoenix and pursue her career while Louis followed his to Hong Kong, she hadn't realized saying goodbye would be so hard. Now, as their last meal together drew to a close, the unresolved issues between them churned in her stomach and guilt rose up her throat like bile. They had made love last night, an encounter that seemed inspired by the mutual realization of their impending celibacy rather than by passion. Although Louis caressed her body with his usual practised skill, he had climaxed quickly and she hadn't. She got out of bed to douche away the stickiness between her legs, feeling empty instead of fulfilled. In terms of closeness, the last minute lovemaking had been too little, too late.

"I packed light," Louis was saying, wiping the edges of his mouth with a linen napkin and pushing back from the table. "As long as I'm going to be in Hong Kong for three months, I might as well have some suits and shirts made while I'm there."

"That's a good idea." Archer tried to sound cheerful as she began clearing the table. The truth was that three months sounded like forever. She and Louis hadn't spent three weeks apart since she was five and he was twelve, let alone the half a year he expected to be away.

From the day his mother came to work for her parents, he'd been part of her life, taking her roller-skating or horseback riding along Wissahickon creek, patching up the bloody knees and scraped elbows resulting from her attempts to keep up with him. How she looked up to him in those days. He'd been like a big brother. Their marriage had seemed inevitable – the most completely right thing she had ever done. How could they have grown so far apart?

She paused in the kitchen doorway, her hands laden with dishes. "Are you sure you don't mind my staying here?"

Louis looked startled. "Don't you think it's a little late for that question?"

At that moment, she would have agreed immediately if he asked her to change her plans.

"I admit, I was a little inconsiderate, expecting you to drop everything," Louis continued. "You worked damn hard to get where you are." His voice deepened, the way it did in business meetings when he wanted to impress people with his sincerity. "I won't be gone for ever. Christmas is just two months away. We'll have some time together then, and I'll be home for good in May. Perhaps this is just what we need, a chance to reassess our importance to each other, to have a fresh start when I get back."

Archer nodded her agreement. Blinking back tears, she carried the dishes into the kitchen and began loading them in the dishwasher. She hadn't realized the slow deterioration of their relationship worried Louis too. He wasn't given to introspection or soul-searching talks, unless it involved something like product improvement. Their marriage was a given, a fact of life both of them had taken for granted. They had been too busy working on their careers to concentrate on their relationship. But obviously, Louis still cared.

Suddenly, the months ahead didn't seem so bleak. They could serve as a hiatus, a chance to erase the slate of hurts they had inflicted on each other recently.

"Well," Louis said, following her into the kitchen, "I

guess we'd better be going." Walking up behind her, he brushed her cheek with his coffee-warmed lips. "I don't want you to worry. Everything is going to work out."

She turned, put her arms around him, and held him tight. She never thought the day would come when he would admit that her art was more than a hobby. And now he had done it. Not in so many words. That wasn't his style. But permitting her to stay home and meet her commitments meant a lot more to her than meaningless protestations. She ought to be ecstatic instead of having a lump in her throat that wouldn't go away.

"Now, now," Louis said, gently disengaging from her embrace and checking his watch, "it's that time."

Her sense of disquiet, of lost opportunities, didn't abate during the trip to the airport. Louis, who concentrated on manoeuvring through the clotted traffic, seemed barely aware of her presence. Was he angry with her, disappointed, or so elated over his new job that he wasn't giving a thought to her disloyalty? His expression gave nothing away. While he continued to stare straight ahead, she studied his profile, wondering how or if he'd have changed when they saw each other again.

With his silver sideburns and firm jaw, he was still a very attractive man and despite their recent problems, she was going to miss him dreadfully.

"If you need anything and can't get in touch with me," he said, breaking the quiet, "call my secretary. I've asked her to regard a request from you as if it were a directive from me."

She nodded and they retreated into silence again, trapped in the snare of their own thoughts. His were of the plans he intended to implement at the Kowloon factory and the satisfaction he felt at finally achieving his goal of being named CEO of a major electronics firm. She, despite concerns about her marriage, found herself reviewing the conversation she had with Liz that morning. By the time the Harrisons reached the airport, they were as far apart, emotionally and mentally, as Singapore Airlines would soon make them in terms of actual miles.

Louis's assistant, Eric Peters was waiting at the departure gate when Archer and Louis arrived. "Eric – over here," Louis called as they neared the younger man.

"How nice to see you, Mrs Harrison, Louis," Peters said.

The two men immediately launched into a discussion of the task ahead. All the while, Archer wished she could take Louis aside and use their last few minutes to, in some way, compensate for their coming estrangement. All too soon the flight was announced, and she embraced Louis one last time.

"I love you, Darling," she said fervently, even though she knew he frowned on public displays of affection. Then she turned to Peters. "My husband tends to overwork on trips like this. I'm counting on you to keep an eye on him."

A feeling of unreality enveloped her as she watched the two men stride confidently out of sight. Regret enveloped her and she angrily knuckled away tears. Louis didn't look back once.

Minutes later, she was back in their Mercedes' reassuring luxury. But she dreaded having to return to a now-empty house. Adjusting the rear-view mirror, she caught an unexpected glimpse of herself. Her mascara had smudged and she looked as woebegone as an unhappy child. Some career woman, she thought bitterly.

Her sense of inadequacy throbbed like a toothache all the way home. She parked the car, rushed into the house and changed her clothes with frantic haste, desperate to be in her studio, creating masterful sculptures that would justify her staying in Phoenix.

Rick's lips parted, displaying his perfect teeth and deepening his dimples as he deposited his Gucci briefcase on the Porsche's front seat. Liz was going to be impressed when she saw the contract it contained, an agreement to furnish all the art for an exclusive resort hotel under construction in Paradise Valley. The gallery had been commissioned to supply three framed prints for each of the four hundred and twenty rooms and suites, original art for the executives offices, and a huge sculpture for the lobby. All told, the deal was worth six figures.

He had been competing with Suzanne Brown and Joan Cawley, two of the most knowledgeable dealers in town. Rick had been forced to use every selling tool in his arsenal, including wining, dining and finally bedding the decorator who was responsible for making the purchase. She'd put her signature on the dotted line over a boozy lunch less than an hour ago. The timing had been perfect.

Eight hours earlier, Rick had crept from Liz's house like a thief in the night, afraid of her reaction if he made the mistake of overstaying his welcome. But now he had something to celebrate, something that would help make up for the lousy sales last night. Heading south on Scottsdale Road, he picked up his car phone and punched in Liz's private office number. "Remember the Hilton deal?" he said without preamble.

"Of course," she responded quickly.

"Well, I just made an even bigger one. I'll be in the office in twenty minutes. Wait for me and I'll fill you in – and don't make any plans for dinner. We have some celebrating to do." He hung up without giving her a chance to say no.

The Porsche's motor hummed smoothly, the car performing like a thoroughbred as he accelerated past the million-dollar homes and exclusive resorts that lined north Scottsdale Road. Tonight, he hoped Liz would respond to him as eagerly.

Rick had been able to walk away from all the other females he bedded, without looking back. He could barely recall their names and faces. But Liz intrigued him. Hell, admit it, she obsessed him.

Ever since shedding his virginity at the age of sixteen in the back seat of his mother's Cadillac, he had dreamed of the ultimate fuck, the perfect combination of time, place and woman. On a scale of one to ten, his encounter with Liz had proven to be a twelve. Now he wanted more of the same, a great deal more – maybe even a lifetime's worth.

He had first heard of Liz Kant two years before when he'd been working as an investment counsellor. His wealthier clients bought their art from her. According to them she had it all – a prestigious place in society, the money to go with it, an impeccable reputation, and the sort of beauty that made women envy her and men want to sleep with her. Sight unseen, she fascinated Rick.

He was determined to meet her – the sooner the better. After learning she was on the Heard Museum's board of directors, he shelled out five hundred dollars to attend one of their fund raisers. It turned out to be a memorable night.

The museum was a Phoenix landmark. Its list of trustees read like an international *Who's Who*. Its world-famous collection of Indian artifacts was housed in a rambling, white-stucco, mission-style building. As Rick strolled down the arched colonnade that led to the entrance, he congratulated himself on five hundred dollars well spent. His fellow party-goers were an affluent-looking crowd who wore their designer dresses and custom-tailored black-tie with casual elan. Jewels – the real thing, not paste – glittered on velvet ear lobes and elegant necks.

Before finishing his first drink, Rick had succeeded in introducing himself to the chairman of a large savings and loan company and the CEO of a major aerospace firm. No doubt about it, he thought, returning to the no-host bar for a refill, the fund raiser was a happy hunting ground for an up and coming investment counsellor like him.

Half an hour before dinner, he made his way to the

flower-bedecked hall where the tables were set up. Glancing around to make sure no one observed what he was doing, he switched Liz Kant's place card so she'd be seated next to him rather than eight tables away. Then he went for a stroll through the museum's sculpture garden. When he returned forty minutes later, he found a stunning redhead in the gilt chair next to his own empty seat.

"So you're *the* Liz Kant," he said, eyeing her appreciatively. She wore black satin pyjama pants and a revealing décolleté top. Diamond waterfalls hung from her ears.

She smiled at him, a thousand-watt winner. "*The* Liz Kant? You make me sound like an institution, and frankly, I've never liked institutions. Sorry, but I didn't catch your name."

"It's Mason – Rick Mason." He grinned back, hoping she would find his dimples as irresistible as other women had in the past.

"You must be new in town," she said in a memorably husky voice. "I don't remember seeing you before."

"I moved here from California a year ago. I'm an investment counsellor – a very good one."

"And a modest one too." She laughed throatily.

"No. Just honest. Now, Liz Kant, why don't you tell me all about yourself."

She looked at him through a fringe of dark lashes. "There's not much to tell. I'm just a business woman."

He leaned toward her, allowing himself a quick glimpse of her cleavage before he met her eyes. "At least one of us is modest," he said, with a self-deprecating chuckle. "But really, I want to know all about you. Do you realize you're the most beautiful woman in the room?"

He managed to monopolize her through all five courses. When the orchestra started playing, he asked her to dance. She was light on her feet, and felt as good in his arms as she looked at a dinner table. Before they parted that night she asked if he had ever considered selling art, and suggested that he consider going to work for her. At the time, Rick had been disappointed. He'd been hoping to interest her as a man, not as a potential employee.

But months later on Black Monday, when the bottom dropped out of the stock market and his clients began complaining about the speculative deals he'd put them in, he remembered her offer. He telephoned for an appointment, and she hired him on the spot.

The gallery had been good for him financially, he thought, pulling up in front. Liz paid a twenty per cent commission on every sale he made. The deal with the new hotel was worth twenty thousand or more to him – a tidy sum in anyone's book. But, as he exited his Porsche, he readily admitted he wanted more than money.

He wanted Liz Kant.

Maryann arrived in Scottsdale a few minutes early for her first date with Reginald Quincy. Parking on a side street so he wouldn't see her ancient Datsun with its, "Life's a bitch and then you die", bumper-sticker, she pulled a compact from her bag. She had applied the war-paint sparingly in honour of her aristocratic escort. She hardly recognized herself without false eye-lashes, frosted eye-shadow and teased hair, but instinct told her Reginald was accustomed to dining with ladies, not ex-bar girls.

Sliding from the front seat, she didn't bother to lock up. Heaven help the asshole who stole her wheels, she chuckled, grinning in spite of the pain of walking in four-inch high heels that tortured her feet but made her legs look terrific.

She'd barely positioned herself in front of the Kant Gallery when Reginald drove up in an emerald green Jaguar, punctual to the minute. Money and manners were an unbeatable combination, she thought, as he uncoiled his six-foot-four-inch length from the leather cocoon of the front seat.

"*Bonsoir, mon amie,*" he called.

Despite the late afternoon's lingering heat he wore a

grey pin-striped suit, custom-made, she assumed, from the perfection of its tailoring, a crisp white-on-white shirt, and what was obviously an old-school tie. She smoothed her recycled dress and patted her platinum curls into place, feeling as excited as a girl on her first date.

Seeing the two of them reflected in the Kant Gallery's windows, she almost laughed out loud. He was so tall and thin and she so short that they looked more like Mutt and Jeff – or Abbott and Costello – than a potential romantic duo.

After making enquiries about her health and her day, Reginald announced that he'd made reservations at L'Orangerie in the Biltmore. "Will that be all right?" he asked solicitously. "Or would you rather dine elsewhere?"

She was suitably impressed. She had lunched at L'Orangerie with Archer once and loved it, although, to her embarrassment, she hadn't enough money in her purse to pay for her share of the bill. The Biltmore, on Camelback Road a few miles from the gallery, was the oldest, most exclusive resort in all Arizona. It had been a favourite watering hole of the world's movers and shakers for decades.

This evening, the food and the service surpassed all Maryann's expectations. Reginald proved to be a perfect gentleman, his courtesy so exquisite that she felt like a bumbling hick by comparison. Whatever lingering doubts she had about his appeal vanished by the time they finished dessert. As he plucked the almost empty bottle of Chablis from its frosted silver container, she noted his tapering fingers and well-buffed nails. Those aristocratic hands probably never had to do anything more demanding than clipping coupons.

"Would you like more wine?" he asked.

"No, thank you kindly, Sir," she drawled. The evening had been fantastic so far and she had no intention of getting tight and spoiling the good impression she hoped she was making. Besides, drinking made her horny, and it was much too early in the game to consider getting it on with the man who sat on the other side of the pristinely linened dinner table.

Maryann was having a hard time imagining Reginald doing anything as undignified as making love – even in the missionary position. Nor could she quite picture herself lying beneath him. Being so tall and thin, he'd probably look like a praying mantis about to gobble up a june-bug.

"I hope you don't mind if I finish the bottle," he murmured. "The wine has a crisp, smoky finesse and 1986 is a very good year. My dear mother always says, waste not, want not."

She had managed not to gasp when he ordered the fifty-dollar bottle of Davoisset-Camus. Never, not in her whole life, had she drunk anything so expensive. Waste not, want not – what a laugh! That fifty dollars would buy her groceries for a week or more.

Thank heavens Reginald had no way of knowing that her uneducated palate couldn't tell the difference between the Davoisset and Ripple. But, as *her* mother used to say, it's the thought that counts. And Reginald was turning out to be a very thoughtful date.

"My dear," he said, clearing his throat with a thin sound, "I've told you all about myself and frankly, I find the recital quite boring. Now, you must tell me all about yourself."

"I haven't been bored for a minute," she responded enthusiastically, although Reginald's life history – which had taken three courses to unfold and had been laced with the names of people and places that meant nothing to her – had left her confused rather than enlightened. "By comparison my life has been quite dull."

"Let me be the judge of that." He took a sip and licked his thin, pale lips. For a moment those lips mesmerized her, reminding her of Bela Lugosi's lips when he'd played

Count Dracula in a film she'd seen on television long ago. She'd been a highly impressionable seven-year-old at the time and had nightmares for days afterwards.

Reginald's voice brought her back to the present. "First of all, *ma petite*," he said, "you bear an old and honoured name. My family has known the New York Van Kamps for decades. In fact, way back when, I think the two families were united by marriage."

New York Van Kamps? Maryann puzzled. What the hell was he talking about? "I come from a little town in south Texas," she confessed. "Van Kamp is mother's name and . . ." She clamped her mouth shut as she realized how close she'd come to revealing her illegitimacy.

"So you use your mother's name professionally?" Reginald queried, oblivious to the enormous blunder she had almost made.

"Yes. You see . . . well," she improvised, "my father's family doesn't approve of my being an artist."

He looked surprised. "*Chacun à son gout*, although I've never understood people who don't appreciate art. We ought to celebrate people like you, people who create beauty. I can hardly draw a straight line myself."

"Why, you sweet thing." The way she pronounced them, sweet and thing became two syllable words. "What a nice compliment."

"It comes from the heart." He reached for her hand and gave it an affectionate pat.

The small kindness touched her deeply. Reginald might not be the handsomest man in the world, but he was certainly turning out to be the most considerate.

"Has anyone ever told you you're one terrific guy?" She gave his hand a little squeeze in return. "Actually, talking about my family doesn't bother me." So saying, she launched into a carefully crafted personal history that could best be called *faction*. "Great grand-daddy on my mother's side had a plantation on the Mississippi and a house on Peachtree Street in Atlanta, but General Grant's army destroyed the plantation and some carpetbag banker wound up with the house."

That much was true. Maryann's mother had been fond of dwelling on the family's aristocratic origins. "Great grand-daddy moved to Texas after the Civil War and tried ranching, but he didn't know a thing about cattle. Sad to say, by the time I came on the scene, the Van Kamps had fallen on hard times." Another kernel of truth. What she didn't add was that great grand-daddy, a blue-blooded civil war veteran, had also been a falling-down drunk and a wife beater, traits he seemed to have passed on to the rest of the Van Kamp men.

"Fascinating," Reginald said. "Tell me about your father's people."

Maryann was enjoying her own inventiveness as she continued to tell a story combining elements of *Gone With the Wind* and *The Grapes of Wrath*. "My daddy was a Rousseaux – a gentleman like you – born in New Orlean's Garden District. He met Mama when he was deer hunting outside of Del Rio. It was love at first sight." Actually, the more proper description would have been "business arrangement". Rousseaux has paid for Maryann's mama's favours, like all the rest of mama's male friends – *Uncles*, Maryann had been taught to call them.

She had actually been naïve enough to feel fortunate, having so many big strapping relatives, all of whom seemed eager to send her to the five and dime with fifty cents in her jeans when they came to visit. Yeah, she thought she was a lucky kid until one of the s.o.bs decided little girls were more his style than aging hookers.

"They were both very young," she continued unabashed, "and Daddy's family was terribly upset when they eloped. He died in a car accident before I was born. Mama never got over it. She passed away right after I graduated from high school." Maryann paused for breath. "My goodness, my tongue's been going like a little old windshield wiper. That will teach you to ask a lady to talk about herself."

"So you are quite alone?"

She nodded and lowered her eyes demurely. "Being alone isn't so bad," she said, doing a passable imitation of *Gone With the Wind*'s long-suffering Melanie Wilkes. "We all have our crosses to bear. I have my friends and my career." She touched the tip of her nose, reassuring herself it wasn't growing like Pinocchio's, because the good Lord knew she'd certainly been telling her share of fibs.

Careers were for the Archers of the world, not for the likes of her. Despite her successes, Maryann still felt like a fraud when she compared herself to other artists. Most of them had educations, degrees from this school or that. The only school she attended was the school of hard knocks. Thanks to their training, other artists could easily switch from one medium to another. By contrast, Maryann had taught herself to use acrylics. Her other medium was crayons. Considering the circumstances, she didn't have to be a genius to realize she would always be second rate.

But Maryann knew that telling guys the truth – that she would gladly trade her palette and brushes for a husband and kids – was bound to scare them away. So she looked up at Reginald, batted her eyelashes and said, "I can't imagine anything more fulfilling than being an artist."

"How I admire you." Reginald lifted his wine glass which now held less than an inch of pale golden liquid. "To you, *chérie* – and to this evening. I've been hoping to meet someone like you for a long time."

Her heart and stomach seemed to fuse into a single incandescently content mass. That makes two of us, she thought. She had been looking for someone like Reginald all her life. His sheer perfection almost overwhelmed her. She was beginning to see him as the flesh and blood embodiment of her dream lover.

"I generally have a post-prandial brandy," he said as the waiter cleared away their dishes. "And I believe they

110

have a lovely, quiet bar for just such a purpose. Can I persuade you to have one with me?"

Feeling a bit like Cinderalla, she agreed at once. "Brandy sounds divine."

The bar proved to be quiet, the ideal place to exchange confidences and come to know each other better. Reginald told Maryann about his lifelong passion for art, and she spoke of her early struggles to become a successful painter and her hopes for ever greater future success. They agreed that women had yet to receive the serious consideration their talents merited in the art world. By the time Reginald delivered her back to the gallery at ten, Maryann was in a fog composed of one part wine, one part brandy, and one part pure happiness. He kissed her hand in farewell and asked to see her again, setting a suitable place and time before saying *au revoir*.

She practically floated the half block to her car and drove home oblivious, for once, to the Datsun's groans of protest. She even failed to be bothered by the ugliness of her neighbourhood as she pulled into her carport. Entering the house through the side door, she deposited her keys on the kitchen counter, slipped off her achingly high heels and began to dance through the house with an imaginary partner cradled in her arms while humming the strains of a Strauss waltz.

La-di-dah-di-dah, she trilled, tossing her bag onto the sofa. She couldn't remember having a better time in her entire life. The evening had been the absolute opposite of her first night out with her ex-husband. What different memories she would have had if only Reginald had walked into her life nineteen years ago instead of Oscar Wanatka.

But, she reminded herself, collapsing on the sofa, someone like Reginald wouldn't have been caught dead in a dry, dusty, one-horse town like Del Rio. The Oscar Wanatkas of the world were the only guys you met in places like that.

It was hard to believe she actually thought Oscar the cutest thing in pants the first time she laid eyes on him. She'd been working the cash register in the Big Bend Café and noticed him immediately when he sauntered in. His broad shoulders positively bulged in his denim jacket. A quick glance and she catalogued his big brown eyes, dimpled chin and even features. Why, he's even better looking than Elvis, she decided.

And then he looked in her direction. His eyes quickly moved from her face to her breasts and her heart responded by beating so hard she thought it was positively going to pop out of her rib cage. She thrust her shoulders back. It was common knowledge that she had the biggest, most shapely boobs in Del Rio High where she'd just become a Junior.

"Can I help you?" she drawled.

"I bet you could, Kid," the man replied, his eyes still glued to her chest.

"I'm no kid!" Maryann bridled, feeling her cheeks blush and her nipples harden under his frank stare. "I'm seventeen years old."

"Too bad you're still jail bait," the handsome stranger replied, "or I'd forget all about having to haul-ass out of here, ask you out and take you for one hell of a ride . . .", sex pulsated in the air between them before he concluded, "in my truck."

"I may not be eighteen yet," Maryann said boldly, "but as you can plainly see, I'm all grown-up."

He grinned. "You got that right, Babe. Say, if I was to ask you out, what the hell is there to do in a one-horse town like this?"

"There's a church social tonight."

He grinned impudently. "That's not exactly my style."

"Well, there's always the drive-in movie."

"What's playing tonight?" he asked.

"Do you really care?" she replied, emboldened by the fact that his jeans failed to conceal a blossoming erection.

112

So began their brief romance. She eloped with Wanatka when he drove his eighteen-wheeler back through town the following week. He was to be her king of the road, her road warrior, her means of escape from a dreary, small town life. Six months later, when he tired of using her for a punching bag, he walked out. Ever since, she seemed destined to attract losers, men who knew more about mean streets than meaningful relationships.

When it came to romance, she had been living a life of diminishing returns until Reginald appeared. Now, as she went into her bedroom to undress, a bright, hopeful light illuminated the darker corners of her mind. Reginald might be the pot of gold at the end of the rainbow, the man she'd been waiting for all her life.

Sleep came swiftly, gently carrying her away into the land of dreams. Behind her closed eyes all was darkness. Suddenly Reginald was there, pouring wine and kissing her hand and telling her what a swell person she was. Only he wasn't Reginald anymore. He was Bela Lugosi in that damn Dracula outfit and he was fastening his thin grey lips against her neck and sucking and sucking. Then he stopped drinking and paused to look at her and his lips were stained scarlet with her blood.

And she screamed and screamed . . .

It hadn't taken Alan long to establish his camp high in the Stronghold. He'd arrived at the *huecos*, natural depressions in the rock that held rain water, late in the afternoon, hobbled Odii and set her to graze before unpacking his gear. He had camped at the same location in the past and the earthen sweat lodge he built was still standing. A few days work and it would be serviceable again.

He spent the waning daylight hours reconnoitring his surroundings to assure himself of being completely alone. Then he gathered wood and built a small, economical fire. By the time he ate a sparse meal of jerky and beans, the stars were out. Leaning against his saddle, he watched them for a while. The winter constellations, the Pleiades, Castor and Pollux, sparkled against the inky black of the unpolluted sky.

It had been too long since he had taken time from the demands of his career to stay in the Stronghold. He could feel himself letting go of the anger, the choking rage that had driven him from Scottsdale. The serenity of the night soothed his injured soul. Yes, nature would make him well again, whole in body and spirit.

The last thought that drifted through his mind before his exhausted body succumbed to sleep, was satisfaction at knowing he would never have to see or deal with Liz Kant and her so-called assistant again.

8

NOVEMBER 16, 1988

One week before Thanksgiving, the Scottsdale winter season was in full swing. It would last five more months. Local businesses had to squeeze an entire year's profit into that period of time. By the end of April the mercury would rise, the winter visitors would leave, and the sun would begin its half year reign over the empty streets. But on this day, traffic clogged the thoroughfares. Hotels and resorts were full. Reservations were required everywhere but MacDonalds, and cash registers bulged with out-of-state money.

Outdoors, the sun shone in a benevolent azure sky and the thermometer reached the eighties. Inside the Kant Gallery, the air was carefully maintained at seventy-four degrees, an ideal temperature for the preservation of art and the comfort of clients and staff.

Seated at his desk, his Bally-shod feet resting on its mahogany surface, his fingers pyramided, Rick found the air conditioning's steady hum to be a soporific. His mind kept wandering. A bemused frown creased his forehead as he thought about the woman in the room just down the hall.

Over the years he'd slept with dozens of broads, interchangeable, disposable females whose names and faces blurred in memory. The experiences hadn't touched his inner core. Now, to his utter amazement, he was in love, gut-wrenching, prick-hardening, soul-shattering love. Liz had every quality he'd ever wanted or admired. She was sexually exciting, mentally stimulating, socially prominent. After their marriage – good God! he was actually contemplating marriage – he would again be a card-carrying member of the beau monde, enjoying the lifestyle he considered his birthright.

Caught in the wayward currents of memory, Rick heaved an unhappy sigh. He and his mother had not been penniless after his parents divorced, he recalled. His father was too concerned with appearances to allow them to go hungry or homeless. But Hollywood was a caste-conscious town. Without Dr Mason's influence and status, Rick had stopped being invited to the homes of boys he'd known all his life. And his mother's fall from grace had been even more humiliating.

As the wife of Beverly Hills' most successful plastic surgeon, Annabelle Mason had been accustomed to an active social life, lunching several times a week with other well-connected wives. Her inside information about which actress had had her tits modified, her behind tucked, her nose bobbed, her face lifted, which aging actor's abdomen resembled a battle field as the result of mismanaged liposuction, made Annabelle tremendously popular with her peers. Divorce from her prominent husband meant instant demotion from Hollywood's A list to somewhere below Z.

A bitter grimace twisted Rick's handsome features as he conjured up images of his own adult life. He had spent it on the outside, looking in, dreaming of regaining his lost place in society. After graduating from college, spending a few aimless years giving skiing and tennis lessons in Colorado and Hawaii, he made up his mind to make a new start, to do something with the expensive education his father had grudgingly paid for. Rick's decision to move to Scottsdale had been based on the city's magnetic appeal to affluent, influential people.

"It's the best kept secret of the rich and famous," his

mother said approvingly when he announced his intention. "I know you'll be happy there. And you'll be spared running into your father's new wife and that brat of hers."

Rick would willingly have travelled a lot further than Arizona to avoid that possibility. His father's big-boobed bride had produced a son and heir, a snot-nosed little son-of-a-bitch who was destined to inherit everything that should have been Rick's.

Fortunately, Annabelle Mason had been right about Scottsdale. The move had paid off beyond Rick's expectations. Now, as he plotted a strategy to win the most desirable woman he'd ever known, he was oblivious to the historical events that accounted for him being in that particular place at that particular time. Sitting in the gallery's climate-controlled atmosphere, he didn't know he owed his job – that Scottsdale owed its very existence – to the mechanics of heat transfer.

In the 1940s, Arizona's economy had been based on cattle, copper and cotton. Although the winter weather was idyllic, the valley was a furnace in the summer and the population of the Phoenix basin hovered near 65,000 hardy souls – give or take a few gila monsters. Scottsdale had been a dry, dusty pit-stop which existed to service the surrounding ranches.

The 1980 census recorded a phenomenal change. The valley's population had mushroomed to a million and a half, and the credit belonged to air-conditioning. Long before the rest of the nation got around to it. Phoenicians installed air-conditioning in their homes, their cars, their hotels and restaurants, the places where they worked and played. The year-round high temperatures and constant sunshine became an asset rather than a liability.

Artists who came to the south-west in search of good light and the good life, found a wealth of new and exotic subjects. Soon after Buck Saunders opened what he called an Art Emporium on Scottsdale Road, galleries began to replace feed stores and gas stations. Luxurious resorts like

117

the Biltmore, Mountain Shadows, the Hilton complex and the Cottonwood, housed the people who bought paintings, prints and sculptures from Suzanne Brown, Elaine Horwitch, Joy Tash, Leslie Levy, C.J. Rein, Liz Kant, and the other dealers whose galleries stood shoulder to shoulder on Main Street, Marshall Way and Fifth Avenue. As the eighties drew to a close, climate, money and art had created a self-perpetuating, symbiotic *ménage à trois*.

But Rick was unaware of those things as he sat in his small office, puzzling over his next move. One month had passed since the night he and Liz made love – thirty days during which their brief intimacy had faded. Liz had a genius for keeping him at arm's length. To win her approval, he had redoubled his sales effort with considerable success. He wanted her unqualified love, but all he got was a series of pats on the back and "well dones".

Instinct told Rick that one man could keep his dream of marrying Liz from becoming reality. Rick had known it the minute he saw that painting in Liz's bedroom. Talk about a picture being worth a thousand words. That damn canvas oozed sexual heat.

To hell with the Indian, Rick thought, sitting up abruptly and pounding his desk with an impotent fist. Longchase wasn't going to wind up with Liz if Rick had anything to say about it. Reaching for his telephone, Rick punched in a Beverly Hills number.

"How's my favourite girl?" he asked when his mother came on the line.

"A little lonely." Annabelle Mason slurred her words so that little came out lishle. "It's lovely of you to call. How's my sweet lambkin?"

She's been drinking again, Rick thought sourly. So what else was new? Annabelle Mason had lots of reason to drink these days. Her alimony cheques hadn't kept pace with the rapidly escalating cost of the good life in Beverly Hills. To maintain her lifestyle, she house-sat a multi-million dollar Bel Air mansion that belonged to a Saudi prince, and she sold gossip – overheard at Spago, the Polo Lounge, or the Bistro Gardens – to the tabloids.

"I'm fine," he replied. "You'd be proud of me, Mom. I've been doing very well at the gallery. So well, in fact, that I was just about to mail you a five-thousand-dollar cheque."

He heard his mother's swiftly indrawn breath. "You're such a good boy," she cooed. "Thank God, you didn't turn out to be a two-timing, stingy prick like your father."

"I'm just sorry it can't be more." Rick paused. "Mom, I need a favour."

"You know I'd do anything for you."

"Do you still have connections with the columnists?" he asked, knowing full well those connections accounted for part of her income.

"Of course, lambkin."

He cringed inwardly, hating that damn nursery name. But he forced a smile into his voice. "I've got an item for you, Mother. Wait till you hear this!"

Alan finished his lunch, added another piece of wood to the fire and rechecked the sky. Dark clouds bunched against the horizon. It was probably raining somewhere along the Mogollon Rim. Higher up in the Tularosas, it might even be snowing. Winter was coming to the mountains.

He'd lived well during the four weeks he'd spent in the Stronghold, dining on rabbit and squirrel stews to which he'd added Apache potatoes and wild onions. He'd ground autumn-dried mesquite beans into coarse flour to make enriched gravies, mixed choke cherries with honey when he craved a sweet. The pure, icy water of mountain streams quenched his thirst. The days and nights of isolation had served him well. His body felt hard and lean, his mind clear. He could think of Liz without pain.

Now, he longed to paint – to express on canvas the serenity he'd found. At night while he slept, the landscape

119

of his dreams was peopled with mystical warriors, mysterious canyons, ancient ruins. The power he'd been granted had been growing larger inside him with every passing day until he ached to release it. This would be his last day in camp. By afternoon the storm would reach the Dragoons. But he had a few hours until then, time for one last sweat bath. He'd return to Scottsdale cleansed in the Indian way.

Keeping an eye on the distant thunder-head, he packed his gear, sweeping the campground of every trace of his stay. While preparing to leave, he heated stones in the fire and then placed them inside the earthen sweat lodge. When he felt warmth radiating through the canvas flap covering the tiny entrance, he checked to make sure Odii was still calmly nibbling on autumn grasses. Then he stripped off his clothes, picked up his full canteen, and slipped inside the lodge.

He poured water on the hot stones. They hissed and sizzled, releasing a gush of steam. With his first deep breath it became a part of his body, searing his lungs. Sweat began the cleansing process as he sat down in the middle of the floor. A film of moisture cloaked his brow, his chest, tickling as it pooled in the hollows of his body before spilling to the dirt. A dozen aggravating itches tormented his body. But he forced his mind away from them, willing himself to drift, to seek that meditative state in which all discomfort is forgotten.

It had been just as hot – no, hotter – on the San Carlos Reservation the summer he came back from Nam. The merciless sun filled each day with a harsh, unrelenting glare that seemed to probe the darkness of his soul. When he bought a pair of sunglasses to shield his eyes, his mother, Natzela, complained that the army had turned him into an Anglo.

"The sun is part of our life," she said. "You are wrong to hide our eyes like a *belagana*."

He didn't know how to tell her he felt safer behind the

dark glass shield. He couldn't verbalize his feeling that a part of him – his youth, his belief in the future – died in Nam. He'd enlisted in the infantry, expecting to be part of the Apache's warrior tradition. But there had been no nobility in the battles he fought – only despair, pain, fear and death.

He spent every day in the jungle praying to survive, to get back to the desert, to his mother and his family – only to return as a stranger, his spirit sickened by all the things he'd seen and done. At night the *chindi* of the dead haunted his dreams. He spent those first weeks back home escaping into an alcoholic refuge, just as his father had after returning from World War II.

His mother had been patient. She didn't pry, didn't ask why he woke up at night screaming, calling out names and words she couldn't understand. She just came in the darkness and held him, her strong, work-calloused hands wiping the sweat from his forehead. He was twenty-two, but at times he felt more unsure of himself than a newly weaned baby. A month went by and then another and still he couldn't paint.

But he could drink.

He had a newly discovered talent for nursing a six-pack from mid afternoon until late evening. When he couldn't afford to make the trip off the reservation to buy beer or whisky, he drank locally brewed mescal.

The afternoon that Hank Begay showed up in San Carlos, Alan was down to his last beer and his last dollar. He sat on a rickety bench in front of his mother's house, nursing that beer and wondering where he'd get another. Then Hank drove up. Alan could still taste and smell the dust that Hank's car had raised from the hard-packed caliche.

"*Ya-te-hey. Qué paso?*" Hank said, as casually as if they had seen each other just yesterday when, in fact, two years had elapsed.

"Not much," Alan replied, mimicking Hank's offhand manner.

"Christ, it's hot." Hank surveyed the barren yard. "I'd forgotten how hot it gets in San Carlos in July. No wonder the white man gave this land to the Apache. No one else," he joked roughly, "would be dumb enough to live here. Now, how about going in the house and getting one of those for me." A nod of his head indicated the beer in Alan's hand.

"Sorry. I'm fresh out."

Hank guffawed. "That's all right. The Bureau of Indian Affairs doesn't permit drinking on the reservation anyway."

Alan assayed a small smile, one of the few since he'd come back to San Carlos. It was one of the ironies of reservation life that Indians were prohibited from buying liquor on their own land. As a consequence, they never learned the art of social drinking. They drank purposefully, to forget. Many of them – his father included – died of cirrhosis of the liver and related illnesses on the supposedly *dry* reservations.

"I've been waiting for you to call," Hank said, joining Alan in the thin strip of shade in front of the house.

"I've been meaning to . . . but . . . you know how it is."

"Yeah, I know how it is. Your mother telephoned me last week and told me *how* it is. You're blowing it, man!" Hank was still sitting on the bench by Alan's side, looking totally relaxed, but Alan could sense the older man's inner tension. "When are you coming back to Phoenix and going to art school, the way you planned before you left?"

Alan tilted the beer can towards his mouth, realized it was empty and tossed it into the yard where it joined the rest of the six-pack sprouting from the parched earth like aluminum flowers. "I've had a little change of plans. Vietnam did that to a lot of us. For some, the change turned out to be fucking permanent." Glancing side-long, he could see anger bunching Hank's harsh features.

In one lithe move the Navajo was on his feet, pulling

Alan up with him. Alan could feel the muscled power in Hank's hands as Hank spun him around. "You listen to me, you chicken-shit. You're not the only kid who went off to fight a war and came back hurting – and you won't be the last! I put in my time in Korea and I know where you're coming from. But, by God, I expected better of you."

"Fuck off. I've had enough lectures from do-gooders to last a lifetime."

Hank shook his head angrily. "The first time I met you, I thought you were special. I never saw an Indian kid with so much pride. When I realized how much talent you had, I thought you could be someone important, someone every Indian child could look up to someday." Hank's voice reverberated in the oppressive, heat-laden air. "Goddamn it Alan, you owe it to yourself, to your people, to use your talent."

In one shattering second Alan lost the alcoholic composure he'd been clinging to for weeks. The rage and despair he'd been suppressing pumped adrenaline through his arms and legs. The need to attack, to make someone – anyone – pay for his anguish, burst from his mouth in a hoarse cry. He backed off and began circling, poised to lash out Apache-style with his feet or his fists. He managed a quick kick to Hank's thigh and a jolting punch that grazed Hank's jaw before the bigger man swarmed over him like a dust devil.

Their unequal battle was soon over. Within seconds Hank sat astride Alan, his hands gripping Alan's arms like a vice. But his face held such a mixture of anger and concern that Alan felt laughter rising in his chest. It erupted in a strangled guffaw he couldn't control. The more he laughed, the more the lines on Hank's forehead deepened. Then, unexpectedly, Hank was laughing too.

And so the healing began.

When they left San Carlos the next day, Alan thought they were returning to Phoenix. Instead, Hank turned his car north toward Navajo country. They arrived at the

123

Begay *hogan*, the traditional circular Navajo house near Ganado that had been in Hank's family for generations, late that night. Alan's baths in the adjacent sweat lodge began the next morning.

He hated them at first, hated the acrid odour of generations of sweat that permeated the darkness. But, despite his discomfort, he began to feel the accumulated horror of Vietnam escaping his pores with the booze-laden sweat that poured from his body.

Four weeks after they arrived, Alan woke one morning to find a stranger standing over his bedroll.

"This is Art Nakai," Hank said with a tone bordering on reverence.

Alan recognized the name of the *hataali*, the medicine man Hank had been studying with for years. Nakai was gaunt, white-haired. One of the last great Navajo medicine men, he was reputed to know eight *healing ways*, complex rituals involving night-long chanting and prayers, the creation of sand paintings, and the administration of herbal medicines. To know one *way* took years of study. To know eight was phenomenal.

"Art and I think you're ready for a curing ceremony," Hank continued. "He's here to determine which one will help you the most."

Alan was about to rise to his feet when Art Nakai knelt by his side, pushing him down with firm but gentle hands. "Stay," the older man commanded in a resonant voice that belied his obvious age.

Nakai closed his eyes and stretched his hands over Alan's body. Within seconds, they began to move, seemingly of their own volition, describing complex arabesques in the air. Alan could feel the hair on the back of his neck rising and goose-flesh erupted on his arms as those ancient hands danced over his body.

After a few minutes, Nakai's eyes opened, he got to his feet and turned to Hank. "Your friend needs a *Beautyway*. I will be back in four days to perform the ceremony. Have everything ready." So saying, the old man exited the *hogan* without a backward glance.

While Alan dressed, Hank explained what lay ahead. "You're lucky," he said. "The *Beautyway* only takes two nights. It's generally prescribed for confused minds. If Art thought you were insane," Hank's leering grin bisected his face, "he would have prescribed a *Nightway*, a *Yeibichai* ceremony that lasts a week and a half."

During the next four days, while Alan and Hank cleaned the *hogan*, gathering firewood and medicinal plants for the coming ceremony, Alan learned more about the Navajo *ways*. They were ritual purifications. Nakai would call on the help of the deities in restoring Alan to a state of harmony with nature, while Hank would complete the required dry paintings, called sandpaintings by Anglos, under Nakai's guidance. In the past there had been almost as many *ways* as there were practitioners. Hank happily spoke of the *Antway*, the *Lightningway*, and the *Coyoteway* among others, each designed to cure a specific range of ailments.

Hank had just spent the last four years struggling to master the *Beautyway*. Truly complex *ways* like the *Mountainway*, took nine nights and could cost as much as a thousand dollars. The *Beautyway* was relatively inexpensive but even so, Alan didn't have the money to pay for it.

Hank happily shouldered that burden. On the appointed evening, his entire extended family arrived at the *hogan* to offer their voices, their prayer, their power, during the *way*. Throughout the hours of darkness, four great bonfires burned outside the octagonal structure. Inside, stripped to a breachclout, Alan sat on a pure white buckskin while Hank created a magnificent painting from coloured sands.

"*Wu, hu, hu,*" the family chanted in unison.

Despite his age, Nakai proved to be tireless. The ritual began at sunset and ended at sunrise. Nakai prayed the entire time. At the end of the first night, he looked so exhausted that Alan didn't think he'd be back. But Nakai was there promptly at sunset on the second day and again, he prayed all night long, dosing Alan with herbal remedies, leading the prayers, guiding Hank through the complexities of the sandpainting.

Alan was never to forget the final words Nakai uttered as the ceremony ended on the morning of the third day. "*In beauty I walk,*" the old man chanted. "*With beauty before me I walk. With beauty behind me I walk. With beauty above me I walk. With beauty all around me I walk. It is finished in beauty.*" Then he turned to Alan and his prayer was a benediction that seemed to pierce Alan's soul. "*May you walk in beauty.*"

Alan returned to Phoenix a few days later, determined to use his power; to learn to paint as no one had ever painted before, *to walk in beauty.* From then on, when he couldn't find inner peace, he returned to the reservation to be with his own people. And when that failed, he would make his way up into the Stronghold to commune with his ancestors and the forces of nature.

Now, feeling totally in harmony with himself and the world, Alan emerged from the sweat lodge to find the storm clouds almost directly overhead. Thunder and lightning, the givers of power, cracked in the sky and made the earth tremble. Still nude, he strode to Odii's side to calm her. He dressed slowly, oblivious to the rain that lashed his back. It was a *male rain,* its torrential strength pouring into the earth to replenish the land, to bring about rebirth.

He offered a quick prayer to the *thunder people* as he mounted the Apaloosa. Beginning his descent through the Stronghold, he felt strong and invincible, a whole man, secure in the knowledge that Liz was finally out of his life.

While Alan rode down through the Stronghold, Hank sat at a desk, staring at a computer screen, grappling with

126

twentieth-century problems. He was updating the records of Alan's widely dispersed inventories.

Four weeks ago the thought of using a computer intimidated him. "I'm a nineteenth-century man," he objected, when Liz insisted he buy one. "I don't like the idea of owning a machine that's smarter than I am."

"I'll call Archer Harrison and see if she can get you a good price from one of W.B.M.'s local dealers," Liz said firmly, as if she were talking to a recalcitrant child. "Accurate records are vital when you're involved with dozens of galleries. I've worked with dealers who don't know how many of Alan's paintings or prints they have in inventory, let alone what they should be priced at. You'd be surprised how often they lose track."

"How the hell can anyone lose track of a two by four canvas?" Hank blustered.

"Things do get misplaced in warehouses and store rooms," Liz explained. "But every now and then a dealer sells something for cash, succumbs to temptation, and pockets the money. The sale is never reported to the artist." Liz's smile was chilling. "No one tries that on me because they know my records are impeccable. I want you to have the same reputation, for Alan's sake."

"You make the art business sound . . ." Hank searched for the right word, "sleazy."

"It can be," she replied without hesitation. "If I don't teach you anything else, I'm going to be certain you learn to keep your back to the wall. Don't give your trust until it's been earned."

"Maybe I'm being naïve, but I'm not sure I can treat people that way."

"Damn it, Hank. You're not teaching school anymore. If you want to protect Alan, you're going to have to change the way you think. Art used to be a gentleman's business. But today, anyone with a little money, a little knowledge, and a glib tongue can open a gallery."

She looked at him sternly. "Forgeries used to be rare. Now, the art world is rife with fraud. There are so many bogus Dali prints on the market that I've advised my clients not to buy one under any circumstances."

"But that's just one artist."

Liz shook her head vehemently. "It's a great deal bigger than one artist. It's an attitude that runs rampant through the art world. There's even a successful painter who makes a fortune selling forgeries that people *know* are forgeries."

"You're kidding!" Hank thought he had heard it all, but Liz managed to surprise him. "If everyone knows what he's doing, how does he get away with it?"

"The critics say the work is important even though they *know* the famous artists haven't really done the paintings themselves, because it makes a statement about the *hypocrisy* of the art world."

Hank shook his head in disbelief. "Sounds like horseshit to me."

"Now we're getting somewhere," Liz said approvingly. "Hang on to that thought and you'll be all right."

She had made her point. The next day Hank purchased a personal computer, a printer and two filing cabinets, and installed them in the den which now served as his office. Liz had come to the house several times after that, patiently showing him how to use the various programs he needed to know.

To his surprise, he enjoyed working with her. She was a clever, sometimes amusing, and always informative teacher. Now, as he finished updating the inventories, he realized how much he was coming to respect Liz . . . maybe even like her. Now how the hell was he going to explain that to Alan?

The architect of Hank's dilemma was struggling with a problem of her own. As Liz studied the sculpture Archer had delivered half an hour earlier, she was uncomfortably aware of Rick standing behind her, peering over her shoulder. He was wearing an expensive, musky cologne that hung in the air, reminding her of the night he spent in her bed. The morning afterward, his scent had lingered in her bedroom until she asked Rosita to give the place a thorough airing.

"I think its perfect for the hotel lobby," Liz said, attempting to give the sculpture her full attention.

She felt Rick's breath stirring her hair. "Archer has outdone herself," he agreed. "The hotel people should be very pleased. They wanted something south-western, something family-oriented that would set the theme for the entire resort, and this really does it."

Liz moved closer to Archer's rendering of a Navajo family, pretending to study the mother's face. "Let me know when you plan to show it to the hotel decorator for her approval and I'll make sure you have my office to yourself."

"She's stopping by later. But I don't anticipate any problems. She approved Archer's preliminary sketches." Rick walked up behind Liz, and put his arm around her shoulders. "How about having dinner with me tonight? I'll let you know how it went then."

Liz smiled weakly. "Another time. I've got a lot to do before I leave town for the holidays."

"What do you mean, leave town?" He sounded like a hurt child. "I thought we'd spend Thanksgiving together."

What in the world was she going to do about him? she wondered, moving away from his encircling arm. Ever since the tenth anniversary show or, to be more accurate, since spending a night in her bed, he had made a practice of stopping by her office on the flimsiest of pretexts, asking her to lunch or dinner.

Having endured a severe bout of rejection in her childhood, Liz was touched by Rick's need to be near her. But she wasn't sure she wanted him there.

To his credit, he'd been working incredibly hard. The

books showed an increased profit over the same period last year. Although she owed that increase to Rick, gratitude wasn't a satisfactory substitute for love.

"You knew the gallery would be closed for the Thanksgiving weekend," she said. "I'm going to New York to do some shopping, see the latest shows, and touch bases with our east coast clients. Did I tell you the Lundgrens are giving a party for me?"

"I love New York. Why don't we go together?" he asked, with an impudent grin.

She couldn't help laughing at his temerity. "Not this time. You know what terrible gossips the Lundgrens are. Besides, I would think you could use a holiday from the art business."

"You can't fault me for wanting to spend it with you." Rick looked thoroughly crestfallen. But then his expression brightened. "Since you're going to be out of town next week, I insist on taking you to dinner tonight."

"I thought we agreed to take things slow and easy for a while."

He squared his shoulders and shot his cuffs, a move that drew attention to his broad shoulders and his impeccably tailored jacket. "You agreed. I didn't!"

Liz threw her hands up. "Now I know why you're such a good salesman."

"We can have an early dinner. I'll make a five thirty reservation at The Glass Door."

She couldn't help laughing. "You win – this time."

Rick walked to the door and stood there. "One thing you ought to know about me," he warned, with the strangest expression on his face. "I always win."

Archer had spent the morning readying the house for her departure, emptying the refrigerator, stopping the paper, arranging for a neighbour to pick up her mail, and packing her clothes. She was carrying her last suitcase out to the car when the phone rang.

"You just caught me," she told Maryann. "Five more minutes and I would have been gone."

"I wanted to say goodbye." Maryann sounded wistful. "I wish you were going with me."

"Me too. It isn't every day someone offers me an all-expenses-paid trip to Santa Fe. I'm sorry about missing your museum show too. I always wanted to meet Roman De Silva. He's supposed to be a real fox." She sighed audibly. "But I couldn't disappoint Reginald."

"I'll give you a full report when I get back," Archer promised.

"Are you sure you don't want to stay in town a few more days and spend Thanksgiving with us? I hate to think of you all alone in a strange city, eating enchiladas when you could be having turkey and trimmings at Reggie's. He says you're more than welcome."

"I'd feel like a third wheel," Archer explained. "Just promise me you'll take the time to get to know him before—"

"Don't you fret about me, Sugah," Maryann interrupted. "Now, before you go, tell me what Liz thought of the maquette you did for the hotel."

"She loved it. Frankly, so do I. It's the best thing I've ever done." Archer smiled into the mouthpiece. "I sent Louis a polaroid of it today. Doing work like that makes my not going to Hong Kong seem less frivolous."

Maryann laughed. "You and your guilt complex. Fess up, Sugah. That's the real reason you're getting out of town. So you won't be reminded of your missing husband every time you turn around."

"Am I that obvious?"

"You are to me. What do you hear from Louis?"

"Not much. With the time difference between Phoenix and Hong Kong, he's asleep when I'm awake and vice versa. I guess closing the factory is a bigger job than he anticipated. He had to get some extra help."

"Male or female?" Maryann asked dryly.

"Female as a matter of fact. Steve Carpenter's secretary is on her way to Hong Kong right now. But you know Louis. To him, a secretary is just another piece of office equipment."

"As Reginald would say, *cherchez la femme*," Maryann replied. "Look, promise you'll forget all about Louis and have yourself one hell of a time in Santa Fe. You've earned it."

"I will," Archer dutifully replied, although in her present state of mind she didn't know if that was possible.

"I'm going to miss you," Maryann said. "Call me when you get to Santa Fe so I'll know you made it, you hear."

Half an hour later, as Archer headed up the Black Canyon highway, she couldn't help wishing Maryann sat by her side. It felt strange, setting out on a five-hundred-mile journey by herself. But the thought of rattling around her empty house was even less appealing. Going to Santa Fe two weeks before the museum show was due to open, seemed like a viable alternative.

Six months ago, if someone had told Archer she would be staying at a hotel in New Mexico by herself over Thanksgiving, she wouldn't have believed it. Holidays were family times, special times. She'd cleaned and shopped and cooked her way through two and a half decades of them.

Six months ago, if someone had told her she and Louis would be living half the globe apart she would have accused them of making a very bad joke. And, had she been able to gaze into a crystal ball and see what was going to happen in Santa Fe in just a few days, she wouldn't have believed that either.

9

NOVEMBER 17, 1988

On the way from the Stronghold to his Pinnacle Peak ranch, Alan decided to stop by the Apache reservation to visit his mother. The home she lived in now was a far cry from the tumbledown, tin-roofed shack he'd come back to after the war. Just one year after Liz began exhibiting his work, his newfound prosperity enabled him to build a sturdy brick house for Natzela. It had four bedrooms, two baths, three fireplaces, and a well-landscaped yard; unheard of luxuries on the San Carlos. Even more astonishing, Alan had paid for it with cash.

Natzela was sitting in the kitchen having a cup of her favourite chicory-laced coffee when Alan arrived late in the afternoon. At fifty-five, Natzela was as lean and gnarled as the trunk of a bristlecone pine. Other Apache women grew more round with the birth of each child. She had grown thinner. She had borne her first at fifteen and the last at thirty, burying two of her offspring in infancy. She loved the six survivors with fierce pride. But Alan, the oldest, the child of her youthful passion, was her favourite.

"It's good to see you, my son," she said, a delighted smile deepening the creases around her mouth and eyes as she rose to embrace him. "How was the Stronghold?"

"Beautiful – quiet – a healing place. I'll take you there next spring when the weather is better," he replied, casting a weather eye outside. The storm, which had pursued him from the Stronghold, lashed the house. Rain beat on the roof and thunder cracked nearby.

"This is no weather for travel." Natzela's glance followed his. "Why don't you put Odii in the shed and stay the night? It's a long time since we talked."

Alan nodded his agreement. He returned to the house fifteen minutes later, drenched to the skin, and went to the bedroom Natzela reserved for his use to change into dry clothes.

When he walked back into the kitchen, his mother had laid the table for supper. While Alan ate a savoury bowl of *posole*, she brought him up to date with the family's recent activities. He got up from time to time to replenish their coffee or add another log to the fire blazing on the kitchen hearth while she chatted about his brother's hardware store in Peridot, his oldest sister's promotion to the position of assistant principal in the Peridot grammar school, and his youngest sister's first pregnancy. "Thank goodness the young ones don't have to leave the reservation to go to school the way you did," she concluded. "All we need now are jobs on the reservation so our young people can find work here instead of having to move to Phoenix."

"There's nothing wrong with living in the city. You make it sound like a fate worse than death."

Natzela cut him a fiercely disapproving glance. "Living among strangers, away from your people and your culture, is worse than death." She had never adjusted to his living away from the San Carlos. It was an old argument, one he was determined to avoid if he could.

"I stopped by today because I have some news of my own," he said. "I've asked Hank Begay to be my master dealer."

A puzzled frown furrowed her forehead. "What does that mean?"

"It means I won't be working with Liz Kant anymore."

Approval flashed in her dark eyes. "Hank is a good man. I'm sure he'll do a better job than the Kant woman. The only thing that *belagana* cares about is money."

"Without that *belagana* I would never have been a success. I wouldn't have been able to build this house, and your grandchildren wouldn't have the chance to go to college. Whether you like it or not, this family owes her a great deal."

Natzela shook her head in vigorous denial, loosening the salt and pepper hair she wore in the traditional *nah leen* of a married Apache woman. "We owe her nothing. Have you become so much a white that you believe the *belagana* deserves credit for your *power*?"

Alan knew arguing was useless. His mother had grown up schooled in the old ways. She saw virtue in all things Apache – and vice in all things white. He quickly changed the subject and the rest of his stay passed peaceably. He went to bed early, woke at first light as was his custom, and spent an hour chopping juniper logs into two-foot lengths and stacking them neatly by the back door. When the pile was high enough to last his mother a few weeks he put the saw, axe and wedge back in the shed.

Natzela had breakfast ready when he opened the kitchen door. Anxious to get home, he ate quickly and got up to clear his dishes.

She ordered him back to the table with a jerk of her head. "I'm not so old and feeble that I can't do a few dishes," she muttered, stacking the dirty plates and silver in the sink. The kitchen had a perfectly good dishwasher, but he had never been able to convince her to use it. When she finished, she turned to face him, a stern look on her face. "The entire family will be here for Thanksgiving. You haven't seen your brothers and sisters for months. I expect you to be here too."

Her tone told him she wasn't about to take no for an answer. Besides, now that he and Liz weren't . . . He refused to finish the thought. "I'll be here," he promised.

135

"Good!" She smiled secretively. "I may have a surprise when you arrive."

Natzela followed him outside while he loaded Odii into the trailer. He pretended not to notice when she slipped the Apaloosa an apple.

"Don't forget, I'm expecting you to be here on Thanksgiving," Natzela called as he climbed into the Blazer's front seat.

The sky was pale and clear, swept clean by the storm, as Alan turned west onto Route 60, headed for Phoenix. And he felt clean too, inside and out. The weeks in the Stronghold had worked their magic. Despite the cold, he opened a window, revelling in the sweet freshness of a new day.

He was more than ready to return to the Anglo world, to get on with his career by choosing a new dealer to exhibit his work in Scottsdale. Elaine Horwitch and Suzanne Brown were the most likely candidates for the job, and he decided to drive by their galleries on his way to Pinnacle Peak.

Three hours later, Alan eased the Blazer down Main Street, taking it slow as he cruised past Suzanne Brown's. She had two large paintings in the window, a Delonna Roberts acrylic and a marvellous pastel by the noted Navajo artist, Clifford Beck. Alan respected Beck as a man and as a peer. If Suzanne Brown's gallery was good enough for Beck, it was good enough for him, Alan quickly decided.

The Kant Gallery was just two doors away. A group of tourists clustered in front, obscuring the view as Alan pulled opposite it. Curious to see whose work would be in the front window, he slowed the vehicle to a crawl and waited for them to move on. As they began to walk away he saw a quarter, then a half, then all of the painting in the window.

Damn! There, boldly displayed, was the last painting he had completed before leaving town. The horse-trailer skidded as he braked to a sudden stop. Odii whinnied in protest but Alan was oblivious to everything but his own anger. That painting should have been on an easel in his studio. What the hell was it doing in Liz's window?

The impatient sound of honking horns urged him to move on, and he began scanning the street for a place to park. When he finally found one two blocks away his fury had reached flash point. He leapt from the Blazer, slamming the door so hard that the vehicle shook, and sprinted to the gallery. A salesgirl was alone in the front room when he yanked the doors open.

"Where the hell is Liz?" he shouted.

"She's not here," the astonished woman answered, throwing a will-you-rescue-me look to Rick Mason as Mason walked into the room.

"Is something wrong?" Mason asked coolly.

"Mr Longchase is looking for Liz," the woman said.

"I'll handle this." Mason dismissed the salesgirl with a reassuring smile, before turning to face Alan. "What's your problem, Longchase?"

"My business is with Liz. Not you."

"She's home, getting ready to go out of town. I'm in charge until she gets back, and I don't appreciate your coming in here like Geronimo, terrorizing the help."

Alan was determined to rein in his runaway temper. His fight was with Liz . . . or Hank . . . not this underling – not today anyway. Turning on his heel, he left the gallery without a backward glance. Hank was going to have some explaining to do, Alan thought, breaking the speed limit as he drove north on Scottsdale Road, and it had better be good.

The fact that Hank's car was blocking the circular drive when Alan got home didn't help his ugly mood. "Hank, where the hell are you?" he shouted, flinging the front door open.

"In here," Hank's rumbling bass answered from the back of the house.

137

When they met in the hall, Hank greeted him with a huge grin before leading the way to the den. "It's good to have you back. You've been gone too long."

"Not long enough for you to get my work out of the Kant Gallery! What the hell is going on?" Alan's fists bunched involuntarily, as he hurried at Hank's heels.

"If you'll give me a minute," Hank sounded like the soul of reason, "I can explain everything."

Alan noticed the computer and the files when he followed Hank into the den. "What's all this?"

"Liz suggested . . ." Hank snapped his mouth shut without finishing.

"Liz suggested?" Alan felt adrenaline pouring through his body as his anger peaked. For the second time in his life, he felt like decking the huge Navajo. "You and I aren't supposed to have a damn thing to do with Liz anymore."

Hank walked to the sideboard and poured himself a short bourbon. The fact that he didn't pour one for Alan was a good indication of his state of mind. "I had every intention of doing what you wanted. In fact, I made an appointment to see Liz the day you left for the Stronghold."

"So what the fuck went wrong?"

"After talking to her, I decided changing galleries wouldn't be in our best interests."

"Who the hell are you to decide what my best interests are?" Alan strode to the sideboard, poured his own drink and swallowed half of it in one gulp.

"I'm your master dealer," Hank said quietly. "I thought that gave me the right to decide who handled your work. Or did I misunderstand my authority?"

Alan couldn't believe what he was hearing. Hank's behaviour was totally out of character. "You ignored my instructions."

"Maybe I don't take orders well," Hank replied grimly.

Alan closed his eyes briefly, seeking the inner peace

138

he'd found in the Stronghold. The last thing he wanted was to get into a brawl with his oldest and best friend. But he wasn't satisfied with Hank's too glib explanation. Alan sensed Liz's fine Machiavellian mind behind Hank's words. "How did Liz convince you not to pull my work?"

Hank was sipping his bourbon as if this were just another friendly disagreement, like the ones they had when they discussed politics. "Liz simply pointed out that there would be a serious lack of continuity if you changed master dealers and major galleries at the same time. I happen to agree with her."

"But you knew how I felt!"

"Think what it will mean to your people, having a man who grew up on the reservation show his paintings at a prestigious museum like the Guggenheim."

Alan shook his head in disbelief. "I don't know anything about a show at the Guggenheim."

"Liz heard from the museum the day you left. They want to give you a retrospective next year."

"I can do a retrospective without being represented by Liz Kant." Alan stared at Hank. "She's got some kind of hold on you, hasn't she?"

Hank glared at him. "I'm going to pretend you didn't say that. Look, I know you wanted to leave the gallery, but you left me in charge. You made a lousy decision, so I unmade it. I had a hundred decisions to make while you were gone. Staying with the Kant Gallery was just one of them. While I was at it, I signed a contract committing you to five more years with Liz. Damn it, Alan, I didn't want to be your master dealer. You were the one who insisted."

"You what?" Alan shouted.

"You heard me." Hank's voice was flat. "I signed a five-year contract with the Kant Gallery. I don't know why you dislike Liz so much, and right now, I don't much care. She's been very helpful since you left."

I'll bet, Alan thought grimly.

"I've always been a man of my word," Hank continued in that same even voice. "If you choose not to honour the contract, you're going to have to fire me."

Alan's eyes bore into Hank's. "You mean that, don't you?"

"I'm afraid I do."

Now, Alan was sure that Liz had found a way to manipulate Hank. Damn her to hell for using an honourable man to get what she wanted. If Alan forced Hank to break his word, it might well signal the end of their friendship. Liz wasn't worth that kind of sacrifice. She had won this skirmish, but Alan would be damned if he'd let her win the war! "From here on, I don't want anything to do with Liz," he said, his level tone matching Hank's. "But I'll honour your damn contract, my friend, because I honour you."

Santa Fe is to south-western artists what Mecca is to Mohammedans – a place of pilgrimage where painters and sculptors worship at the shrine of predecessors like the Taos Ten or Georgia O'Keefe.

Archer had been to Santa Fe several times to deliver sculpture. But her stays had been brief. In the past, she had always hurried home to take care of her family. Now, waking up in a strange bed, it felt peculiar to realize she could stay as long as she liked. She had checked into La Fonda, the inn at the end of the Santa Fe Trail, late the previous afternoon. There were other, more luxurious hotels to choose from, but she loved the historic building. Like all the other buildings in Santa Fe, La Fonda boasted pueblo architecture. Archer's fourth floor room was furnished in a south-western style that echoed the city's unique ambiance.

Smiling as she got out of bed, Archer began to consider how she would spend the next two weeks. Now that she was actually in Santa Fe, her refusal to accompany Louis to Hong Kong seemed perfectly logical. She needed to immerse herself in a south-western culture, to spend time in the various Indian pueblos clinging to the banks of the Rio Grande, if she intended to continue doing the sort of authentic, carefully-researched sculpture that was becoming her hallmark.

Thank heaven, Louis had accepted the fact that she couldn't go helter-skelter to Hong Kong, not when she had the opportunity to do a museum show with an internationally acclaimed artist like Roman De Silva. Stretching, she walked to the window, thinking how much she had to be grateful for. When Louis got back home, they could concentrate on their marriage. In the meantime, Santa Fe lay at her feet.

Her room's antique heating system rattled into life as she finished dressing. The city nestled at the foot of the Sangre De Cristo mountains, at an altitude of 7,400 feet. Knowing it could get bitterly cold in mid November, she took her sheepskin-lined jacket from the closet, walked out of the room and headed for the elevators.

Ten minutes later she was seated at a table in the coffee house adjacent to the hotel lobby. The odour of yeast breads, spices and expresso combined with the damp smell of winter woollens and warm bodies in a pungent but not unpleasant mix. The small room was as crowded, and the croissants as meltingly delicious, as she remembered from her last visit.

Calories be damned, she thought, savouring every buttery morsel of pastry. A cosy fire blazed on a large hearth, the juniper logs crackling and sputtering merrily. Customers, arriving in a steady stream, somehow managed to find places at the already crowded tables. Looking around, Archer realized she was the only person sitting alone. For a moment she felt a twinge of shame for taking up an entire table. Ordinarily, she'd have finished quickly so someone else could have her place. But today, when the waiter asked if she would like her cup refilled a third time, she replied, "Yes, thank you."

Santa Fe was a present she had given herself and she intended to enjoy every moment of her stay. Relaxing, she began a slow survey of the room's inhabitants. Like most of her fellow artists, she was a confirmed people-watcher. Form, shape, and line are the sculptor's lingua franca, and Archer read character from the way people sat or moved.

An Indian woman at a corner table with a group of Anglos was the first to catch Archer's eye. The woman's face, all chiselled planes and angles, was a sculptor's dream. Suddenly, Archer recognized her. She was Grace Medicine Flower, the famous potter. Looking further, Archer's eyes lingered on a young couple. Their bodies touched from shoulder to thigh as they gazed at each other. Newlyweds, she decided – or lovers who wished they had stayed in bed instead of going out for breakfast.

Next, an imposingly large man caught her eye. The span of his shoulders made his sturdy wooden chair look fragile. He had salt and pepper hair, a ruddy complexion that exuded health and vigour, and lively blue eyes set deep beneath a powerful brow. He leaned back, his legs spread in a macho pose, holding court while his table-mates paid him rapt attention.

The man's spread-legged attitude reminded Archer of a nude male model who sat just that way for one of her life-drawing classes, offering his genitals to view as if they really were the family jewels. The memory made her squirm with annoyance.

Suddenly, everything about the man across the room, from his posture to his obvious self assurance, rankled her. He wore a workman's shirt and pants, and high laced boots with the sort of thick rubber soles that looked like tire-tread. He's probably one of those shit-kicking types who thinks muscles are more important than brains, she concluded.

Before she could look away, he turned and gave her a very thorough, appraising look. Feeling herself redden, she fumbled in her wallet for a tip and stood up abruptly. As she walked out of the room, she felt sure his eyes were following her. It took an act of will not to turn around to see if she was right.

She left the coffee shop hurriedly, suddenly aware of being a woman alone in a strange city. But her uneasiness was banished by the city's charm as she stood gazing around Santa Fe's central plaza. The air was cold, crisp, and sparkling, like *brut* champagne.

The square hadn't changed since her last pilgrimage to Santa Fe two years before. But then, it hadn't changed much in the last century. An ornate Victorian bandstand stood at its centre, with walkways radiating from it in all directions. Galleries, boutiques and restaurants occupied the buildings lining three sides of the plaza. The north side was taken up by the palace of the Governors, a rambling, three-hundred-year-old structure that housed the history museum. Indians from the Rio Grande pueblos sat in front of the Palace, selling pottery, jewellery and baskets.

Archer's destination, the art museum, was diagonally across from La Fonda. Like the hotel, its architecture evoked the city's pueblo Indian origin. The building's interior was quiet as she pushed open the heavy front doors, the lobby empty but for a woman who sat behind a semi-circular information desk.

"Can you tell me where the De Silva–Harrison show is going to be?" Archer asked.

The woman looked up from the book she'd been reading. "In the new wing," she said, pointing the way. "You can't miss it."

There were few other visitors on the premises as Archer passed through a series of rooms where the museum's permanent collection was on display. Heading down a ramp, she reached a pair of thick glass doors that divided the older section of the building from the new. Pushing them open, she shivered with anticipation. Two more weeks and her own work would be displayed here!

At first, she assumed that the large room was empty. But then, as she walked around a partition, she saw a man standing with his back toward her. From his clothes, she guessed he must be a custodian. As if sensing her presence, he turned around.

She recognized him at once. It was the man from the coffee shop. Her first instinct was to leave but, seeing him head in her direction, she decided to face him down.

"Can I help you?" he asked, with a lazy, knowing smile.

Although Archer was tall, this man towered over her. It made her feel distinctly uncomfortable. He must be six foot three or four, she thought. "I was wondering if this is the space where the De Silva–Harrison show will be on exhibition."

"That it is." His eyes moved over her body as intimately as a lover's hands.

She refused to let him know how self-conscious he made her feel. "Do you know when they'll be mounting the show?"

"Sometime next week, at least that's what they tell me."

"Thank you," she said, turning quickly and heading for the exit.

"You're from out of town, aren't you?" He reached her side in time to open the doors to the old wing.

Nodding, she hurriedly retraced her way through the museum.

"Do you like Mexican food?" he asked, easily matching her rapid pace with his long-legged stride.

"I don't see that it's any of your business."

He ignored the rebuff. "If you're still around the square at lunch, you ought to try The Shed. It's just down Palace Avenue a couple of blocks from here. They make the world's best blue-corn enchiladas – but make sure to ask for extra cheese."

"I doubt I'll be in the area," she snapped, as she left the building.

But three hours later, she was still prowling the shops and galleries that lined the plaza. Her stomach rumbled and the thought of blue-corn enchiladas made her mouth water. Workmen usually know the best places to eat, she rationalized. Just because this particular man had an insolent, familiar manner wasn't any reason to deny herself the pleasure of a delicious lunch. A brisk walk brought her to the north-east side of the square. From there, she followed her nose.

A blend of a half dozen different chilies, fresh tortillas, cheeses and spices wafted from the restaurant's courtyard entry. Archer followed a waitress to a table by a window, ordered blue-corn enchiladas with extra cheese and a Dos Equis to go with them. She had just taken her first frosty swallow of beer when a flurry of sound made her look toward the entrance. To her dismay, the workman had just walked in, and it seemed every waitress was vying for the job of seating him.

"I'm meeting a friend," she overheard him say before he headed in her direction.

If he thinks I'm that friend, he's in for a rude surprise, she vowed.

"I see you took my advice." He grinned down at her impudently. "Do you mind if I join you?"

"I mind very much."

"Oh come on, Archer," he pulled out the chair opposite hers, "that's no way to act."

"If you don't leave me alone right now," she sputtered, "I'll have the management call the police!" And then she realized he had called her by name. "How do you know who I am?"

"I saw your picture in the catalogue the museum did for the De Silva–Harrison show."

"You have me at a disadvantage – since you know my name and I don't know yours."

His grin broadened. "Permit me to introduce myself. I'm Roman De Silva."

Alan's first night back home was plagued by bad dreams. He woke at first light, dressed in jeans, a plaid Pendleton shirt and Kaibab moccasins and headed for the stables at the rear of his property. Odii greeted him with a soft nicker. She needed exercise after the long hours in the trailer on the way home, but thirty minutes after saddling up, he returned her to her stable.

He'd been away from painting too long. Now, the need to express himself on canvas burned inside him. He rubbed the Apaloosa down, grained her, forked some fresh hay into her stall and, not bothering with breakfast himself, went directly to his studio. The free-standing, twenty-by-thirty-foot adobe structure was separated from the main house by a large patio. Like the house, it was built in the Santa Fe style with softly rounded walls and a flat roof supported on massive beams.

Alan unlocked the door and went in, pleased to see the place was clean, tidy, and ready for him. Hank's doing, he realized, regretting the harsh words they exchanged the day before.

Sky-lights and a north-facing wall of windows provided good natural light. Storage shelves lined one side of the room and racks for finished paintings took up another. A traditional beehive fireplace bulked in one corner. Ordinarily, Alan would have taken time to build a fire, but now that he was back in his studio again he lusted to paint.

Moving purposefully, he quickly assembled the tools of his trade. Unlike some painters, he preferred to stretch his own canvasses and kept a dozen on hand. Selecting one at random, he placed it on a sturdy easel. He gathered tubes of Grumbacher oils, a variety of brushes from fifty-dollar sables to inexpensive synthetics, several conté pencils, a much-used palette, jars of turpentine and linseed oil, and placed them on a large table next to his easel.

Then he stepped back several paces and studied the canvas, waiting for an idea to suggest itself. If someone had come up to him then and there and asked how he knew what to paint, he wouldn't have been able to answer. The concepts seemed to bide their time somewhere in his mind, like flowers waiting to be plucked. If he looked at a canvas long enough, he would have a vision of the painting he wanted to do. Every time he assembled his materials, the miracle happened, the power flowed through him.

Other artists had different ways of explaining the phenomenon laymen call inspiration. At a recent opening, Archer Harrison had told him she felt as if her sculptures already existed in the clay, and that all she did was free them. The great Navajo artist, Chethlahe Paladin, claimed to get his ideas from a deceased painter who talked to him.

Alan knew the how and why didn't matter. The creative urge existed in all peoples and all cultures, and had done from the dawn of mankind. When he stood in front of a canvas, he felt a part of a great unbroken chain of painters that had its beginning in the Stone Age artists who worked in the caves of Lascaux and Les Eyzies. Those long-gone masters seemed to whisper in his ear, offering encouragement and guidance. If there was such a thing as atavistic memory, he suspected it resided in artists. Theirs was, he believed, the oldest profession.

Now, standing in front of the blank canvas, the vision came to him as he knew it would. Picking up a conté pencil, he began to sketch freehand, moving with unconscious grace – swaying, dipping, bending, rising on his toes, dancing with the drawing. He pulled back to use the full, free sweep of his arm to create a bold outline, and stepped close to pencil in details as the figure of an elderly warrior began to materialize. The drawing was born in one continuous effort. There was joy in its birth, a river of pleasure that flowed from his imagination through his fingers.

An hour after he'd begun, the sketch was finished. He took a deep breath and put the conté pencil on the table, his concentration broken for the first time. He'd drawn with the left side of his brain. Now, the analytical right side sought flaws in what he'd done. His eyes narrowed as he looked at his work.

The warrior was old, with the exhausted nobility of a man whose battles have all been well fought. But something was missing, some key ingredient that would make the painting more than just a portrait of an Apache elder statesman.

The answer came in a radiant burst of understanding. Alan retrieved the conté pencil and drew a single budding rose in the old man's hand. He stepped back again and this time, he knew the drawing was complete.

Next, he filled his palette with large squibs of colour – ochre, burnt sienna, zinc white, payne's grey – the monochromatic shades he used for underpainting. His movements intensified as he attacked and retreated, placing a slash of colour here, another there. He worked with controlled fury, seeking to master himself and his talent, to create a canvas as fine as his inner vision had promised it could be.

Three hours later, the underpainting that gave his work its remarkable depth had been completed. The exultation of creation ebbed as he stepped back to survey what he'd accomplished. Noontime sun flooded the overhead skylights and molten beams of gold touched the canvas with magic. This is what it's all about, he thought. The rest of it – working with galleries, dealers, collectors – was bullshit. He felt best in his studio, with a palette in one hand, a brush in the other – facing a canvas. It was what he'd been born to do.

Filled with a renewed sense of purpose, Alan took one last look at the work in progress and then, suddenly aware he hadn't eaten all day, returned to the main house. Hank was in the kitchen, pouring a cup of coffee when Alan walked in.

"Care to join me?" Hank asked politely, although his tone held no welcome.

"Make mine black." Alan looked around the immaculate kitchen. "Have we got anything to eat?"

"I was about to make Navajo tacos."

"Sounds good to me."

Hank turned his back and busied himself at the kitchen counter.

Clearing his throat, Alan launched into the speech he had rehearsed earlier that day, while riding. "I owe you an apology," he said. "You were right last night, and I was wrong. I hope you'll forgive my bad temper."

"Why the about face?" Hank asked, putting a cast-iron skillet on the stove and filling it with oil.

"I left you in charge. We both know I didn't give you a chance to say no. I had no right to question your decisions. From here on, I intend to give you a free hand."

"Are you sure that's what you want?" Hank asked, forking flattened circles of bread dough into the pan.

"I came home to paint – and that's what I intend to do. But more important, it's time I got on with the rest of my life as well."

"You lost me." Hank turned the sizzling fried bread over.

"It's not very complicated. I haven't had a relationship with a woman since Liz and I broke up."

"What does that have to do with what we've been talking about?" Hank lifted a steaming sphere of golden brown fried bread from the hot fat, set it on a paper towel to drain, and turned to face Alan.

"The only way I'm going to put my relationship with her into perspective is to get involved with someone else. I'll be forty in a few months. It's time I got married and started a family."

"You're Roman De Silva, the artist?" Archer gasped. "Why in the world did you take so long to tell me?"

Roman looked at her, thinking her photograph hadn't done her justice. "The timing didn't seem right."

"Do you realize I've been wondering why the hell you were following me?"

She looked very angry and very pretty – a devastating combination. He responded by leaning across the table and kissing her squarely on the mouth. She tasted of beer, menthol cigarettes, cinnamon Certs, and something he recognized as uniquely her. In fact, he was so intrigued by the flavour that he was about to try for seconds when she pushed him away.

Blinking furiously, she took a deep breath. "I'd heard you were the Peck's Bad Boy of the art world, Mr De Silva, and, so far, you've more than lived up to your reputation."

"I'm glad I haven't disappointed you."

"This morning, I was convinced you were one of the museum custodians – and a very forward one at that. What were you doing there?"

"Hoping you would show up. I tried to catch up with you when you left the coffee shop this morning, but you disappeared. Now, turn about is fair play. What are you doing in Santa Fe so soon? According to the people at the museum, you weren't expected for ten more days."

"My plans changed." Suddenly, unhappiness clouded her grey eyes. "I should be home working, but I decided to play hooky."

She's a serious one, he thought, wanting to see her smile again. "As you've probably heard, I'm a bit of a

150

truant myself. I hope you'll let me play hooky with you while you're here."

Before Archer could respond, their waitress delivered a fragrant platter laden with blue-corn enchiladas. Roman ordered the same for himself and urged Archer to dig in. To his pleasure, she didn't seem compelled to indulge in meaningless chit-chat while she ate. Instead, she gave the food the attention its excellence merited. Meanwhile, he gave her the single-minded attention he felt she deserved.

He had been aware of her from the moment she walked into the hotel restaurant that morning. A rare and unusual beauty he thought then, taking note of her slim figure, ash blonde hair, and flawless skin; the kind of woman he would enjoy painting – or bedding. He hadn't known who she was at first. Then it hit him. Her picture hadn't done her justice. She had to be Archer Harrison.

He'd been in love with her work from the first time he saw it featured in *Southwest Art* magazine a year before. He related to her sculpture at once, felt psychically connected to it, and made up his mind to meet its creator. Arranging the museum show had been relatively easy. But he hadn't expected Archer Harrison to be beautiful. He counted on responding to her on an intellectual level.

Now, as he watched her eating – saw the delicate interplay between teeth, tongue and lips – he found himself responding in a purely physical way. His heart rate accelerated and his palms began to sweat. He shook his head, as if that could dispel the foolish ideas crowding it.

"Is something wrong?" Archer asked, looking up from her food.

"Everything's perfect," Roman replied.

He began to eat as soon as his food arrived and was halfway through the meal before he realized he hadn't tasted a thing. What the hell was happening to him? He hadn't experienced this breathless sense of wonder for more years than he cared to remember.

A decade ago when his wife died of cancer, all Roman

151

knew of love and joy seemed to die with her. He buried the part of him that believed in happiness, certain he would never experience it again. But as he looked across the table at Archer Harrison, he felt as young and hopeful as a boy waking up on a birthday.

When she walked into the coffee shop that morning, what he had experienced could be best described as a *coup de foudre*, a thunder clap that left his head spinning and his heart pounding in his chest. He had tried denying it, spent the rest of the morning telling himself he was indulging in a forty-six-year-old man's romantic notions. He didn't even believe in love at first sight. At least he hadn't, he realized, until now.

10

NOVEMBER 23, 1988

Dust devils sported across the terrain, tossing dried bolls of tumbleweed in the air like children playing with balloons. The breeze tore ragged plumes of smoke from the chimney of Natzela's house on the outskirts of Peridot.

The family had already gathered when Alan arrived for Thanksgiving dinner. Assorted trucks and four-wheel drive vehicles crowded the driveway. They were, he noted with pleasure, relatively new and well cared for – a pleasant contrast to the rusted, battle-scarred car the family had owned twenty years before.

Alan's male relatives, brothers, brothers-in-law, cousins and uncles were in the living room, gathered around the television, watching football when he walked in. Twenty-three-year-old Hazous, his youngest brother, was the first to greet him.

"How're they hangin?" Hazous asked, clasping one of Alan's grocery-laden arms.

"A hell of a lot bigger than yours," Alan replied, bringing a rough shout of laughter from the other men in the room.

They were a handsome group – slim, wiry, with chiselled, weather-worn faces, black hair and hooded eyes. Today they wore their best jeans, flannel shirts, and cowboy boots. Alan, who thoroughly disliked suits and ties, felt instantly, completely at home, as he never did at Anglo gatherings.

"Ma said to tell you she wanted to see you right away."
Hazous grinned and shoved Alan toward the back of the
house. "Has she got a surprise for you, you lucky dog."

The mingled aromas of traditional Anglo and Apache
foods made Alan's mouth water when he walked into the
kitchen. A thirty-pound turkey roasted in the oven while
posole, a stew made with hominy, simmered in a huge
cast-iron pot on top of the stove. It would take a strong
man to carry it to the table at supper time. Alan's sisters
had contributed dozens of blue-corn tamales and fresh
fried bread for the holiday feast. Platters of fried chicken,
bowls of potato salad and coleslaw, and trays of cakes
loaded with thick, creamy icing burdened the kitchen
counters.

Family members all brought what they could afford. In
keeping with Apache tradition, the strong cared for the
weak, the haves for the have-nots, the young for the old.
The grocery sacks in Alan's arms held a cornucopia of fresh
fruit, apples, pears and out-of-season grapes and peaches
which were unavailable at reservation grocery stores. They
also held candy and small gifts for the children, and two
bottles of Seagram's Crown Royale for the men.

In all, forty people crowded the house. The home he'd
built for his mother served as a *gowa*, a centre for the entire
clan. Surrounded by his family, Alan's spirits lifted with
pride and the sense of a job well-done. The Longchases
had been born in a shack which offered scant shelter
from the elements. The so-called necessities, food and
clothing, had been in short supply. And yet here they
were; successful, educated men and women, making a
contribution to their tribe and their country. That his
wealth had paid for their triumphs didn't even occur to
Alan.

"You're late," Natzela scolded from her place at the
kitchen table where she'd been shelling peas.

"Now, Ma," Alan's sister, Anna, jumped to his defence,
"Alan has a long drive from Scottsdale. You can't expect

154

him to arrive as early as the rest of us, when we live just around the corner."

One by one, his female relatives demanded a moment of his time – a special greeting, a hug or a kiss. Not until they finished did Natzela speak again.

"It's good to see you with your family. This is where you belong, my son." Suddenly, a sly smile blossomed on Natzela's face. "Remember the surprise I promised you?" Gesturing that she expected him to follow, she handed her bowl of peas to Anna and walked to the back door.

Unaccountably, the other women began to giggle and whisper. Natzela stopped in her tracks, turned and silenced them with a fierce matriarchal scowl before preceding Alan into the back yard.

He was immediately engulfed by a tide of children from toddlers to teens, who shouted his name before hurling themselves at him. Kneeling to receive their greetings, he relished the powdered scent of the babies, the sweet shy kisses of his nieces, the manly handshakes of his nephews. Still kneeling, he distributed the gifts he'd bought. While the children scurried off to compare presents, he stood up and found himself facing a strange woman.

"Celia, this is my son, Alan," Natzela said, beaming with satisfaction. "Alan, I'd like you to meet Celia Atcittie. She teaches third grade in the Peridot school. She is not of our *Ki*," Natzela concluded, her tone imparting significance to the statement.

Apaches always married outside of their clan. Alan belonged to the *Tu'agaidn*, the White Water people. Celia, he soon learned, was a member of the *Tisk'adn*, the Cottonwood Standing people.

Apache social structure is governed by rigid rules. Alan had broken those rules by courting a *belagana*. Natzela, who clung tenaciously to all Apache traditions, believed that marrying a white woman would have caused Alan's ultimate reincarnation as a mule. She wanted him to marry

155

a woman of his people, and now she seemed to have chosen a likely candidate.

So this is my mother's surprise, he thought, looking at Celia. The young woman had raven black hair that hung loose and straight, halfway down her back. Her face was rounder than most Apache faces – one of her ancestors had undoubtedly suffered reincarnation as an owl for marrying a Pima or a Papago – but her cheekbones and chin were well carved, and her rich brown eyes were fringed by the thickest black lashes he'd ever seen. Her body was ripe and full, like fruit grown in a gentle summer. Although he never did well when it came to guessing a woman's age, he thought she couldn't be more than twenty-two or -three. She's lovely, he realized.

"I've heard a great deal about you," Celia said, offering her hand, "and I love your work."

Her grip was firm, her skin soft. "It's a pleasure to meet you," he replied with genuine warmth.

In the old days he would have met someone like Celia Atcittie at a squaw dance. If she struck his fancy – and her clan was in no way related to his – he'd have managed to arrange a series of accidentally-on purpose meetings. Assuming that she returned his interest and began seeking him out, he'd have asked an uncle to take an offering of horses to her father as a bride-price. If the offer was accepted, Alan would have claimed the girl as his wife and she'd have come to live with his family.

"Celia's father serves on the tribal council," Natzela said. "You should have seen her *nai'es*. People came from hundreds of miles away to attend."

The White-Painted Woman puberty ceremony, or *Nai'es*, lasted four days and was so expensive that few families could afford to host one anymore. Natzela was telling him, in her round about way, that Celia's family was well off – and that Celia herself should be considered a real catch.

"Now, Mother Longchase, you're embarrassing me,"

Celia said, blushing prettily. "I'm sure Alan doesn't care about things like that."

Mother Longchase? Alan mused. No one called Natzela mother other than her daughters or her daughters-in-law. This girl must be very special indeed.

The insistent clamour of children's voices kept him from further speculation.

"Your nieces and nephews have been talking about you all morning," Celia said. "Is it true that you always play a few games with them?"

"Yes, it is," Alan admitted. Of all the family's adult males, he, the childless one, took the greatest pleasure in the family's numerous offspring.

He could sense his mother's approval as he permitted Celia to lead him to the milling youngsters. Celia's hand was warm and her smile even warmer as she said, "We've been playing blind-man's bluff. The children have been waiting for you to get here so you could take a turn at being it."

The youngsters screamed with delight as she tied a blindfold over his eyes. Snarling with pretended rage, he pretended to be a ferocious warrior, stalking them around the grassy yard. The more daring rushed up and tagged him, *counting coup* before darting away, trailing laughter.

Within minutes, Alan's senses became accustomed to the dark. With hands outstretched, he attempted to catch first one scampering youngster and then another. Stepping forward and feeling the ground through the thin-soled Kaibab moccasins he always wore at home, he was aware of someone coming near just as he heard a throaty laugh. He reached forward, expecting to grab a child by the shoulder. Instead, his right hand came in contact with a woman's rounded breast.

The children, shrieking with delight, drowned out the sound of Celia's surprised gasp. Unlike Alan, the youngsters could see the flush that started at Celia's neck and quickly reached her rounded cheeks.

157

Ripping off the blindfold, Alan smiled into Celia's eyes. "This game has unexpected pleasures."

Her blush deepened as his bold gaze roved her body. Yes. His mother had chosen well, he thought.

"Now, it's your turn to be it," he said.

Before he tied the blindfold over her eyes, their glances met and held. He read the message in hers quite easily. There was no guile in Celia Atcittie's frank gaze. She obviously liked what she saw. Her approval was as soothing as balm, and he found himself responding in kind.

After the game resumed, he stood on the sidelines, watching. Even blindfolded, Celia moved with fawn-like grace. She was pretty, intelligent, and obviously good with children. Some day, she was going to make a wonderful wife and mother. Then, recalling his recent resolve to marry and start raising a family, he looked at her with growing interest. Could Celia be the woman he'd been seeking?

Although Reginald and Maryann had seen each other two or three times a week ever since their chance encounter at the Kant Gallery, she had never been to his home. Now, as she drove to Clearwater Hills, an ultra-exclusive gated community in Paradise Valley, she was thrilled at the prospect of sharing Thanksgiving with him, seeing his art collection for the first time. It seemed to signal a change in their relationship, a growing seriousness on his part.

Reginald was so dignified, so reserved, so undemonstrative – not that she was complaining, mind you – that she still didn't know where she stood. Her hopeful heart kept hearing wedding bells while her more cautious mind told her to beware.

She still didn't feel at ease in his company. Reginald was so alien to her experiences with the opposite sex that he might as well have been from another galaxy. The men she met in bars liked to screw before the first date. But Reginald seemed perfectly content to take her to expensive restaurants, to spend a small fortune on her without expecting anything in return.

From past experiences, she had concluded that dating was little more than an acceptable form of prostitution, a quid pro quo for money spent and services rendered. A cheap dinner had to be repaid with touchy-feely, a more expensive one with a fuck, and concert tickets called for a well-done blow job. She could write a book on date-rape.

By contrast, Reginald seemed perfectly content with holding her hand and giving her a gentlemanly peck on the cheek when he said good night. And he was generous to a fault. She was giddily close to falling in love with him.

Pulling up in front of the gate that controlled access to Clearwater Hills, she gave her name to the guard on duty. While he checked his admittance list for her name, she glanced in the Datsun's rear-view mirror. As part of her new, ladylike image, she had abandoned false eyelashes, sculptured nails, and her fetish for dresses that vaunted her abundant cleavage. She wanted Reginald to think of her as the sort of woman he'd be proud to introduce to his mother. Although that meant making over her appearance and curbing her tongue, it was a small price to pay.

She shivered with anticipation as the guard indicated she could drive right on in. She'd never been in a gated community before, and had been firmly convinced that people who lived in such places thought they were a hell of a lot better than the poor folks they locked out. But dear Reginald was nothing like the snooty, rich bastards she'd imagined living behind the gates of Clearwater Hills. He had told her to take a left and then a right turn, and then go to the end of the street. His home, he explained, stood at the crest of a small hill.

A mountain is more like it, she thought, as her wheezing

Datsun protested the road's steep incline. Heights gave her the heebie-jeebies, and she was wondering if she had sufficient courage to go another foot when the end of the street came into view.

Beyond it stood the most splendid house she'd ever seen. She forgot to be scared as she surveyed her destination – a turreted Spanish mansion that reminded her of photographs she had seen of the Alhambra. The long driveway was paved with yards and yards of imported glazed tile she would have loved to use in her bathroom – if she could afford it. Feeling vaguely sacrilegious, she braked to a stop and stepped out onto its glistening surface. The goddamn Datsun was going to leak oil all over the place. She had considered renting a car for the day so Reginald wouldn't know how broke she was, but had decided to invest in a new Liz Claiborne outfit instead. Now, smoothing her new dress over her hips, Maryann resolutely marched to the front door and rang the bell.

Within seconds, a blatantly handsome young man in an immaculate black suit answered her summons. "You must be Miss Van Kamp," he said. "Mr Quincy asked me to show you into the drawing room. He'll be right with you."

"Thank you kindly," Maryann drawled. It was her first encounter with a real, honest-to-God butler, and she tried to get a good look at this one without seeming to stare. He appeared to be in his late twenties. Beneath his perfectly tailored jacket and sharply pressed trousers, she detected a heavily-muscled body. Dressed differently, she would have taken him for a body-builder – maybe even a gay body-builder, she thought, taking a second look. Something about him sent alarm signals racing along her spine as she followed him along a wide passage to a pair of mahogany doors.

He opened them and motioned Maryann into the room. Not wanting to appear like a hick, she managed to stifle a gasp of pleasure. It was the most beautiful room she had ever seen. This wasn't *Better Homes and Gardens* – it was *best* homes! The elaborate inlaid parquet flooring was covered with fine oriental carpets in the softest pastel shades. She wasn't knowledgeable enough to identify the exact period of the furnishings, however they were obviously – even to her untutored eyes – French, authentic, and expensive. But their beauty was easily eclipsed by the art that hung on the walls. Maryann was immediately drawn to a large Cassatt, a tenderly rendered portrait of a young mother and child. She walked toward it with reverential awe.

"I thought you would like that one," she heard Reginald's familiar voice behind her.

"Like it? I love it!" she exclaimed, turning to face him.

He was casually dressed in soft flannel slacks and a wine velvet smoking jacket that softened the lines of his angular frame. Standing on tiptoe to brush a kiss against his cheek, she decided that he looked quite handsome.

"You look very *distingué* today," she said, trying to throw the word in so casually that Reginald wouldn't know she'd spent hours poring over her old French vocabulary book.

"*Merci, mon amie,*" he replied, a welcoming smile warming his face. "Before we settle down in front of the fire, how would you like to see the house?"

"I'd love it," she replied with heartfelt enthusiasm.

The tour began back in the vaulted entry. It was, Maryann now realized, situated in the tower she had observed from the outside. A magnificent tapestry hung on one side and a stair with an elaborate wrought iron banister climbed the other.

"The banister is art deco," Reginald explained, "a Guimard, circa 1910. Isn't it wonderful?"

Maryann nodded her agreement although, to be honest,

there was something upsetting about the way the wrought iron writhed and twisted, like a nest of snakes.

It took an hour to tour the mansion's ten thousand square feet. Reginald proved to be a delightful guide, reciting the provenance and personal history of each antique and artwork in his considerable collection. The library, in addition to hundreds of beautifully leather- and gilt-bound first editions, boasted a large Nevelson wall sculpture.

Reginald owned three O'Keefes. The best, a hard-edged painting of a ram's skull, hung in what he called his morning room. A Bonheur, bucolic and peaceful, was in his bedroom along with a Morrisot. Maryann felt a special thrill when she saw her own painting in a small room Reginald described as his private hide-away.

"I like to read and listen to music in here," he explained, indicating a complicated-looking stereo and a comfortable leather chair. "Sometimes, when I'm tired or depressed, I just sit quietly and look at your paintings. It's very sooth-ing. I'm never lonely when I'm with my art."

"You sweet thing," Maryann replied, thinking it was the nicest compliment anyone had ever paid her. "A terrific guy like you should never want for company."

Reginald took a handkerchief from his breast pocket and pressed it against his lips. "If you knew me better, you'd realize I've led a rather solitary life."

"Why didn't you ever get married?" she asked, giving voice to the question she had been holding in check ever since they met.

"I was never fortunate enough to meet the right woman." He cleared his throat and dabbed at his lips again. "A man in my position, well, I have to be careful. It's hard to know if someone likes me for myself, or for the Quincy name and fortune."

On impulse, she took his hand and kissed it. "If you saw yourself the way I see you, you wouldn't worry. You're the nicest man in the world, and that isn't something money can buy."

He sighed. "I wish I could believe you."

"You can," she answered vehemently.

Suddenly, a little awkwardly because of their height difference, he pulled her into his arms. The top of her head came halfway up his chest, and he ran one hand through her platinum ringlets. "You're a very special woman. I never thought I would be fortunate enough to meet a lady with your talent and *joie de vivre*."

She wanted to hug him back hard, but you didn't just go throwing your arms around someone as reserved as Reginald.

"Now, how about some sherry?" he asked, gently releasing her.

"I'd love some," she replied, although the only sherry she ever tasted had been cheap, and tasted medicinal.

The house was so big that she would never have found her way back to the living room without Reginald leading the way. She grinned, thinking it would be a good idea to leave a trail of bread crumbs when she went to the bathroom.

They spent the rest of the afternoon sipping sherry in front of a blazing fire and talking about painting and painters. Reginald's knowledge of art history far surpassed her own, but he knew nothing about the creative process and questioned her at length.

Never before had she attempted to analyse why she painted the things she did. "It's like I have something to say," her brow furrowed as she struggled to explain something she had only intuited, "and I just can't hold it in. I'm not very good at expressing myself in words. But most of the time, painting is easy for me."

"Where do you get ideas?" he asked.

"I wish I knew. They just seem to be floating out there, and I kind of snag them, like a fisherman hooks a trout."

"Fascinating," he exclaimed. "Tell me more."

By the time the butler – whom Reginald introduced as Keith – announced dinner, Maryann was slightly tipsy from too much sherry, and exhausted by the endless questions and the need to formulate careful answers. She felt as if she'd been through an interrogation. Not that she minded. No man had ever shown the slightest interest in her artistic life. She was flattered and touched as, arm in arm, they walked into the dining room.

Two places had been set at the head of an enormous table exquisitely arrayed with an orchid centrepiece, fine bone china, gold tableware and deeply-etched crstal. It was a far cry from the five-and-dime dishes and jelly-jar glasses she had grown up with.

An hour and a half later, after a five-course meal, she had more than eaten her fill. "This has been the best Thanksgiving ever," she said, refusing a last glass of Mums. A warm glow spread from the top of her head to the tips of her toes, enveloping her in a feeling of well-being.

"My sentiments exactly," Reginald replied.

Sighing, she got to her feet. "I mustn't overstay my welcome."

"You could never do that," he assured, as he followed her into the hall. It had grown dark outside and she could barely see his face.

She wanted to go home, take off her control-top, support pantyhose, and rub the circulation back into her feet. "All good things must end," she replied.

"Will you see Miss Van Kamp out?" Reginald asked, as the butler materialized out of the gloom. "I hope you don't mind my not seeing you to your car, my dear, but I want to call my mother and tell her about our lovely dinner." He bent down, and kissed her cheek. "Thank you for brightening a lonely bachelor's holiday, *chérie*," he said in farewell.

"I hope you enjoyed your visit, Miss Van Kamp," Keith added, preceding her to the enormous mahogany doors and holding them open.

The butler's manners were so polished that she didn't understand why he made her so ill at ease. But she couldn't help feeling relieved when she was alone again in her Datsun. The car sputtered and groaned to life and she headed down the drive. Then, she couldn't resist taking one last look in her car's rearview mirror. To her surprise, Reginald was standing in the door with Keith by his side. They seemed to be having an animated conversation. Strange, that someone as reserved as Reginald would be on such familiar terms with a servant.

Archer couldn't remember the last time she felt so content. Everything about the day had been delicious, from the croissants she and Roman De Silva shared in the coffee shop at La Fonda that morning, to a long walk through Santa Fe's quiet streets, to cooking Thanksgiving dinner together. His expertise in the kitchen had been a surprise, but then the man had been completely unpredictable from the moment he introduced himself, a marked contrast to staid, predictable Louis.

During lunch at The Shed one week before, Roman had volunteered to act as her guide in Santa Fe. She grudgingly accepted his invitation to tour the local museum the next day and soon discovered their shared passion for fine Indian crafts – Navajo rugs from Burnt Water and Two Grey Hills, black on black pottery from Santa Clara, Hopi baskets from First Mesa. Their mutual dislike of what Roman called the splash, dash, trash school of art, was another bond. It seemed perfectly natural to spend more of each ensuing day with him. It's just an innocent friendship, she told herself when doubts began to keep her up at night. Besides, she would be heading back home in a week or two, and there was no reason to think she would ever see Roman De Silva again.

Now, she pushed back from the table, stretched and patted her full stomach. "You get an A for your cornbread stuffing. Where in the world did you learn to cook?"

His expression sombred. "I used to watch my wife in the kitchen. But I couldn't boil water until she died. Afterward, cooking was a matter of survival."

The day after they met, he had told Archer about his wife's death, the pain of loss still clearly written on his face. At the time, she found herself wanting to take him in her arms, to comfort him as she had so often comforted her sons, and the tenderness of her feelings had taken her by surprise.

"I don't think I'll be able to eat again for a week," she said, getting to her feet and beginning to stack the dishes. "It's hard to believe just a week ago I was feeling sorry for myself because I was going to be alone for the holiday."

"You made a lonely bachelor very happy," he said, pushing back his chair. "Now, how about doing the dishes together?"

She cocked one eyebrow. "Don't tell me you do dishes too?"

"I'm an equal opportunity employer."

Despite his aggressively macho exterior, Roman had proven to be as egalitarian as the most ardent feminist could have wanted. While she rinsed and stacked, he stored the leftovers and tidied up. He was an intriguing mixture of intellectual and homebody – a man with strong opinions and a gentle soul. Roman was, she admitted with sudden insight, the sort of man she would have married had Louis not been part of her life from childhood.

When Archer and Roman had finished their chores, they returned to the living room carrying cups of brandy-laced coffee. It had been snowing all day and the wind soughed eerily as it danced around the house, seeking entry. The drifts had deepened while they ate, and the path Roman cleared from the drive to the house had disappeared completely. Archer felt an absurd desire to go out and play, to make a snowman or have a snowball fight or hurl herself into the deepest drift and make angel's wings with her arms.

"It's been a perfect day, thanks to you," looking out of the window. She had never known a man like him. He made no demands. In fact, he seemed to approve of everything she said or did. By contrast, she was always trying to please Louis and never quite succeeding. With Roman, she succeeded without even trying.

Getting to know him had been an incredible experience, exhilarating, and a little frightening. She felt alive again, young and reckless. "You had better take me back to the hotel," she said reluctantly, "before we get snowed in."

The sofa creaked and she realized he must have got to his feet. "Would that be so bad?" he asked softly, coming up behind her. She could feel the heat of his body as he moved closer. And then he pulled her to him.

Everything she had ever been taught, everything she believed about fidelity and the sanctity of her marriage vows, told her to thank him for his hospitality and be on her way. But the strength of his arms, the comfort she felt in them, made her want to nestle closer. Wavering between desire and decision, she stood as frozen as one of her sculptures.

"You must know how I feel about you," he whispered, nuzzling her hair, his breath warm on her cheek. "Please don't go. Stay with me tonight."

She turned, planning to insist he take her home. But he continued to hold her close, so that the act of turning brought her face within inches of his. Without meaning to or even knowing she would, her arms stole around his back.

With a start, she realized he felt completely different from Louis. Roman was a big, bulky man. His body had power, solidity, sheltering strength.

He continued to hold her gently while their hearts steadied and she slowly relaxed in his arms. It had been a long time since he'd held a woman this way, Roman thought. The smell, the feel of her was intoxicating, filling him with tumultuous anticipation. Tilting her head up to

167

his, their lips met. He kissed her deeply, gently, for a very long time before he let her go.

"I didn't plan it this way," he said, looking deep into her eyes, seeking answers to questions he didn't dare verbalize. "God knows, I didn't plan it. I know you're married. Loving you is all wrong. But it's the best thing that's happened to me in a long, long time."

He felt her stiffen, saw sudden wariness on her face, but refusing to let her go, he stroked her the way he would stroke a high-strung thoroughbred. "Please, hear me out," he murmured against her hair. "I gave up on life after my wife died. All I've done since is go through the motions. Painting was the only thing that gave me pleasure until you walked into that coffee shop a week ago. I feel alive for the first time in years."

Archer shuddered with a mixture of pleasure and guilt. Standing in Roman's arms was sweet torment. How could she tell him he had done the same thing for her? If she did, there would be no turning back from this moment. Her conscience bade her to leave now, for both their sakes. But nothing in the world could have driven her from his arms. Wanting him with an aching need that rooted her in place, she said, "Heaven help us both. I'll stay."

Wordlessly, he picked her up and carried her down the hall to his room.

For the first time since they met, he seemed unsure of himself. "This is the hard part, getting undressed in front of a woman you love for the first time," he said huskily. "I'm not the best looking man and God knows, I'm not young anymore."

"You're beautiful to me," she said. At that moment, right and wrong ceased to exist for Archer. Roman filled the empty, echoing spaces in her heart as no one had before.

"We could undress each other," she suggested, wanting to help him past the awkward moment.

He reached for her with startling swiftness, his powerful

hands fumbling with the tiny buttons that closed her blouse while she tugged his turtle neck sweater over his massive shoulders. The bunched muscles in his arms and shoulders exuded power. He was a big, raw-boned man and despite his self-deprecation, in superb condition. A fine mat of silver hair covered his chest, tapering to a tantalizing V as it reached the hard wall of his abdomen.

When she reached for his belt buckle, he tried to touch her breasts and their arms tangled. "This is killing me," he groaned. "I want to touch you, and I want to undress you, and I can't do both at the same time."

Breathless with haste, they stripped off the rest of their clothes without exchanging another word. Now, nothing prevented Archer's eyes from following that tantalizing trail of hair streaking down Roman's belly. She expected him to begin making love to her immediately. Instead, he backed away.

"Is something wrong," she asked, although his erection gave evidence that everything was very right.

"I just want to look at you," he said.

She shivered and her nipples hardened in the cold air while his eager eyes traced every line of her body. She thrilled to the touch of his eyes as she would soon thrill to the touch of his hands, mouth and tongue. Her bones seemed to melt with longing.

There would be time for regret and recriminations tomorrow and all the tomorrows to come, she thought, as Roman finally took her in his arms. This one night she would forget her past and her future, the life she had apart from this place and time.

This one night belonged to the two of them.

The stars were hidden by scudding clouds when Liz emerged from the St Moritz lobby. She had spent the last five days in New York, shopping, theatre-going, visiting museums and galleries, and looking for a space in which to open her own. With Alan firmly back in the fold, committed

169

to five more years with her, there was no reason to delay her plans. She would not, could not permit the failure of their relationship to spell the failure of her career.

The thought of the borrowed money was an additional incentive. Tonight, at the party the Lundgrens were giving to introduce her to their friends, she would announce her intentions.

Now, as a cab jolted to a stop in front of the hotel with a squeal of its brakes, she began to plan exactly what she would say.

"Where to, Lady," the driver asked as she settled herself into the vehicle.

"Sixty Sutton Place," she replied, giving him the Lundgrens' address.

Tonight, her last in town, would not be wasted. Howard and Skip had promised to invite a number of New York art collectors who had yet to make their way west. Liz was looking forward to the opportunity to convert them. She intended to return to Scottsdale with a number of prominent names to add to her mailing list.

Fifteen minutes later she got out of the cab at her destination, scarcely bothering to glance at the black ribbon of the river to the left. The view would be far better, she knew, in the Lundgrens' sixteenth-storey apartment – a spacious residence they had purchased years before for a fraction of its present astronomical worth. No doubt about it, Lundgren had an almost uncanny knack for making good investments. As she recalled, he'd been one of the first to buy Alan's canvasses.

Damn. There she went, thinking about Alan again. You fool, she thought, stepping into the elevator and pushing the button for the sixteenth floor.

Arriving in front of the Lundgrens' door, she checked her watch. There was nothing worse than having a guest of honour arrive before everyone else. But it was almost eight in the evening and she could hear the muted sounds of a party as she rang the bell.

A liveried servant admitted her to a spacious octagonal mirrored entry. She saw herself reflected again and again in the smoky glass as she handed over her fur. "Please tell the Lundgrens that Liz Kant is here," she said.

"If madame would like to freshen up, the facilities are through that door, and to your left." The servant gestured across the entry before leaving her alone.

Deciding to take advantage of the momentary respite, she followed his instructions. The door led to a hall carpeted in muted shades of peach and hung with some of the paintings the Lundgrens had purchased from her gallery. It was a terrible place to display even a small part of their collection, she decided, with a spasm of annoyance.

Pushing open the first door on the left, she walked into a well-appointed powder room. Two women sat at a dressing table chattering intently as Liz made her entrance. Hearing the door close, they glanced her way.

She gave them one of her best smiles. "Good evening. I'm Liz Kant."

"I must say, I'm surprised you came," the younger of the two said, jumping to her feet.

The second woman gave Liz a speculative once over. "I've heard a great deal about you Miss Kant."

But neither of them offered her name or her hand, and both of them beat a hasty retreat.

Liz grimaced. If these were the so-called art collectors she was supposed to charm, it was going to be a long evening.

She'd just finished re-applying her lip gloss when the door opened again. This time, Skip Lundgren paused dramatically on the threshold. She was wearing yet another Krizia, and this one was as inappropriate to a woman of her age and figure as the one she had worn to the tenth anniversary gala.

"I was afraid you wouldn't come, but Howard said, 'Oh no, Liz will be here. She's a fighter. She won't let something like a silly article take the wind out of her sails.' And my Howie was right. Here you are."

Although Skip was flighty, Liz had never seen her so rattled. "Of course I'm here. Why wouldn't I be?"

"Because of the article in *Galaxy*." Skip fluttered her lashes and wrung her hands. "Don't tell me you haven't seen it. The timing couldn't be worse. Of all nights for that article to appear. Most of my guests are died in the wool liberals. I'm afraid your credibility has been badly hurt."

"I'm still not following you." Liz was beginning to feel like a guest at the Mad Hatter's tea party.

Skip had been holding something in one of her hands. Now, she thrust it at Liz. It proved to be the latest issue of *Galaxy*, a tasteless tabloid noted for lurid stories.

"I never read that trash and, frankly, I doubt if your guests do either," Liz said. "From the way you described them, the *Wall Street Journal* or the *New Yorker* should be more their style."

Skip scowled. "Well, Liz, you had better read this!"

Liz accepted the paper reluctantly. An article on the second page had been circled with a red pen. It featured a photograph of Alan, smiling at her. The caption read, " 'Happier days for jet-set art dealer. Liz Kant and famed Apache artist, Alan Longchase'." The picture was flattering to them both. The story was not. Liz read it with increasing dread. In eight cruel column inches, she was portrayed as a prejudiced, greedy art dealer who used Indian artists, and particularly Alan Longchase, only to cast them aside when they no longer served her purposes. Her eyes stung with repressed tears as she handed the paper back.

"Of course you're going to sue," Skip said, making it sound more like a statement of fact than a question.

"No," Liz replied. "All I'd accomplish would be to draw attention to a filthy pack of lies. The people at *Galaxy* knew that when they printed them."

"But what am I going to tell my guests?" Skip wailed.

"You don't need to tell them anything," Liz replied, squaring her shoulders and stiffening her spine. "I don't intend to dignify the article by paying any attention to it."

The evening proved to be one of the longest, most miserable in her life. Facing a room full of strangers, laughing and sipping champagne as if she hadn't a care in the world when all the while the pain of those cruel words etched into her soul, was one of the most difficult things she had ever done.

To her credit, she did it well. She left the Lundgrens at ten with her head held high, and a parting smile on her lips. Returning to her suite, she locked the door behind her and, dropping all pretence, threw herself down on the bed and wept. Who would want to hurt her, and know just how to do it?

Alan, the answer came, like the tolling of a judgement bell.

11

NOVEMBER 24, 1988

Having spent a sleepless night, Liz flew back to Phoenix the morning after the Lundgren's party. Her eyes felt grainy, her mouth tasted stale from smoking too many cigarettes, and the face in the mirror when she put on her make-up was not the face of a winner. She looked drained, and blush didn't completely conceal her pallor. One agonizing question kept reverberating through her mind. Who had given *Galaxy* that story? How many people knew she had refused Alan's marriage proposal?

The article had been full of inside information about both their public and private relationship. Although it came to a series of wrong and highly damaging conclusions, she couldn't deny they had a fundamental basis in truth. Someone had to be responsible for its publication, someone who knew a great deal about her – who had a strong motive for wanting to hurt and humiliate her. Try though she might, she could only come up with one person who fitted those particular qualifications.

Alan. It had to be Alan.

How he must hate her. First, she refused to marry him. Then she thwarted his attempt to leave her gallery. Of course it had been in his own best interests. But he would never accept that. So he'd found the perfect revenge.

By the time her plane landed at Sky Harbor airport late in the afternoon, she was in a fever to confront him, to get whatever was going to happen over and done with. She told Ramon, her driver, to take her to Alan's Pinnacle Peak ranch, and then settled back against the Cadillac limousine's plush upholstery, willing herself to relax and prepare for the coming encounter.

Forty-five minutes later, when Hank opened the door to her third ring, his eyebrows elevated in surprise. "Liz, what in the world are you doing here?" he asked, stepping outside and pulling the door closed behind him.

"I have to talk to Alan. Is he home?"

"Yes. He's been painting all day. But I don't think barging in on him is a very good idea. You're obviously upset about something."

"You're damn right I'm upset." Liz pulled the dog-eared tabloid from her bag. "Read this."

Hank took it from her hand and spent a moment scanning the contents. "Is this why you want to see Alan?"

"I have to know if he had anything to do with it." Liz could barely restrain her impatience. "Are you going to keep me waiting on the doorstep all day?"

Hank reluctantly ushered her inside. "I'm sorry. You took me by surprise – coming here." He looked down at the tabloid still clutched in his massive hand. "This whole thing has taken me by surprise. But I'd be willing to swear that Alan had nothing to do with this, this . . ." his voice trailed after him.

She followed him down the quiet hallway, past the living room and into the den. Not so long ago, she had been welcome in this house. Its sturdy oak and leather furniture gave it a warm masculine feel. Alan's favourite paintings hung on the walls side by side with museum-quality Navajo rugs. How many times had he taken her to task for having a similar rug on her office floor?

"Would you like a drink?" Hank asked.

"I just flew in from New York and I'm very tired. I want to get this over as quickly as possible."

Hank swung his massive head from side to side, like a bear at bay. "You'll be making the mistake of your life.

I told you how hard it was to get Alan to honour that contract of ours. Things are just beginning to get back to normal around here. This isn't the time to rock the boat."

"The person who planted that story is responsible for rocking the boat," Liz reminded him.

"But I'm damn sure Alan had nothing to do with it." Hank paused, his eyes seeking hers. "You know Apaches. They're intensely private, Alan more than most. To be *ni'a tago ahi*, someone who tells stories about others, is one of the worst things an Apache can do."

"I've had a long trip and I'm very tired. I want to see Alan. If you don't want to go with me, I'll understand."

"If you're determined," Hank said, handing back the tabloid, "I'd better go with you."

Liz permitted Hank to lead the way through the house and across the patio to the studio, although she could have found her way blindfolded. Alan had his back to the door when they walked in. A cheerful fire burned in the beehive fireplace and the air was fragrant with the scent of juniper logs and turpentine. He was working on a life-size portrait of an Apache girl, who, even at this early stage in the painting, Liz could see was stunningly beautiful. Moving with inborn grace, Alan let his brush dance across the canvas. The painting was superb, a worthy rival to her own portrait. A pang of jealousy twisted her stomach as she realized the girl must be very special to him.

"What do you think, Hank?" Alan asked, obviously unaware of her presence. "Should I tell Celia I need her to sit again tomorrow? I could call and ask her to join us for supper. She could pose for me afterward."

"Alan," Hank cleared his throat, "you've got company."

Alan's welcoming smile faded when he saw Liz. "What are you doing here?"

She tore her gaze from the painting. "I have a question to ask. But before I do, I want you to swear you'll give me a straight answer." She blinked once, pressed her lips firmly together to keep them from quivering, and held out the copy of *Galaxy*. "Are you responsible for this?"

Alan's eyes flicked over the page, contempt and anger twisting his finely modelled features as he thrust the tabloid back in her hand. "I know nothing of it."

"Have you told anyone else why I'm not your master dealer anymore? Your family, your mother – that girl in the painting?"

Alan's eyes burned into hers. She saw rage in them – and something else she couldn't quite decipher. "You never learn. You never change. You never will. Do me a favour and get out of my house before I do something we'll both regret."

She fled the studio, raced through the house and out of the front door to her limousine without even saying goodbye to Hank.

Her heart was still beating erratically when the chauffeur pulled up in front of the gallery. What a fool she'd been. Hank had tried to warn her. But no, she had to have her way and confront Alan.

He was right. She didn't learn. She just kept right on doing things that pushed them further apart.

Rick had asked the staff to notify him the minute Liz returned. He was in the storage room, checking invoice sheets against inventory when one of the sales girls buzzed him on the intercom, alerting him to Liz's presence.

Play it cool, he cautioned himself, knocking on her office door.

"Who's there?" she called out.

"It's me, Rick."

She was pacing the floor, white-faced and distraught when he walked in.

"You look like you could use a drink," he said.

A visible shudder ran through her body. "Make it a brandy, a double."

He went to the bar and poured a generous measure into a delicate snifter. "What's wrong, Liz? I wasn't expecting you back for a few more days."

"I had something urgent to take care of here."

"That's not much of a vote of confidence," he said, placing the drink in her shaking hand. "Everything's gone well in your absence."

"I'm sorry, Rick. I didn't mean to imply you weren't capable of running the gallery for a few days. You're more than capable. In fact, I don't know what I'd have done without you these last few months."

He took one of her hands and pressed his lips against the palm. "I'm glad you feel that way. Now, how about telling me what's got you so upset?"

She backed off, walked to her desk, picked up her bag, and pulled out a dog-eared newspaper. So she's seen the tabloid, he thought, recognizing the page she held out. The article had turned out even better than he'd hoped.

"Have you read this?" she asked.

"One of the sales girls showed it to me. My God, Liz, talk about cheap shots. How in the world did that lousy rag get the story?"

"I don't know," she said wearily. "I thought Alan might have something to do with it, but I was wrong."

"How can you be sure?"

"I stopped by his ranch on my way from the airport. He denied knowing anything about it."

"And you believed him?"

She nodded.

"Hell, Liz, you know him better than I do." Rick paused for a long, pregnant moment, taking care not to let satisfaction show in his eyes, convinced he'd driven the final nail in the coffin of Liz and Alan's relationship. "Any other suspects?"

"Not a one. All I want to do right now is forget the whole thing."

"Tabloid!" Rick said. "What tabloid?"

She rewarded him with a small smile. "You have a way of making me feel better."

"If I ever get my hands on the person who planted that story . . ." He didn't finish the sentence, but the implied menace hung in the air. "The thought of someone hurting you. It kills me. This may not be a very good time, but it's time I spoke my mind. Hell. You must have guessed by now. I'm in love with you."

"Oh, Rick." Her voice was tight with repressed emotion, "I just can't deal with that now."

For a moment, Rick stared off into space. She hadn't reacted quite the way he hoped. But it wasn't a rejection either. All she needed was a little time to get used to the idea. She'd come around, he reassured himself. After all, nothing was more compelling, more irresistible than love.

"It's all right," he soothed. "We can talk later, when you're ready. Now, I want you to forget about everything that's upsetting you. How about having dinner with me tonight? I'll bring you up to date on what's been happening around here."

"Not tonight, but I'd like a rain check."

"Whatever you say," Rick acquiesced at once, heading for the door. He was content to leave her office, knowing he'd won a major battle. Next week or the week after, he felt sure he'd win the war. Liz Kant wouldn't cut him off the next time he said he loved her.

"For Chrissakes, Archer, you were gone long enough to open six shows," Maryann pouted. "I missed you. Reginald and I had this heavenly Thanksgiving dinner at his place and I didn't have a soul to discuss it with afterward. What the hell was so fascinating in Santa Fe that you decided to stay an extra week?"

Archer toyed with her empty coffee cup, trying to come up with an answer that would satisfy Maryann. The sunny breakfast room where they sat had always been one of Archer's favourites. Now she found herself resenting its memories of meals shared with her husband. The house, the furniture, even the clothes hanging in her closet seemed to belong to a stranger – a proper society matron rather than the reckless creature who had fallen in love with another man.

Maryann leaned toward her. "Well, give," she urged.

"The show was a terrific success," Archer replied, determined to confirm her reply to a neutral topic. "There were hundreds of people at the opening, and the art critics were very kind. One of them even compared my work to Maillol." She shrugged. "You know how those things go. We were asked to do a lot of interviews after the show and that took a few days."

"We?" Maryann's eyebrows arched. "You must be talking about Roman De Silva. What's he really like? Is he as hard to get along with as they say?"

"He's nothing like that!" Archer declared hotly.

"Don't bite my head off. You've got to admit that the guy is always taking potshots at somebody; the critics, the dealers, artists who get big bucks for rolling nude bodies across a canvas or draping a bridge in sheets."

"All he does is say in public the things you and I have said in private."

Maryann studied Archer intently – speculatively. "My, my. Aren't you bent out of shape? What's going on? Is De Silva the reason you stayed in Santa Fe?"

Archer stared out the window, oblivious to the glorious December day. She'd come home in an emotional turmoil, needing time to sort out her feelings, to start getting her life back in order, to get used to being Mrs Louis Harrison again. During the three weeks she had been away, she managed to convince herself that no real harm would come from taking time out of her life to be with Roman – a few weeks of happiness isolated from the reality of who and what she was. She couldn't help loving him, hadn't planned it – and she had sworn to close the door on those feelings when she returned to Phoenix.

The rationale had worked beautifully while she was four hundred miles from home. Knowing their time together would be finite made it all the sweeter. But the sweetness left a bitter after-taste. She'd been a naïve fool. There would be no forgetting Roman, no putting him aside like last year's fashion. He was a part of her. All the clichés she'd ever heard or read about love had turned out to be true after all. Not a second passed that she didn't miss him, want him. She couldn't eat, couldn't sleep, couldn't even think straight.

Her feelings for Louis had been very different when they were dating. She had assumed it was because they grew up together, knew each other too long and too well for her heart to skip a beat every time she saw him. Now she wondered if she ever loved her husband; or was what she felt for him really love and what she felt for Roman merely physical attraction? Her life was a mess and she had no one to blame but herself. She needed to confide in someone, and Maryann sat there, waiting. "Promise you'll never repeat what I'm about to tell you."

"Does that mean what I think it means?"

Archer nodded.

"Oh, Sugah," Maryann leaned across the breakfast table and gave her a reassuring hug, "tell me all."

Once Archer began to talk she found she couldn't stop. She started by describing the chance meeting at the coffee shop and went on to detail the lunch at The Shed when Roman surprised her with a kiss. For the next twenty minutes she permitted herself to relive the days they spent learning about each other – the mutual tastes they discovered by going through galleries and museums, driving to Taos with the radio playing softly, feeling as if they were the only two people in the snow-clad world. It had been an enchanted time. One quiet night they even

181

played Bach together, Roman on the classical guitar while she played piano.

"I know it doesn't excuse what I did," she concluded, "but Roman made me feel like a whole person. For the first time in my life I was able to relate to a man, as a woman and as an artist."

Maryann had sat through the entire recital, smoking and nodding occasionally, her blue eyes widening. "I only have one question," she said when Archer finished. "What the hell are you going to do?"

Archer couldn't meet her eyes. "I promised myself I'd never see him again."

"What!" Maryann's voice rose. "You tell me you met a cross between Rhett Butler and Picasso and you're not going to do a thing about it? Honey chile, you listen to me and listen good. I've been looking for someone like Roman De Silva all my life . . ." She stopped short as if she couldn't deal with the enormity of Archer's decision. "Shit! If you don't want him, how about passing him on to me?"

"I wish I could . . . I wish I could be sure he'd meet someone as caring as you."

Maryann shook her head in disbelief. "Look, I know you're married. However, from what I've seen, the marriage hasn't amounted to a hill of beans for a long time. Correct me if I'm wrong, but this past year you and Louis have just been going through the motions. You tell me you've met this terrific guy and you're madly in love – only you don't plan to do a thing about it. Damn it, Archer, this is the twentieth century. People get divorced all the time and for a lot less reason."

"I know all that. Roman and I had this same talk before I left Santa Fe." Archer closed her eyes, trying to shut out the memory of the man she loved, pleading with her to give their relationship a chance. "Don't you see, I can't just sit down and write my husband a letter saying, 'Sorry, but the last twenty-four years were a mistake.' I put my heart and soul into our marriage and so did Louis. We have two wonderful sons and a wonderful life."

"No you don't! You had a wonderful life. What you have now is a habit. Trust me, there is a difference. For all you know, Louis is in Hong Kong this very minute screwing his secretary."

Archer bit her lip. "I don't believe that! But even if I did, I'm the one who sent him off by himself. If our marriage fails it will have been my fault."

Maryann jumped up so abruptly that her chair fell over. "Archer, I love you like a sister. But this time I've got to say it. You're full of crap! The world you live in, the one where people have houses with white picket fences and have 2.3 perfect children, doesn't exist anymore. I'm not sure it ever did. If you insist on sacrificing yourself on the altar of a worn-out marriage, don't come to me for sympathy."

Despite the considerable amount of money he had spent at the gallery, Liz didn't care for Reginald Quincy. And after a day like the one she had just endured – the long flight home, the terrible scene at Alan's, and Rick's confession – all she wanted to do was go home and hide. But a collector like Quincy was too important to ignore. Meeting him at her office door, she managed a welcoming smile. "This is an unexpected pleasure," she said, ushering him into the room.

"*Pour moi aussi*," he replied, giving her office a very thorough scrutiny. "My mother always said you can tell the quality of a person by the way they've decorated the place where they work. You, my dear, have done a superb job."

"Thank you Mr Quincy," she replied. "Can I get you a drink?"

"Some white wine would do nicely. And please, call me Reginald."

"Then you must call me Liz," she said, pouring a single

glass of white wine and handing it to him. If she joined him in a drink he'd stay longer, something she hoped to avoid. Perching on the edge of one of the Barcelona chairs, she looked up at her guest. "What can I do for you today, Reginald?"

He folded his slender frame onto the sofa. "I'm thinking about buying some more of Maryann Van Kamp's work, and I was hoping you could give me additional information."

So that's why he's here, Liz thought. He's snooping. "I'd be happy to talk about her art," Liz responded.

"How long has Miss Van Kamp been with the gallery?"

"Three years. When she came to me, she wasn't represented by anyone else. Alan Longchase is the only other artist I've taken on under similar circumstances."

"You must have considerable faith in her talent." Satisfaction warmed his ascetic features.

"I do."

"Would you say her work is a good investment?"

"As an ethical dealer, I can't tell you what her work will be worth in the future."

He looked mildly amused. "Come, come, Liz. I've been buying art for three decades, and I've yet to meet the dealer who didn't tout his merchandise for its potential appreciation."

"You've met one now," Liz said firmly. "We are not talking about a proven artist like Longchase. I can almost guarantee his work will be worth a great deal more in the years ahead. Mind you, I said *almost*. But I would still strongly suggest that the only proper reason to buy an artist's work is because you love it and want to live with it. Maryann is an entry-level painter and, although she is an extraordinarily good one, I can't give you any assurances about the future value of her canvasses."

To her surprise, Reginald nodded in agreement. "I'm glad to know you're so forthright. But I didn't come here to discuss Maryann's future. I'm really more interested in her past."

"Then you've come to the wrong place. I'd be happy to talk about any aspect of Maryann's professional life, but I will not discuss her private one. However, I do have a biography we give to all her collectors."

He put his empty wine glass on the table. "You gave me one when I bought my first Van Kamp. Is there nothing more you can tell me?"

She got to her feet, hoping he would realize the interview was over. Damn the man. If he wanted to know about Maryann's past, why didn't he ask her? "I can assure you Miss Van Kamp is a fine, caring person, a gentlewoman in every way that matters, and an excellent artist. Everyone in the gallery is very fond of her. Does that answer your question?"

"A gentlewoman you say." He paused as if he needed time to consider the idea. Finally, he nodded and headed for the door. "I couldn't agree more. You've been most helpful, Liz."

Now what was that all about? she wondered after he'd gone. Something about him made her intensely uneasy. But she couldn't quite define it, and in view of her other worries, her concern about Reginald Quincy soon faded. Returning to her desk, she picked up the copy of *Galaxy*, reread the article, and then deliberately shredded the paper.

She had an enemy somewhere out there. But all she could do was wait for him or her to make another move.

12

NOVEMBER 30, 1988

One hour after he watched Archer's Mercedes receding down Canyon Road, Roman made up his mind to follow her. He spent the next few days making preparations – hiring a security company to keep watch on his house, a handyman to take care of the grounds, emptying the refrigerator, cancelling the paper, and asking a neighbour to collect his mail until he could send a forwarding address.

Then he loaded his van with essentials: finished paintings, canvas, stretcher bars, his brushes, a large box of paints, sketch pads and pencils, two easels, a tool box, a carton of books he couldn't bear to leave behind, his guitar and his stereo system, all the things that had been essential to his solitary existence.

After his wife's death, he had immersed himself in painting. It helped him endure his grief, gave him a reason for getting up in the morning and allowed him to go to bed at night tired enough to sleep. It was art, his quest for the ideal place to paint, that ultimately led him to Santa Fe and a newly-solitary lifestyle.

He never expected to fall in love again, had thought himself content with work and a few friends. But having met Archer, he knew he'd just been marking time. Fate had dealt him a second chance at happiness. He wasn't the sort of man to fold his cards before he'd played them out.

Sure, falling in love with a married woman didn't sit well with Roman's conscience. He didn't fancy being a home-wrecker. However, from everything Archer said about her relationship with her husband, the marriage was dead. She and Louis just hadn't taken time to give it a proper funeral.

Roman had lived long enough to be painfully aware that the consuming need he felt for Archer happened once in a lifetime; twice if you were very lucky. He knew, from the agonizing experience of having his wife die before her thirty-fifth birthday, that a lifetime could turn out to be terrifyingly short. You had to grab at all the joy that came your way – cling to it, nurture it. He had made up his mind to do just that, for Archer's sake as well as for his own.

So he loaded his van and drove the five hundred miles to Scottsdale, stopping on the way only to fill the gas tank. He pulled up in front of the Kant Gallery at three in the afternoon, shut off the ignition, and sighed with satisfaction, heedless of the knotted muscles in his shoulders.

Just knowing he was in the same town with Archer made him feel better. Stretching, he glanced through the windshield inquisitively. Main Street had changed very little since his last visit. How long ago had it been? Three years or more. But he still had vivid memories of his meeting with Liz Kant back then.

She had been in the front room when he strolled into her gallery, propelled by curiosity to see the place that was dominating the world of south-western art.

Liz had recognized him immediately. "What an unexpected pleasure this is," she said, coming across the floor to greet him. "I'm a great fan of yours, Mr De Silva."

He had heard a great deal about her, but nothing other people said fully prepared him for her beauty. His painter's eyes avidly drank in her red hair and ivory skin, the sculpted perfection of her features, even as he drawled, "Thank you kindly, Mam," doing his best Gary Cooper imitation.

"I'd be delighted to give you a personal tour of the gallery." She skewered him with a devastating smile.

Few men could resist Liz if she made up her mind to charm them. At first, Roman proved no exception. He found himself following her like an eager, tail-wagging puppy at its mistress's heels. But, by the time they reached her office, he had his libido back under control.

"Can I get you something? Perhaps a drink?" she asked in a husky, seductive tone, touching his arm intimately as she guided him to a sofa.

Not for a minute did he flatter himself that she wanted him personally. But he felt certain she was hell-bent on adding him to her stable of artists. He had been equally determined to resist her blandishments.

A stubborn woman, that one, he thought as he stood outside her gallery again. Would she remember that first meeting as vividly as he did?

Back then, he recalled saying, in his usual shoot-from-the-hip fashion, "What it boils down to, Liz, is the fact that I don't trust art dealers. As far as I'm concerned, they're a pack of unscrupulous parasites. My work is handled by an old friend in New York, someone I trust. I see no reason to make a change."

She hadn't taken it well. In fact, she told him never to darken her door again – or words to that effect. He grinned, thinking she was going to be one very surprised lady when she heard what he had to say today. But first, he had to find a phone.

Half an hour later he was cooling his heels in the gallery's front room, waiting to see Liz. He supposed that making him wait was her way of punishing him for the things he said the last time they talked. But, he admitted ruefully, he would wait until hell froze over if it gave him a chance to see Archer. And being represented by the same gallery was bound to present him with lots of legitimate opportunities.

188

Five minutes passed while he paced the tiled floor under the watchful eyes of one of the staff. "I'm sure Miss Kant will see you soon," the woman said, after Roman checked his watch for the third time.

"She'll see me now," he replied, turning and heading for Liz's office.

On the way through the gallery Roman passed several pieces of Archer's work he hadn't seen before, and he felt his aggravation evaporating. Let Liz cool her heels, he decided. He wanted to study the sculptures. They were good, damn good. Archer probably didn't even know how talented she was. With few exceptions, women artists were constantly being put down by someone; the critics, the collectors, even their own husbands if they had the misfortune to be married to chauvinistic jerks. Roman had never been able to figure out why so many men thought ovaries and artistic excellence were paradoxical.

He was so engrossed in Archer's work that he didn't hear Liz approach. "What an unexpected pleasure this is," she said, repeating verbatim the words she used the last time their paths crossed.

So she does remember, he thought, turning to greet her. "Thank you kindly, Mam," he drawled, refusing to be outdone.

"It's lovely to see you again."

"The feeling is mutual," he replied in kind. He was content to bide his time and allow her to play the gracious hostess. Not until he was comfortably ensconced in a leather armchair across from her desk, with a glass of vintage Kentucky bourbon in his hand, did he broach the reason for his presence.

"Considering our last meeting, you're probably wondering why I'm here."

"I assumed it's a social visit," she said smoothly.

"As you undoubtedly recall, I'm not the social type. I'm here because I have a proposition for you."

"Personal?" she queried, a deliciously wicked gleam in her eyes, "or professional?"

Roman chuckled appreciatively. "Strictly professional. Are you still interested in handling my work?"

"I seem to recall you saying something about art dealers being parasites the last time we discussed the matter."

"You have an excellent memory. However, I believe the exact quote was 'unscrupulous parasites'."

"Have you changed your mind about gallery owners?"

"Not a bit," he replied.

"Then what made you change your mind about my gallery?"

"That, Miss Kant, is a personal matter."

She leaned back, seemingly untroubled by the rebuff. "Archer told me your Santa Fe museum show was a great success."

He nodded, trying not to reveal the warmth he felt at the mention of Archer's name. Are they close friends? he wondered.

"Mr De Silva, the last time we met, you were completely honest with me. I intend to be just as honest with you. Three years ago you weren't willing to consider showing your work with anyone other than your trusted friend in New York. A few weeks after opening a show with a sculptress I happen to represent, you make the trip from Santa Fe to ask me to carry your work. While I make a policy of not interfering in my artists' lives, I do need to know anything that might reflect on the gallery. I'm neither naïve nor foolish, and I usually put two and two together."

"And what have you come up with?" he asked quietly.

"You're here because of Archer Harrison."

He sipped his whiskey, wondering if he was that transparent. Or was Liz that intuitive? "That's an interesting theory. But all you need to know is that I'd like you to represent me. And you still haven't given me an answer."

Dazzling him with a high voltage smile, she leaned across her desk to shake his hand. "Frankly, Roman De Silva, I don't give a damn why you're here. Whatever your reasons, welcome aboard."

Two hours later, an exultant Liz accompanied Roman to his car. She stood on the sidewalk, watching until his van turned a corner and disappeared from sight. Then she walked back through the gallery, shut her office door firmly, and let out a triumphant whoop.

Sitting down at her desk, she glanced through the contract Roman De Silva had just signed. It gave her the exclusive right to represent him west of the Mississippi for a period of three years. In addition it stipulated that he would do an annual two-person show with Archer Harrison. Throughout their meeting, Roman's demeanour had been friendly and cooperative, a far cry from the man she remembered.

He had unloaded ten paintings from his van after the preliminaries were settled, and she had been pleased to see they were major works of art. Apparently, he wasn't going to send his best pieces east, leaving her to sell the leftovers. It had taken half an hour to inventory and price them, and another hour to put five of them up on the walls. She planned to hold the other five in reserve, for private showings to her best clients.

Representing both Longchase and De Silva would raise the gallery's cachet to new heights. Nothing she had said to Roman three years ago, promises of monthly advertising in the most prestigious magazines, of a yearly all-expenses-paid show, had any effect on him. She had reluctantly concluded that he couldn't be had, not for love or money.

How wrong she'd been. Roman could be had, given the proper incentive. It was perfectly obvious that he was interested in Archer. No, Liz thoughtfully amended. Interested didn't seem the right word. A man didn't uproot himself, leave home and hearth behind because of mere interest. He had to be head over heels in love.

Rick washed his hands carefully, checking his nails to make sure no grime hid under them. Then he took a paper towel, dampened it and mopped his face, removing any trace of sweat. He had worked like a stevedore, hanging and storing De Silva's paintings. They were huge, awkward to handle, and as far as Rick was concerned, they didn't look any better or any worse than anyone else's work. But Liz said De Silva was an important artist, a genius – another one of those bastards who had it all.

What had she called him? A towering talent. An elemental force in the art world. With that kind of PR, how could De Silva lose? Bitterness welled inside Rick. Other men were getting theirs. He was sick and tired of waiting his turn.

He took a moment to study himself in the mirror over the sink. A bit of styrofoam popcorn clung to his Perry Ellis jacket. The damn storeroom was full of the stuff. Half the time when he worked there, he came out looking as if he'd been caught in a blizzard. He picked the offending fragment off and disdainfully dropped it on the floor. Then he finger combed his hair, straightened his tie, and practised his smile.

A few seconds later he paused in front of Liz's office door, reassembling his features into a suitably ardent mould. Their relationship was stalled and going no place. He'd been waiting for the right moment to make another move. Thanks to De Silva's unexpected appearance, Liz was in a terrific mood. It was now or never, Rick thought, knocking on the door.

"Come in," she called.

There was a genuine sparkle in her eyes, a warmth he hadn't seen for a long time. She looked chic, expensive, and utterly desirable. Heat pooled in his groin. He had to force away the mental image of himself unbuttoning her

192

blouse, freeing her breasts. "That was quite a coup," he said, "signing Roman De Silva to a contract."

"I can't tell you how much it will mean to us. He's one of the top painters in the country. Did you know we're the only gallery outside of Manhattan to carry his work?" She didn't wait for his answer. "I want you to spend the rest of the week calling our major clients and inviting them in to see his work. The ten paintings he left with us should be gone by the end of the month."

De Silva's canvasses were priced between twenty-five and a hundred thousand dollars. Calculating quickly, Rick realized he stood to make a fortune from selling them. "I'll get right on it," he said.

"I knew you would, but that's not why I asked to see you. I'm in the mood to celebrate."

"Then I'm your man. What will it be? Dining, dancing, theatre?" Or bed? he thought hopefully.

"Actually, I was thinking of doing something a little more complicated."

"Whatever it is, I'm still your man. You know I'd do anything for you, Liz."

"I'm counting on it." Taking his arm, she walked to the sofa and pulled him down next to her. "Even though you weren't with the gallery this time last year, you've probably heard about my annual New Year's Eve party. It gives our patrons and artists a chance to mingle in an informal setting, and it's my way of saying thank you to all the gallery's friends."

"I've been looking forward to it." His voice throbbed with sincerity.

"I'd be grateful for your help."

He looked into her eyes, wondering just what kind of help she wanted and what she meant by grateful. Was he finally going to be invited back into her bed? "As I said before, I'd do anything for you. I thought you knew that."

"It will mean a lot of extra work."

"You haven't been listening. Have you forgotten I'm in love with you?"

"No, I haven't forgotten. You've been good for me and the gallery. That's why I want you to be my host on New Year's Eve."

Bingo! he thought. The party was the social event of the season. As far as he was concerned, asking him to host it was the same as telling the world they were a twosome. His patience had finally paid off. Giving her his best smile, he reached for her hand. "It would be my pleasure. How about having dinner with me so we can go over all the details?"

Archer couldn't concentrate on driving. She was going to have an accident, she thought, easing off the Mercedes's accelerator. She couldn't think of anything beyond the fact that she would see Roman in just a few minutes. He was here. In Scottsdale. If she had any doubts about how much she meant to him, they were swept away by his unexpected arrival.

Throughout her marriage, she had moved from city to city like a camp follower when her husband's career required it. Now, a man had disrupted his life and his career to be near her. Archer had never felt more loved. But that feeling was treacherous in her position, she reminded herself. Much as it thrilled her, Roman's presence added to her burdens.

She came home, determined to forget him. After that hadn't proved possible, she steeled herself to endure the pain of giving him up. It had seemed simple and straight forward when she left New Mexico. Like a *penitente*, a flagellant from the hills north of Santa Fe, she even took a perverse pleasure in her own misery, as if being wretched atoned for her guilt in some way. Now, delight and remorse vied for control of her emotions.

"I'm in town, and I'm here to stay," Roman had said when he telephoned.

"What? Where are you?"

"In a restaurant called The Sugar Bowl, on the corner of Scottsdale and Main. Do you know it?"

"Of course. It's half a block from the gallery. But Roman . . ."

"No buts," he interrupted. "Just promise to meet me here in two hours. We'll talk then."

The Sugar Bowl was a pink confection of a building, a Scottsdale landmark. Roman was waiting outside, peering eagerly up and down Scottsdale Road when she arrived on foot, having parked half a block away. At the last second, he seemed to sense her presence and turned around.

"I missed you so much," she said, walking straight into his wide-held arms.

He pulled her even closer. "I missed you too. You'll never know how much."

Hearing an appreciative sharp wolf-whistle from a passing pedestrian, she extricated herself from Roman's embrace and, stepping back, searched his face. "You look wonderful."

"So do you." His broad grin matched hers. Their eyes caught and held. His were so filled with love that her knees went weak and she had to lean on him for support. Still staring at each other and grinning like children on a school holiday, they walked into The Sugar Bowl arm in arm.

Sunshine streamed through the restaurant's windows. Uniformed waitresses bustled around the large room, brandishing pots of coffee and plates laden with the rich desserts that had made the establishment popular. A low hum of conversation permeated the air. It was an ordinary scene in every way, Archer thought. But for her, it was a most extraordinary day. Feeling like a child who has been given an unexpected gift, she couldn't stop staring at Roman.

"I still can't believe you're here," she said, after they were seated and had ordered coffee.

"You didn't give me much choice."

"The problem is, I'm not sure what to do about it."

"You could be happy," he replied quietly.

"It's not that simple. Having an unplanned affair in Santa Fe was one thing." Her hands fell to her sides, like wilting flowers. "But continuing that affair here is another. I can't ignore my duty to my husband, my family."

"Duty is for soldiers."

"No matter how hard I tried, I couldn't stop thinking about you, missing you, and hating myself for it."

He reached for her hands and, needing his warmth and strength, she clung to him.

"I feel the same way."

"Knowing that doesn't make it easier."

"What would?"

"Being able to forget you," she answered honestly.

"I won't let that happen."

Tears stung her eyes and she blinked them away angrily. "I have something to say that you aren't going to like. Promise you'll let me say it without interrupting."

Although he looked unhappy, he nodded his assent.

"What happened between us was wonderful. But I've felt terrible about it ever since I came home. I fell in love with you in Santa Fe. Here, in the city where Louis and I share our lives, all I can think of is that I committed adultery."

As she spoke the blood drained from Roman's face and his grip on her hand became painful. "Don't you ever talk about us that way," he said. "You make what we have sound dirty. Damn it, Archer, we are in love, we did make love. Nothing can change what happened. The only mistake is the fact that you insist on throwing away your life – and mine."

"You must understand that we can't go back to what we had in Santa Fe. My husband and my sons will be home for the holidays in a few weeks. I need to get my life back together for their sakes."

Roman was on the brink of saying, "What about me,

what about us?" But he couldn't ignore the sorrow in her eyes, the dark shadows under them. She looked as if she hadn't been sleeping well. He hated being the cause of her problem, but he couldn't give her up without a fight either.

For a second, he was at a loss for words. What he had to say cried out for a more romantic language, like French or Italian. Finally, he said simply, "I love you. And I know you love me. But I'm not going to pressure you. We'll take it one day at a time and see what happens."

"I'm going to be worried about you if you stay here, worried that you're lonely, that you've given up too much for me." Sagging lower in the booth, she murmured, "I wish you'd go home."

"You are my home," he replied. "But I promise that the day you can look at me and say you don't love me anymore, I'll leave."

"Oh Roman," she sighed, "what the hell are we going to do?"

He reached across the table, tracing the curve of her tear-stained cheek with a finger tip. "Find me a place to live, for openers. I have the feeling I'm going to be here for a while."

"You're home early," Rosita said, giving Liz an appraising look. "And I can see you're happy about something. Can I get you something to eat?" she asked. "You haven't been eating enough."

Liz shook her head. "Actually, I came home to take a nap. For the first time in weeks, I feel as if I could sleep for hours."

"*Bueno.*" Satisfaction warmed Rosita's brown eyes. "I'll hold all your calls."

"Wake me at six," Liz said, over her shoulder, heading for her bedroom. "I have a dinner date with Rick Mason."

Normally, she didn't take naps. But she hadn't slept

well for weeks. Now, she felt as if she could snooze for hours. It had been a busy, exciting day, the best she'd had in a long time. She stripped to her bra and panties and lay down, sighing with contentment. Stretching luxuriously, she reviewed the last few hours. De Silva was a fascinating man – a genius. For the first time since Alan tried to pull out of the gallery, she felt its future was assured. Snuggling under the covers, she relaxed, just drifting.

Her eyelids closed, she breathed deeply, evenly, as sleep folded her into its embrace. Then, suddenly sensing someone's presence, she sat bolt upright. It was Alan. Unaccountably, he was wearing a tuxedo. The ruffled white shirt accented the smooth bronze of his skin, the ebony black of the jacket matched the colour of his shoulder-length hair. Why hadn't Rosita let her know he was there?

"I had to see you," he said, closing the bedroom doors. "I know the truth – all of it."

"And you don't mind?" she cried out. "You don't hate me?"

"Of course not. You should have told me long ago. My poor darling, how hard it must have been on you. Will you forgive me, take me back?"

"Alan, darling, I've waited for you so long." Her feet seemed to float across the carpet as she crossed the room. And then she was in his arms and their bitter quarrels were swept away by their first kiss. She parted her lips, savouring the sweet taste of his tongue.

He pressed the full length of her body against his, brushing the corner of her mouth, the hollow of her neck, her closed eyes with his lips while she clung to him.

She'd wanted this, had dreamed of making love to him again. That it was finally happening didn't seem possible. But reality was the strength of his arms as he swept her off her feet and carried her to the bed. They undressed each other urgently. He was so beautiful as he stood naked before her, his chest smooth and hairless, his muscles clearly defined under the satin sheen of his skin. Her eyes slid down his torso, seeing him strong and ready for her. She lay back on the bed, revelling in his weight as he joined her.

"I've wanted you for so long," he breathed into her mouth, kissing and laughing with the joy of being together.

She ran her fingers along his back, glorying in every remembered detail of his body, her hands cupping the muscled hardness of his buttocks while he kissed her breasts in turn, sucking her nipples. She moaned, feeling her need for him deep in her abdomen. His mouth was honeyed nectar, his fingertips fire and ice as he explored her eager body. She strained against him. To delay any longer was madness, yet she wanted to see him, touch him everywhere. Pushing him down gently, she said, "Be still. Let me pleasure you."

And then, leaning over him, she kissed his chest, tracing the curve of his pectorals, tonguing his nipples, feathering his body with her fingers and her hair. Moving down, she found his navel and pressed her tongue into it while her hands stroked his thighs, drawing closer and closer to the heat of his sex.

Alan groaned beneath her as desire welled in his throat. "Oh God, Liz."

She caressed his shaft and, lowering her head, took the glistening tip into her mouth, loving the taste of him. He had a beautiful cock, straight, broad, eager, as it thrust into the willing warmth of her throat.

He groaned again and reached for her, pulling her up and turning her in his arms so that she lay beneath him. "Now," he said, "it's my turn. I'm going to kiss every inch of you."

He began with her fingertips, sucking each one in turn. Moving on, he nibbled and tongued the sensitive skin of her inner arm. She trembled with desire as he reached her breasts. Taking his head between her hands, she urged him lower . . .

199

And then Rosita called through the bedroom door. "It's six o'clock, time to get up."

Liz opened her eyes, groaning with frustration. The room was empty. It had been a dream. The real world was Rick, and their dinner date.

13

DECEMBER 19, 1988

In December most Scottsdale art dealers, anticipating a gift-buying bonanza, feature exhibitions of miniatures – tiny paintings and small sculptures at affordable prices. Convinced that asking her artists to produce works of a specific size belittled their talent and integrity, Liz shunned the practice. Besides, she reasoned, as she stood in her office looking out of the window at the sculpture garden, it wasn't good business. If she was going to sell a work of art as a Christmas present, it might as well carry a high ticket.

Although candelabras outlined the gallery's roof, and wreaths hung from the windows, the trappings of the season didn't lift her spirits. Peace on earth, good will toward men, were just so many words as far as she was concerned. The holidays had never held a special place in her heart, but this year it had been especially hard to take part in the season's bonhommie.

Her calendar had been filled with dinner parties, formal balls, and open houses. Being seen at the right places, socializing with the right people, was an important part of her business. In the past, Alan had been her companion as she moved through Scottsdale's glittering social scene.

This year, she had asked Rick to serve as her escort. She knew from the looks they got when they walked into a room together, that other women envied her his company. But she still missed Alan. Almost five months had gone by since she refused his proposal of marriage. As Liz stared out of the window, her thoughts focused inward. She couldn't help speculating on how she would handle things if fate should give her a second chance. Suppose she told Alan the truth? Would he forgive her for ten years of lies? Would he understand why she had been compelled to tell them in the first place. Or would he be even angrier than he had been the day she confronted him with the *Galaxy* article?

Bowing her head, Liz closed her eyes. She had to stop doing this to herself. She had to get a grip on her emotions – concentrate on the business at hand. Alan and Hank were due at the gallery any minute to choose paintings for the Guggenheim retrospective. She needed to be ready for them. Biting her lower lip, she crossed the room to the closet that held her files.

Over the years, she'd had every one of Alan's paintings photographed before selling it to a collector or shipping it to another gallery. The resulting slides had been clipped to three-by-five cards on which title, price, date of completion, and ultimate disposition were recorded.

She kept the cards in a fireproof file. Now, as she took it from a shelf, she noted that the file was almost full. Hurring back to her desk, she put it down and was jotting a note to herself to buy another when she allowed the pen to fall from her hand. There would be no need to buy another file. Hank was now the guardian of Alan's artistic history.

One by one, the ties that bound Alan to her had been severed. At least she had the satisfaction of helping him achieve the career his talent merited. Someone else, perhaps even the lovely Apache girl in the painting, would one day give Alan children. But Liz had given him the world.

When she had started in the art business twenty years before, a retrospective for a forty-year-old painter would have been unthinkable. Such exhibitions were supposed to crown a long career, and they were often held posthumously, when the artist being honoured was no longer in a position to enjoy it. In this era of instant gratification and fifteen-minute fame, major galleries and museums – apparently unwilling to await the test of time – were holding retrospectives for relatively young men.

While she didn't approve of the practice in theory, she was too good a business woman not to take advantage of it for Alan's sake. The show at the Guggenheim would mark him as one of the most important contemporary artists in the world. Nothing must be allowed to prevent that from happening, she reminded herself sternly, certainly not her tangled emotions.

Alan had dressed casually in faded jeans, a soft chambray shirt, boots, and a denim vest. As he walked into the living room, he was surprised to see Hank nattily attired in a new three piece suit, an oxford cloth shirt and subdued paisley tie.

"Did Liz specify formal wear?" he teased.

Hank frowned. "Liz calls it power dressing, and I'll be damned if it doesn't work."

Alan was uncomfortably aware of how close Hank and Liz were becoming. It annoyed him. Hell. It infuriated him. "You ought to dress like yourself, rather than a trumped-up yuppie."

"If we don't leave soon," Hank said, seemingly unperturbed by Alan's outburst, "we'll be late."

"I'll be ready in a few minutes," Alan replied. He pulled his car keys from his pocket and tossed them to Hank. "I've got a call to make before we go. Why don't you bring the car around front?"

After Hank left, Alan walked to the living room windows and gazed out at the nearby hills. There was no phone call. He simply needed time to himself.

"Liz . . . Liz," he said into the quiet room, as if testing his own reaction to the sound of her name.

Why did just thinking about her still have the power to make him angry? He felt unsettled, lacking the harmony that was essential to an Apache's sense of well-being. It was as if he had woken up this morning to find the sky green and the trees blue. And all because he faced a meeting with Liz.

She had the ability to twist things, to change and shape them to her own desires. Because of her, his life hadn't turned out the way he expected. Before joining the gallery, his biggest ambition had been to earn a living as an artist. Today he was a millionaire twice over. But it hadn't been his goal. Having made enough to satisfy his daily needs, the extra money meant almost nothing to him. He felt suspended between two worlds, the Anglo and the Indian, unable to leave one behind and give his whole heart to the other.

"All set?" Hank inquired, returning to the living room.

"As ready as I'll ever be," Alan replied.

"Just promise me one thing," Hank said, leading the way out to the car. "No fireworks today. No arguments. Let's just stick to business and choose the paintings for the retrospective."

"Are you speaking as my master dealer or as my friend?"

"Both," Hank replied firmly.

Two hours later, Alan was struggling to follow Hank's instructions. Liz had been sitting close to him while they reviewed the slides of his work. Now, she leaned over his shoulder as he held one up to the light, and her breast brushed his back. Damn the woman. Did she have any idea what her touch still did to him?

Perhaps his mother was right about Liz being an *odii*, a love witch. Nothing else explained her continuing power over him.

"Is that the last slide?" she asked.

"Yes," he replied, pretending to study it although he recalled all his paintings as vividly as if they had just been completed.

"I'm afraid that's not one of my favourites." She

sounded as if she was afraid her comment might offend him.

"Nor mine," he agreed, returning the transparency to the file.

"It doesn't matter," Hank interjected, offering the list he'd been compiling. "You've already chosen fifty paintings. That's more than enough to give the Guggenheim what they want."

"That's it, then." Liz checked her watch. She was surprised to see that two hours had passed since Alan's arrival. She'd kept the entire afternoon open in anticipation of a difficult and time-consuming job. But, no matter how far apart she and Alan had become personally, they were obviously still in tune artistically.

"This is one of my favourites," Hank said, picking up a slide of a painting that currently hung above the fireplace in Alan's living room. "I'm going to miss it while it's in the Guggenheim." Nodding at Liz, he added, "You were absolutely right years ago when you suggested that Alan collect his own work as an investment."

Laughing lightly, she gestured toward the pile of slides on the coffee table. "As you see, I followed my own advice." Of the fifty paintings they had selected that afternoon, fifteen belonged to Alan and twelve to her. The remaining twenty-three were owned by major collectors who would gladly relinquish them for the three months they would be on display in the museum.

She smiled at Hank, grateful for his steadying presence. Being so close to Alan had been unnerving. How could Alan be so calm, she wondered, when her own heart was beating so rapidly? Surely, if she meant anything to him at all anymore, he would have revealed it by the tone of his voice, the expression in his eyes. But he'd been all business from the minute he and Hank walked into her office.

Hank returned her smile. "It's been a very pleasant afternoon. Seeing those slides was like seeing old friends.

And it's nice to know you two can still agree on something."

"This time, we had no reason to disagree," Alan replied curtly.

Stung by Alan's response, Liz got up from her place beside him, walked to her desk and sat down. "There's one more thing I want to discuss before you leave. I'm going to suggest that the Guggenheim call the show *The Sacred Circle*, but I wanted to run it by the two of you first. The name would acknowledge the American Indian belief in a sacred circle."

Alan blinked. Liz had never shown any interest in his culture before. The fact that she was aware of the concept of a sacred circle of life, and wanted to make the concept part of the retrospective's title, came as a surprise – a very pleasant one. "I'd like that very much," he said.

"I'll suggest it to the director of the museum the next time we talk," she replied.

"That wasn't so bad, was it?" Hank asked fifteen minutes later, climbing into the Blazer's passenger seat.

"It wasn't bad at all," Alan admitted.

But his thoughts were chaotic as he drove back to Pinnacle Peak. The meeting had gone well – almost too well. Could he have been wrong about Liz all these months? Was their estrangement as much a product of his own bad temper and injured pride as it was of anything she had said or done?

What was it she tried to tell him on that terrible night? Something to the effect that he didn't know everything about her. Perhaps he didn't. She had certainly surprised him today. Maybe, just maybe, the two of them still had a chance.

Roman De Silva glanced at his watch and then back at the canvas he'd been working on. It wasn't going well, but that wasn't too surprising. He found it hard to concentrate on anything other than the fact that Archer would be there in just an hour.

God, he was going to miss her. Louis Harrison was due back from Hong Kong tomorrow and the thought of their reunion twisted in Roman's gut. It was going to be one hell of a Christmas. He had agreed not to see Archer while her husband was home. Even worse, Roman had reluctantly faced the fact that reunion might go hand in hand with reconciliation.

"Hell," he said out loud, "hell and damnation." The bleak mood he was in made painting impossible.

Three weeks before, when he arrived in Scottsdale, he'd been too relieved at the prospect of being with Archer again to look beyond the moment. They had spent a couple of idyllic days searching for a rental that suited his needs before finding one in Carefree, a town snuggled into a rocky escarpment twenty miles north of Scottsdale. The adobe house, perched on five cactus-studded acres, had been built by an artist and it had a big studio. Anticipating a long stay, Roman had taken a year's lease.

Since moving in, he made a habit of telephoning Archer first thing in the morning. They talked for half an hour or more before saying goodbye. He spent the day trying to concentrate on his work but somehow, there was always something else he wanted to discuss with her and he'd find himself reaching for the phone. There had been luncheons, dinners, long drives through the desert, hikes in the red rock country around Sedona.

Roman had done his level best to live from day to day, to ignore her Louis's pending return. But now, putting his paints and brushes away, he ruefully admitted he'd been living in a fool's paradise. The fact that the woman he loved belonged to someone else filled him with impotent fury.

When Archer pulled up in the drive an hour later, Roman was already out in the front. "Thank God, you're early," he said. "I've been wearing a path in the grass, waiting for you." Taking her hand, he led her into the quiet house. "It's crazy. You just got here, and I'm already starting to miss you."

She looked as stricken as he felt. "I wish you'd go back to Santa Fe to be with your friends over the holidays. I hate the idea of you here alone."

"It wouldn't work," he replied. "I'm not good company for myself when you're not around, let alone anyone else. I'd just be thinking about you every minute, wishing we were together." He closed the doors and pulled her into his arms, needing the feel of her body against his to stave off the reality of her return to her husband's bed.

They'd held hands, even embraced since he'd moved to Carefree, but he had respected her determination to keep their relationship on a platonic level, although it was the most difficult thing he'd ever done. Climbing Everest would have been easy by comparison. Now, feeling her respond to his kisses, he looked into her eyes and finding the answer he sought, began to undress her there in the entry.

"This is all wrong," she gasped as he pulled her sweater over her head, leaving her hair tousled around her shoulders.

"No, it isn't. We're right together and that's all that matters."

And then there was no need or time for talk as he kissed her. He had never known a need like the one that drove him now – a hot urgency to possess her, to erase the future and the past in one violent coupling.

Reginald sat in his study, sorting through an enormous stack of mail. He opened the Christmas cards first, thinking that the best thing about the holidays was the renewed contact with old friends. Most of his were married and had children. It was immortality of a sort, and he envied them for it. Perhaps one day in the near future, he would be able to assure the immortality of his own lineage.

Finishing with the cards, he looked over the rest of

the mail. There were the usual bills, and the predictable number of requests for donations from charitable organizations. They were like bloodhounds, he thought angrily, sniffing out the fact that you had money the minute you arrived in town and deluging you with their needs forever after. He tossed their printed pleas aside. Then a large, white envelope bearing Liz Kant's name, caught his attention. Another show? he wondered.

Tearing it open, he saw an invitation to a New Year's Eve party. There was, of course, no question but that he'd attend, even though it meant cutting his holiday visit to his mother short. She would understand when he explained his reasons.

More than anyone else, his mother had taught him the value of associating with the right people – and Liz Kant was certifiably the right people, a woman of impeccable breeding and exquisite taste. As long as he limited his social life to the right people, he would avoid the difficulties that had plagued him in the past.

The months he'd spent in Scottsdale had been *très merveilleux*. How fortunate he was to have met someone like Maryann so soon after he arrived, and what a difference knowing her had already made. He'd always admired creative people, writers, musicians, but especially artists. To find talent and *savoir-vivre* embodied in one lovely human being seemed the answer to his prayers. Satisfaction warmed his eyes as he reached for the phone.

Maryann was sitting at her kitchen table, working on her Christmas list. As usual, she'd left her shopping until the last minute and, she thought unhappily, for the usual reason. She ought to have a bumper sticker made that read, So many presents, so little money. Her biggest problem was getting an appropriate gift for Reginald. She was afraid to buy him something too personal, and she really couldn't afford the sort of things they carried in pricey stores specializing in goodies for people who had everything.

Getting up, she retrieved a bottle of Manischevitz from a cupboard, poured herself half a tumbler, swallowed deeply and looked around the room. How could she afford to buy Reginald anything when she'd already spent so much on clothes for their dates?

She was contemplating that unhappy truth when the phone interrupted her musing. "Good morning, you'all," she drawled.

"Good morning to you, my dear," Reginald responded happily.

The man must be a mind-reader, she thought. "How nice to hear from you. I hope you're not calling to break our lunch date tomorrow?" It was to be their last before Reginald left. When he told her he planned to spend Christmas with his mother in Boston, she had been disappointed. She'd been hoping for a repeat of their Thanksgiving dinner.

"You know I wouldn't dream of breaking a date with you," he said. "Actually, I'm calling to make another one, or at least to ask if you're free. I just received an invitation to Liz Kant's New Year's party, and I'd be honoured if you would attend the event with me."

"I got my invitation days ago," she blurted, and then, realizing how awful that sounded, she added, "Liz always sends them to her artists early. It's a command performance as far as we're concerned."

"I quite understand, my dear. But I hope you haven't already asked someone else to serve as your escort." He sounded as if he'd be genuinely upset if she went with another man.

"No, I haven't. In fact, Sugah, I was planning on asking you."

"We can talk about it tomorrow," he replied.

"*A demain, ma chérie,*" she said, feeling proud of her carefully enunciated French.

Putting the phone back in its cradle, she took another sip of the deep purple vintage, wiped her mouth on the back of her arm, and gave the room a fierce scowl. Coming up with plausible excuses to keep Reginald from seeing her house was exhausting her inventiveness. But she had a gut-level instinct that she mustn't do anything to spoil the lady-like image she had so carefully cultivated.

Besides, it really wasn't that far from the truth. She had blue-blood on both her mother's and father's sides. The fact that she had been born on the wrong side of the blanket, so to speak, and that her life had taken a few unpleasant turns, couldn't be held against her. One day, she was going to level with Reginald.

But not just yet.

Feeling events crowding in on her, she sat back down at the kitchen table and put her head in her hands. Reginald, Reginald, what to get Reginald? It had to be special, but not too personal – and valuable despite the fact that she didn't have any money.

Suddenly, the solution to the problem was so obvious that she couldn't believe she'd been puzzling over it for weeks. She was an artist – and he collected art. She'd give him something of hers. Nothing big, mind you. Any artist with half a brain knew better than to give away his or her work. Perhaps a sketch, nicely framed and matted.

Whistling cheerfully, she headed for her studio.

Archer returned home early in the afternoon, emotionally and physically drained, her body as bruised and sore as if she'd been forced to have sex. But her conscience wouldn't permit her to use that excuse for what had happened in Roman's entry hall . . . and then again in his bed. Despite her determination to keep their relationship on a purely platonic level, she'd been a more than willing participant in their passionate encounter. How many times had he brought her to orgasm? She blushed as she realized she'd lost track. Now, parking the car in the garage, she anticipated taking a much needed hot bath.

Letting herself into the house, she paused in the kitchen,

listening to sounds overhead. "Who's there?" she called out loudly, although fear shivered through her body.

"It's me. I'm home," Louis's voice floated down from their bedroom.

This can't be happening, she thought. He wasn't due for twenty-four hours. She had planned to pick him up at the airport.

Instead, he must have come home while she'd been in Roman's bed. Archer clasped her hand to her mouth, stifling a moan. She had spent hours thinking about Louis's arrival, wondering how he would look, what she'd say to him, how it would feel to be together again? She'd been praying their reunion would miraculously erase her passion for Roman. Instead, she was filled with self-loathing as she headed upstairs.

"Where have you been?" Louis sounded aggrieved when he met her at the bedroom door. He looked tired, bleary-eyed, "I've been home for hours."

"I wasn't expecting you, and I had some last minute shopping to do," she replied, surprised at how easily the lie came. Was this the way it was going to be from now on, lying and cheating? she wondered, despising herself.

"I've got a horrible cold." As if to offer proof, he coughed harshly. "In fact, it feels like pneumonia. So I decided to come home ahead of schedule."

"Can I get you anything?" she asked, feeling herself flush with guilt.

"I was about to take a hot shower. You might unpack for me."

While she waited for him to emerge from the bathroom, she dealt with his luggage with hurried efficiency. Then she sat at her dressing table, deftly re-applying her make-up, powdering and lipsticking away every trace of Roman's fierce kisses. She dabbed White Shoulders on her neck, her arms, and in the deep crease of her breasts, brushed her long blond hair vigorously, fluffed it around her face and sprayed it into place. Louis would probably accuse her of making their bedroom smell like a French whorehouse when he came out of the shower, but at least she didn't smell of Roman.

She had just finished when Louis walked back into the room. A bath sheet draped his body from waist to calves. Jumping up, she was about to walk into his arms when he gestured her away. "Unless you want to catch whatever I've got," he rasped, "you'd better keep your distance."

"You sound terrible," she commiserated. And then, ignoring his protests, she hugged him hard. He felt smaller. Diminished somehow. Had she gotten so used to Roman's comfortable bulk that she'd forgotten the feel of her husband's body?

"Really, Honey," Louis said, pushing her away and snuffling, "I don't want you to catch this bug. It would be a hell of a Christmas for the boys if we were both sick. When are they due home anyway?" He took a pair of pyjamas from his armoire.

"Tomorrow. But don't count on seeing too much of them."

"I'm afraid you'd better not count on seeing too much of me either. I've got a hell of a lot to do at the office." A coughing spasm doubled him over.

"But you're sick," she protested. "And we haven't been together for months. For heaven's sake, Louis. It's Christmas. Can't that damn company get by without you for a few days?"

Louis didn't reply. Instead, he cut her a chilling glance that told her that nothing had changed. He was still more married to his career at W.B.E. than he had ever been to her.

"I'm going to bed," he said. "I need some rest if I'm going to be well enough to go to the office tomorrow."

"Is there anything I can do for you?"

"I could use a cup of tea with honey." He pulled down the spread, crawled into bed, curled up in the fetal position and looked at her through bloodshot eyes.

213

"Try to have that tea ready before I doze off, Sweetheart."

"Of course," she murmured, leaving the room hurriedly.

When she returned a few minutes later, he'd already fallen sound asleep and she didn't have the heart to wake him. She tiptoed away, Maryann's words echoing in her mind.

"You had a good marriage," Maryann had said. "What you have now is a habit."

Perhaps Maryann was right, Archer thought miserably, but habits can be very hard to break.

14

DECEMBER 31, 1988

Archer sat at her dressing table finishing her make-up while across the room, Louis fussed with his black bow tie. On other, happier evenings he had asked her to tie it for him. But tonight he seemed to consider it a point of honour to do it himself. The silence, a very different silence from the quiet of the empty house during his absence, throbbed with things unspoken. Their growing estrangement, as tangible as a living presence, filled the air.

His holiday homecoming had been a disaster from his unexpectedly early arrival while she'd been with Roman to this New Year's Eve. Although it seemed like a tasteless joke or a bad dream, they were actually planning to attend Liz's party with Roman De Silva and Louis's secretary, Stacy Howard. How in the world could she have permitted things to reach this state?

Looking back, it all seemed inevitable, as if an evil genie had taken control of all her life.

It had begun innocently enough. The day after Louis came home, she had asked if he would mind including Maryann in their Christmas dinner plans. She'd been prepared for an argument. In the past Louis had avoided having unescorted females at their dinner table, complaining that they tended to monopolize the conversation. This time he had exuded affability.

"That sounds fine to me," he said. "I hate to see anyone spending Christmas alone. While we're at it, let's invite

Stacy Howard too. She says her friends made their holiday plans long before she got back from Hong Kong. The poor kid doesn't have any place to go."

"Who in the world is Stacy Howard?"

"My new secretary." Louis looked puzzled. "Don't you remember my telling you about her?"

"I guess so." Archer suddenly recalled Louis telling her that Steve Carpenter's former secretary had been sent to Hong Kong to help out. The woman's name had been Stacy Howard.

"Stacy has been a Godsend," Louis continued. "This was her third trip to Hong Kong and she really knows her way around."

"Why don't you invite her when you see her at work tomorrow?"

"I think she'd feel more comfortable if the invitation came from you," Louis replied.

Archer acquiesced at once, knowing they had reached a quid pro quo: she could invite Maryann if she invited Stacy Howard too.

From a social standpoint Christmas dinner started pleasantly enough. Louis's eggnogg, a culinary chef d'oeuvre whose recipe had been handed down to him by his mother, helped relax everyone. Mark and David, newly home from college, were in boisterous good spirits. Louis played host to the hilt, giving Stacy Howard a tour of the house while Maryann and Archer retired to the kitchen.

"So that's Louis's new secretary," Maryann said under her breath while spooning peas and pearl onions into a serving dish. "I'll bet she does a hell of a lot more than type and file."

Archer was pouring gravy into a sterling silver boat, but she stopped and looked across the room at Maryann. "What's that supposed to mean?"

"Girls as stacked as Stacy Howard aren't hired for their shorthand."

"Don't be ridiculous." Archer turned back to the stove.

"Stacy has been with W.B.E. for several years, and Louis says she's the best secretary he ever had."

It was just like Maryann to see sex around ever corner, Archer thought, with a twinge of aggravation. True, Stacy Howard was well-built. The secretary had a pleasant face. She would have been quite attractive if she did more with make-up, and wore something other than a severe business suit. But Louis had always regarded secretaries as a sort of ambulatory office machine. Infidelity was her own sin, not his.

Although Louis and Stacy sang each other's praises when the dinner conversation turned to their activities in Hong Kong, Archer didn't detect any unusual intimacy in the way they treated each other. She felt certain her husband's interest in the girl was purely professional. It wasn't until dessert, when Maryann mentioned Liz's New Year's Eve party, that the impending calamity began to coalesce.

"I've read about Liz Kant's New Year's gala in the society pages every year. How I'd love to go." Stacy sighed and stared down at the damask table cloth. She sounded like a little girl who has been shut out of a candy store after all the other children have gone in. Then, to Archer's surprise, Stacy glanced across the table at Louis, an obvious plea in her eyes.

He responded to that plea with unexpected gallantry. "Surely, Archer, you must know some unattached male who could provide Stacy with a suitable escort."

It had been the strangest moment of a strange afternoon.

"Oh, please," Stacy said. "I'd really love to go. You see, I don't even have a date for New Year's Eve. It would mean so much to me to be with . . ." she hesitated, "all of you."

"I can think of someone who might be available," Maryann offered. "Archer and I know an artist who just moved to town. Roman De Silva. I doubt he has a date."

217

"He's the man who did that Santa Fe show with you, isn't he?" Louis asked.

Wishing she were somewhere else – another planet would do nicely – Archer nodded yes.

"Do you think this De Silva would be willing to take Stacy to the party?"

'Really, Louis, I hardly know the man and, in any case, he's much too old for Stacy," Archer protested, wondering if her words rang as false to Louis as they did to her.

"He's only forty-six," Maryann interjected, smiling with seemingly angelic innocence. "That's not a bit too old for you, is it Stacy?"

"Of course not!" The younger woman made a moue. "In fact, I prefer older men. They're so much more intelligent and interesting than men my age."

"And a hell of a lot richer. Too bad for us single girls that most of them are taken," Maryann replied curtly.

From then on the dinner party did not go well. Mark and David excused themselves from the table after dessert and went off to find more congenial company. Stacy left soon afterward as well, thanking Archer profusely for her hospitality.

While Louis walked Stacy out to her car, Archer cornered Maryann in the kitchen. "How dare you suggest Roman take Stacy to Liz's party?"

"I thought you needed a chance to compare the men in your life," Maryann shot back. Then her voice softened. "Really, Archer, it's for your own good."

"My good, my ass!"

But the comparison was to prove unavoidable. The next morning Louis insisted she call Roman, practically putting the phone in her hand. Roman had sounded surprised to hear from her, and even more surprised when she made her request. But he agreed at once as she knew he would. And so it had been arranged.

And now Archer faced a New Year's Eve party with her husband and her lover both in attendance. Applying a last stroke of mascara to her lashes, she studied herself in the mirror, amazed that her inner turmoil wasn't at all evident. The unhappiness, concern, and almost insupportable guilt that made her palms sweat and her stomach churn, had all been camouflaged by her carefully applied maquillage. Satisfied with her appearance, she got to her feet and turned to face her husband.

"Ready when you are," she said.

A fourteen-foot tall blue spruce, decorated with miniature Kachinas, Indian pottery and beeswax candles, barely filled one corner of Liz Kant's twenty-by-forty living room, scenting the air with a resinous perfume. Red and green Hopi ceremonial sashes, interwoven with pine boughs, garlanded the fireplace and the large arch that led to the entry hall. Outside, luminarios lined the drive and patios. The pungent aroma of traditional south-western cuisine, tamales, fajitas, tacos and enchiladas, wafted from the kitchen where the caterer and his staff were in the midst of final preparations for the New Year's Eve celebration.

Rick had put in fourteen-hour days, making arrangements for the party while carrying on with his other duties at the gallery as well. Now, looking around the house, he congratulated himself on a job well done. The evening promised to be the social event of the holiday season.

Liz looked stunning, he thought, watching her confer with one of the help. Cerise didn't suit most redheads, but Liz was breathtaking in a beaded red dress that caressed her breasts, waist and hips – a Mackie, Rick supposed, from the sophisticated sensuality of the style.

As Rick strolled over to her, his mother's advice echoed in his mind. "If you want to be successful," Annabelle Mason often said, "you have to look successful. That means driving the right car, wearing the right clothes, being seen at the right places with the right people." How his mother would have loved seeing him tonight, acting as the host at Liz's party.

"I don't know how I can thank you for all the time and effort you put in," Liz said. There was a sparkle in her eyes, a glow on her cheeks that had nothing to do with make-up. She looked, he realized with sudden insight, like a woman in love. "Let's take one last tour of the house and make sure everything is ready," she said.

Not trusting himself to speak, he placed her hand in the crook of his elbow. This was going to be the best night of his entire life. He just knew it. Swallowing the unexpected lump in his throat, he replied, "Lead the way."

Rick had proved himself to be the most valuable employee in the gallery's ten-year history, Liz mused while they toured the house together. Despite the hours he'd spent making arrangements for the party, his sales hadn't declined at all. The gallery's profits were holding steady. She had been more than able to meet her bills, including the payments on the large and as yet unused loan.

If the evening went as well as she expected, it would be due in large part to Rick's efforts. He had been there when the caterers came earlier in the day, setting up bars in the dining room and den, and stocking the kitchen with food. He supervised the installation of a wooden dance floor in the centre of the living room. And he personally checked the credentials of the half a dozen valets who were waiting outside to ferry her guests' cars back down the mountain to a lot he had rented off Camelback. Yes. Rick had proved to be an invaluable employee.

But could she ever again permit him to be anything more? She still wasn't sure.

Maryann tugged a girdle over her panty hose, hoping the latex would reduce her hips a couple of inches. The new outfit she'd bought, the sixth since she started dating Reginald, had been on sale or she would never have afforded it. Unfortunately, it had been a size too small. Four days of absolute starvation and a large dose of laxative had just about taken care of the problem. She was counting on the girdle to do the rest.

Earlier that day, she had laid the black taffeta skirt and matching blouse out on the bed. Archer had insisted she buy the outfit, although Maryann had been convinced it made her look like Vampira. Hell. Considering Reginald's pale skin and the fact that he'd be in black too, they might be mistaken for Count Dracula and his bride.

But now, as she finished dressing, Maryann had to admit she'd been wrong. The collar-to-hem black made her seem taller and . . . more important – every inch a lady. Gazing in the mirror, she felt as if she were seeing herself for the first time, a new self she could be proud of, the kind of broad who really had her shit together.

You're a Rousseaux, she thought, even if her parents never married, and Rousseauxs stand tall. Draping Archer's silver fox stole around her shoulders, Maryann cast a last approving look at her reflection, turned out the lights, and walked out of the room.

Fifteen minutes later, she was on her way to the Hilton Hotel on north Scottsdale Road where Reginald would pick her up. Thank heavens, he believed her story about having to take a room at the hotel because of a broken hot water heater that couldn't be fixed until the holiday. But one of these days, she was going to run out of excuses and he would see the way she was living. What then? she wondered. Would he accept her present poverty as easily as he had accepted the highly edited story of her past? Or would he start asking questions she didn't dare answer?

Roman hated formal affairs. In his rented tux, he thought he looked more like a waiter in an Italian restaurant than a sophisticated man-about-town. All he needed to complete the image, he reflected wryly, was a white napkin draped over his forearm. But he would have cheerfully dressed up in a gorilla suit if it meant seeing Archer.

Three weeks ago, when the engraved invitation to Liz's

221

New Year's Eve party came in the mail, Roman tossed it in the trash with the rest of the junk mail. He was not, had never been, a party animal. Having to mingle with people he didn't know was bad enough at exhibitions of his work, but they were a necessary part of his career. Parties were not.

Then Archer telephoned with her bizarre request and his plans changed.

"Are you sure you want me to do this?" he'd asked, wondering why Archer was breaking her own self-imposed rule about not seeing each other during the holidays.

"Absolutely," she replied in a tone that brooked no argument. "My husband is standing right here, and he'd be very grateful if you could take his associate to Liz's party."

So that's it, Roman thought. It's Louis's idea. The situation instantly piqued his curiosity. "Tell your husband I'd be delighted." Then Roman couldn't help adding, "God, how I've missed you."

"We'll pick you up at eight. And thank you very much." Archer had hung up without another word.

During the brief conversation, Roman had been intensely aware of Louis Harrison's presence on the other end of the line. Where were they when Archer telephoned? The den, the breakfast room? The bedroom? And what were they doing? Unable to deal with any of his questions, he'd thrown on a sweatsuit and gone running.

Now, waiting for the Harrison's to arrive, he allowed himself to think about the evening ahead. Double dating with Archer, her husband, and Stacy Howard, had the makings of a very bad drawing room farce. Who would kiss whom when the clock struck twelve?

"I'm still not sure I'm doing the right thing, going to this damn party." Alan looked from Hank to Eleanor Tsosie, who was now Hank's fiancé.

Looking tall and attractive, standing by the side of the

man she loved, Eleanor Tsosie was all woman, with a woman's concerns.

"I know how you feel about Liz, so maybe I'm being selfish," Eleanor answered, "but this is my first black-tie affair, and I could use some moral support. You had damn well better be there, Alan Longchase, since you're the reason Hank and I are going."

"Besides," Hank chimed in, "you'll be doing me a favour. The *Galaxy* article caused a lot of talk. Having you show your face tonight should put an end to some nasty gossip."

"All right. You've convinced me."

Hank had been pushing Alan in Liz's direction ever since the meeting about the Guggenheim retrospective. He'd been singing her praises, had even mentioned that he'd be happy to retire as a master dealer when and if Alan saw fit to work with Liz again.

"I'm glad you're seeing things my way," Hank said.

"Have I ever told you how bossy you are?" Eleanor quickly rose to Alan's defence.

Alan couldn't help grinning at the two of them. They made quite a couple. Although Liz's invitations specified formal attire, Hank and Eleanor had chosen to make a statement by wearing traditional Navajo clothing. Standing side by side in Alan's living room, they looked nothing short of spectacular – like royalty of an ancient and exotic lineage. Hank wore jet black trousers, a black shirt, black cowboy boots, and a high-crowned black hat, accented by a massive silver and turquoise concho hat band. Several strands of chunky turquoise nuggets draped his massive chest.

Eleanor was wearing a velvet triple-tiered, floor-length skirt and a long-sleeved top. A row of silver buttons ran up the front of her high-necked blouse and down both sleeves from shoulder to cuff. Silver and turquoise bracelets covered her wrists. A large squash blossom necklace and matching earrings completed the outfit.

"You look beautiful, Eleanor," Alan said, leaning down to kiss her cheek. "I'm sure you and Hank will be the hit of the party. And if Hank doesn't treat you right, just let me know."

"Are you sure you don't want to drive with us?" At times Eleanor sounded almost as parental as Hank.

"Thanks, but no thanks," Alan replied. "I'm not sure how long I'll be staying." Or if I'll come back here tonight at all, he silently added, wondering if Liz was anticipating the evening with the same high hopes.

"Have a terrific time at the party," Keith muttered, helping Reginald with his coat.

"I assure you, I will," Reginald replied curtly. Earlier that day, he had instructed Keith to wash and polish the Jaguar and park it in the circular drive. Keith had done as he was told, but he'd pouted all day. The man was getting to be a real problem, Reginald reluctantly admitted. Perhaps the time had come to give him notice. He would be so much excess baggage if things worked out with Maryann.

Just thinking about her soothed him, slowed his respiration and relaxed the lines around his mouth. To his surprise, he actually found himself whistling "Auld Lang Syne" as he inserted his key in the Jaguar's ignition. He had missed Maryann even more than anticipated when he went home to Boston to spend Christmas with his mother.

But, it had been the right thing to do. Having the opportunity to talk to his beloved mother helped Reginald solidify his plans. He'd barely been home an hour the first time he broached the subject of Maryann.

"You're going to love Miss Van Kamp," he assured the elegant grande dame who, amazingly, had actually given birth to him – although he couldn't imagine Grace Quincy doing something so unladylike as spreading her legs, even in a delivery room.

They had been sitting in the north parlour, having tea. Poised on the edge of a tapestry-covered *bergère* chair,

Reginald felt very much like a boy instead of a mature man. "I haven't had any problems since I started seeing Maryann."

"None?"

"Not one!"

"If Miss Van Kamp is responsible," Grace Quincy replied with a reluctant nod of her carefully coiffed head, "I'm sure we will get along beautifully." She was meticulously dressed in a casual tweed suit, made to her measure by an English tailor. A perfectly matched strand of pearls hung from her neck and she fingered them slowly.

Reginald was still awed and chilled by his mother's studied perfection. She never had a hair out of place, a run in her stockings. Nothing ever marred her composure. He had spent his entire life trying to live up to his mother's standards, and failing miserably. How different Maryann was, how warm, how accepting. "I'm so anxious for you to meet her," he concluded lamely.

"And so you should be." Grace picked up a Spode platter laden with watercress finger-sandwiches and offered them to him. "I want to hear all about this paragon."

Although he detested watercress in any form, he dutifully took one and bit into it.

"Is she one of the New York Van Kamps?" Grace queried, with a lift of her brows.

"No. Maryann's from old southern stock. I believe you've heard of the Rousseaux family." Reginald washed down a half-chewed mouthful with a generous swallow of tea.

"So she's a Rousseaux?" Grace's glacial tone thawed slightly.

"Yes. But her mother and father died when she was quite young." He cleared his throat. "Really, Mother, you will adore her just as I do. She's so much fun to be with, so talented, and quite the lady in a Texas sort of way."

"Texas?" Grace's eyebrows arched even higher. "I've never associated with anyone from Texas. They have always seemed like such crass people. Really, Reginald, from the little you've chosen to share with me, your Miss Van Kamp doesn't seem entirely *comme il faut*. While I have no objections to your immediate plans, I want you to promise to have her investigated – discreetly but thoroughly. I won't accept your proposed union until I know exactly who this woman is."

"Of course, *Maman*," Reginald replied.

"I can only hope she's truly worthy. You know what happens when you associate with the wrong sort of people."

He pretended to study his well-buffed nails. No one knew the consequences of associating with riff-raff better than he did. "I assure you those days are past. I'm well, and I'm in love. Why can't you be happy for me?"

Grace's answering look destroyed Reginald's buoyant mood. "You know the answer to that."

"I may have given you cause for concern in the past, but those days are over," he assured her. He was finished with psychiatrists, not that they had ever really helped him. No matter how many hours and dollars he spent on analysts, how many rest cures he had or how many prescriptions he took, the problems which began in his teens had lingered on. But, ever since meeting Maryann, he'd been completely free of them. Deep down, he had always known that all he ever needed was a good woman, someone who loved him for himself and not his money.

Now, putting the key in the Jaguar's ignition, Reginald rejoiced at having finally found her. This New Year's Eve was going to be very special indeed, he thought, turning the car toward the Scottsdale Hilton.

Archer sat alongside Louis in the Mercedes' front seat. Although the heater warmed the interior, she shivered and pulled her mink coat tighter.

"You're sure this is the right place?" Louis asked, turning into Roman's drive.

"According to the directions Mr De Silva – that is

Roman – gave me, this is it," Archer replied. She'd been wondering whether to use Roman's first name or his last in front of Louis, and hadn't made a decision. If she called him Roman, would Louis wonder about the extent of their friendship? On the other hand, wouldn't calling him Mr De Silva sound overly distant? Lord, how had she got herself in this mess?

"He certainly lives in the boon-docks," Louis grumbled before exiting the car. Impeccably turned out in black tie and a black double-breasted cashmere coat, he looked every inch the successful business man as he walked to the front door and rang the bell.

Roman answered at once. Light spilled from the house, silhouetting both men. Roman towered over Louis, diminishing him. Archer heard the deep resonance of Roman's voice, although she couldn't distinguish his words. In the darkness she couldn't see either man's face, but they appeared to be chatting amiably as they returned to the car. She fought down a hysterical giggle as Louis got in the front seat and Roman in the rear.

"Good evening, Archer," Roman said with perfect aplomb, reaching across the back of the seat to shake her hand as if they were no more than casual acquaintances. "It's nice to see you again."

"It's nice to see you, too," she replied, astonished that she managed to sound equally cool and collected. She had never considered herself to have any acting talent. But tonight she had damn well better give a performance worthy of an Oscar.

A stream of luxury cars, Mercedes, BMWs, Cadillacs, Porsches, and Jaguars, were heading back downhill as Alan drove up the steep road to Liz's house. Pulling in behind a newly-arrived limousine, he waited until it disgorged its passengers before stepping from the Blazer and handing his keys over to a valet.

Standing near the front door, waiting for Hank and

227

Eleanor, memories of other nights and other parties spun through his mind. He had hosted Liz's New Year's Eve parties many times. Over the years, the party had evolved from a casual get-together to an increasingly more formal event. Tonight, it felt a bit strange to be just another invited guest.

He was grateful to have his musing interrupted by Hank and Eleanor's arrival. Time to forget the past and get on with the future, he thought, walking into the house behind them.

"Shall we find our hostess?" Hank's voice rose above the din.

"You go ahead. I think I'll look around first."

Liz stood at the far end of the room, beneath the Christmas tree. She was laughing, talking with half a dozen people. Her mahogany hair hung loose, brushing the top of her bare shoulders. He drank her in, revelling in her beauty, her self-assurance. Although he couldn't hear what she said, there was no mistaking the warmth in her eyes when she greeted Hank and Eleanor, drawing them into the circle of her friends.

Had she truly changed as Hank claimed? God, how Alan wanted to believe it could be true. Her magnetic appeal was as potent as ever and he almost permitted himself to respond when he saw Rick come up behind her, put a proprietary arm around her waist and whispering something in her ear. Liz smiled, pointed across the room, and Rick hurried away. Although Alan tried to tell himself that the brief encounter was meaningless, his desire to greet Liz was quickly replaced by the need for a drink, something potent.

The den was crowded when he walked into the room. Working his way through the well-dressed throng, he found a place at the bar beside an Anglo male with Hank's height and heft.

"I'll have a double Scotch on the rocks," the man said in a resonating baritone.

"Would you make that two?"

The stranger turned, revealing a powerfully-hewn face that reminded Alan of Michelangelo's bust of Brutus. "They say brilliant minds think alike. This is one hell of a crowd. Does Liz Kant do this often?"

"Once a year," Alan replied.

The bartender placed two half-full whiskey glasses on the bar. The stranger handed one to Alan and then drank his own in one long swallow.

"I'd like another," the baritone voice rumbled above the din. "How about you?"

Alan downed his own drink and nodded.

"I hate these damn affairs." The man handed Alan a refilled glass, picked up his own and took another huge swallow.

Again, Alan matched him, gulp for gulp. "So why are you here?" he asked.

"A woman."

Alan grinned sympathetically. "Enough said," he replied.

The stranger studied him briefly, smiled broadly, and held out his hand. "Unless I'm mistaken, you're Alan Longchase. It's a pleasure to meet you. I'm Roman De Silva."

"I'll be damned. I heard you joined the gallery. I'm an admirer of your work."

"And I of yours. I was hoping you'd be here tonight," De Silva's boisterous laugh boomed over the din. "I think that calls for another drink."

They spent the next twenty minutes talking easily and drinking hard before De Silva excused himself, saying, "I guess it's time I did something about that woman problem of mine."

Fortified by liquor and soothed by masculine camaraderie, Alan replied, "Good luck."

"I'm going to need it." Roman grinned wolfishly.

"That makes two of us."

They shook hands a bit self-consciously, as if they both realized they had revealed more of themselves than they intended.

Liz was talking to one of the caterer's helpers when Alan walked up behind her and touched her shoulder. She spun around.

"Happy New Year, Liz," he said.

"Now that you're here, it is," she replied huskily, her eyes full of emotion before she lowered her gaze. "You just missed Hank. His Eleanor seems very nice."

"She is," Alan responded. "By the way, I just met Roman De Silva. He's very personable."

She laughed. "That's one way to describe him."

After everything they had been through – the disappointments, the battles, the heart ache – it felt strange to be engaging in cocktail party chit-chat.

"I have very good news," she said. "The Guggenheim has agreed to call your retrospective *The Sacred Circle*. And they want as many members of your family at the opening as possible."

"That is good news." There was so much more he wanted to say, words of regret – and perhaps of reconciliation. But any thought of uttering them died as he felt a hand pounding him on the back in a too-hearty greeting.

"Quite a bash, isn't it?" Rick said, moving to Liz's side. "You're probably the only man in the world who can imagine how pleased I was when Liz asked me to be her host tonight."

"He's your host?" Alan felt as if a vice were constricting his chest.

"Yes. He's been the biggest help." She gave Rick the same warm smile she had bestowed on Alan just moments ago. "Rick, would you get some champagne for the three of us?"

Alan knew he had to get away from the two of them before he did something he would regret. "Don't bother. I'm not staying."

"But you just got here," she protested.

Managing to ignore Rick, Alan looked deep into Liz's eyes. "Goodbye," he said, knowing that this time it was forever.

He stopped on the way out to tell Hank he was leaving. Then, in a fury of impatience, he waited for the valet to appear with his Blazer. What a fool he'd been, allowing himself to think, even for a moment, that he and Liz still had a chance. She was welcome to her young Anglo lover, and he to her.

Roman was feeling the effect of the drinks he'd had with Alan Longchase, but he wasn't drunk yet – not by a long shot. In fact, he was damn certain no amount of liquor would get him drunk tonight. There would be no drowning his sorrows, no forgetting them. Finding Stacy Howard alone in a corner of the vast living room, he said, "I hope you managed to amuse yourself while I was gone."

She was holding a glass of Chablis in one hand while smoothing her beige polyester gown with the other. "I could spend the rest of the night just looking at the way other women are dressed. Apparently, I've got a lot to learn."

"Nonsense. You look just fine," he replied, although even his undiscerning eye had noticed the poor cut of her dress, the way it managed to make the least of what was a sensational figure. She would have been exceedingly attractive, he realized, if she hadn't gone to such obvious pains to appear business-like.

"No, I don't, but I will one of these days." Steel hardened her breathy voice. "I'm very grateful to you for bringing me. Have I thanked you yet?"

"At least a half a dozen times."

Maryann, Reginald and the Harrison's were at the opposite end of Liz's living room, having a somewhat stilted

231

conversation when Roman De Silva approached them with Stacy Howard on his arm.

Lordy Lord, Maryann thought, De Silva is a hunk. And incredibly talented to boot. Lucky Archer. "Hello, you two," she said. "Roman De Silva, Stacy Howard, I'd like you to meet my dear friend, Reginald Quincy."

Reginald, who had been deep in a conversation with Louis, barely nodded at the newcomers before turning his full attention back to Louis. "Maryann tells me you're the new CEO of World Business Electronics. How about a little inside information. Should I be buying their stock?"

"I'd recommend it highly." Louis sounded supremely confident. But then, Maryann recalled, he usually did when he was talking business. "We're in an acquisition mode," Louis continued, lowering his voice conspiratorially. "I'll be starting up a series of maquiladores in Mexico in the coming months. Considering the tax shelter aspect, and the reduced labour costs, our profits will soar."

"You really should follow his advice, Mr Quince," Stacy gushed. "Louis is the resident genius at W.B.E."

"It's Quincy," Reginald corrected, "Reginald Ambrose Ardmore Quincy."

There was something about Stacy, probably the way she looked at Louis like he was some kind of oracle, that made Maryann feel like giving her a good poke with a sharp stick. Anxious to get away from the mismatched foursome she had helped create, Maryann tugged on Reginald's arm. "I'm sure you two men could talk business all evening, but this is supposed to be a party, and I could use a drink."

"I didn't mean to ignore you, my dear. If you will excuse us?" Reginald said to the others. "This lady's wish is my command."

"What's your pleasure, *mon amour*?" he asked, catching a waiter's eye.

"I'd just adore some more bubbly, and it does seem *à propos* tonight." Maryann, who had seen the phrase in print but never checked its pronunciation, had said a-prop-us.

232

To her surprise, Reginald burst out laughing. "You are so divinely funny sometimes. And you're absolutely right. Champagne is perfect on New Year's Eve. But I need something a bit stronger . . . for Dutch courage." He ordered wine for her and vodka on the rocks for himself.

Dutch courage? she mused. Why does he need Dutch courage. Surely he didn't feel as out of place as she did? He belonged at a party like this one, while she still felt like an impostor at a fancy dress ball.

When their drinks were delivered he raised his glass. "To the most wonderful woman I have ever known – with the single exception of my own dear mother."

"Why thank you kindly, Sir. From what you've told me about your mother, that's quite a compliment." Any time a man compared you to his mother, he had to be getting serious. And he'd called her *mon amour*. Now that was really intense for Reginald.

So far, it had been a terrific night. Reginald had been a fab escort, complimenting her effusively on her appearance when they met at the Hilton. He'd given her an orchid, pinning it to her bodice with trembling fingers as if he were a high school boy on his first formal date rather than a wealthy socialite. It touched her more than anything he could have said.

They'd had a light dinner at the hotel before leaving for Liz's. Several times during the course of the meal, he'd seemed about to say something. But each time, he bit his lip and sat in almost stunned silence while she struggled to keep the conversational ball bouncing. Now, he had the same peculiar expression on his face as he took her hand.

"Let's find a quiet place where we can talk."

"I don't think that's possible in this crowd," she replied, looking around.

But she was wrong. A few minutes later he pushed open a pair of doors at the end of a long hall and they found

233

themselves in Liz's empty boudoir. The bed was piled high with furs and overcoats, the lights dimmed. Reginald led Maryann to a pair of chairs opposite the fireplace. They looked up simultaneously and saw a painting of a nude woman hanging above the hearth.

"I'd give my soul to own that," he breathed.

Maryann whistled. "Well, if that doesn't beat all. I'd heard rumours about Longchase painting Liz in the buff."

Reginald's eyes pinioned the portrait and his inhalations quickened. A tremor ran through his body before he tore his glance away. "Never mind that now," he muttered, seemingly to himself.

Maryann felt her skin goosebump. There was something about the way he looked when he saw the painting, something she couldn't quite define, that bothered her. If he just once looked at her the way he looked at that damned canvas, she'd probably run a mile and never see him again.

"*Revenons à nos moutons*." Reginald's reedy voice brought her back to the moment. "I wanted to speak to you in private because this is a very important night, the sort of night people remember all their lives – the way they remember where they were when the Japanese bombed Pearl Harbor."

She nodded as if he were making perfect sense. The poor guy seemed totally strung out.

"I'm not doing this very well." He licked his lips. "You see, most people don't recall the night they got engaged. And it always seemed to me that the date was as significant as the day the wed. So I thought if I asked you on New Year's Eve, we'd always remember it."

"Are you saying what I think you're saying?" Suddenly, Maryann's heart was trip-hammering in her chest.

Reginald fell to his knees. "I was hoping you would do me the honour of being my wife." He reached in his jacket pocket, produced a jeweller's box and snapped the lid open. A headlight clinker of a diamond – four carats at least – effervesced in the gloom.

"Oh, Reginald, honey, I accept," Maryann exclaimed before he had a chance to change his mind.

She sobbed with happiness when he slipped the ring on the fourth finger of her left hand. Her buzzard's luck had finally come to an end. No more holding back, no more being scared to fall in love for fear her affection wouldn't be returned. Reginald was hers, and she was his. It was the most excruciatingly wonderful feeling. She was going to have a home, a husband and, the good Lord willing, children. She wanted to shout with glee, to dance around the room. But that wouldn't be ladylike, she reminded herself sternly.

Instead, she took Reginald's cool, bony hand in her own small, warm one. "I promise," she said fervently, "to make you the world's best wife. To honour and obey until death do us part."

He looked down at her and something in his eyes seemed to thaw. Their gazes met and held as he pulled her into his arms. But then, just before their lips met, his eyes drifted back toward the painting of Liz and a strange, almost pained expression played across his face.

As far as Liz was concerned, the New Year's Eve party ended with Alan's abrupt departure. After that, the gay sounds of the celebratory crowd rang hollow in her ears. She had wandered from one conversational group to another, barely grasping what people were saying. When the last of her guests finally left five hours later, she was exhausted.

Rick, on the other hand, seemed energized. He'd been Johnny-on-the-spot all evening, supervising the caterers, charming the guests. "That was some party," he said enthusiastically.

"I suppose so. I'm just relieved it's over for another year."

"Where's your New Year's spirit? The evening's young!"

"It's four in the morning."

"Not too late to have some more champagne, I hope. I saw a bottle of Tattinger's in the fridge and set it aside just for us."

"I've had enough to drink," she replied. "Why don't you take it home with you."

He seemed oblivious to her mood. Moving behind her, he began to knead her shoulders. "I give a wonderful, rejuvenating back rub."

Reaching up, she pushed his hands away and turned to face him. "Rick, I don't mean to be unappreciative. You've been an immense help and there will be a substantial bonus in your paycheque – but the evening is over."

He looked confused, even dismayed. "You know I don't want a bonus. I didn't work my tail off for money. I did it for you. I thought you and I had something going."

It was truth time for both of them, she realized grimly. Seeing Alan and Rick together earlier in the evening, she had finally faced the inevitable knowledge that Rick would never be able to substitute for Alan. No one would. "I'm afraid I haven't been fair to you. I like you a great deal, Rick, and I'm terribly grateful for everything you've done. You've been there when I needed a friend. But," she paused, "that's all you will ever be."

"I know you don't feel the way I do . . . not yet – but I'm willing to wait. You saw what a great team we made tonight."

"I've kept you waiting long enough, Rick. It can't go on," she said wearily.

"What do you mean? What the hell are you talking about?" There was a desperate, wounded look in his eyes she'd never seen before. She was suddenly glad Rosita was nearby in the kitchen.

"I know I've treated you badly, and I can't tell you how sorry I am. I'll understand if you want to quit the gallery on the spot."

236

"Quit?" He seemed close to tears. "I love you. You asked me to be your host tonight. I thought . . ."

She interrupted. "I know it doesn't help to say it. I didn't plan to mislead you. Asking you to be my host was a business decision, not a personal one. Everyone at the gallery likes you. I do, too, very much, but I don't love you – and tonight I finally realized I never will."

15

JANUARY 7, 1989

Saying goodbye was much easier the second time around, Archer admitted as she watched Louis pack. He was methodical and efficient, putting everything in its proper place so his custom-made suits and shirts wouldn't be wrinkled when he arrived in Hong Kong.

She had packed for him during the early years of their marriage, but he no longer needed her to perform even that small service. They seemed to be facing, or at least nearing the end of their life together. It was due, she thought, to something intrinsically wrong with their relationship, something aside and apart from her feelings for Roman. Now, knowing how completely she could relate to another man, she realized how incompletely she had always related to her husband.

They talked, but they didn't communicate. She knew the details of his life, his favourite meal, the sort of suit he preferred to buy, the way he liked his coffee, what drink he would order under what circumstances, which magazines he read, which political party he favoured, but she knew nothing of the essence of the man. She could only surmise the source, the internal wellspring that fed his need to succeed in the world of business.

After having him home for two weeks she longed to shout, to scream out her unhappiness, to precipitate a confrontation and get it over with. Their time together had deteriorated into a series of uneasy silences, punctuated by brief exchanges about what to have for dinner or which television programme they intended to watch on the rare evenings he didn't return to the office. They hadn't really talked, not once.

"Well, I think that's everything," he said, zipping his carry-on bag closed while he scanned the room for anything he might have left behind.

"I can always mail anything you've forgotten." She might as well wrap and ship their marriage too, she thought bitterly. He'd forgotten how to be a husband and, to her dismay, she'd forgotten how to be a wife. Perhaps she never knew. They lived together, shared a bedroom and a bed, even made love without touching mentally or emotionally. Throughout the holidays, she had been plagued by a gnawing sense of futility, an empty echoing void in the place inside her where happiness used to reside.

Louis checked his watch before picking up his luggage. "We've got a little time before we have to leave for the airport. How about a drink?" He coughed dryly, the last remnant of the chest cold he'd brought home. "I could use a Scotch."

"Sounds good to me, as long as it's a small one since I'll be driving." She followed him down the stairs, painfully aware of how different this leave-taking was from the last one. Then, she'd dreaded his departure. Today, she could hardly wait for him to go so she could get on with her life. How she despised herself for feeling that way.

He put his bags down in the entry and preceded her into the den. It was a large room with a panelled ceiling, dark leather furniture, half-timbered walls, and a fifteen foot long antique bar. When they built the house, Louis had insisted on attempting to replicate a men's club he'd visited during a business trip to London. She had argued the point, saying it was impractical, expensive, and out of keeping with the rest of the décor. But, in the end, she had given in. Instead of looking old and lived in, the room had proven to be kitschy, a triumph of conspicuous consumption over good taste.

Louis walked behind the bar and reached for a bottle of Glenlivet.

"I'm sorry it wasn't more of a holiday for us," he said, pouring drinks for them both, "sorry I had to spend so much time at the office."

"I'm used to it."

"Well, I just wanted you to know I'm sorry."

Her simmering anger flared. "No you're not. Why the hell go on pretending? This was supposed to be a vacation, but you went to work every day. And I know damn well you loved every minute of it. There's never been any question about your priorities."

"You're being unreasonable. We're still in a bind at the office. If I want my appointment as World Business Electronics CEO to be permanent, I've got to prove I can do the job."

"You could have spared a few hours for us, for our sons. Fortunately they were too busy, or too politic, to notice their parent's marriage is in trouble."

He reached across the bar, tilting her chin so her eyes met his. "You're wrong, Archer. I am sorry I wasn't able to spend more time with you, sorry that our marriage isn't going the way we'd both like."

An angry laugh burst from her mouth. "I find that a little hard to believe."

"Really, Archer, I don't think this is a laughing matter." Louis splashed another inch of liquor in his glass. "I don't want to leave home with things the way they are, but I don't have any choice. You know that. The company needs me."

"What about my needs?"

"You'll do just fine. You're one of the strongest women I've ever known. Sometimes I think you're stronger than I am."

"When I hear you say something like that, I can't help

wondering if you're ever going to come home." Or if I want you to, she almost added.

"Don't be melodramatic. I'll be back soon. And when I am, I promise that we'll work everything out."

"Are you sure that's what you want?"

He looked at her sharply. "I want to do what's best for all of us – me, you, the boys. Don't you?"

"Of course," she replied automatically. The problem was, she could no longer be certain what was best.

Rick studied his reflection. From his forty-dollar haircut to his pin-striped suit to his Pima cotton shirt to his Sulka tie and Italian shoes, he looked every inch the successful financier. *Perfectomundo*, he grinned, testing his smile.

Whistling cheerfully, he locked the door to his furnished apartment and took the elevator to the basement garage. He caressed the Porsche's well-polished side, admiring the job the detailer had done before pulling out his car keys. The car was a beauty – reliable, always ready to respond to his demands. When he slid into the front seat, the leather enveloped him like a well-fitting womb. It was going to be a fan-fucking-tastic day, he thought, pulling out of the garage. Stepping into the accelerator, he took a sensual pleasure in the car's throbbing power.

A lesser man might be suffering at a time like this – but he'd never thought of himself as run-of-the-mill. One week ago, he'd endured what could have been a telling blow in the form of Liz Kant's rejection. Most men he knew would have gone home and spent the next few months licking their psychological wounds. But he didn't believe in crying over spilt milk. Getting even was more his style.

It took an hour, driving in the typically heavy winter traffic, to travel from his Scottsdale apartment to the main branch of the Arizona Bank on the up-town, up-scale end of Phoenix's Central Avenue. He parked the Porsche diagonally, taking up two spaces in the bank's garage, retrieved his Vuitton briefcase from the back seat and swung out of the low-slung vehicle in one lithe, athletic movement. It was another perfect January morning, he noted, pushing open the bank's massive glass doors.

"I'd like to see the new accounts manager," he told the young woman behind the information desk. She was an exceptionally pretty brunette. Another time, he might have flirted with her and asked her to join him for a drink after work. But since the débâcle with Liz, he had made up his mind never to mix business with pleasure again. And today, he had very important business.

The girl eyed him up and down appreciatively. "If you'll follow me, I'll show you to his office."

Minutes later, Rick was comfortably ensconced in a leather armchair, facing one of the bank's young vice presidents.

"How may I help you, Mr . . . uh?" the VP asked.

"Mr Mason," Rick replied coldly. Guys like this self-important VP were a dime a dozen. "I want to establish a new account for the Cochise Memorial Art Trust."

The banker reached into one of his desk drawers and removed a few forms. "The Cochise what?"

"Memorial Art Trust." Rick enunciated each word impatiently. "I'm the trustee for an organization that's raising money to build an art school on the San Carlos Reservation."

"That sounds like a very worthy cause. Is it non profit?" the banker queried, working on his forms.

"Of course."

"How much will you be depositing today?"

Rick smiled confidently, knowing the man was about to be impressed. "Two hundred thousand dollars," he said. The money came from an account he'd opened in the Caymans while on vacation a couple of years before. At the time, he had been intrigued by the idea of banking in a place where the normal rules and regulations covering financial transactions didn't apply. Today, he was using his life savings to establish bona-fides with the Arizona bank, to get them accustomed to his depositing and withdrawing large amounts of money.

When he sauntered from the building an hour later, after having been invited to join the exclusive Arizona Club on the top floor of the building and then being given a tour of the premises, the Cochise Memorial Art Fund was in place. A second account, opened under an assumed name, would be set up as soon as he had some false ID. There was no trick, Rick thought gleefully on his way back to the gallery, to laundering money. He'd seen it done on television dozens of times.

All he had to do now was get his hands on the slides of Alan Longchase's Guggenheim show and he'd be on his way. Liz, my lovely, he chortled, you're in for one hell of a surprise.

Maryann stepped from her car and, for the first time looking toward Archer's house, she didn't have to repress a feeling of envy. Archer's home was lovely, but it couldn't hold a candle to the one that would soon be hers.

As she shut the Datsun's door, her four-carat diamond caught the sun, splintering the light into a rainbow of colours. Never in her entire life had she expected to own a jewel like it. Her first husband hadn't bothered with an engagement ring. He'd given her a plain gold-plated band the day they married. When he walked out six months later, the brass underneath was already showing through. By contrast, Reginald had promised that her wedding ring would be even more spectacular than the one he'd given her for their engagement. She could hardly wait to see it. Holding her hand in front of her face so she could admire the diamond, she trotted to the front door and rang the bell.

Five minutes later she and Archer sat across the table in the sunny, yellow breakfast room, two Bloody Mary's in front of them. Maryann studied Archer's face, noting how weary the other woman seemed. Obviously, Archer could use some cheering up and these days, Maryann was feeling like little Miss Sunshine. "You look like you just lost your best friend – or your husband," she said. "Since I'm still around, when's the divorce?"

"Why are you so damn sure there's going to be one?"

"You should see yourself. Honeychile, I've seen farmers who looked happier after losing a crop and finding out the bank wouldn't extend their loan." Maryann took the celery out of her Bloody Mary and bit into it, crunching loudly.

"There isn't going to be a divorce . . . at least not soon. I don't think Louis wants one. Before he left he apologized for having spent so much time at work. In fact, he promised we'd work things out when he came home."

"So he doesn't know about Roman?"

"Good Lord, no!"

"Did he say anything about Stacy?"

"Why should he?"

Maryann shrugged. "After seeing the way she fell all over him at Liz's party, I figured the two of them were making it."

Archer frowned. "Louis isn't like that."

"Oh for Chrissake, Archer, be real. All men are like that. Stacy Howard has the hots for your husband. She'll get him in the sack sooner or later. You can make book on it. Frankly, I don't know why you care, considering Roman's hanging around to pick up the pieces."

"I don't know how you can be so sure of things. I'm older than you and I've been married for two and a half decades, but right now I'm not sure of anything."

Maryann sighed. She'd been bursting with good feelings ever since Reginald's proposal. Although they'd publicly announced their engagement at Liz's party, Maryann had yet to have a private moment to share her happiness with Archer. But obviously, this wasn't the right day.

"I just don't understand you. Roman is obviously the guy for you. I thought, especially after Liz's party, that you'd put two and two together."

"I did, but I came up with five. I guess I used to see things – people, situations – as black and white. Now all I see is the grey. I'm so torn between Roman's needs and Louis's that half the time," Archer gave a queer little laugh, "I can't even make up my mind to go to the bathroom."

"Sugah, you've got a bad case of mental constipation. You've got to stop trying to figure things out with your head, and start listening to your heart."

"Is that what you're doing?"

Maryann held her ring up to the light. In the week since Reginald put it on her finger, it had become a habit, a gesture she repeated every time she sensed the tiniest cloud on her horizon.

"Is that what you're doing?" Archer repeated.

"Not exactly. I'm not going to pretend I'm madly in love with Reginald, at least not like you are with Roman, but I do love him. You've got to try to understand. I've been sucking hind tit my whole life and let me tell you, it's been slim pickings. So, no, I'm not following my heart. The damn thing has been broken too many times to pay any mind to anyway." She paused, and took a long swallow of her drink. "Reginald is a terrific guy, and I think we can have a very good life."

"I know you want me to be happy for you," Archer said, "and believe me, I'd like to see somebody's dreams come true. But are you absolutely sure this is what you want?"

"I've never been surer. The main thing is, I respect Reginald and he respects me. You have no idea how wonderful it is to have a man more interested in my mind than my tits. Happy marriages have been built on a hell of a lot less."

"Reginald seems so . . ." Archer looked at Maryann.

245

"Hell. I don't know any easy way to ask this. But Reginald is so obviously a snob. Does he know about your family?"

"If you mean, does he know my mother was Del Rio's town whore, the answer is no. But I don't happen to think the past is anywhere near as important as our future. I'm going to do everything in my power to make him happy, to be a good wife."

Archer grimaced.

"Now don't go making faces. He wants companionship and so do I. We've talked about having children. Trust me, Archer. Reginald is the man I've been waiting for my entire life. Anyway, I didn't come over today to get into a heavy-duty discussion." No way was Maryann going to let Archer bring her down. Not today. "I came over because I wanted to ask you to be my matron of honour."

Alan sat astride Odii while Hank rode his bay mare. There was a wintry chill in the morning air and the horses' breath condensed around their muzzles in vapour-laden clouds.

"Pretty country," Hank observed, gesturing toward the cactus- and rock-strewn hills they rode through.

Alan nodded. Few people would describe the rugged, inhospitable hills behind Pinnacle Peak as pretty. But, like Hank, he found them so. "I'm going to miss this place," he said.

"What are you talking about, missing it? Don't tell me you're leaving again. Christ, man, you just got back from the Stronghold a couple of months ago." Hank reined his bay to a halt, blocking the trail.

"I need a change."

"Don't you think it's time you told me what the hell is going on? You haven't been acting like yourself for months, not since the morning you asked me to be your master dealer."

Shrugging, Alan kneed Odii past Hank's bay and the two men rode silently for a while, the quiet broken only by the chuffing of the horses, the clinking and creaking sounds of the saddles and bridles. As they topped a small rise Alan reined Odii in. Telling the truth would be painful, but dealing with it alone was worse. "You're right as usual. I do need to talk to someone."

Hank dismounted and, holding his reins loosely, let his mare graze on the sparse winter ground cover. "Ready when you are," he said.

Alan dismounted too. "It started the night of the tenth anniversary show. Or rather, that's when it really ended. When I went to the gallery the second time that night, I had half a mind to try and work things out with Liz, as least as far as our business relationship was concerned. I got there at eleven. You know how her openings are. They go on forever. But the gallery was already closed. So I figured I'd just drive on to Liz's and have it out."

Hank seemed about to say something, but Alan silenced him with a gesture. He wanted to get this over. "When I got to Liz's," he continued, "all the lights were on and the front door was unlocked. By then I was sure . . . oh, hell, I don't know what I was sure of. I just went in. God, how I wish I hadn't." His jaws clenched, his voice lowered, his gaze fell. "I found her in bed with Rick."

Hank reached for his arm. "Fuck. I'm sorry. I know that must have been rough. Did they see you?"

"No. They were too busy." Alan leaned his forehead on Odii's shoulder. "I didn't have any claim on Liz that night, any more than I do today. But no matter how I try, I can't seem to get past . . ." He took a deep breath. "Seeing them together again on New Year's Eve made me realize I had to put some distance between us."

Hank's dark eyes held a world of sympathy. "I understand why you feel the way you do, but I'd be willing to swear Liz isn't involved with Rick anymore." He was about to say that he and Liz had been working together twice a week for months and that she never even mentioned Rick's name. And then Hank realized he couldn't, unless he was prepared to break the solemn promise he made to Liz when they struck their deal.

"You're entitled to your opinion, but I know what I saw." Abruptly, Alan turned away and mounted up.

"You could always stake Mason out in the desert, Apache style," Hank said, trying to lighten Alan's mood.

"Don't think it hasn't occurred to me."

"Where will you go?"

"I've talked to Roman De Silva about leasing his house in Santa Fe."

"When are you leaving?"

"Soon."

"Do you still plan to do your annual show at the Kant Gallery?"

"I have to. It's in the contract you signed." Alan made no effort to disguise the despair he felt. Looking down at Hank, he said, "I'm going to let her run."

Leaning forward in the saddle, he urged Odii into a canter and then a flat-out gallop. Racing across the open ground, he experienced a feeling of freedom. On horseback, he was in touch with his roots, with his Apache birthright. But he knew the feeling wouldn't last.

The Appaloosa was in a lather when he finally reined her in, turned in the saddle, and looked back down the trail to wait for Hank. Begay was a lucky man, a man who knew exactly who and what he was, a Navajo in love with being a Navajo – and in love with a Navajo woman.

"You're going to kill yourself one of these days, riding like that," Hank scolded, joining Alan a few minutes later.

The two men kept their own counsel as they rode back to the stable. They unsaddled and rubbed their mounts down without exchanging a word. Hank finally broke the silence as he followed Alan into the house.

"You've confided in me. I think it's time I confided in you. I know seeing Liz with Rick had to hurt like hell. But there's something about her you ought to know."

Alan turned abruptly and faced the bigger man. "Hank, I love you like a brother. But don't push me. I know you like Liz. Hell, you've made that plain as day. But you don't know her the way I do."

Hank drew closer. "What if I told you I knew her better?"

"Damn it, Hank. I don't want to hear this. If Liz has her hooks in you, Man, I pity you."

Archer stared across Roman's dining room table, memorizing his face as if they were never going to see each other again. She couldn't seem to get her fill of looking at him. Cold logic, buttressed by her sculptor's discerning eye, told her he wasn't conventionally handsome. His brow was too heavy. In self-deprecation, he jokingly described it as Neanderthal. His nose – broken while wrestling in college – was crooked, and his jaw was too square. He had a wrestler's thick neck and heavily-muscled, sloping shoulders. His hands were large, the fingers often paint-stained. And when it came to clothes, he was the complete antithesis of Louis's unfailing sartorial splendour. Yet, gazing at Roman over the brim of her coffee cup, she thought he was the most beautiful man she'd ever seen.

"So nothing's changed," he said, not even attempting to mask his disappointment.

"I'm afraid not. Louis was so distant the entire time he was home, even more involved with his job than he was before he left the first time, that I was sure he would bring up the idea of a separation."

Roman looked at her sharply. "Why are you waiting for him to make the first move?"

"It's the least I can do, considering the circumstances."

"By that, I assume you mean me. Damn it, Archer, when are you going to figure out that falling in love isn't a sin?"

She just stared at him.

He got up and began to stack the dinner dishes. "I wish

249

you could find a way past your guilt. Sooner or later you're going to have to make a decision about your marriage."

She looked up at him. "Am I horrible, expecting you to wait while I make decide what to do?"

"You are," he said bluntly.

"Maybe you should go back to Santa Fe and pretend you never met me."

"Sometimes, I'd like to. But it's too late for simple, easy solutions – for either of us." Shoulders hunched, he stalked into the kitchen.

She followed, still talking, desperate to justify her lack of resolve. "Before Louis left, I felt certain our marriage was over. I intended to suggest that we use the rest of his trip as a trial separation. But he seemed so unhappy that day I took him to the airport, and so sincere about wanting to work things out."

Roman turned to her. "What about me? I'm sincere too, and I'm unhappy – damn unhappy."

Archer scowled. Damn Roman, damn Louis, damn all men for being so eternally convinced life revolved around what they wanted. "You knew, that first day in Santa Fe when we had lunch at The Shed, that I was married. You could have walked away from me then and there, and none of this," she paused, feeling her anger build, "none of this would have happened. I didn't ask you to come here."

She'd never seen him so upset. "You're right about that. You didn't ask me in so many words. But, damn it, Archer, you did it in every other way. Did you really think I was going to stay in Santa Fe and pretend you didn't exist?" He didn't give her a chance to respond. "I wouldn't love you if you were the sort of woman who slept around. I could have a fling with a woman like that and forget it the next day. In fact, I have."

Archer could feel herself reddening. "So I'm not the first married woman you've slept with. How many others have there been?"

"This isn't about me," he snapped. "It's about you. You

and Louis." Unexpectedly, an embryonic smile twitched the corners of his mouth. "I think we're having our first fight. Do you realize we've known each other less than two months under incredibly stressful circumstances, and we've never even been close to an argument before?"

"You're impossible," she said, refusing to let her anger go so easily.

"No, I'm not." He grinned foolishly. "Difficult, maybe. The media always says I'm difficult. But not impossible. No one's ever said I'm impossible."

Turning, she rewarded his nonsense with a small smile. He bent to kiss away the frown between her eyes. He'd been close to blowing it, saying things that would rise between them like a wall. No matter how bad her marriage might be, she would carry the scars of its failure for the rest of her life. Despite the love they shared, they could not forge in a few weeks or months, the powerful ties of mutual history that bound her to her husband. Deep down in an aching place in his gut, Roman knew he might have to love her enough to give her up.

16

FEBRUARY 9, 1989

February is prime time in Scottsdale. The holidays have come and gone, the presents are all paid for. Galleries, like predators on a blood trail, scent money in the air – big money. So did Rick. He checked his watch. Six fifteen in the evening, time to get on with it.

He'd had his tuxedo cleaned after Liz's New Year's Eve party – a mistake, he realized, considering how immaculate it looked when he put it on. He'd have to get it good and dirty before the night was over. Patting his jacket pocket, he felt for the duplicate of her house key. Getting a wax impression had been easy. All it took was access to her purse, and some wax to make an impression.

On his way out, he stopped to pick up the crowbar he'd left by the front door. Any other night he'd have taken the elevator to the garage, but tonight he didn't want to be seen with the crowbar in his hand. He hurried down the hall to the stairway and pushed open the fire door. Shivering in the cool, stagnant air, he blinked, waiting for his eyes to adjust to the gloom. The sound of his patent leather dress shoes pinged off the steps and he plunged down them two at a time, not caring if he tripped and fell and messed himself up.

His fists were clenched, his shoulder muscles tense when he reached his car and unlocked the driver-side door. Putting the crowbar on the front seat, he leaned against the roof, hating what he was going to have to do

252

later on. That morning, he'd lovingly washed and waxed the automobile, enjoying the feel of the sleek cold metal under his hands. The Porsche never let him down. Take good care of a car and, unlike a woman, it took care of you. Tonight he would have to break that rule, and it hurt. It hurt like hell.

He straightened up abruptly. What was the matter with him, carrying on about a car? Fuck. In a few more weeks, if everything went according to plan, he'd be able to buy a Maserati or a Rolls. Just take it one step at a time, he cautioned himself. Tonight he had a window of opportunity, a chance to find the Guggenheim slides, and he had to make the most of it. Alan Longchase's annual one-man show would keep Liz busy for hours, and she'd given her busybody housekeeper, Rosita, the night off. Liz's house would be empty. It was now or never.

"Do it, Man," he exhorted himself.

Just that afternoon, her royal majesty, Liz fucking Kant had said, "Be sure to get to the gallery no later than six."

He'd bowed and scraped as usual, saying, "You can count on me." She would be furious when he didn't show up on time. But the bitch wouldn't question why he was late once he showed her the car.

He ground his teeth, working the muscles in his jaw as he put his key into the Porsche's ignition. The motor came to life instantly. Grasping the steering wheel and closing his eyes, he steeled himself for what was to come. Then he checked his watch again. He had twenty minutes to reach Liz's turnoff, park on a side-street, and wait until he saw her drive past. Pulling out of the subterranean garage, he glanced up at the sky. Clouds rolled overhead, hiding the moon and stars. He grimaced with satisfaction.

What he had to do tonight was best done in darkness.

Liz pulled into her private parking place behind the gallery at precisely six thirty, half an hour before her clients would begin arriving for Alan's annual one-man show. If everything went in accordance with her carefully laid plans, it would be the biggest, best attended show of the Scottsdale season. She couldn't afford another fiasco like the tenth anniversary gala.

To her surprise she saw Alphonse, the caterer, pacing up and down in front of the back door. The diminutive man rushed to her as she slid from the Corniche's front seat.

"Madame Kant, I have been waiting half an hour for someone to arrive." In his agitated state, his authentic Brooklyn accent broke through the phony French one.

She scanned the alley for Rick's Porsche. "I'm terribly sorry you had to wait, but Mr Mason had strict instructions to be here to let you in."

Alphonse had a look of injured dignity as he said, "Madame, I am not used to being treated in such a cavalier fashion. If this had happened with anyone but you, I would have driven away. Unfortunately, with just half an hour to prepare, I cannot guarantee my usual excellent service."

"I'm sure you'll manage. I'll put my entire staff at your disposal." Opening her beaded evening bag, she retrieved a heavy ring of keys and headed for the door, with Alphonse and his retinue of helpers at her heels.

The storeroom and offices at the back of the gallery were dark. There was no indication Rick had been there that evening. The rest of the staff, as well as the string quartet she'd hired to play that night, were waiting at the front door. She brushed aside all their questions about Rick's whereabouts.

While her staff scurried about doing Alphonse's bidding, she inspected the exhibition one last time, trying to view it the way a collector would. Alan's one-man show took up four major rooms at the front of the gallery. After learning that Alan didn't want Rick to hang his paintings, she had tackled the job herself. Now, walking the exhibition, she had to admit she'd done well, seducing the eye from canvas to canvas in a seemingly effortless flow.

Alan's work, more powerful and emotion-filled than any he'd done before, seemed to leap from the gallery's stark white walls. Some potent emotional impetus had driven him to new heights of excellence. It showed in every one of his new paintings. If only she had been the source of his inspiration. But she suspected that honour belonged to the Apache girl whose portrait now hung on the power wall.

Squaring her shoulders and holding her head high, Liz returned to the front room. Tonight, she would formally introduce Hank to all of Alan's patrons as his new master dealer. Then Hank would announce the dates for the Guggenheim show. The news of a major museum retrospective should have a highly favourable impact on sales. The opening seemed destined to be enormously successful from a financial standpoint. From a personal one, it was going to be one of the most difficult evenings of her life.

Tonight, she was going to meet the girl in the painting.

Alan rang Celia Atcittie's doorbell promptly at seven. "I can't thank you enough for doing this for me," he said, after they exchanged greetings. "This is one opening I didn't want to attend by myself."

"Thank your cousin, George," she replied, "not me. If he hadn't approved of our little charade, I wouldn't have been able to go with you tonight." Her brown eyes glittered with mischief. "Perhaps, if I had known you were going to ask me out again, I wouldn't have accepted your cousin's proposal of marriage."

"My cousin is a very lucky man," Alan replied sincerely. "He's going to have a beautiful wife."

She wore a gold lamé sheath that accentuated her exotic sensuality. Celia, he realized, had no undergarments on. Her firm breasts tilted upwards, her nipples erotically visible through the thin metallic fabric. He dismissed a brief twinge of regret at losing her to another man, even one of his *Ki*. Celia deserved someone who could love her with a whole heart, and that, Alan would never be able to do.

"I'm really looking forward to tonight – especially to meeting Liz Kant. Your mother has told me a great deal about her." Celia smiled enigmatically.

"Sometimes my mother talks too much."

"She says Miss Kant is an *odii*. That it will take someone with *diyi ncahi*, strong power, to fight her."

"My mother believes in the old ways."

"And you? Alan Longchase, what do you believe in?" she challenged.

What questions the girl asked, he thought, pondering his answer. "I believe in the wisdom of Cochise, the courage of Geronimo, in the power of the Ghans, in always painting the truth . . ." he smiled at his own earnestness, "and I believe if you keep me here talking much longer we're going to be late."

He looked around the small apartment, seeing what a cosy nest Celia had made for herself. The girl's coat was draped across the back of a chair and he walked over and picked it up. "It's a time to go," he said, offering the coat.

"Ready when you are, Lover," she murmured in his ear, taking his arm and leaning against him seductively.

Alan stepped back, his eyes widening. "Lover?"

"Just practising. You do want people to think we're a happy couple, don't you?"

"Yes."

"Well, Alan Longchase, if I were dating you instead of being engaged to your cousin, you can be damn sure I'd do a lot more than just call you lover."

256

He returned her warm smile. She had more spirit than he realized. Celia's youth and beauty would undoubtedly arouse Liz's envy, and tonight, he was in the mood to see Liz Kant squirm.

Maryann couldn't remember feeling more anxious in her entire life, not even when she eloped with Oscar. For the first time since she and Reginald started dating, he was going to see the way she lived.

She had spent the last two days giving her place a real military spit and polish, washing windows, waxing floors, scouring her bathroom until she could have eaten from the toilet bowl. The house smelled of lemon oil, soap, and the two dozen red roses Reginald sent yesterday. But all the work in the world couldn't hide the fact that it was dump-city.

She sat on the edge of the sofa, chewing her cuticles, heedless of the effect on her fresh manicure. If only she'd told the truth up front she wouldn't be in this fix. Every time he asked her out, she had promised that the next time she would tell him to pick her up at home. There had been three and a half months and dozens of dates worth of next times.

What the hell was he going to think tonight? Would he hate her, want to end their engagement? If he did, she'd have no one to blame but herself. How did that poem go? Something about what a tangled web we weave when first we practise to deceive. Holding the fourth finger of her left hand up to the light, she couldn't help wondering if she'd still have the right to wear her engagement ring tomorrow?

Reginald's mouth pursed with distaste as he pulled up in Maryann's driveway. There must be some mistake, he decided, turning on the Jaguar's interior light to double check the directions she'd given him. Surely she didn't actually live in this rundown neighbourhood?

But, no. There couldn't be any error. He'd followed her instructions to the letter and they had delivered him straight to this cheap, misbegotten part of town. He eased out of the car, stepping carefully across the rutted, weedy asphalt of her drive, as if he feared his thin-soled Bally dress shoes would be permanently ruined by contact with such a plebeian surface. A hand-written note by the doorbell warned callers to knock loudly, as the bell didn't work.

Maryann answered his summons quickly, a bright smile on her face. "Hello, Dear. You're right on time. I hope you didn't have any trouble finding me."

Reginald stepped through the entrance warily, wondering what horrors lay in store for him inside. "Well," he hesitated, "I've never been in this part of town before, but your directions were accurate."

"I've chilled some bubbly," she said, pointing at a cheap, plastic ice-bucket on the coffee table, from which a bottle of Dom Perignon incongruously protruded.

He stood by the door, looking around the room, unaware that dismay and disappointment had drawn his features up into a pained rictus. The house had no formal entry. He'd walked directly into the living room, a dingy space whose freshly painted walls merely served to accent the worn carpeting underfoot. Seeing a narrow hallway to the left and an opening into a kitchen on the right, he blurted, "Where in the world do you paint?"

He'd been longing to visit her studio, the sanctum sanctorum where she created the canvasses he so admired. Surely she didn't create those lovely works in this hovel?

"Wouldn't you like some champagne before you see it?" Her voice had lost some of its characteristic brightness.

"Yes, of course," he replied, remembering his manners. This was the woman he planned to marry, he reminded himself, and there had to be a perfectly good reason for her life-style. He just had to be patient until she explained.

Maryann bent down and picked up the Dom Perignon, hoping her hand wouldn't shake. From the minute he walked in the door, she knew that having him see her home was a mistake, a terrible miscalculation on her part. She'd been praying that he'd be able to accept her for what she was. Now she knew that would never happen.

Reginald hadn't asked her to marry him, he had proposed to the woman he thought she was – a woman who bore only a surface resemblance to her true self. The look of disgust, a look he seemed unable to repress as he studied the room she'd so carefully cleaned, told her everything she needed to know. Somehow, she'd have to come up with a good reason for the way she was living, something he'd be able to accept.

"I'd better do that," he said as she fumbled with the champagne bottle.

His long, aristocratic fingers twisted the wire seal off expertly. The cork zinged open with a festive sound and he caught the frothing liquid in the flute she handed him. At least the glasses were genuine crystal, purchased while she was making big bucks in Vegas.

He held his up to the light appraisingly. "Waterford," he commented, looking only marginally pleased before he put it down untouched.

"Let me show you where I work," Maryann said, "although I must apologize for the house. It belongs to an old spinster aunt of mine who is in the hospital, poor thing. It may not be much, but she treasures it. She asked me to move in and take care of it until she gets better, and since I'd just sold my condo and was looking for a house in Paradise Valley, I thought, why not?"

Maryann knew she was talking too fast and too much

as she led Reginald down the dark hall to the room that served as her studio, but she couldn't seem to slow down. "Now it looks as though poor Aunt Harriet is going to have to go into a nursing home and the house will have to be sold. But I'm glad I tried to help her. You see, she doesn't have anyone else." She finally ground to a halt, like the Datsun when it was being uncooperative.

"Quite commendable of you, my dear," Reginald said, his tone a bit warmer. "I must admit, I was quite surprised to see you were living in a neighbourhood like this. But family, especially the older generation, must come first. I imagine living here has been quite a sacrifice on your part."

Maryann stepped into the bedroom that served as her studio, flicking on the cheap overhead light fixture. "Oh, it has," she replied, relieved that he seemed to be swallowing her story. "The only things I brought with me were my easel and the living room furniture. But the worst of it is trying to paint without a real studio. The light in here, as you can see, is just terrible."

Reginald pursued his lips, studying the paintings that were stacked against the walls. "Still," he said, "despite the obvious drawbacks of working in such a place, you've managed to turn out some rather nice things. The paintings are quite lovely, even if the house isn't. How long have you been here?"

"I moved in just before we met," Maryann responded promptly.

"So these paintings were done here?" He looked around the ten-by-ten space as is he couldn't quite believe it.

She nodded.

His only answer was a sigh that sounded as if it had come from a broken woodwind.

"Would you like more champagne before we leave for the gallery?" she asked, distractedly running her fingers through her platinum curls.

"*Cela va sans dire*." He shook his head from side to side in a series of jerky bobbles. "Really, *ma chérie*, I must admit I'm quite distressed to find you living in a place like this. It's one thing to play the good Samaritan. It's another to . . ." he faltered.

"I understand completely," she said, leading him back to the living room.

She wrapped her arms around herself to hide her trembling. She'd come terribly close to losing him. But, God willing and the creek didn't rise, he'd bought her story about poor maiden Aunt Harriet.

As he handed her a brimming glass, her engagement ring caught the light, a beacon of hope in the drab room.

Liz stared at her watch, wondering where in the world Rick could be. In the past, despite their aborted romance, he had been completely reliable. Nothing short of a disaster would have kept him from showing up on time.

Her short-handed staff had to scurry to keep up with sales. Although it was only eight, red circles had already been pasted next to half of the paintings on display. She looked around the room, sensing the well-dressed crowd's buying fever. She'd never been able to figure what triggered that fever, but once it started it guaranteed a sell-out show. Seeing other collectors getting out their chequebooks seemed to trigger a primordial response in all the rest. What she privately thought of as the lemming syndrome was certainly operative tonight, she thought, as another anxious buyer demanded her attention.

"I've got my eye on one of the paintings in the other room," the buyer said, "and all your sales people are busy. Would you mind helping me?"

Liz was writing up the sale when she heard a hubbub coming from the front of the gallery. Her firm script wavered. Alan's arrival was the only thing that could have created such an excited burst of sound. Her first thought was to turn the rest of the paperwork over to one of her staff and go to welcome him. But knowing he wouldn't be alone, she continued writing methodically.

She was congratulating the buyer and arranging for Rick to deliver and hang the painting when she sensed Alan's presence and turned to face him. He looked heartstoppingly handsome in a fringed, beaded doeskin shirt and creamy leather trousers that moulded to his body.

"Alan, I was afraid all your paintings would be sold before you got here."

"I wouldn't have missed this for the world." He gave Liz a cheerless smile that sent chills racing down her spine. "I'd like you to meet," he paused long enough to exchange a significant glance with the young woman by his side, "my very good friend, Celia Atcittie."

Liz's mouth dried as she studied the other woman. This was the moment she'd been dreading ever since the night she and Alan broke up, the moment when he introduced her to a woman of his own tribe, someone he would want to bear his children. But not even in her worst nightmares had Liz imagined a girl as lovely and desirable as the one she faced. Alan will marry this one, Liz thought, forcing herself to smile.

In sharp contrast to Alan's Apache costume, Celia wore an abbreviated gold lamé dress that showed off her youthful breasts and long, slim legs. Liz was uncomfortably aware of how desirable the young woman looked. She herself had dressed carefully for the evening, choosing a beautifully draped ebony De La Renta that made a perfect backdrop for her pale skin and red hair. But now, as she took in Celia's bold sensuality, Liz suddenly felt old and inappropriately garbed, like a woman attending the opera in widow's weeds.

"How nice to meet you," she said with a warmth she didn't feel. "Hank has told me a great deal about you."

But she didn't tell me you were two decades younger than I am, she reflected, or that you looked like an Apache Venus. Liz felt every one of her forty-two years as she stopped a passing waiter and ordered champagne for the new arrivals.

Rick used the duplicate key to let himself into Liz's house. Fortunately he was prepared for the fact that the lights all came on all when he opened the front doors. So much the better, he thought. It would save him the time and trouble of turning them on.

Logic dictated that the slides would be in the room Liz used as an office, so he went there first. He searched the desk, the closet and an antique Mexican sideboard she used to hold files, with frantic haste. He found her personal financial records, bundles of letters, folders on other artists and galleries, clippings from newspapers and magazines, all meticulously catalogued. When he finished he knew a great deal more about her. But he still didn't know where she kept the damn slides of the Guggenheim paintings.

Next he searched the den, the library, the living and dining rooms, prying into a multitude of cabinets and drawered tables. He remembered noticing a built-in desk in the kitchen, but it proved to contain nothing but Rosita's recipes and coupons she'd clipped. Finally, he headed for Liz's bedroom where seductively treacherous memories lay in wait.

How many times had he relived what happened here, stroking himself to completion while he imagined Liz beneath him. The nude portrait over the fireplace beckoned him, and, for one agonizing moment, he allowed himself to acknowledge what he'd lost when he lost the woman who posed for it. Ignoring its power required a conscious act of will.

Ten minutes later Rick finally found what he sought in the octagonal cabinet next to the bed. He hurried back down the hall and out of the front doors, making sure they locked behind him. When Liz discovered the box missing, she would undoubtedly call the police. They would certainly wonder what a thief wanted with worthless slides when the house held valuable jewels and silver.

He headed back down the mountain, turned left on Camelback and sped eastward until he reached a sparsely-settled area. Turning off the ignition, he opened the door and took the crowbar from its place on the front seat. The night was quiet and still, the nearest house half a mile away. He'd scouted this area two weeks ago. It was undeveloped, devoted to small ranches, the sort of place where you could commit a rape without being caught in the act.

He broke out in a cold sweat as he hefted the heavy crowbar in both hands and walked to the front of the car. Raising it overhead, he brought it down full-force on the highly polished right front fender. The metal shrieked in protest and glass burst from the headlight with a sharp crack. A sliver hit his forehead and stuck there. Wincing with pain, he pulled the shard out, feeling blood beginning to trickle down his temple. Ignoring the wound, he raised his arms a second time. Heedless of the tears oozing from his eyes, he struck the sleek vehicle again and again.

"I'm so sorry, Baby," he moaned, wreaking destruction on the car's satiny metallic surface.

When he finished, the right front headlight and fender had yielded up an ugly harvest of broken glass and dented metal. Examining the results of his onslaught, he sobbed just once. Damn Liz Kant to eternity. It was all her fault. She was going to pay dearly for what he'd just done. His poor, poor car.

Shuffling back to the driver's door, he felt his stomach heave. Vomit filled his throat and he turned aside, spewing his dinner onto a clump of cactus, not caring that a few clotted fragments mingled with the blood that already stained his previously immaculate shirt front. When his gut stopped contracting, he took the crow bar and threw it as hard and as far as he could into the darkness.

Half an hour later, Rick staggered into the Kant Gallery. As the opening-night crowd parted to make way for him, a hush enveloped the front room. He knew he looked terrible, even worse than he anticipated when he planned his cover story.

"Get Liz," he said weakly to one of the sales girls before collapsing into a chair by the front desk.

By nine, all but two of Alan's paintings had sold. He didn't even bother to calculate his share of the proceeds. Tomorrow he would be on his way to Santa Fe. Thinking about leaving Scottsdale and Liz behind helped him get through the evening. So had Hank, whose self-assurance burgeoned as he publicly assumed the mantle of master dealer. There had been a spattering of spontaneous applause when Liz made the formal announcement, and an even louder response to Hank's disclosure of the retrospective. He and Alan had been overwhelmed by well-wishers.

Celia had played her rôle to the hilt, overplayed it actually, acting as if she and Alan were the hottest of lovers, clinging to his arm, posing for photographers while looking up at him adoringly. He was going to have some explaining to do when cousin George saw those pictures in the morning papers.

"This is so much fun," she cooed, sipping champagne. "Quite a change from a school teacher's life."

"I'm glad one of us is having fun."

Suddenly, the devilish gleam that livened Celia's eyes was erased by a look of dismay. Her voice seemed overloud in the room's sudden silence. "Oh my God," she gasped, "who's that?"

Alan turned in time to see Rick collapse into a chair by the front desk. Blood ran down the side of Rick's face, his clothes were a mess, his eyes dazed. While Alan watched, transfixed, Liz hurried to Rick's side.

"Rick, I've been so worried about you," she said, her voice trembling with anxiety. "What in the world happened?"

"God, I'm sorry I'm late." Rick groaned, reached for her hand and held on hard. "I was on my way here when a dog ran in front of my car. I swerved to avoid it and ran into a tree. My poor car is a mess."

"Never mind the car. What about you?" She knelt by his side. "Are you all right? Should I call a doctor?"

A tall grey-haired man stepped from the circle around them. "I'm a doctor, Miss Kant. I'll be happy to take a look at Mr Mason if you like."

She nodded her assent. "Help me get him to my office."

Supporting Rick between them, they made their way through the crowd. As Alan watched her walking away, her arm around Rick's waist, any shred of doubt he may have had about their relationship vanished.

"Wow!" Celia commented when they were gone. "Are Liz's openings always this dramatic?"

Maryann and Reginald had been at the bar at the back of the gallery when Rick arrived and, like many of their fellow guests, they didn't know about his accident. It had been, from Maryann's point of view, a very satisfying evening. Reginald seemed to have bought the story about her Aunt Harriet, hook, line and sinker. Better still, even though it was clearly Longchase's show, someone had bought one of her paintings.

Reginald had been suitably impressed when he'd seen the red circle next to the canvas. "Too bad," he'd commented. "I was thinking about buying that one myself."

"Reginald, Sugah," she'd drawled, "you don't need to buy my work. After we're married you can have first pick."

She hadn't even been jealous when Reginald bought an expensive Longchase just a few minutes later, although she usually felt a pang whenever someone she'd brought to the gallery decided to purchase another artist's work. After all, she'd consoled herself, anything that Reginald bought would soon be hers.

Now, having spent two hours standing in a pair of impossibly high heels and making polite chit-chat, she felt tired and a bit cranky. "I promised to go and see Aunt Harriet at the hospital first thing in the morning," she said. "Would you mind leaving soon?"

Looking down at her, Reginald nodded. "I'm a bit weary myself."

For him, it had been a most unsettling evening. His brain throbbed. The headache that began when he stood in Maryann's living room drinking champagne had grown increasingly more malevolent as the evening wore on. He wanted to believe Maryann's story about helping an aging relative. But could he trust her?

Doubt nibbled at his reservoir of belief on the long drive back to her house. He barely pecked her on the cheek by way of good night kiss before leaving her on the doorstep of that odious house.

Could it be, he pondered, reaching his own front door forty minutes later, that Maryann wasn't the women she seemed? He regretted aborting his early attempts to learn something of her background. At the time, he hadn't considered getting professional help. In fact, he had actually felt embarrassed after questioning Liz Kant.

Now, all the grating little things he'd observed, things he'd ascribed to Maryann's Texas upbringing, jumped to the forefront of his mind. Her funny accent and occasional mispronounced word, the fact that he'd never met a single member of her family, things he'd deliberately ignored, took on monumental significance. Perhaps he ought to telephone Liz again in the morning and see what he could learn?

Reginald climbed out of the Jaguar wearily, the headache pulsating behind his brow, a nerve under his left eye twitching. Keith was waiting for him in the entry hall.

"You look tired," Keith said, slipping Reginald's coat from his shoulders. "Do you want me to give you a massage tonight?"

"That would be very nice," Reginald replied, grateful for his butler's ministrations.

"Is something wrong, Boss?"

"I'm not sure," Reginald replied wearily.

Tomorrow, he thought, tomorrow he was going to deal with his doubts. Much as he hated the idea, despised the thought of anyone prying into his personal life, he'd have to hire a private detective.

He couldn't possibly go through with marrying Maryann Van Kamp until he knew who she really was.

17

FEBRUARY 25, 1989

When she looked back, Liz would always be surprised that the phone call hadn't come in the middle of the night. In films, that was the traditional time for people to be notified of impending tragedy. Instead, it had been a cheerfully blue-skied February afternoon, and she had been in her office going over ad-copy for the upcoming De Silva–Harrison show when the telephone rang.

"A Mr Jacob Kantorwitz is asking to speak to you," one of the staff had informed her. "He says it's urgent. Will you take the call?"

Liz's throat constricted and her stomach spasmed. Twenty-three years had passed since she last heard the name, Jacob Kantorwitz. What could he possibly want? Did she know how successful she was – would he want her to recompense him for continuing to keep the secret of her past? Of course. That had to be it. Money. The Kantorwitzs always needed money. God knows, they never had any of their own.

"Put him on," she replied, struggling for self-control during the brief silence while the call was transferred.

"Is that you, Rachel?" a man asked hesitantly.

"Jacob?" He sounded so different. She hardly recognized the deep masculine voice, but then he had been barely fourteen the last time they spoke.

"She wants to see you," Jacob Kantorwitz said bluntly.

"And what does he have to say about it?"

269

"Nothing. He's been dead for five years."

"Why wasn't I notified?" She began to tremble.

"He didn't want you to know."

"Aaah." She sighed her comprehension. Of course he wouldn't have wanted her to know. For him, she had ceased to exist the day she left.

There were a thousand questions she could have asked Jacob – should have asked. But the words wouldn't come. Fear, concern, anger and guilt battled for supremacy over her emotions.

She had known Jacob as a boy and loved him, but she didn't know the quiet uncommunicative man on the other end of the line now. Could she trust him? His words gave nothing away. If he was bitter, avaricious, or just disinterested and uninvolved, he maintained a careful monotone.

"Will you come?" he asked.

Every instinct told her to say no. She had long ago closed the book on the early chapters of her life. Not once in all the intervening years, had she felt the slightest inclination to re-open it.

"She's dying," Jacob said into the pregnant pause.

All doubts were swept from Liz's mind. This was no quest for money – although that would have been far easier to bear. "I'll be on the first plane tomorrow."

Los Angeles and Phoenix are just three hundred and seventy miles apart and Air West makes almost hourly flights from Sky Harbor to Los Angeles International. Although she travelled widely, Liz had avoided her birth place for two and a half decades. Now, as the limousine took her from the luxury of the confectionary-pink Beverly Hills Hotel to the gritty realism of West Hollywood, she realized the environment had changed almost as much as she had in the intervening years.

A mustard-coloured haze overlay everything – the nearby hills, the gleaming glass cubes of high-rise buildings. Once-proud palm trees struggled upward in an inhospitable sky, their brown fronds drooping sadly. There were more people, more cars than she remembered, and the city seemed destined to choke on both.

The sidewalks grew dirtier, the pedestrians less well-groomed as the limousine drove east on Hollywood Boulevard. The fabled Walk of Stars had become an unappealing honky-tonk where bewildered tourists brushed shoulders with hustlers, pimps, runaways, and prostitutes. No matter the cost, the personal anguish, the nights when she had been beset by almost insupportable regret and loss, she had been right to leave. She had found a better, freer, wider world, and had invented Liz Kant in the process.

As the driver turned south into the warren of narrow streets between Sunset and Santa Monica Boulevards, she began to pick out a few familiar landmarks, a tired park with brown stubble grass and wilting shrubbery where she had played in girlhood, a Kosher butcher shop, a book store that specialized in Hebrew periodicals and texts. This was the Hollywood uninitiated travellers never saw, a teeming ghetto of ethnic neighbourhoods.

And then she saw the first of them, a group of bearded men dressed all in black, clustered on a corner like so many crows. She averted her gaze, forcing the interior of the rented limousine to become her horizon.

She barely had time to compose herself when the driver announced, "You're here, Miss Kant."

The building in front of her had changed little since she last saw it. Built in the early twenties, it had passed its prime long before she lived within its confines.

"I'll be a few hours," she told her driver. "Wait for me." And then, straightening her spine, she climbed the steps that led to the small lobby.

Her nostrils were immediately assailed by the scent of cooking and cheap disinfectant that overlay the building's overall odour of mustiness and decay. The once attractive art deco floor was scabbed with concrete where missing

271

tiles had been patched. The hallway was painted institutional green, and decorated with graffiti. Apparently, the current residents specialized in four-letter words.

As Liz walked toward the back of the building, a woman dressed all in black, a babushka on her head, came out of one of the apartments. The woman's face registered her disapproval as she absorbed Liz's expensive clothing and her sweep of red hair.

Welcome home, Liz thought, experiencing the instant rebellion such looks had elicited throughout her childhood. She had never belonged here, she reminded herself, fighting down the wave of misery that threatened to overwhelm her now that she was back. Her departure had been as inevitable as death and taxes.

Apartment 8–A was at the end of a long, poorly-lit hall. She hesitated in front of the door, took in the double locks and the *mazuzah*, both a form of protection against the world's evil, and then knocked firmly.

Jacob Kantorwitz answered at once. A weary-looking man dressed in a rumpled black suit, his hair hidden by a battered fedora, his prayer shawl hanging out from under his suit jacket, he stood there momentarily speechless as he took her in. Despite his full beard and the long side-locks of the devout male Hassidic Jew, there was no denying the familial resemblance.

And then he reached for her hand, shaking it formally. "I wasn't sure you would show up. Please, come in."

"I said I'd take the first plane in the morning," she replied sharply, unnerved by the encounter.

"Ah yes, I remember that about you. You always kept your word. As I recall, my sister, Rachel, was a stubborn girl who always meant what she said, and said what she meant. At least that much hasn't changed." A gentle smile softened his features.

"Your sister, Rachel, hasn't existed for two and a half decades. My name is Liz, Liz Kant," she reminded him. "I had it changed legally."

"Of course." He paused and ran his tongue over his lips. "Forgive me . . . Liz."

The years hadn't been kind to Jacob, she thought, still holding her brother's hand. Just thirty-eight, three years her junior, he looked ten years older – his beard shot through with grey, his blue-green eyes a pale, watery version of her own.

"I'm almost bald and I wear glasses for reading," he said, seeming to read her mind. "But you . . . you look wonderful."

Crying would have been easy, but she refused to give in to tears even though they welled in her eyes. "I didn't know what my reception would be. I feel like a returning prodigal."

"Risen from the dead," Jacob replied, grinning broadly. "It's not every day a man sees a ghost. Did you know father had the Kaddish said for you?"

She nodded. The Kaddish was the traditional Hebrew prayer for the dead. "He threatened to the day I left."

She could still hear the rancorous words her father had flung at her during the argument that propelled her from this apartment forever.

"You are a Hassid, and Hassidic women are not supposed to get an education," Moishe Kantorwitz had said, his voice as cold and final as a tomb. "Learning is for men. It was bad enough that you should have gone to a public school for twelve years. That must be where you got all those liberal ideas."

"You're right! That's where I got them," she shouted back. "God knows, there are no new ideas in this apartment. You're still living in the fifteenth century."

"Blasphemer," he said. "How dare you take the Lord's name in vain? Tomorrow I will see about arranging your marriage. Perhaps a husband will be able to teach you some sense."

"This isn't some backward Polish village," Liz had bellowed, not caring if the neighbours heard the quarrel through the building's thin walls. "It's twentieth-century America. I don't have to marry some man just because you say so. Damn it, Father, I'm not a piece of property to be put up on the auction block."

Just then, her mother had come into the room and Liz had looked at her pleadingly, desperate for an ally, someone to take her side in the struggle over her future.

Malka had averted her eyes. "You must do as your father commands. Reb Lipshitz is a fine man. You will see. He didn't even mind that we had no dowry to give him on your behalf."

"What the hell does Reb Lipshitz have to do with this?" Liz exclaimed.

Her father and mother exchanged a single knowing glance.

Liz felt as if she'd been hit in the solar-plexus. She gasped for breath. "Do you mean to tell me you've already chosen my husband without even consulting me?"

"Of course," Moishe replied, grabbing Liz by the wrist. "It's our custom. Your mother's father chose me, and I have chosen for you. It has been that way for hundreds of years. Who are you to want to change things? What makes you so special?"

Liz bit her lower lip so hard that she drew blood. They would never understand. Never. Her only hope was to stand up to them now, before it was too late. "To hell with custom. I'm going to accept the Stanford scholarship no matter what you say."

"If you leave this house," her father let her wrist go and thrust her away from him so that she stumbled awkwardly, "you will be dead to this family. You will never see your mother or your brother again. I will have the Kaddish said for you."

Liz had brushed past Jacob who was standing in the living room, wide-eyed at her temerity. No one tried to stop her when she packed her meagre belongings, although she kept on hoping against hope that her mother would try. She left the apartment within the hour. Her mother had been weeping in the kitchen, Jacob had gone out, and her father was sitting in the living room in stony silence as she shut the front door behind her.

After spending two weeks at a friend's home, Liz had moved into the dorms at Stanford. By then, she had made up her mind to start a new life, completely free of all the constraints, the hide-bound rules that had governed her life as a Hassidic Jewess. The first step had been choosing a new name. The second had been creating a believable background for herself.

She told all her new friends that she had been orphaned at an early age. It wasn't very far from the truth. Although she faithfully wrote to her mother once a week during her first year at college, the letters went unanswered. The second year Liz wrote once a month. By the time she graduated with honours, she had stopped writing altogether. She turned her back on the past as totally as if she had been born the day she entered Stanford. The habit of secrecy, so difficult at first, became as much a part of her as her red hair and turquoise eyes.

Now, pushing the bitter memories away, she looked at Jacob. "When Mother didn't answer my letters, I knew Father must have carried out his threat."

Jacob shook his head sadly. "It was all so long ago. We weren't even permitted to say your name after you were gone. I didn't think I would ever see you again."

"Did you want to?"

"Not right away. Father was so angry. He took it out on me and Mother. I'm afraid I blamed you." Jacob shrugged. "But we can talk about that later. Mother is waiting to see you."

Liz followed him down the hall, girding herself for the coming meeting.

Malka Kantorwitz lay in the same bed, in the same room her newly-wed husband, Moishe, had brought her to forty-six years before. She had been fifteen years old then, and pretty enough to turn men's heads. Moishe Kantorwitz had not been the man of her girlish dreams. Small, stoop-shouldered, he was a locally renowned Talmudic scholar. It was, so her parents told her when she wept the night before her wedding, an honour to marry such a learned man, a *zaddik*.

Now Malka looked up to see the fruit of that enforced, passionless union standing in her bedroom doorway. She had wronged this child years ago, just as her parents had wronged her. This was, Malka knew – although the doctors had yet to tell her she would soon die of cancer – her last chance to make amends. "How good it is to see you," she said softly, lifting a waxen hand toward Liz.

She's so frail, Liz thought, her knees suddenly weak as she took in the pale wraith on the bed. Her mother had been healthy and full of life the last time they saw each other. Now death was plainly written on Malka's ravaged features. She was propped up on pillows, and her skin was almost as white as the worn linens.

"Come here," Malka rasped. "Let me look at you."

Liz moved to the bed, sat down on the edge carefully, and kissed her mother's cheek.

"You're so beautiful." Malka reached forward to run her emaciated hand thrugh the luxuriance of Liz's hair. "To force a woman with such hair to wear a wig for the rest of her life would have been a crime."

"Father didn't see it that way," Liz said softly, remembering the hated acrylic monstrosity she'd had to wear. She'd been so ashamed of that wig. Her classmates had teased her mercilessly until the day a gang of girls had attacked her on her way home from school, calling her yid and kike before yanking the wig off her head and trampling it under their feet. Liz had come home with a split lip and a bloody nose. But those girls had unwittingly done her a favour. She had never worn a wig again.

"Being a Hassid is not easy," Malka said. "Wigs, side

curls, a kosher kitchen, black clothes, they are the price of our faith."

To say nothing of feminine subservience, Liz was tempted to say. But she kept her counsel. She hadn't come all this way to fight old battles.

"We must talk." Malka's voice was as frail as her body. "But I hardly know where to begin." She reached for the water glass on the night table by her side, took a pill from a brown vial and swallowed it down.

"Are you in pain?" Liz asked, searching her mother's face.

"It will pass."

"I'll leave you two alone for a while," Jacob said from the doorway.

But neither woman heard him go.

"Twenty-four years ago," Malka began, looking directly into her daughter's eyes, "I permitted your father to do you a great wrong. I had to see you to ask your forgiveness."

At last, Liz let the tears come. A lifetime of guilt and self-hate burst from her. "I'm the one who needs to be forgiven, for abandoning you."

Maryann sat at the bar in Rick's Place, one of her favourite haunts in her pre-Reginald days, feeling she'd come full circle. Here she was, alone again, drowning her sorrows in a singles bar.

Reginald had pulled a classic disappearing act. She hadn't heard from him for three weeks, not since the evening when she finally let him see the way she lived. The flowers, the phone calls, stopped. So did the dinners, the nights at concerts and the theatre. The clock of her life had struck midnight and whammy, the carriage had turned into a pumpkin and the horses into mice. Or was it meece? She could almost feel that old buzzard's luck settling on her shoulder.

Despite her incessant calls to Reginald's house, all Keith

would tell her was, "Mr Quincy was called out of town unexpectedly."

Out of town, my ass, Maryann thought, taking a deep draught of her strawberry daiquirí. At first, desperate to make things right, she actually sank low enough to try and con her way past the guard on the Clearwater Hills' gate. But the s.o.b. had seen through her story and refused to let her in. All the guard had to do, Maryann thought, swirling the slushy daiquiri through her teeth, was take one look at her Datsun and he knew she didn't belong in an up-scale place like the Hills.

Face it, she admonished herself, it's over. Reginald was long gone by now. She finished her drink, pushed it in the bartender's direction, and was about to order another when she heard a vibrant masculine voice over her shoulder.

"Can I buy you another one of those?"

Swivelling her barstool, she turned to confront a good looking guy in his late thirties or early forties – with lots of strawberry-blond hair, freckles splashed across his nose, a deep tan, and friendly hazel eyes surrounded by laugh lines.

"Whiiiy not?" she drawled, offering him a mega smile.

Her antenna had gone on full alert when she had strolled into Rick's Place half an hour ago. He'd glanced around in the semi-dark room and seemed to notice her right away. But he had taken a seat halfway down the bar and sat hunched over, as if the troubles of the world rested on his broad shoulders.

Now, he took the stool next to hers. Casually dressed in grey flannel slacks and an opened-necked sport shirt in a wild Hawaiian print, he looked like a yuppie surfer. While she wondered whether he'd begin the conversation by asking what she was doing alone in a bar at three in the afternoon, or by suggesting they compare signs, he ordered drinks for them both. His was light beer.

"Do you live around here," he asked.

"No. I live on the west side."

"You don't work," he commented, checking his watch, "or you wouldn't be in a place like this in the middle of the afternoon."

"You're a regular Sherlock Holmes, aren't you?"

"Am I right?"

"Maybe I'm independently wealthy."

"Good! Then you can buy the next round."

Five minutes later she told him her real occupation and her name.

His was Malcolm Murphy – but his friends called him Murph. Murph was a rep for a sporting goods manufacturer.

"I'm my own best customer. I use what I sell," he said.

That explains the athlete's body and the tan, she thought. Three weeks ago, despite his easy smile and well-developed build, she wouldn't have given Murph the time of day. But, in view of Reginald's desertion, she felt ready for anything – especially a good-looking guy who wanted to buy her drinks.

"Tell me about the man who put that diamond on your finger," Murph said, paying for their second round.

Maryann looked down at her engagement ring, thankful that the pain of Reginald's rejection had finally been lulled by liquor and masculine attention. "Oh that doesn't mean a thing," she said firmly. "It's a keepsake."

"Good," Murph replied. "I'm glad you're not spoken for, because I want to buy your dinner."

Dinner led to dancing and they were still together at eleven. Murph was easy to talk to, Maryann reflected, the kind of guy who wouldn't sit in judgement because a girl happened to be born on the wrong side of the tracks or the wrong side of the blankets. He wanted to know all about her and she told him damn near everything. He hadn't put any moves on her either, which was too bad because the booze made her decidedly horny. How long had it been since she'd been with a man in the biblical sense. And was there any other way that counted? she giggled to herself.

By his own admission, Murph had broken up with his steady a few weeks ago and been celibate since. "Nowadays," he said, "you have two choices. You can die of loneliness or you can take your chances with herpes or AIDS."

"Tell me all about it. You're damned if you do and damned if you don't. Personally, I'd prefer to be damned for doing," she tittered, dropping her hand on his well-muscled thigh.

He ordered a last round of drinks, and put a companionable arm around her waist. Then, as his hand came in contact with her breast, she realized there was nothing companionable about his intentions.

"How about coming back to my place?" he said huskily. "My apartment complex has a heated pool."

"I don't have a bathing suit."

"I was counting on it."

Murph lived in Mesa, a good forty miles from her house in Sunnyslope. Maybe she was crazy, she thought twenty minutes later, for climbing into a car with a perfect stranger. But he promised to deliver her back to her Datsun whenever she said the word, and there was something about him that inspired trust. They necked a little before he started the motor and, she decided happily, if he made love half as well as he kissed, she was in for a memorable night.

His one-bedroom apartment on Baseline near Fiesta Mall was comfortably cluttered without being the typical bachelor pig-sty. She'd seen a lot worse. To her surprise, he offered her the bathroom and a huge terry bath sheet so she could undress without being self conscious. She emerged a few minutes later, modestly swaddled from underarms to ankles.

While she changed, he had stripped too and the towel

280

that circled him from waist to thigh revealed a chest full of strawberry-blond hair and a conspicuous bulge at his crotch. Another good omen, she thought.

"Now for that swim," he said, taking her arm and leading her outside.

They had passed the pool on the way from the parking lot to his front door. The water, in the chill late February night, sparkled blue-green under a thin layer of vapour. "Are you sure we won't get caught skinny dipping?" she asked, surrendering to a brief moment of timidity.

"You don't know Mesa, do you?" Murph replied. "Look around. Do you see any lights on? In this town, they roll the sidewalk up at ten. Everyone is sound asleep except you and me."

He was right. Other than the pool lights, the apartment complex was dark.

He pulled off his towel and dived into the water so abruptly that all she saw was the flash of his white buttocks. While he swam a length underwater, she dropped her towel and jumped in too. As promised, the water was as warm as chicken soup.

Maryann had learned to swim on the banks of the Rio Grande, skinny-dipping with the local band of urchins, and she could manage a thrashing dog paddle if she had to. But Murph was a symphony in the water, his fluttering feet creating a crescendo of bubbles while the steady pull of his arms established the beat. He swam eight impressively skilled laps while Maryann bobbed in the deep end, before he joined her at the edge of the pool.

"That was really something," she murmured appreciatively.

"I swam freestyle in college," he told her, barely breathing hard, "but you need to keep it up. Another two laps and I'd be dying."

Glancing down at her naked breasts, he seemed to run out of conversation. An awed, "Holy shit!" was all he managed before he reached for her.

His mouth was warm, his lips and tongue tasted of chlorine and beer. She'd never done it in a pool – at least not in the deep end – and with a lesser athlete than Murph they might have both drowned. But he soon proved how completely at home he was in the water. Holding the side with one hand, he lifted her breasts in turn, suckling greedily.

"It's not true," he said, finally coming up for air.

"What's not true?" she asked, looking into his hungry hazel eyes.

"I've heard guys say a handful is all you need, but you, Maryann, are living proof that you can't get enough of a good thing."

Not waiting for her to reply, he let go of the edge, took her breasts between his large hands, gently squeezing them together until he fit both nipples in his mouth at once. His engorged penis brushed against her legs and reaching down, she pulled him between the warmth of her thighs. He groaned deep in his throat, a primordial sound that sent shivers down her spine, and then he parted her legs and dived under water.

Most men give lousy head in bed. Even underwater, Murph was superbly skilled, so skilled in fact that she choked down a triumphant orgasmal scream before he came up for air. Turning her so that her back touched the tile's slick surface, he held to the edge with one hand and pulled her close with the other, kissing her long and hard.

"Guide me in," he said, placing her hand on his penis.

It pulsed with life under her fingers. She opened her legs to receive the pleasure-pain of his first powerful thrust. From then on, she stopped worrying about someone seeing them.

"Oh God, that feels good," they said in tandem.

Murph was no wham-bam lover, she learned as he built a rhythm of long, slow strokes that she felt at the very top of her womb. He worked both their bodies with the compulsion for physical perfection that was the legacy of his athleticism. When she tired of his frontal assault, he carried her to the steps and asked her to kneel.

This time his eager cock found new, untested ground, while his fingers filled the emptiness it had so recently occupied. They came simultaneously, and their shouts should have roused the dead – but not a single light flickered on in the quiet complex.

They floated side by side afterward like salmon who have spawned, waiting for their hearts to quiet and their lungs to stop labouring. Later, wrapped in towels once more, they returned to his apartment. Too tired to go home, Maryann crawled into his bed and slept dreamlessly in the hollow created by his abdomen and chest.

He took her out for breakfast the next morning before taking her back to her car. "I'll call you," he said before he drove away. Somehow, despite a life of dashed hopes and broken promises, she managed to summon up enough faith to believe he would keep his word.

Reginald sat down and crossed his thin, elegantly-trousered legs. When he'd begun his search for a discreet private investigator three weeks before, he'd never imagined finding him in a place like this.

Now, Reginald looked around Charles Davis's office appreciatively. The walls were panelled, the furniture excellent reproduction Sheraton. Davis himself had turned out to be the biggest surprise of all. Reginald had been afraid he would have to deal with a lower class individual, someone who wore a battered hat, smoked foul-smelling cigars, and said things like dese and dem. But Charles Davis wore three-piece suits, French-cuffed shirts, had a fine-boned, Anglo-saxon face and spoke with a familiar Boston accent. Two weeks before when Reginald had employed him, Davis had promised both discretion and thoroughness.

"What have you uncovered in the course of your investigation?" Reginald asked after making himself comfortable.

Davis tilted his head and looked over the rim of his tortoise-shell glass frames. "Your Miss Van Kamp has quite an interesting history. To begin with the basics, she's a thirty-six-year-old divorcee. She hasn't seen her ex-husband in years. She divorced him for desertion and, apparently he owes her a tidy sum in back support."

Reginald nodded impatiently. So far, the things Davis reported were already known to him.

"Mis Van Kamp is an artist and is represented by the Kant Gallery where she is well thought of. I spoke to Liz Kant myself, pretending to be a potential buyer, and she assured me that Van Kamp is a talented painter with a fine future."

"I know all that," Reginald snapped. He hadn't given Davis a large cheque just to be told things any fool could learn by picking up the phone. "Please, get on with it," he commanded, not bothering to disguise the irritation in his voice.

"Mr Quincy, you asked me to do a thorough job. If you'll let me continue, I'm sure you'll be more than satisfied with my services. I spent considerable time checking into the subject's background. She was born in Del Rio, Texas. Her mother was unmarried, and there is some question as to who her father might have been. No one claimed the honour, but that's not too surprising in view of the fact that Miss Van Kamp's mother had a reputation for selling her sexual favours."

Reginald felt the blood drain from his face. "She wasn't married to one of the Rousseauxs?"

"She was never married at all. I hesitate to use the word prostitute, since she was never arrested on that charge, but it does seem to characterize her lifestyle. From what I learned in Del Rio, Maryann Van Kamp didn't share her mother's vocation, at least not while she lived there."

"What in God's name are you saying?"

"After her divorce, Miss Van Kamp held down a variety of jobs, car hop, cocktail waitress, that sort of thing, to pay for art lessons. A few years ago when she was in financial difficulty, she spent several months in Las Vegas working as a bar-girl."

Reginald struggled to control the white hot rage blossoming in his stomach. "I'm not sure I understand."

Davis gave him a do-you-really-want-me-to-spell-it-out? look. When Reginald didn't respond, Davis shrugged and went on. "As a bar-girl, Van Kamp was supposed to get johns to pay for her drinks. If they wanted a roll in the hay, she paid the owner of the bar a cut of her take. From what I heard, she was damn good in the sack. A natural, you might say." Davis rolled his eyes. "Like mother, like daughter."

Reginald was swallowing bile. He felt deathly ill. "What can you tell me about Maryann's finances?" he rasped. Despite the fact that what he'd just been told made marriage out of the question, he desperately wanted to believe Maryann had been motivated by genuine affection for him, rather than financial need.

"I guess you'd say she was down and out. Her credit rating stinks," Davis replied. "She has a savings account with fifteen hundred dollars in it, and her chequing account had an average balance of five hundred dollars over the last year. She has a habit of robbing Peter to pay Paul if you know what I mean. She's been spending a great deal of money on clothes lately, and payment on her Visa is overdue." The detective looked smugly satisfied as he continued. "In view of your request for privacy, I conducted the investigation myself rather than turning it over to one of my men. Consequently, I was following Miss Van Kamp personally last night when she picked up a man at Rick's Place. That's a singles bar."

"Go on."

"Miss Van Kamp returned to the man's apartment and

after a brief interval, they came out wrapped in towels. They took a nude swim and then had sexual intercourse in the pool, vaginally and anally."

Reginald felt feverish.

Faithless bitch. Seductress. Liar.

"Are you still all right, Mr Quincy?" Davis asked.

Not trusting himself to speak, Reginald nodded. Damn, damn, damn her to eternal hellfire. He'd trusted her, cared for her, and she had made a mockery of his tenderest feelings. All the sweet things she said to him were lies. Every kind word, every loving gesture, more lies. Maryann Van Cunt had been after him for only one reason – she wanted to get her greedy, grasping hands on the Quincy money. The hair on the back of his neck rose as he realized how well she had practised her deceit.

"Miss Van Kamp," Davis droned on, "owns her own home in Sunnyslope. She payed thirty-five thousand for it, and the mortgage balance is twenty-seven thousand and change."

Reginald felt beads of sweat pop out on his forehead. So she'd been lying about the house too. Her devotion to a dying aunt was nothing more than a sham.

Had the bitch told him the truth about anything?

18

MARCH 10, 1989

Liz stayed in California long beyond her original plans. At first she used the extra days to get to know her mother and brother all over again – to integrate the girl she had been with the woman she had become. It had been a period of healing and re-awakened love.

Malka Kantorwitz, having lived beyond her doctor's most optimistic predictions, died in her sleep a week after Liz arrived in Los Angeles.

Liz had called Rick several days earlier to say she wouldn't be back as scheduled. Now, she telephoned him again. "I've had another change of plans," she explained. "I won't be back for a few more days."

She had been expecting Rick to object, to say he was carrying too much of a load and that she was needed in Scottsdale. Instead, he replied, "If I were vacationing at L'Hermitage, I wouldn't be in any hurry to get back either. Stay as long as you like. You've earned some time off."

"Thanks for your co-operation," she replied. "One of these days I'm going to find a way to show how much faith I have in your ability."

She spent five more days with Jacob, first seeing to their mother's funeral and then closing the apartment. She and Jacob said their goodbyes at Los Angeles International Airport. He was planning to emigrate to Israel while Liz was returning to Arizona. Dismayed by the depth of her loss as she said farewell to her newly-rediscovered brother, she found herself clutching his hand as if she were the child and he the parent.

"Don't look so sad," Jacob said, patting her shoulder. "I'll be back for the unveiling in a year."

"As much as I would love to see you, you don't need to come all the way back from Israel to see to mother's tombstone. I can take care of it."

"You've come a long way in the last two weeks," he replied, "but you still don't understand me – or our faith. Getting together one year after a death, listening to a rabbi say the prayer for a Woman of Valour over our mother's grave, is an important tradition. You may look at the whole thing as a bother, a bit of medieval foolishness. But traditions come from common sense – an understanding of human nature. The next time we see each other we won't be thinking of mother the way she was these last few weeks. We'll be able to dwell on happier times."

Just then her plane was announced and Liz hugged him hard. "A year it will be. Good luck in Israel. I hope it turns out to be everything you want."

Back in the familiar comfort of her own home, Liz felt certain Jacob had made the right choice about his future. Hassids had power in Israel these days. He would undoubtedly do well there. She could only hope the choices she had made about her own future would be as wise. For Jacob was running to something, while she feared she was running away.

Glancing at her watch, she put the morning paper down on the coffee table. There was nothing more to be gained from analysing her motives. Her plans were made. Hank was due any minute. The time had come to end his tutelage, to cut the last tie that bound her to Alan.

When the doorbell rang, she called, "I'll get it, Rosita," and hurried to answer it herself.

Hank stood there, a solemn look on his face. "I was very sorry to hear about your mother," he said.

"I got your card, and the flowers were lovely. I wish you had known Malka. She was quite a woman."

"Then you must take after her," Hank responded sotto voce.

Rosita appeared almost at once, carrying a tray laden with cups of steaming hot chocolate, the spicy Mexican variety, and cinnamon-dusted churros she had made early that morning.

"*Buenas dias*, Rosita," Hank said, taking the tray from her hands. Although he and Liz still had an occasionally adversarial relationship, he and Rosita had hit it off from the start and the housekeeper always prepared special treats when she knew Hank was coming.

"I'm glad you're here," Rosita said. "Liz has hardly eaten since she got back from California. Perhaps you can convince her to take better care of herself."

"I'll do what I can," Hank replied.

He was as good as his word. During the next half hour, while he kept the conversation to inconsequential matters, he tried to persuade Liz to join him as he consumed three churros and several cups of Rosita's specially-blended chocolate himself.

But Liz had no appetite. She was anxious to get on with their business and wasted no time after the dishes had been cleared. "You've come a long way since we began working together," she began.

"That's quite a compliment, coming from you."

"I had my doubts about your ability to become a competent master dealer. Now, I understand why Alan chose your for the job."

"That cuts both ways. Five months ago when you telephoned and insisted we meet, I would have avoided it if I could. If you hadn't been willing to teach me, I'd have made a terrible mess of Alan's affairs."

She smiled. They were beginning to sound like a mutual admiration society. "Things worked out for both of us. I kept Alan's work in the gallery and you got the help you needed. However, I didn't ask you here to talk about the past."

Hank's brow furrowed. He had a what's-Liz-up-to-now? look on his face that almost made her laugh. So much for their mutual admiration society, she thought. "You don't need to look so concerned, Hank. I wanted to see you in person to tell you that the time has come to end our sessions."

Hank's frown deepened.

"From everything you said on the phone," Liz went on, "you didn't have any problems you couldn't handle while I was gone. The dealers, the collectors, the museum people, all turn to you now when something comes up. The show at the Guggenheim is set. You're more than capable of carrying on without any help. Another month and the Scottsdale season will be over." She hesitated, but asked her next question anyway, even though she knew it was none of her business. "Will you be joining Alan in Santa Fe this summer?"

"For a while. Eleanor has two weeks vacation coming. She's going with me."

"I'm sure Alan will be delighted to see you both." Liz closed her eyes briefly, warding off the pangs of loss. First Alan, now her mother and Jacob, even Hank. She was so tired of having to say goodbye.

Then, gathering her courage, she said, "Since it looks like we may not see each other for quite a while, there's something else I want to tell you."

Rick paced his cramped living room, reviewing his accomplishments. What a stroke of luck it had been, having Liz leave town unexpectedly. Now that she was back he was constantly looking over his shoulder, wondering if or when she would catch on to what he had really been doing.

The bank accounts were in place, the slides of Longchase's Guggenheim paintings were in his possession, and he'd completed the list of potential clients. He even had a first-class, one-way ticket to Acapulco in his briefcase. The time had come to put the rest of his plan in motion. Still, he hesitated.

There had been a moment on the night of the Longchase opening, seeing the genuine concern in Liz's eyes after he walked into the gallery covered with his own blood, when Rick had actually considered abandoning his carefully-crafted scheme. That night he realized Liz cared for him. The problem was she didn't care enough. And by her own admission, she never would.

He had to start taking care of number one, he admonished himself; looking ahead instead of looking back. That meant getting to work. But instead of making himself comfortable on the sofa and picking up the phone, he stood rooted in place. Being at home in the morning, if you could call a lousy apartment with rented furniture home, felt strange.

In his year and a half with the gallery he'd grown accustomed to hustling clients from breakfast to the cocktail hour, and often on into the evening if the client happened to be female and lonely. Selling expensive art to a woman like that was laughably easy. A few dinners, a sympathetic ear and he had her opening up her chequebook – her legs too if he was in the mood.

He'd done almost as well with the gallery's other, less vulnerable clients. The secret of selling was to find out what the customer wanted and then deliver the goods.

"Art buyers aren't just purchasing paintings or sculpture," Liz had told him when he first went to work for her, "they are buying into a whole concept of themselves as people with taste and breeding."

How right she had been. Selling expensive art had as much to do with snob appeal and social cachet as it did with aesthetics. No one exemplified that simple fact more than the couple whose name appeared at the head of the list on Rick's coffee table. He walked across the room, settled on the sofa, picked up his hand written notes and read the first names. Howard and Skip Lundren. They lived in Manhattan he recalled, but loved spending time in Scottsdale where they could play at being big fish in a little pond.

Lundgren was in what he laughingly referred to as the trash business, although what he actually did was own a number of highly profitable landfills. He'd made a fortune as a glorified garbage man. But Rick knew that Lundgren's wife wasn't satisfied with just being wealthy. Skip, bless every carefully-frosted hair on her head, aspired to being a member of the haut monde. That made the Lundgrens ideally suited to Rick's needs.

Reaching for the phone, he resolutely punched in their number.

"What's on your mind?" Hank gave Liz a searching look.

She took a deep breath and wet her lips. She wasn't quite sure why she wanted Hank to be the first person to know about her past. No, damn it, she was sure. Hank was her link to Alan, a tenuous tie at best, but all she had. Alan might hate her forever. Somehow, that made winning Hank's approval and understanding even more critical. "I want to tell you about my family."

He looked perplexed. "I was surprised when you telephoned to cancel our meetings because your mother was ill. You never even mentioned her before."

"Would you tell me something?"

He nodded, his dark eyes probing hers.

"Have you ever been ashamed of being a Navajo?"

"Sure." The beginnings of a smile illuminated his features, making him look less forbidding, more accessible. "I guess there comes a time when every kid wishes they were someone else. My younger sister used to be convinced she was adopted. But she outgrew it."

"I didn't," Liz said quietly. "I've spent my entire life feeling ashamed of who and what I was. You see, my name isn't Liz Kant. It's Rachel Kantorwitz. I was born a Hassidic Jewess."

Hank's eyebrows threatened to meet his hairline. Liz had always been chary of talking about her past, he recalled. Being a well-reared Navajo, he never asked her any personal questions. Occasionally, she had offered some tit-bit about her past – that she had graduated from Stanford with a minor in art and a major in business, gone on to New York where she successfully managed a number of galleries befome coming to Scottsdale to open her own. He assumed that she came from an upper-class background. But now, confronted with the truth, he remembered their first meeting at The Glass Door, when he had wondered what tribe she came from.

At last he knew.

Liz's voice returned him to the present. "I grew up in a small Hassidic enclave in Los Angeles. My father was a *zaddik*. He devoted his life to studying the Torah, instead of making a living."

Hank looked even more perplexed.

"Do you know anything about Hassids?"

"About as much as you know about traditional Navajo ceremonies."

"Hassids are the strictest, most devout of the Jewish sects," Liz explained. "They are the living representatives of an ancient tradition. Hassidic men wear side-curls, prayer shawls and phylacteries tied to their wrists, and both sexes dress in black."

Hank nodded his comprehension. "I've seen pictures of them. But," he halted for a moment and scratched his head, "I'm having a hell of a problem equating those pictures with you."

"Nevertheless, I was born a Hassid. For the first time in my life, I think I'm going to be able to accept it. You see, I turned my back on my roots a long time ago. I ran away from home a week before my eighteenth birthday. Stanford University had just offered me a scholarship," she said, beginning the story that she concluded half an hour later with the recounting of her trip to Los Angeles and its outcome.

"So you see, I was ashamed of who I was . . . and then I was ashamed of being ashamed. I got trapped in an endless round of denial and deception."

"Why are you telling me?" Hank asked when she finished. "Alan's the one you ought to be talking to. I don't see why you never told him the truth."

She had been expecting the question. "Do you remember the way he was when he first came to the gallery?"

"Of course. Having you take him on was like a dream come true."

"You must realize how much he needed someone like Liz Kant to believe in him. After we fell in love, I was afraid to tell him the truth. By then I knew how much he valued honesty, and my entire adult life had been a lie. So I kept putting off telling him, and the longer I waited, the more impossible it became."

"Everything you say is true, but I still don't understand. You and Alan were so close . . ."

"Were we?" Liz interrupted. "I'm not so sure. I was never able to forget that he was an Apache, and I don't think he completely accepted the fact that he had fallen in love with an Anglo. Do you realize that Alan never once took me to his reservation, never introduced me to his family?"

"I didn't know." Hank's eyes narrowed. "Does anyone else know about your past?"

"Just my brother, Jacob. He's my only living relative. And now you."

"May I tell Alan?"

"No," she said firmly. "You have to promise me that you won't. Too much has happened. We can't get back what we lost. In any case, he's involved with another woman, a woman who can give him the children he's always wanted."

Hank and Liz stared at each other wordlessly for one long moment, each wanting to say more – but knowing it would be pointless.

Rick arrived at the gallery late in the afternoon, sauntering through the front door with the casual insouciance of a man who didn't have a care in the world, even though he felt thoroughly wrung-out by the long hours he'd already put in on the phone back in his apartment.

"Liz has been asking for you," the girl at the front desk said.

"Tell her I'll be right there," he replied, fixing a confident smile on his lips.

Instead of going directly to her office, he went to his cubicle at the back of the gallery to give himself time to calm down. Sitting down at his desk, he took an immaculate, monogrammed handkerchief from his pocket and wiped his brow. Liz couldn't possibly know anything. He'd sworn everyone he spoke to that morning to secrecy.

There were the usual messages on his desk from customers who wanted him to come out and rehang a painting, and decorators who wanted to see the gallery's portfolio. He ignored them and, refolding the handkerchief, returned it to his pocket. There were a dozen reasons why Liz would want to see him, he reassured himself, none of which had anything to do with the calls he had made that morning. But his hands were icy when he reached for the ringing telephone.

"Rick, I want to see you in my office," Liz said without preamble.

"I'll be right there," he responded.

Although his underarms were damp as he walked into her office a few minutes later, his smile never faltered. "What can I do for you?" he asked amiably.

"Do you have a little time?"

Rick kept his voice steady. "I always have time for you."

"First, I want to say I'm very grateful for the way you've handled yourself the last few weeks. From all reports, you did a terrific job of managing the gallery in my absence."

"I was just doing what I get paid for."

"Thanks in part to my confidence in you, I've been able to consider a new venture." She took a cigarette from the open pack on her desk and Rick hurried to offer her a light.

"Six months ago," Liz went on, "I borrowed a great deal of money with the intention of opening a gallery in New York."

"I didn't know." Rick could feel the hair on the back of his neck prickle. Half the phone calls he made that morning had been to collectors in New York.

"I was a bit premature in taking out the loan. But now, I think the time is ripe to put that money to use."

All Rick could manage was a nod. He had no idea what the hell she was talking about.

"I'm planning to open a gallery in New York, hopefully somewhere on 57th."

Rick sagged into the chair across from her desk, his spine almost melting into its contour. Not trusting himself to speak, he continued to smile although the muscles in his cheeks ached from the effort.

"What do you think of the idea?" she asked.

"Exciting," he croaked, pausing to clear his throat, "very exciting. A gallery on 57th will certainly put you in the centre of things. You can count on my help."

"I was hoping you'd feel that way." Liz gazed at him intently. "How would you like to manage this gallery permanently? It would mean a substantial raise, and I'd be willing to give you a virtually free hand here. In time I'd even consider letting you buy in."

Excitement coursed through him. A substantial raise would undoubtedly put him in the six-figure income bracket, and a hell of a lot of prestige went with the job she was offering him. A couple of years and he'd be somebody, a person to be reckoned with in the art world. It was a sweet deal any way he looked at it.

Liz's eyes continued to probe his. "Well, Rick, what do you say?"

God-all-mighty. What could he say? He'd been handed the opportunity of a lifetime – and it was too fucking late. Christ! If only she'd made the offer yesterday, before he started calling people. His smile froze on his face.

"Great," he muttered.

Maryann put down her paint brush and stepped back. Shit. The new painting was out of balance, the colours garish. She'd been creating a steady stream of crap for a month, making mistakes she hadn't made in years. At times like this she couldn't help wondering if she had any talent at all. If she didn't need the money so badly, she would have taken great delight in trashing the still-wet painting.

Instead, she headed for the bottle of Scotch she kept in the kitchen. She'd just filled a glass when the telephone rang. Please let it be Murph, she thought as she picked it up and said, "Hello."

"Maryann, this is Liz. If you've got a minute, we need to talk."

Maryann's heart sank. Liz sounded serious. "I was just taking a break from work."

"Your work is what we need to talk about. The canvasses you delivered while I was out of town are disappointing," Liz said, her soft tone belying the harshness of her words as she went on. "They just aren't up to the gallery's standards. In fact, I'd like you to pick them up."

"I'm sorry. I know I haven't been doing well, but I've had some personal problems."

"If you want to stay with the gallery, you're going to have to learn to separate your private life from your creative one," Liz admonished, adding, "I don't mean to sound harsh."

Next she'll say this hurts me more than it hurts you, Maryann thought, wishing she could get angry. Unfortunately, Liz was only saying what Maryann already knew. "I guess it won't make any difference if I tell you I've been doing my best."

"If you keep on doing your best I'm sure things will work out. They usually do," Liz replied brightly, too brightly, as if she was trying to convince both of them that she believed it. "Don't forget to pick up those paintings and if you've got some others finished, I'd be happy to look at them."

After Liz said goodbye, Maryann continued to stare at the telephone, wondering what else could go wrong in her life? She didn't have to wait long to find out. This time Murph was on the other end of the line.

"Before I say anything else," he began, "I want you to know how much I like you."

Here it comes, she thought, another stab in the back.

"I had a terrific time the other night, and I had every intention of seeing you again. But . . . remember me mentioning I'd broken up with someone I'd been seeing for a long time?"

Maryann grunted her assent.

"Well, that someone is back in my life. If she wasn't, I guarantee I'd be calling to ask you out to dinner instead of saying goodbye. All I can say is I'm sorry."

"It's all right, Murph. I understand, and I appreciate your letting me know." It wasn't much consolation, but at least she wouldn't spend the next few weeks wondering why she didn't hear from him, and thinking she'd struck out again.

Screw it, she thought, returning to her studio. Screw everything, Liz, Murphy, the whole fucking phony art world, but especially Reginald Ambrose Ardmore Quincy. It was his fault she couldn't keep her mind on her work. Even if he was out of town the way Keith said . . . well, they had telephones out of town, didn't they?

Taking a palette knife, she slashed at the failed painting, puncturing the canvas in half a dozen places. And then she began to weep. Tears spilled down her cheeks in black streaks, coloured by the heavy coat of mascara on her lashes. She could feel her nose turning red the way it did when she cried. But for once in her life, she didn't care how she looked. Sitting down on the only chair in the room, she gave in to great heaving sobs.

Just when she thought she had a terrific future and someone to share it with, that rotten old buzzard's luck came home to roost. Shivering, she wiped her damp eyes and tried to turn off the negative thoughts that crowded her mind. Get back to work, that was the thing to do. Wiping her dripping nose with her shirt sleeve, she took the tattered canvas from the easel.

She was underpainting a new one when the phone rang for the third time that afternoon. It's just got to be Reginald, she thought, trying to pour out a flood of positive vibrations as she rushed to pick up the receiver.

"Hello," she breathed into the mouthpiece, trying for her most irresistible little-girl voice.

"Is that you, my dear?" Reginald asked, sounding as if he'd spoken to her just the day before instead of ignoring her existence for a month.

"Reginald, you naughty boy," she chided, trying not to sound shrill, "I've been worried out of my mind about you. Where in the world are you, and why haven't you called?"

"I'm in Boston," he said, although she'd have sworn, from the clarity of their connection, that he couldn't be more than a few miles away. "I've always been meaning to telephone, but I wanted to be sure I had good news."

"Then something is wrong?"

"It's Mother," he replied. "She had a heart attack. The doctors have discussed the need for a triple bypass. You have no idea how frantic I've been. I couldn't bring myself to talk to anyone about it – not even you. But Mother's so much better that I expect to return to Scottsdale in a few days."

"I've missed you. You'll never know how much I've missed you," Maryann said fervently, so happy to hear his voice that she almost wept again. Then, remembering her impassioned night with Murph, she silently vowed she wouldn't look at another man as long as she lived.

"How is your Aunt Harriet?"

"How sweet of you to ask," she replied. "I wish I had good news like you, but she's worse."

She could have sworn she heard a muffled laugh before Reginald replied, "Please give her my best. And now, my dearest, I want to make sure you'll be free when I get home. I'm very anxious to see you."

So great was her relief that her knees suddenly gave way and she slid to the floor. "I'll be waiting for you, Darling."

"Good. I'm planning a very special party in your honour when I get back."

"Ooh, you know how I feel about parties," Maryann cooed. "I can hardly wait."

19

MARCH 25, 1989

Maryann turned from side to side, enjoying her reflected image. If you've got it, flaunt it, she thought, staring into the deep valley of her own cleavage. Her breasts rose from her dress's plunging neckline like twin Vesuviuses. Her life had been shaped by possession of size forty double D mammary glands, her history recorded in the names of the men who had lusted after them, and her new outfit – bought especially for this evening – showed them off to perfection.

Tonight she would be the guest of honour at Reginald's home. He had told her it would be a coming-out party of sorts, a long-awaited chance to meet all his friends. She felt so proud. Intending to do right by him, to make his friends sit up and take notice, she spent hours looking for just the right outfit. Archer had been too busy to act as a fashion consultant, but that no longer mattered. After all those months of pretending to be a real lady, Maryann had almost convinced herself she was. Her taste was as good as anyone's.

For the first time since she'd started dating Reginald, she felt totally satisfied with her appearance. Considering all the drab outfits she'd worn on their previous dates, he was in for a surprise when he saw how dishy she could be if she gave herself half a chance. Humming "This Could be the Start of Something Big", she turned out the bedroom light and waltzed into the living room. The bleak

301

sense of gloom and doom that had hovered over her like Los Angeles smog during Reginald's absence, had been replaced by euphoria.

"Are you free the evening of March 25?" he'd asked when he got back from Boston. "I think it would be the perfect night to have our little get together."

"I can't tell you how much I'm looking forward to meeting your friends. Who have you invited?" She'd expected him to name names she knew from reading the society columns.

"Shame on you," Reginald scolded. "I'm not going to tell you. I want the evening to be a complete surprise."

"I just want to be sure Archer is at the top of the guest list."

"But her husband is out of town. And I'm only asking couples."

"Pretty please?"

"Now, Maryann," Reginald said sternly, "I'm quite sure your friend wouldn't want to come by herself. And, this may sound a bit old-fashioned, but I don't want to be put in the position of arranging a date for a married woman."

"I guess I understand," Maryann had said, trying not to sound too disappointed.

"I'll tell you what. Why don't you keep the party a secret. If Archer doesn't know about it, her feelings won't be hurt."

Despite Maryann's prying and teasing, Reginald refused to tell her anything more.

The next day she couldn't help telling Archer about the party. "I hope you aren't upset about not being invited," she finished.

"Not a bit," Archer had replied equably. "Reginald is quite right about not wanting an extra woman, especially if he's planning a sit-down dinner."

Now, turning out the lights in her bedroom, Maryann felt sure she was in for the time of her life. Waiting for the

302

limousine Reginald was sending, she refused to dwell on how much she was going to miss Archer tonight. Having a familiar face at the party would have been reassuring. But Maryann was determined not to let anything negative spoil her enjoyment of the evening. When she and Reginald came back from their honeymoon, she'd make damn good and sure to have Archer over to the house whenever she pleased.

Sitting on the arm of the sofa carefully so as not to crease her new dress, she closed her eyes and surrendered to the fantasy of what life would be like once she became Mrs Reginald Quincy. She pictured herself hostessing a series of teas, brunches, lunches and dinners – attended by Archer and Liz and anyone else she wanted to entertain in the lavish home that would soon be hers. Before long the society columnists would be begging for invitations. She'd be the hostess the Quincy name deserved. Her tables would be set with fine bone-china and heavy silver, and she'd serve real gourmet food like that nouvelle pizza from California.

She was brimming with happiness, her living room awash with positive feelings when a knock on the front door roused her from her reverie. She rushed to open it and there stood Reginald's butler, Keith.

"Good evening, Madame," Keith said, his respectful tone clashing with the way his eyes roved her body before catching and holding on her cleavage. "You're looking especially lovely tonight, Madame. If you're ready, Mr Quincy is most anxious for the party to begin."

Reginald paced from room to room, too keyed-up to sit calmly waiting for Maryann's arrival. All his senses were heightened in anticipation of the evening. His beloved paintings seemed to glow with colour as he went from room to room. The complex counterpoint of a Haydn concerto, piped through the house on the intercom, flowed over him. As he walked into the turreted entry the scent

303

of fresh flowers filled his nostrils, the crisp aroma of white carnations subtly mingling with the sweet bouquet of virginal white roses. Burying his face in the bouquet, he breathed in deeply.

Intensely, almost painfully aware of the rhythmic pounding of his own heart, he felt more alive than he had at any time since coming to Phoenix. Remembrance of other nights like the one he anticipated brought a surge of warmth to his groin, and his penis strained against the silken fabric of his boxer shorts.

When Keith escorted Maryann into the drawing room a few minutes later, Reginald was ready for the evening's entertainment to begin.

Quel horreur, he thought, surveying the dress. Had she just once worn such a blatantly tacky gown on their previous dates, it wouldn't have taken a private detective to tell him who she really was. He had to give Maryann credit. She had played the loving little lady to the hilt. Marriage to her would have been the grossest *mésalliance*.

Maryann had been looking around the empty room, patting her hair, smoothing her dress with nervous little gestures. "Where is everyone?" she asked, wondering why the house seemed empty. She half expected guests to pop up from behind the furniture, shrieking "Surprise!"

"I thought we'd have a private drink before the evening begins, just the two of us," he replied, barely able to conceal his distaste as he gripped her arm and propelled her toward a chair.

"I just can't stand surprises," Maryann said, settling herself. "Look," she indicated her own naked arms, "I've got goose-bumps, just wondering what you're up to. Sugah, you've kept me in suspense far too long. Won't you tell me who all's coming?"

"My guests are most anxious to meet you, my dear," he replied. "I think we're going to have a splendid time tonight. Just splendid. But first things first." He reached for the iced Moët et Chandon nestling in a silver wine bucket on the coffee table.

There was no reason to prolong the overture to the evening, to go on with the charade of being a devoted fiancé – except for the exquisite pleasure he took in putting off Maryann's punishment. She looked up at him so trustingly, her bovine eyes as placid as a cow's and just about as intelligent.

"Ooh," she cooed, "you know I adore bubbly."

It was an expression he'd come to detest. A woman of genuine breeding would never call a wine like Moet-Chandon bubbly. As he recalled, Maryann had used the expression the first night they met. He should have taken notice then, should have got a warning signal from her lower class usage of the King's English.

Thinking back, there were dozens of things that should have alerted him to her true nature. But, in his desire to start a new life, he'd permitted himself to be taken in. Now he realised that even her skills as a painter were marginal. She was no Cassatt or O'Keefe. In a burst of fury, he'd slashed his own Van Kamps the day he learned the truth about their creator. Destroying the paintings had given him fleeting satisfaction. But it was nothing compared to the satisfaction he would experience by this evening's end.

His hands clenched involuntarily as he thought of all Maryann's lies. Tomorrow or the next day, he would telephone his mother and tell her the engagement was off. How he dreaded hearing her response. She might not actually say, I told you so, but he damn well knew she would be thinking it. Never again would he make the mistake of trusting or confiding in a woman. No matter what happened tonight, it couldn't possibly pay Maryann back for the injury she'd inflicted.

"To our little party," he said, draining his glass.

"To our party," she echoed, looking around the room as if she expected new arrivals to materialize out of the woodwork.

He reached for her hand and helped her to her feet. "Let me show you to one of the guest rooms so you can freshen-up."

Squeezing his hand, she smiled back. "You're so thoughtful."

He had to bite his lip to keep from laughing as he opened the drawing room's double doors. The Haydn concerto effectively masked any other noises in the house as he led her upstairs. Looking back over his shoulder, he saw her ridiculous dress shimmering in the gloom, her white face rouged and mascaraed to excess. Painted slut.

"When are our guests arriving?" she asked, as he threw open the door to one of the guest rooms. All the lights were on inside and she blinked, owl-like, in the sudden brightness.

"They should be here by the time you finish powdering your nose," he soothed.

Stepping into the bathroom, Maryann locked the door behind her. A quick survey assured her she was alone. It was a perfectly ordinary john – if you considered opulence ordinary – with soft grey porcelain fixtures complete right down to a bidet. Silver wallpaper and dove grey towels, the terry cloth so thick and luxurious that it looked like velvet, were reminders of Reginald's wealth. But she ignored them and rechecked the lock on the door before lowering herself on the pot to take a long overdue, nervous pee.

No doubt about it, she was spooked. Something was wrong. She'd felt it from the moment Keith arrived on her doorstep. He'd been civil enough, but there was a peculiar, speculative look in his eye every time she caught him glancing at her in the limousine's rearview mirror. Reginald had the same peculiar expression when he greeted her, although he'd quickly buried it under a welcoming smile.

She'd expected his home to be blazing with light and full of people when she arrived. Instead, it had an almost ominous quiet. There were no caterers bustling about like they did at Liz's parties, no musicians, no smell of food to indicate a celebration was in the offing. It didn't add up. And that death's head grin Reginald gave her before she shut the bathroom door had been positively unnerving.

Suddenly, she longed to be safe within her own four walls. She looked around the bathroom, searching for another way out. Seeing a narrow door, she tiptoed over and opened it ever so quietly. Row upon row of dove grey towels were stacked on the closet shelves in front of her. She bit her lip hard. Seeing her own frightened face in the mirror over the sink brought her up short. She was being ridiculous, imagining bogeymen lurking behind closed doors and disaster waiting around every corner.

She could almost hear her mother saying, "Maryann, Sugah, you've got too much imagination and not enough common sense!"

All the negative vibrations she'd been sending out would ruin the evening if she let them. Standing in front of the mirror, she forced herself to smile brightly.

"You're going to have the time of your life tonight," she promised her reflected image. "This party is for you, and you're not going to let a bad case of jitters spoil it."

Reaching into her evening bag, she took out her lipstick, powder and blush and began working on her face.

Reginald watched Maryann disappear into the bathroom and waited until he heard the lock click into place before stepping into the darkened hallway where Keith waited. "You can bring your friends in now," he said.

Keith nodded. "They're in the next room. We're ready to rock and roll."

By the time Reginald saw the handle of the bathroom door turn again, signalling Maryann's imminent re-appearance, Keith's three friends were standing near the guest room's king-size bed. In the past, Reginald had enjoyed this sort of evening more if the men who participated were young and well-built. Tonight, Keith had chosen his cohorts exceptionally well.

The biggest of the threesome was also the most physically intimidating. He was a rugged-looking brute, unshaven, with a broken nose and a boxer's heavily-muscled body. A thick penis bulged against his jeans. Reginald's eyes lingered on it appreciatively before he turned to the other two men. They were better dressed, but a quick glance revealed they were equally aroused, excited by the imminent prospect of taking part in a gang-bang.

Reginald retreated to the throne-like chair he'd asked Keith to place at the side of the bed earlier in the day. He had just taken his seat when Maryann made her entrance. Her eyes widened when she saw the men grouped around the bed.

"Who the hell are these jerks?" she demanded angrily, mingled fear and surprise widening her eyes.

"Don't be rude to our guests, my dear."

She looked at him in disbelief. "These are your friends? You've got to be kidding."

Feeling she'd walked into the middle of a bad dream, she closed her eyes firmly. Please God, don't let this be happening, she prayed. But when she opened her eyes again the men were still there, and Reginald still sat on the chair by the bed with that awful smile on his face.

Archer looked up from her book to the clock on the mantle. Maryann must be at Reginald's mysterious party by now, she thought. It was an event Archer was only too happy to miss, but she hoped Maryann was having the time of her life. If anyone deserved a little happiness, Maryann did. The problem was, Archer couldn't quite accept Reginald as its source. Something about him bothered her.

Despite Maryann's firm belief that he was a sweet, considerate man who wanted nothing more than to settle down, Archer couldn't quite figure him out.

Stretching, she got up from the sofa to put another log on the fire. Once Maryann and Reginald got married, she was going to have to put her personal prejudice aside. For a moment she considered picking up the phone and wishing them both well.

No, she decided almost at once. They were in the middle of a party and Reginald would undoubtedly resent her intrusion or worse still, think she was angling for a last minute invitation.

Returning to her place on the sofa, Archer curled up again, staring into the flames. Tomorrow morning Maryann was bound to telephone and tell her all about the evening.

Maryann screamed as the men grabbed her and dragged her to the bed.

"For God's sake, Reginald, don't just sit there," she sobbed, struggling against her captors. "Call the police."

"You don't seem to understand. These are our guests, my dear. You're supposed to keep them entertained."

She screamed again and kept right on screaming, kicking, clawing, scratching as her clothes were torn away. And then she realized no one would hear her. Reginald's house was far from the nearest neighbour. Fighting was useless. The cavalry wasn't going to ride to her rescue.

She stopped resisting as Keith and the other men forced her down on the bed. Don't fight a rapist or you might get killed, isn't that what the police advised? Shutting her eyes tight, she made up her mind to play dead. A mouth closed on one of her naked breasts while a pair of strong hands forced her legs apart. But a series of disjointed words filtered into her consciousness. Tits . . . ass . . . cunt. They were talking about her as if she were a piece of meat, and she knew they would use her like one.

Then, hearing Reginald's voice, she opened her eyes. He was looking directly at her, into her, through her, as he took her engagement ring from her hand.

309

"She's all yours, *messieurs*," he said, pocketing her diamond.

It was the final indignity. That ring had been her talisman. She wailed out her anguish and terror.

Her cry was still vibrating on the air when the men began to work on her in earnest. Hands, lips, tongues, were all over her body – probing, squeezing, hurting. She tried to find a hiding place inside her mind, to shut out what they were doing to her. Concentrate, she commanded, willing herself to visualize the first painting she had ever sold, and the wonderful feeling she had when she got paid for it.

Someone forced her legs so far apart that her hip joints ached. Cold air chilled the most intimate parts of her body. A penis pressed hard against her vagina, but she was too tight and dry to permit easy entry. It pressed harder. God, it hurt. She heard a moaning sound, and realized she had made it. The man inside her pushed faster and deeper, his groans joined hers.

Then a weight pressed on her rib cage and a rank odour filled her nostrils. Someone's hand prised her jaws apart. She gagged as an engorged penis violated her mouth. She could almost ignore what was being done to the lower part of her body, but the organ in her mouth thrust so deep into her throat that she gagged. She swallowed convulsively, choking on her own vomit.

They came at her in pairs now, and she lost track of who was doing what to her until they turned her over onto her stomach. Then a new kind of agony raced up her rectum, erupting from her mouth in a tormented scream. She didn't know when she fainted. When she revived, she swam up through a grey mist to find they had finally finished. The four men were gone. Turning on her side, she vomited over the edge of the bed.

"God, Keith, you went too far again," she heard Reginald saying somewhere in the background.

"Don't blame me," Keith replied. "You're the one who

gives the orders. If you'll get the hell out of here, I'll take care of things."

The bedroom door shut with an explosive crash and Maryann knew she was alone with Keith.

"You'd better get dressed," he said.

She wanted to get out of that room – God, how she wanted that. Brushing at the vomit that fouled her face and hair, she tried to sit up. Pain shot through the lower part of her body. Looking down, she saw her own blood mingled with the semen that soiled the sheets. Swaying to her feet, she willed her legs to carry her to the bathroom. Keith trailed after her, carrying her clothes.

"I'd make it fast if I were you," he warned.

She shut the bathroom door and staggered to the sink. Turning on the taps, she rinsed her face. Then, soaking a hand towel, she dabbed ineffectually at her stained and bruised thighs and crotch. Putting on her clothes took a supreme effort of will. Her dress was torn and she had to hold it together with one hand. She supported herself with the other, leaning against the walls as she dragged herself from the room.

The house was utterly quiet but for the continuing sounds of the Haydn concerto. She tried to concentrate on the purity of the music, to ignore the fact that she had to rely on Keith to help her down the stairs and out of the front door. He put a towel on the limousine's back seat and indicated she was to sit on it.

"I'd catch hell with the boss if I let you ruin the upholstery," he explained.

She closed her eyes, refusing to think about what had happened. When they pulled up in her drive, Keith had to help her to the door. She couldn't stand the thought of him touching her, but she was too weak to do anything about it. He half carried her into the living room and deposited her on the sofa, and then he left without another word.

Reginald's party was finally over.

She didn't know how much time passed before she had

the strength to get up. The need to bathe away the blood and semen that caked her thighs and buttocks finally drove her to her feet, but her legs couldn't support her. She crawled into the bathroom, stripped off her clothes, and began to fill the tub. Glancing down at her own body, she saw a mass of purpling bruises where powerful hands had held her. Teeth marks rimmed both her nipples. An aching circle on her naked stomach told her someone had put out a cigarette there. It must have happened after she fainted. Oh God, why hadn't she been able to faint earlier?

She bathed thoroughly, drained the tub, refilled it and bathed again, sinking beneath the water to wash her hair. When she felt able to stand, she got up and douched. And then she refilled the tub a third time. Don't think about what happened, she ordered herself, knowing it would drive her crazy if she did.

But it was impossible not to think about it. The pain of her torn rectum and vagina were an unbearable reminder.

The police. She could call the police and have Reginald and Keith and those other men thrown in jail. But what good would that do? They would all be out on bail in hours. Reginald's money guaranteed it. And then what would happen to her? Would they come after her again. She looked at the pale circle on her left hand where her engagement ring had been just hours before.

Shivering in the now-cold tub, she knew she would never be safe again. "Oh, Momma," she whispered, "I'm so scared."

She began to dry herself and then realized she would have to go into the dark hall to get to her bedroom. The thought was utterly terrifying. Choking back a sob, she wrapped a towel around her body and lurching rather than walking, plunged into the dark bedroom. She flicked on the light and screamed as she saw a white-faced apparition in the mirror. It was the bag-lady who haunted her dreams. And then she realized the haunted eyes, sunken cheeks and bleeding lips were her own.

While she got into her nightgown and bathrobe an awful knowledge began to work on her mind. She would never be able to get past this night. The love she counted on had never existed. The future she dreamed of was gone. All she had was a past she couldn't face. She didn't want to know what lay in store for her, didn't think she could endure living through another day. Burying her face in her pillow, she cried until she had no more tears. But crying didn't help. It would take a river, an ocean of tears to wash away this night.

When she felt stronger she got to her feet and headed for the bathroom again. Ignoring her reflection in the mirror over the medicine cabinet, she concentrated on reading the labels on the prescription bottles inside it. Phenobarbital, valium, demerol, aspirin, the roll call of panaceas for loneliness and despair. Thank God, the small brown vials, accumulated over the past couple of years, were more than half full. She carried them to the kitchen, spilled their contents on the counter, filled a tumbler with Scotch and began swallowing.

Before she fully realized it, the glass was empty and the counter bare. It was so easy, she thought, returning to the living room, so simple. No one would ever be able to hurt her again.

She made it to the sofa just as her legs gave way. Reclining against the upholstery, she closed her eyes, feeling her own heart slow, thinking about all the things she would never do, the paintings she would never paint, the friends she would never see.

Hell. Who was she kidding? She only had one real friend. Archer. She hadn't said goodbye to Archer.

Sliping from the sofa, she crawled to the phone and dialled with already numb fingers.

Darkness began its final assault as she waited for an answer. The phone slipped from her hands. She felt herself

313

sinking into pitch black emptiness. But then a warm, white light ignited in the void. Her dead mother materialized from the incandescent blaze and came toward her, smiling and beckoning. Maryann longed to seek shelter in her mother's arms, to be finally home, safe.

Then she heard a female voice. "Who's there?" it said. "Who is this?"

"It's me, God, your friend Maryann," she tried to answer. But the words wouldn't come. In their place, a feeling of pure joy rushed up her throat and exited her mouth in a shuddering last breath. How thrilled she was that God's voice had turned out to be female.

Across town, Archer repeated, "Who's there?" several times before she hung up.

20

MARCH 28, 1989

It was a perfect March day – ideal for picnics, long leisurely walks, making love outdoors, revelling in the joys of life rather than wallowing in its sorrows. The wrong sort of day for a funeral, Archer thought, glancing out of the Mercedes' windowshield at the mild-mannered sky. Roman sat across from her, his competent hands gripping the steering wheel, a scowl furrowing his brow.

"I keep on asking why . . . why things like this happen?" she said.

"You know what they say." He looked as miserable as she felt. "Shit happens."

"I just can't get it through my head that Maryann committed suicide."

"Are the police still investigating the accidental overdose theory?"

"Nobody takes as many drugs as Maryann did by accident." Archer pushed her sunglasses firmly back on the bridge of her nose, hiding her red-rimmed eyes. "I'm certain Reginald knows much more about what happened than he's admitted."

"I don't like the man any better than you do. But other than intuition, have you got anything to go on?

"Not much. But I know that Maryann was with him before she died. I told you about the party he was giving to introduce her to his friends. She was so excited about it. Why would she kill herself just when her dreams were coming true?"

Roman's knuckles whitened on the steering wheel. Was he thinking about his wife's death? Archer wondered.

"I wish I had some answers for you," he said.

Opening her bag, she took out a tissue and wiped her nose. "I miss her so much."

Reaching across the front seat, Roman pulled her closer. "Believe me, I know how much you're hurting right now."

"Thank God you're here," she snuffled, feeling comforted by the solid warmth of his body.

"Did you tell the police about Reginald's party?"

"Yes."

"And . . ."

"Detective Gonzalez promised to look into it. But, in the long run, what difference does it make?" Archer could feel herself growing weepy again. "Nothing can bring Maryann back."

Rick took his most sombre suit from the bedroom closet, laid it out on his bed, and checked his Rolex. He had forty-five minutes to finish dressing, pick Liz up at the gallery and get to the funeral home, barely enough time even if he moved at top speed. But he couldn't seem to make himself hurry. Hell. He hated funerals. Always had, always would. They made him feel lethargic and depressed. And he couldn't afford either today.

His first instinct had been to refuse when Liz asked him to drive her to the services for Maryann. But he didn't dare do anything this late in the game to arouse Liz's suspicions. He'd been working at top speed, spending hours on the telephone, depositing cheques, moving money from one account to another, while still putting in the required hours handling the gallery's legitimate business. The prolonged all-out effort had exhausted him. Thank God, he only had three weeks to go.

Shaking his head, he picked up his trousers and pulled them on. Maryann's troubles were over. But his would just be starting if he didn't get a firm grip on his emotions. The prospect of spending the day with Liz unnerved him. He'd have to be on guard every minute, say and do the right things, make certain the wrong people didn't get a few minutes alone with her. It was going to be a bitch, he thought, adjusting his balls to the left of his crotch and zipping his fly.

An hour later, he exuded a properly solicitious manner as he helped Liz from the air-conditioned comfort of his Porsche into the cascading sunlight of the funeral home's parking lot. To his surprise, dozens of people were milling around.

"Quite a crowd," he commented.

"Archer and I were afraid the only mourners would be people from the gallery," Liz replied. "I guess we needn't have worried."

In unrelieved black, she looked unexpectedly frail. He he had to fight down the old, familiar tug of caring. She's really taking it hard, he realized, before he spied the Lundgrens out of the corner of his eye. Damn the luck. They were the last people he expected to see. He hadn't given a thought to the possibility of them flying in for the funeral. If he had, he would have done his best to prevent it.

He tried to steer Liz away from them, but it was too late. The Lundgrens were already hurrying their way.

"What a sad occasion," Howard Lundgren said, shaking Rick's hand.

"We have several of Miss Van Kamp's paintings." Skip Lundgren grabbed one of Rick's arms and gave it an intimate squeeze. "We intended to buy more," she rattled on, "but I guess that's out of the question now."

Liz seemed barely aware of what they were saying. Her eyes had been searching the crowd. "If you'll excuse me," she said, "I need a few minutes to myself before I give the eulogy."

"Of course," Rick murmured, releasing her arm and

317

restraining the wild urge to push her away from the Lundgrens.

"Liz seems pretty shaken by this whole thing," Howard commented after she had gone.

"She's very upset." Rick lowered his glance. "We all are."

"I guess this wouldn't be the right time to talk to her about the Cochise Memorial Art Fund?" Skip said.

Rick could cheerfully have strangled Skip then and there. His anger must have been evident because Howard spoke up at once.

"For God's sake, Skip, when will you learn to keep your big fat mouth shut. Rick explained the need for secrecy when he telephoned to make the offer. If Liz doesn't want to know the details until the night of the party, that's good enough for me!"

Rick took a linen handkerchief from his breast pocket and wiped his brow. "Thank you very much, Sir. I'm sure your wife didn't mean any harm, but I would appreciate it if she didn't talk to Liz today . . . at all."

"Mum's the word," Howard said, giving his wife a fierce glare. "Right, Skip?"

Skip batted her lashes at Rick. "Can't you take a little joke? I have no intention of breaking my word. And now, Rick, since we've flown all the way from New York to attend this shindig, how about sitting next to little old me during the service?"

"I'd be delighted," he replied, placing her hand in the crook of his elbow. Damn right, he'd sit next to her. He didn't plan to let her out of his sight until she was on her way back to where she came from.

No way would he permit a stupid bitch like Skip Lundgren to become his Achilles' heel.

Liz entered the chapel, pausing to get her bearings. Most of the local art world had taken time off to attend the funeral. She saw dealers she never had time to talk to during the frantic six-month Scottsdale season. The members of the Scottsdale Art Commission were seated side by side in a back row, deep in conversation. World-famous Navajo painter, R. C. Gorman, sat near the middle, taking to Danny Medina and Thom Romeo, the editor and publisher of *Art Talk*.

Moving down the centre aisle, Liz picked out other familiar faces. Amado Pena, Katalin Ehling, Delonna Roberts, Ed Mell, Nancy Young and Shirley Estes were gathered on one side of the aisle and Clifford Beck, Lawrence Lee and his wife, Mary Wyant, on the other. Liz couldn't remember seeing more talent assembled in one place.

And then she spotted Alan Longchase seated toward the front of the room, and her breath caught in her throat. She hadn't known he would be there. Automatically nodding at people she knew, Liz made her way toward the casket, moving with a robot's jerky steps.

"Are you all right?" Archer asked, taking her bag from the chair she had saved.

Not trusting herself to speak, Liz nodded a greeting. Roman De Silva was seated by Archer's side, holding her hand as if it were the most natural thing in the world. So she had been right about the two of them, Liz realized. How lucky they were to have each other today of all days.

Sunlight, muted by its passage through a pair of stained-glass windows, sifted onto Maryann's coffin, glancing off the bouquets and wreaths surrounding it. The air had a cloyingly sweet, hot-house scent. *Adonai elohenu, Adonai echod*. The Hebrew affirmation of faith rose from some long forgotten corner of Liz's mind. She wished she could say the *Kaddish*, but the solemn words drifted just out of reach in the recesses of her mind.

Biting her lower lip, she recalled her last conversation with Maryann. She couldn't help wondering how much that conversation had to do with what had happened. If

319

only she had postponed making that call for a week or two. She would have given a great deal to take back what she had said.

Missed opportunities, her life was full of missed opportunities; a tide she somehow never took at the flood.

Liz looks ghastly, Archer thought. But then, she realized she probably didn't look much better herself. She held onto Roman's hand and tried to concentrate on the casket, the flowers, the organ music. Maryann may have done without during her life. But Archer had chosen the best of everything for her funeral, paying for it with her own money. How strange the business of death was, the dollars-and-cents decisions the mind had to make while the heart cried out for relief.

But there would be no relief this day, she knew. No comfort that wrongs would be righted and justice done. Detective Joe Gonzalez had confirmed that when they spoke outside of the chapel. It had been their third meeting in as many days.

Gonzalez was a short, heavy-set man with the shrewdest brown eyes she'd ever seen, eyes that didn't go with his perpetually hang-dog expression. He looked as if he'd seen every one of humanity's foibles and they'd ruined his day, his week, his life.

After expressing his sympathy, he said, "I'll be filing my preliminary report this afternoon but, in view of your suspicions about Quincy, I wanted to tell you how things are going." He paused. "If you feel up to it."

She swallowed hard. "I want to hear it all."

"Before I begin, you ought to know that Quincy's butler, Keith Wilson, backed up everything Quincy said." Gonzalez reached in his jacket pocket and produced a dog-eared notebook. "Now, about that party Miss Van Kamp discussed with you. According to Quincy, he never intended to give a party in Miss Van Kamp's honour. Quincy asked Miss Van Kamp over to the house to tell her, as gently as possible, and I'm quoting him directly," Gonzalez said, looking at his notes, "that the engagement was off."

"Do you believe him?"

"What I do or don't believe has nothing to do with it. The only thing that counts is proof, incontrovertible evidence I can pass on to the district attorney. And frankly, I don't have any. Keith Wilson says he took Van Kamp back to her own home about eight thirty. According to Wilson, she was in tears the entire time because of the broken engagement."

"What about Maryann's neighbours? Did they see anything?"

"You know the neighbourhood. People who live in places like that rarely cooperate with the police. My men went up and down the block, but no one saw or heard a thing."

"Hell," Archer muttered.

"My sentiments, exactly," Gonzalez replied. "By the way, I ran a make on Quincy and Wilson. As I expected, Quincy is clean. But Wilson has a rap sheet – arrests for male prostitution, shop lifting, possession. And there was a more serious charge, a rape."

Archer shuddered involuntarily, thinking of Maryann spending her last hours alone with Reginald and a man like Keith Wilson.

"I wasn't going to discuss this with you today," Gonzalez continued, "but I guess I might as well get it over with. Miss Van Kamp's body had numerous bruises and contusions. The autopsy revealed that she had sexual relations before her death and, from the physical evidence, she was probably raped."

Archer sagged against Roman.

"I've heard you can match sperm to blood-types," Roman said. "Couldn't you find the rapist that way?"

"Not without a suspect." Gonzalez' hang-dog expession intensified.

321

Archer stiffened. "You're not going to give up?"

"I have to wait until we get the final lab results. But I'm afraid, considering the lack of evidence and the fact that there was no suicide note, this will go down as just another accidental overdose."

Now, with Maryann's funeral service about to begin, Archer couldn't stop thinking about the detective's parting words.

Trying to be as inconspicuous as possible, Reginald waited to enter the chapel until the service began. He wouldn't have been there at all if Keith hadn't talked him into it.

"Hell, Boss. It will look damn suspicious if you stay home," Keith had said.

"But I told the police Maryann and I broke up the night she died," Reginald objected.

"All the more reason for you to go to her funeral."

"*Merde*. I never expected her to kill herself."

"Neither did I. It's not like she was a virgin or anything. Shit! A broad who has been around the block a time or two shouldn't have gone off the deep end over a little sex." Keith had given his shoulders an eloquent shrug. "Most women would have enjoyed it."

"You should have stopped when I told you to!" Reginald insisted.

"If you recall, I did stop," Keith proclaimed his innocence. "It was the other guys who kept going after she passed out."

But Keith had been right about one thing. Attending the funeral was the prudent thing to do. A shiver of apprehension trembled through Reginald's bony frame as he settled into a back row seat while an organ thundered the strains of a requiem.

Alan had lost buddies in Vietnam. But those deaths had a predictable inevitability. There had been no predicting Maryann's end. The last time he saw her, she had been so full of life. Just thirty-six, a few years his junior, she would never finish another painting, see another sunset, laugh at a joke, love a man. Ah, there was the crux, the key word, Alan mused. Love. Had Maryann ever known the sweet solace of love?

For that matter, had he?

He'd flown in for the funeral, not only to pay his last respects to a friend and fellow artist, but – he was forced to admit – to see Liz. The past months had taught him one thing. Like it or not, he was tied to her by bonds so strong that time and distance hadn't succeeded in breaking them.

He'd been aware of her presence as soon as she arrived, had looked over his shoulder to watch her slow progress toward the front of the chapel, only turning away at the last moment so their eyes wouldn't meet. Expecting Rick to be by her side, Alan had been surprised to see her take a seat in the front row next to Archer Harrison.

Mid way through the service there was an anticipatory hush as Liz rose and moved to the lectern. When she turned to face the assembled mourners, Alan's chest tightened. She was pale, her eyes shadowed. Sorrow diminished other women. But it gave her beauty a new, haunting dimension.

"It is an honour to be asked to pay tribute to someone as talented as Maryann Van Kamp," Liz began quietly, as if she were talking to herself, "an honour I will do my best to deserve. As an art dealer, I have known many artists. Maryann was a genuine original, as a human being and as a painter. She brought joy and laughter to her friends, and beauty to the world through her work . . . and that's not a bad way for any of us to be remembered."

Holding the lectern for support, Liz paused and looked out over the crowd. There was such pain in her eyes when they finally met Alan's that he had to glance away.

Memories of the countless hours they had spent together held him captive while time and space drifted away.

Finally, he permitted Liz's voice to bring him back to the present. "Like many creative people, Maryann lived a lonely life," Liz was saying. "I think she would be surprised to see all of you here today – surprised and a little nervous. Maryann hated openings. She was never sure of her talent, her place in the art world.

"She was not the biggest or best selling artist in my gallery, but her talent shone as brightly as anyone's. Contrary to the public's perception, it is the fate of most artists to be forgotten. If they haven't achieved fame during their lifetimes, one can almost guarantee that their names will quickly fade into obscurity after they are gone.

"Today in your presence, I would like to make a promise. I will not let that happen to Maryann Van Kamp. If I have my way, and most of you know me well enough to realize that I usually do, Maryann's work will be more sought-after ten years from now than it is today."

Liz's voice had been growing in strength, and now it rang out. "When the history of south-western art is written, she will have an honoured place in it."

As her last words echoed in the large hall, Alan felt a thrill of pride. He decided to seek a moment alone with Liz to tell her how much the eulogy had moved him.

But Alan's plans evaporated when he saw Rick get up and help her back to her seat.

Although Reginald sweated profusely throughout the service, he couldn't help congratulating himself for having the daring to attend. *L'audace, toujours l'audace.*

He had been surprised by the number of mourners. But most of all, he was astonished by Liz's emotional eulogy. Reginald knew he had made a fatal error when it came to Maryann's background and breeding. It never occurred to him that he might have misjudged her talent too. Could the little whore really have had a spark of genius? Could it be that her work would actually increase in value over the coming years? What a fool he'd been, destroying Maryann's paintings in a fit of pique. Suddenly, he lusted for those lost canvasses.

After the pallbearers carried the coffin up the aisle, Reginald jumped to his feet. Moving quickly, he elbowed his way through the crowd, blinking rapidly as he emerged into the sunshine. Outside the building, people were clustering in little groups, their voices subdued. He stood conspiciously near the chapel doors, preparing, as Maryann's former fiancé, to receive their condolences.

To his eternal discomfort, no one approached him. Fidgeting, he shifted from one foot to another. He considered leaving, but it was imperative he talk to Liz before the day was over. After what seemed an eternity, he saw her emerging from the chapel on the arm of the Arts Commission chairman.

"I think your idea of having a Van Kamp retrospective at the Scottsdale Art Centre next autumn is wonderful," Reginald overheard her saying before she and the commissioner parted company.

Mon Dieu, a retrospective of Maryann's work boded very well for the future value of her paintings. He had to talk to Liz. Now!

Hurrying to her side, he blurted, "Did you really mean what you said about Maryann having a place in art history?"

Liz looked right through him.

Although he felt himelf flush, he refused to be put off. "If it would help my fiancée to gain proper recognition for her talent, I would be happy to purchase several of her paintings from you at whatever price you . . . that is, we, deem fair."

Liz turned and fixed him with an icy stare. "From what I've heard, Miss Van Kamp was not your fiancée the night she died. First you broke her heart, and now you want to profit from it. There's no way in the world I will allow you

325

to capitalize on this tragedy. As far as you are concerned, Maryann's work is not for sale."

Archer had watched Liz and Reginald with morbid fascination. Seeing Reginald recoil from Liz's angry words, Archer realized there might be a way to get to him after all.

Turning to Roman, she said, "I have to talk to Reginald."

"Are you sure you want to?"

How she loved him for looking so concerned. "No. It isn't something I want to do. It's something I have to do."

"Do you want me to go with you?"

She squeezed his hand for luck. "This is something I have to do myself."

Reginald was halfway to his car when she caught up with him. "Leaving so soon?" she asked loudly.

He looked startled. "Oh, it's you, Archer."

"Aren't you going to the cemetery?"

"I'm afraid this whole sad affair is more than I can bear."

She caught him by the arm, forcing him to face her. "What's the matter? Don't tell me you have a guilty conscience."

"I don't know what you're talking about," he replied, trying to pull free.

She held him firmly, her strong sculptor's hands tightening their grip. "I think you know a great deal about what really happened to Maryann."

"You're being ridiculous."

"I don't think I am," she proclaimed, "and neither does Detective Gonzalez."

She noticed a nerve under his left eye twitching spasmodically. People had begun to look in their direction. Archer raised her voice, suspecting Reginald would hate it if she made a scene. "You were the last person to see

326

Maryann. She was a happy woman before she went to your house. But she left it and went home to commit suicide. I think you have some explaining to do, a hell of a lot of explaining.''

His cool demeanour had been evaporating under her verbal assault. "You can't prove a thing.''

"I wouldn't be so damn sure.'' Now her voice was loud enough to carry to every corner of the crowded parking lot. "Maryann was raped the night she died. Is that how you always break your engagements?''

A shudder ran through Reginald. He could feel himself being censured, judged by the people who surrounded them. God. After today, he wouldn't be able to hold up his head in Scottsdale. And sooner or later, his mother was bound to hear that he'd been involved in another scandal.

"Leave me alone,'' he said, looking from Archer to the multitude of curious bystanders, "all of you, just leave me alone!''

Breaking Archer's hold, he hurried toward his waiting limousine, the nerve under his eye tap dancing. Yanking the door open, he threw himself into the back seat.

"You look awful,'' Keith said, allowing the engine to idle. "What the hell happened?''

"That's none of your fucking business, you son-of-a-bitch. Shut up and get the hell out of here.''

After they pulled away from the kerb, Reginald pushed the button that raised the glass divider between the driver and passenger compartments. He didn't want to look at Keith, let alone talk to him. The entire Maryann débâcle was Keith's fault, from beginning to end.

By late afternoon Archer and Roman were seated in a booth at The Glass Door, two steaming cups of Irish coffee on the table in front of them.

"Remind me never to cross you,'' Roman said, his eyes filled with admiration.

327

"I think I got to Reginald. At least I tried."

Roman reached across the table and took her hand. "You're quite a woman."

"I just wish I could have done more for Maryann."

"The crowd at the chapel was a real tribute."

"If only she had known how many people really cared about her." Archer's eyes brimmed with tears.

"Go ahead and cry." Roman handed over his handkerchief. "You've been holding it in too long."

She wiped her eyes brusquely, almost angrily. "I've already cried a lake, a river, a whole Mississippi, but it doesn't help." Reaching for the coffee, she took a large swallow. It burned its way down her throat, helping melt the lump that had been there ever since she watched Maryann's coffin being lowered into the ground.

"I know it's not much comfort right now, but the pain does go away."

"The only thing that would give me any comfort right now," Archer replied grimly, "would be knowing that the person responsible for Maryann's death was going to pay for it."

Reginald spent the afternoon in the room he once described to Maryann as his private hideaway. Four weeks ago her paintings had hung on its walls. Now, the blank spaces seemed to stare down on him accusingly. He tried reading the latest bestseller but couldn't concentrate on the printed word. Then he put on a tape of Vivaldi's *Four Seasons*, hoping to lose himself in the music. But that escape failed miserably too. Last, he poured himself a large snifter of Courvoisier and gulped it down.

There was no getting around the awful truth. He had been publicly humiliated. That he, Reginald Ambrose Ardmore Quincy, the scion of an old and powerful Boston family, should have been treated like a pariah, was unthinkable, intolerable. He should never have gone to the funeral.

Jumping to his feet, Reginald began pacing the room. If it hadn't been for Keith, he would have stayed at home. But for Keith, there might not even have been a funeral. It was Keith who hired those thugs, Keith who was at the bottom of all his troubles.

Keith. The name worked on his brain like acid on metal. Reginald's rage, ignited by self pity and fuelled by liquor, reached spontaneous combustion.

Rushing from the room, he burst into the cavernous entry hall. "Keith," he shouted, "get your ass in here this minute."

His voice bounced off the three-storey tower and echoed in the still air.

"I said get your ass in here," Reginald shouted again when the other man failed to appear.

Reginald didn't wait for a response. He hurried down an adjacent hall to the kitchen. The maid and cook were seated at the table, having coffee when he pushed the door open with an audible thud. Ordinarily, Reginald would have chastized them for loafing, but right now his mind was totally preoccupied with Keith's perfidy.

"Where's Keith?" he demanded, ignoring the frightened look on the women's faces.

The maid rose to her feet, her hands working at the edges of her apron. "I believe he went to his room, Sir."

Spinning around, Reginald stormed out.

"If I was you," the cook said after he was gone, "I'd spend the rest of the afternoon in the kitchen."

"But I'm supposed to clean Mr Quincy's room," the maid responded.

"I wouldn't go near the place, the way he's acting. Did you see the look in his eyes? If the pay wasn't so good, I'd be thinking about quitting."

Reginald was unaware of the mutiny brewing in his kitchen. He took the stairs two at a time.

Keith's room was at the end of a long hallway. When

Reginald reached it, he flung the door open so violently that it rebounded in his face, infuriating him even more.

Keith was on his bed, his pants undone, his penis engorged, a copy of *Hustler* in one hand, his dick in the other, and a joint dangling from his lower lip. His eyes had the unfocused look that drugs always produced in them.

"I told you not to smoke that shit in my house," Reginald cried out.

"It's my first joint in months." Keith sat up and fumbled with his fly.

"Lies, lies, lies." Reginald's voice rose with each succeeding word.

"I swear, Boss, I won't do it again."

The tic under Reginald's eye flared up. He could feel it twitching and pulsing, as if it had a life of its own. "Damn you," he roared. "You're no different from Maryann. The two of you are incapable of the truth. But that's what I get for dealing with scum."

His penis finally tucked in his pants, Keith got to his feet, flexing the muscles in his arms in a decidedly menacing manner. "If I were you, I wouldn't be calling people names."

"That's it. You've overstepped the bounds once too often. I want you out of here before the day is over," Reginald gave him a parting glare before leaving the room.

Keith pursued him down the hall. "What the hell do you mean by that?"

Coming to a stop so suddenly that Keith bumped into him, Reginald drew himself up to his full height and looked down at the younger man scornfully. "I know you're not very bright, but surely you understand simple English. You're fired. Pack your things and get out of here before I call the police."

"Look, Boss, I know you're upset about Maryann. But you're not thinking very clearly." Keith's tone was reasonable. The look in his eyes was not. "I know you better than you know yourself. Sooner or later, next week, next month, you'll be wanting to have another little party like the one we had the other night. And where will you be without me then?"

Not wanting to hear another word, Reginald resumed his hurried passage down the hall. Grabbing his arm, Keith detained him. It was the second time that day that someone had laid hands on Reginald.

"Don't touch me," he warned. "I'll call the police if you aren't out of here in an hour."

Keith laughed mirthlessly. "Go ahead, you fucking pervert. Call the police and I'll tell them everything about the other night with Maryann, and all the other nights in all the other towns."

Reginald slapped Keith with all his force. The next thing he knew, they were grappling with each other, pushing and shoving as they reached the top of the stairs.

Keith's hands were a powerful vice that held him fast. In an effort to break free, Reginald clawed at the other man's face, raking it with his nails. When Keith let go to touch the blood that now streamed down both of his cheeks, Reginald pushed Keith away as hard as he could. To his shock, Keith pushed back.

For a second, Reginald teetered on the top step, struggling for balance. And then he was falling, banging against the banister and the steps, tumbling head-over-heels. He clutched at the wrought iron baluster, tearing out a nail, but the cold metal repelled his frantic grasp. His last rational thought was, this can't be happening.

Feeling his femur snap and his ribs shifting in his chest, he began screaming, a long agonized wail that forced its way past the blood that was pouring from his mouth. The scream was still caroming off the rafters as Reginald's lifeless body came to rest at the foot of the stairs.

21

APRIL 22, 1989

Rick pried one eye open and then the other, staring at the woman in bed next to him.

She gazed back myopically.

"Well, hello there," he said, momentarily unable to remember either her name or where they were. He squinted at the unfamiliar room, taking in his hastily discarded clothing, his jacket tossed on a chair, his trousers and shorts jumbled together on the floor – and his brief amnesia disappeared. He was in Acapulco, having occupied the most expensive villa at the Las Brisas resort for the last three gloriously drunken days.

"Hello, yourself," the woman said, stretching luxuriously.

The sheet slid down, revealing magnificent breasts, crowned by the biggest rosy-brown nipples Rick had ever seen. He still couldn't think of her name but her remembered those nipples, the taste and texture of them in exquisite detail.

She smiled at him, her vapid pale-blue eyes as intelligent as a parakeet's. Come to think of it, she had been a much better fuck than a conversationalist.

Taking what the gods so generously offered, he moved over and took one of those memorable nipples in his mouth. It hardened instantly. He sucked with pleasure, and then turned his attention to its twin.

The woman moaned, reached for his cock, and began to

stroke along its length, circling the tip until he rewarded her efforts with a tiny viscous spurt. She massaged the fluid into his skin as if it were the most expensive face cream before disappearing under the sheet to take him in her mouth. It was then that a name of sorts came to him. He decided to call her Deep Throat. It was the last coherent thought he was to have for some time.

Three hours later, having bidden Deep Throat a grateful farewell, he sat by his villa's private pool. After ordering a Margarita from a hovering, pink-jacketed waiter, he lay back in the lounge chair. There was nothing like sun, sea air, and a well-made drink to soothe the senses. The bartender at Las Brisas was a genius when it came to Margaritas. Rick never had better.

In fact, the resort more than lived up to its reputation as a luxurious vacation hideway. Shading his eyes, he raised his head to gaze down over the tiled roof tops of Las Brisas' *casitas,* following their well-groomed descent to Acapulco Bay. According to his travel agent, this was one of the most highly touted views in the world, superior to the view of Rio from Sugar Loaf.

Far below, the Pacific had an opalescent shimmer. Overhead the sun shone in a faultlessly blue sky. Palms, flowering bougainvilleas and other greenery he couldn't identify, festooned the gardens that tumbled down to the shore, filling the air with a spicy scent. His villa, at a mere seven hundred dollars a day, was the best Las Brisas had to offer, a sybarite's dream complete with its own pool and spa as well as the services of a full-time maid. Totally secluded, it was still close enough to other resort hotels to make nightly forays to local hotspots convenient.

Best of all, Acapulco, or at least its gringo section, was literally crawling with good-looking broads. There were so many tight asses and up-tilted tits beside the various hotel pools that he hardly knew where to begin. So much pussy, so little time, he chuckled to himself. When he tired of romping with leggy beauties, he could retire

333

to the serenity of his hill-top hideaway and wallow in self-absorbed splendour. Adjusting his position so that the sun would reach his inner thighs and complete his near-perfect tan, he closed his eyes.

His escape to Acapulco had been almost too easy. The way had been paved with Liz's client's money. The cheques had started coming in a month before. By mid April, the early trickle had turned into a flood. He'd been so busy transferring money from one account to another that he hadn't had time to do much legitimate selling. Fortunately Liz had been too busy making plans for her New York gallery, as well as arranging Maryann's fall retrospective at the Scottsdale Art Centre to take notice of what he was or wasn't doing.

But she'd be forced to take notice today.

Narrowing his eyes against the sun's glare, he checked his watch. In just six hours Liz Kant was going to have the surprise of her life. How he wished he could be there to see how she handled it.

Although he hated to admit it, he missed her. The one thing that could have improved his stay in Acapulco would have been having her by his side. For a moment he succumbed to the fantasy of a bikini-clad Liz, her breasts barely covered by a wisp of cloth and that glorious red-thatched mons . . . hell, he wouldn't want anything covering that at all.

Swallowing the last of his drink, he turned off the day-dream before it aroused him. Forget Liz, he admonished himself, and concentrate on the cool two million earning interest in the bank this very minute. He planned to have one hell of a good time with that money, to really indulge himself. But more important, he intended to use it as seed money to harvest an heiress. Planning, it was all in the planning, just as tennis was all in the grip.

"You've been working so hard," Liz had said when he told her he needed a few days off to visit his ailing mother. "I just want you to know how much I appreciate everything you've done for me and the gallery. Take as much time as you need and don't worry about a thing. And Rick, if there's anything I can do to help, anything at all, don't hesitate to ask."

She'd been so damn sympathetic and concerned that he'd practically gagged on her kindness. She even wanted to drive him to the airport, an offer he quickly refused. He had flown to Acapulco the next day under an assumed name.

Trouble hadn't surfaced until he arrived. As he checked into Las Brisas, he spotted a familiar face in the lobby. At first, he wasn't sure it was Archer's husband, Louis Harrison. The guy was tanned, wearing the briefest pair of trunks, and he had a stunning, twentyish blonde on his arm. Rick had only seen Harrison a couple of times at Archer's shows, and then he'd worn conservative suits. But, after taking a better look, Rick had no doubt about the identity of the man in the lobby.

The girl looked vaguely familiar too. Rick, who prided himself on never forgetting a face, finally realized where he had seen her before. She had been with Roman De Silva at Liz's New Year's Eve party. Stacy something or other, he recalled. But this Stacy was a hell of an improvement over the earlier edition.

While Rick continued his circumspect observation, Harrison bent down and kissed the woman. It wasn't a fatherly kiss either. This was a full-blown smacker, complete with probing tongues and a slight erection on Harrison's part. Christ. They almost got it on while half a dozen hotel employees watched appreciatively.

When the passionate exchange ended, Harrison finally looked around to see who had witnessed the embrace. His eyes met Rick's and flicked away without a trace of recognition. Harrison seemed too concerned with having a blossoming hard-on in the middle of a fashionable hotel lobby to really be aware of anyone or anything else.

Rick had turned away quickly. A light sweat slicked his

palms and under-arms as he contemplated the possible consequences of Archer's husband telling her when and where he had seen Rick. For one frantic instant, he thought about blowing town immediately. But common sense prevailed. What the hell! He was dead sure Harrison hadn't recognized him. And even if he had, the man was hardly likely, in view of the circumstances, to tell his wife anything.

No, Rick thought, feeling the sun beat against his face, his luck was holding. He was absolutely safe.

It was Rosita's day off and Liz was alone. She had come home early, planning to pamper herself. Filling a steaming tub, she added bath oil and settled in for a long soak.

There had been little time to think in the last few weeks. She had hurried through them at a frantic pace, setting up Maryann's retrospective while planning the Kant Gallery's 89/90 season.

Now, relaxing in the perfumed water, Liz reviewed the season that had just ended. Thanks to Roman De Silva's coming to the gallery, and her staff's outstanding performance, the gallery would record the most prosperous six months in its history. But the cost had been high. Alan was gone from her life. He seemed permanently settled in Santa Fe and one of these days she would undoubtedly hear that he and Celia were getting married.

Then there was Maryann. To have been so brutally raped, and then cast aside like a piece of garbage, went beyond tragedy into the realm of pure horror. If anyone deserved to die, it was Reginald Quincy. How ironic that his accomplice should also be his killer.

If the season had one shining virtue, one person she could think about with unqualified satisfaction, it was Rick. Despite their personal problems, he had performed above and beyond the call of duty again and again. The trust she had in him was the single most important factor in her decision to finally open that New York gallery.

336

How good it would be to get away, she thought as the doorbell rang. "Go away," she muttered, sinking deeper into the tub.

She wasn't expecting company and wasn't in the mood to deal with anyone. But her unexpected caller didn't give up. Whoever it was rang again and again.

"Damn," she muttered, rising from the tub and pulling on a floor-length terry robe.

Her bare feet left a wet trail on the floor as she padded down the long hall. Thoroughly annoyed, she scowled and yanked the door open.

Howard and Skip Lundgren stood there. The look of dismay on their faces, when they took in her dishabille, was mirrored by the expression on Liz's as she noted that Howard was in black tie while Skip wore an Ungaro that Liz had contemplated buying.

"What are you doing here?" she gasped.

Blushing scarlet, Howard turned to his wife. "We do have the right day, don't we? Damn it, Skip, this is April 22 isn't it?"

"Of course it is!" Skip declared.

"Right day? What are you talking about?" Liz asked, automatically ushering them into the house.

"We're here to pick up our Longchase." Skip pouted as she surveyed the dark, empty entrance. "Rick said you were having a cocktail party for all the buyers. Where is everybody?"

"Cocktail party? Buyers?" The Lundgrens were good clients, but they were taxing her patience.

"There must be some misunderstanding," Lundgren muttered, trying – unsuccessfully – not to stare at Liz's cleavage.

She clutched her robe closer and led them to a conversational grouping in a corner of the living room. "I think you'd better tell me what this is all about."

"I hardly know where to begin." Lundgren's voice sounded overly loud in the quiet room.

"At the beginning," Liz prompted.

He pulled out a handkerchief and mopped his brow. "About six weeks ago Rick Mason called us in New York, with a fantastic opportunity. He told us the Longchase paintings slated for the Guggenheim, the twenty-seven you and Alan owned between the two of you, were for sale. Rick guaranteed the paintings would double in value after being exhibited in the museum. Of course we were immediately intrigued."

"Why didn't you call me after talking to Rick?"

"He swore us to secrecy. He said you didn't want your clients and friends to accuse you of favouritism when it came to choosing the buyers, that you had asked him to take on that responsibility. Considering the investment potential, and the fact that there were only so many paintings, it made perfect sense to us."

"He said you wanted it to be a complete surprise when you learned who the buyers were." Skip chimed in.

Surprise didn't begin to describe it, Liz thought. Panic, bewilderment, and anger barely did justice to what she felt.

Just then Skip jumped up and walked to a painting on the far wall. "This is the one we chose from the slides Rick sent," she said, indicating a superb canvas of a Ghan dancer.

"How much did you pay for it?" Liz's throat felt painfully dry.

"Seventy thousand dollars," Lundgren offered, "and we believed it was a bargain at that. Mason told me to make the cheque out to the Cochise Memorial Art Fund. He said you and Longchase would use the money to build an art school on the reservation, and I could deduct the entire purchase price from my taxes because the fund was non profit."

Liz shuddered. How easily Rick had taken them in. But, she reflected, he had taken her in just as easily.

Before she could ask any more questions the doorbell

rang again. This time she opened it to see another pair of familiar faces, the Almquists from Chicago.

"What's this? A costume party?" Almquist blustered, looking at Liz.

"I wasn't expecting anyone," she replied, struggling to stay calm. Her nice quiet evening had turned into a waking nightmare.

"Aren't you going to invitie us in?" Almquist asked, taking his wife's arm and barging past Liz. Seeing Lundgren in the living room he shouted, "Howard, what the hell is going on?"

Liz hurried after them.

"It's quite a story," Lundgren said, rising to greet the newcomers, "and not a very pleasant one."

By five thirty, twenty-seven eager couples had arrived, ready to celebrate. Elegantly-dressed, they wandered through the house eyeing Liz's Longchase collection. Several of them, seeing the painting they had purchased from Rick, declared "That's mine," and simply took it down from its place on the wall as if defying Liz to do something about it.

One woman, her face red with anger when she didn't see the canvas she had bought, shook her diamond be-ringed finger in Liz's face and shouted, "What the hell are you going to do? I want some goddamn action, and I want it now."

A swelling chorus of "Me toos," reverberated through the room.

As the unexpected gathering built its own ugly momentum, Liz left the room to telephone Rosita. The housekeeper showed up quickly with a niece and nephew in two. While Rosita and her niece began preparing hors d'oeuvres in the kitchen, and the nephew tended the well-stocked bar in the den, Liz was finally able to excuse herself to dress. Retreating to her room, she sagged onto her bed.

She knew she ought to be making plans to deal with

339

the disaster, but despair welled in her mind. Rick had pulled the art scam of the decade, maybe of the century. It had been brilliantly planned, carefully executed. He had walked away with two million dollars. She doubted there was any hope of tracing the money, let alone getting it back. Rick was too clever not to have found a way to launder it. Somehow, she would have to pay it all back, every penny. But money wasn't the main issue.

Integrity was. Her reputation was at stake.

She'd been lucky with the gallery from the start. Sure, she had worked hard. But all the hard work in the world wasn't as important as simply being fortunate enough to be in the right place at the right time. Scottsdale and south-western art had come into their own in the years since the gallery opened. Thanks to her involvement with artists like Longchase, Harrison, and De Silva, Liz had developed a name for being a ground-breaking, far-sighted dealer.

Tonight, the time had come to pay her dues.

Think, she ordered herself, as she began pulling clothes from her closet. There was no way she could ask Alan to pay for Rick's sins. If she could help it, Alan would never know what had happened.

When she walked into the living room fifteen minutes later, she knew what she had to do and how to do it. Resolve stiffened her spine as she began speaking in an authoritative, steady voice.

"As most of you already know," she began, confronting her hostile audience, "I am as dismayed as any of you by what has happened. Although I knew nothing of Mr Mason's plan, I accept full responsibility for his actions. I intend to pay every penny back."

At first a satisfied sigh rippled through the crowd. But Howard Lundgren spoke up. "I don't want your ⸻ said. "I want my painting. My wife has a ⸻d for it in our living room and I've told my friends about buying it. If I don't get that painting I'll be a laughing stock."

"Those of you who bought canvasses in my personal collection can take your paintings home tonight," she said. But her words were lost in an angry tumult.

"Where the hell is Longchase?" someone shouted. "Does he know what's going on – or is he in this thing with Mason?"

"I never trusted that Indian," someone else announced to no one in particular. "He really acted peculiar the night of the tenth anniversary show, and he hasn't been around town for months. What's he trying to hide? Why isn't he here right now?"

Liz had to raise her voice to be heard. "I'm sure he'd be here if he knew what happened."

"That won't wash," an irate collector interrupted. "How do we know Longchase didn't put Mason up to the whole thing? If you ask me, Longchase and Mason split the money and skipped town."

"Let's call the police," Wilma Almquist shrilled.

Liz knew the time had come to play her best card. First she gave Wilma a withering look that quietened her. Into the ensuing silence, Liz said, "My first thought, when the Lundgrens told me what had happened, was to call the police immediately. But," she paused, letting the *but* sink into their minds, "the only reason to call the police would be to charge Rick with his crime – to have him found, arrested, and brought to trial."

A chorus of "Amens," greeted that statement.

Liz ignored them.

"While having Rick arrested, assuming the police find him, would be gratifying, I don't think it would be wise."

To her satisfaction, the gathering quieted again. Everyone was giving her their full attention. "Each of you has worked hard to achieve a high standing in your respective communities." Again, she waited, watching her clients nod in agreement. Vanity and pride were their joint weaknesses, the weapons she would use to insure their cooperation.

"If you publicly brand yourselves as victims of this scam, every con man in the country will consider you fair game. Worse still, you'll be a laughing stock among your friends and business associates. I wouldn't want that to happen to any of you. And I'm quite certain you wouldn't want it either."

She ignored the low rumble of accord. "I'm sure the tabloids would have a wonderful time with the story. But, if you still want me to call the police I'll be only too happy to oblige. After all, it would save me a great deal of money."

Clenching her jaws in determination, she started for the phone. If no one stopped her she would have to make good her threat. Time seemed to pass in slow motion while she drew closer, one fateful step at a time. Blindly, she picked up the receiver and held it to her ear. She reached out, her index finger poised to dial when Howard Lundgren leapt to his feet and raced to her side.

"What the hell do you think you're doing?" he demanded. "Do you want to ruin all of us?"

Almquist joined them and wrenched the instrument from Liz's hand so forcefully that he twisted her wrist. But she ignored the pain. She had won!

"I agree with everything you've said so far. We've got to keep this thing from going public," Almquist loudly proclaimed as if it had been his idea. "But what about Longchase? You haven't convinced me he isn't in on the deal."

Liz whirled to confront him, frustration thinning the slender thread of her control. "What would it take to prove Alan is as much an innocent victim as you are?"

"I'd believe it if I heard it from Mason," he said.

"Would you settle for a letter in Rick's own hand," she bluffed, "saying Alan had nothing to do with any of this?"

342

To her horror, Almquist called her bluff. "Yes. That would do nicely," he said.

"Then I'll find Rick Mason and get a written confession," Liz responded with a confidence she didn't feel.

An hour later an accord had been reached. The Longchase paintings in her possession would be given to the individuals who had paid for them. Those who bought paintings in Alan's private collection would take her post-dated cheques. In addition, they would be given first choice of future Longchase work at a twenty per cent discount, which Liz and the gallery rather than Alan, would absorb.

After the details had been settled, she logged out the paintings and then sat down with her cheque book and began writing. Thank God she still had the half a million dollars she had borrowed. In addition, she would have to use up all her other financial resources.

The worst moment of all came when Almquist told her he'd paid one hundred and fifty thousand dollars for the nude painting in her bedroom. "I want to see it . . . now," he said in a tone that brooked no argument.

"I'll pay twice what you gave Rick for it," she replied, suspecting she would have to take out a second mortgage on her house to make good on the offer.

Almquist smirked. "I'm not going to agree to anything, until I see the painting."

"Follow me," she said, getting to her feet. Although the effort to carry herself proudly cost her dearly, Liz led the way into her bedroom and flicked on the lights.

Almquist's expression never changed as he looked at the painting. Clearing his throat, he finally said, "Make it four hundred thousand and you've got a deal."

Although there would now be no question that she would have to take out a second mortgage, Liz returned to the living room, wrote the cheque and handed it over with a smile. "By the way," she said, watching Almquist stuff the cheque in his wallet, "I don't ever want to see you in my gallery again. Do we understand each other?"

Almquist smiled. "Now, now, Liz. You've just blown a million and a half dollars. You're going to need a good customer like me to help make up your loss. Call me the next time you get something special."

"I'm never going to need a customer like you again," she replied, feeling a small moment of satisfaction as Almquist's grin vanished.

By nine the house was quiet. Rosita's niece and nephew had helped clean up and then gone home. Liz and Rosita sat in the kitchen, having a cup of hot tea.

"I can't believe Mr Rick would do something like this." Rosita's lined features betrayed her shock.

"He took me in completely too," Liz replied. "The worst of it is that no matter what I said tonight, a few people still think Alan had something to do with the theft."

"That's ridiculous! There isn't a finer man than Mr Longchase."

"I know it, and you know it." Liz's hands began to shake, forcing her to put down her tea cup.

"*Pobrecita*," Rosita murmured. "*Madre de Dios,* so many troubles. First your mother and now this."

"I'm not worried about myself. I'm concerned about Alan. How in the world will I ever be able to tell him what happened? He'll blame me, and he'll be right. I hired Rick. I trusted him. I gave him access to all my files."

Rosita crossed herself. "I know I shouldn't wish evil on anyone, but Señor Mason – he's an *hombre muy malo.* If you like, I will consult a *bruja* to see what can be done about this man."

For the first time that night, Liz laughed. The idea of a witch sticking pins into a Rick doll was eminently satisfying. "Thanks, Rosita," she said, "but I plan to take care of Mr Mason myself."

344

If I can find him, she silently added. And that was a very big if.

Archer paced up and down in front of the Sky Harbor gate where Louis was due to appear. Determination gave her grey eyes a steely gleam. The next few hours would see her future settled. She no longer shrank from the task. Maryann's death had made her take a long, hard look at where she had been and where she was going.

She could finally face the fact that her marriage to Louis had been motivated as much by rebellion as it had been by love. Once she said her vows she had been determined to have the ideal marriage, to prove her parent's predictions of disaster wrong. But she and Louis had never really been suited to each other. Their needs differed almost as much as their goals. Without realizing it, she'd come to think of marriage as a prison and Louis as her jailer.

Stopping in mid stride, she took a seat and pulled a pack of cigarettes from her bag. When Louis walked through the gate fifteen minutes later, she was stubbing it out.

His home-at-last smile changed to a look of disgust. "When did you start smoking again?" he asked without a word of greeting.

"When Maryann died," she answered levelly, stepping back to look at him.

At Christmas he'd been tired, ill, overworked, and had looked it. She had been expecting him to look even worse today. But the man who stood in front of her wasn't an exhausted, over-stressed executive. This Louis had a golden tan. Colour flushed his cheeks, and the grey that had so gracefully adorned his temples was gone. He's touching up his hair, she realized, thunderstruck. Louis glowed with health, like a man who had been on a vacation rather than a soldier returning from the corporate wars.

"You look wonderful," she said sincerely.

"You look pretty terrific too, except for that damn cigarette. I thought we agreed to give them up years ago."

"You agreed. Not me. But let's not fight about it your first five minutes home." So far they hadn't embraced. Realizing she didn't care filled her with an unanticipated sense of loss.

"We've got a few minutes before I can get my luggage," he said. "Why don't we have a drink?"

"Fine with me." In fact, it was more than fine. She'd been about to suggest it herself.

"We need to talk," he said earnestly, taking her arm.

She nodded. The things she had to say clamoured for expression, but it was only after they were seated in a booth in the airport's cocktail lounge that she began. "I hate to welcome you home this way, but there's something I have to tell you."

"There's something I have to tell you too," he said, studying the surface of the table as if it were the Rosetta Stone, "but you go first."

She had rehearsed what she planned to say so many times that she thought saying it would be easy. Now she realized it was going to be the hardest thing she'd ever done. "I wish I could think of some way . . ."

A frown knit his forehead. "You're not sick, are you?" he interrupted, "and the boys, they're fine?"

"It's nothing like that." She hesitated. "It's just that . . . well . . . we haven't been close for a long time." Seeing that he intended to interrupt her again, she hushed him with a gesture. "I know you said you wanted to work on our marriage when you got home. But I don't think there is enough of our marriage left to make it worth working on. I don't know how else to say this except to just say it. I want a divorce. I've fallen in love with someone else."

There. It was finally out.

She had been watching Louis carefully to see how he would react. His worried frown was replaced, first by a look of curiosity, and then by speculation.

"It's De Silva, isn't it?"

She nodded, wondering how in the world he knew.

346

She and Roman had been so circumspect on New Year's Eve.

"Well, I'll be damned!" he exclaimed.

She would never forget what he did next.

Louis began to smile. Then he chuckled and the chuckle escalated into a full-blown belly laugh. "Oh, my God," he chortled, unable to control his booming voice, "oh, my god. The four of us double-dated."

She expected anger, recriminations, anything but hysteria.

He took a large swallow of his V.O., sputtering in the glass as a new wave of hilarity swept over him. "To think I've been worried sick about how to tell you I wanted a divorce – and you beat me to the punch. Oh, Archer, you've always been one step ahead of me."

"Then you're not angry?"

"Angry? Hell, I'm thrilled." He finished his drink and signalled for a refill. "This calls for a little celebration."

Archer knew it was unreasonable, but she found herself considering physical violence. Punching Louis in the nose would do nicely for a start. It wasn't supposed to be happening this way. Her imagination had conjured up a scene out of Tennessee Williams, something seething with raw emotion, and Louis was giving her Laurel and Hardy instead. "So you think my wanting a divorce is a reason to celebrate?"

Louis chuckled again. "Archer, I've been half out of my mind for the last three months, trying to figure out how to tell you I wanted out of our marriage, that I'd fallen in love with someone else."

"Stacy!" Archer declared. She'd been so consumed by her relationship with Roman, and then so devastated by Maryann's death, that she put Stacy Howard completely out of her mind. "Are you in love with your secretary?"

"Yes."

"We sound like a soap opera. Maryann tried to tell

347

me you were having an affair with Stacy, but I refused to believe it."

"And Stacy tried to tell me you were having one with De Silva, but I refused to believe her."

"How long have you two been involved?"

"A couple of months. It started after we arrived in Guadalajara in January. We were having dinner and drinks one night and . . . oh, hell. You don't want to know the details."

He was right. She didn't. "Are you happy?" she asked.

"I am now." Louis sighed heavily. "I didn't want to hurt you. It's been eating away at me, the thought of making you unhappy. In fact, when I got off the plane I still wasn't sure I could go through with asking for a divorce, especially after the promises I made at Christmas."

"You're sure you're not angry?"

His eyes seemed to focus inward as he pondered her question. "I'm a man, Archer, so yes, a part of me is angry. You're still my wife and thinking about you making love to some other guy, well, it isn't easy."

At that moment she knew how much she still cared about him and their marriage, how much of her past she would be giving up. "I feel the same way when I think about you and Stacy." She shook her head sadly. "Why did it have to end this way?"

"I've asked myself the same question."

"Did you come up with any answers?" She pulled a cigarette from her purse, certain that this time he wouldn't object.

"Sort of. Or I should say, Stacy did. I'm not a religious man as you know, but Stacy is a real church-goer."

A regular little saint, Archer thought, giving in to a moment of pure venom.

"Anyway, she was reading something from the Bible the other day and it really hit home – something about a season for all things, a time to reap and a time to sow. I wish I could remember it exactly."

Archer groaned.

"The way I see it," Louis continued, "you and I had our season, our time in the sun. But it's time to move on. Life doesn't stand still. We had something pretty wonderful for a while, but it's gone now."

"You make it sound so simple. How about regret? Don't you have any?" She looked into his calm hazel eyes. If they were truly the windows of the soul, his must be in pretty good shape because he gazed back at her serenely.

"I wouldn't be human if I didn't have regrets," he said. "I'm going to miss you and the life we had. And I'm worried about how this will affect my permanent appointment as CEO of World Business Electronics."

"Oh, Louis. You and that damn company!"

"You've never understood how much it means to me."

"And you never understood how much art means to me," she couldn't resist saying. "I guess, considering how little we have in common, the miracle is that we stayed together as long as we did."

He finished his drink. "The big question is where do we go from here?"

"Are you concerned about how our sons will take the news?"

"We did a good job raising them. That's one thing I'm very proud of. They're fine young men and I'm sure they'll handle it well." He checked his watch. "I imagine my luggage was ready and waiting some time ago."

"So that brings us back to where do we go from here? Do you want to stay at the house tonight?"

"Stacy is expecting me. And I suppose you and Roman have plans as well."

Her eyes brimmed as relief, gratitude, regret, and an echo of the affection they'd once shared threatened to overwhelm her. "I'm going to miss you. I feel as if we're admitting that the last twenty years were a mistake."

Leaning forward, Louis took her chin in his hand, the familiar gesture that always indicated his utter sincerity.

"Don't ever say that. We had a good run and we gave it our best shot. I hope we can stay friends, see each other from time to time. No matter what went wrong between us, we have two wonderful sons." He paused. "I want you to have the house."

She tried to say something but he covered her mouth with his hand.

"No! Don't start objecting, damn it. I know you don't need my help financially – that's always been a part of your problem – but I worked like a dog to give you the things your father gave you. I want you to have the house. In fact, I insist on it. My lawyer will get in touch with yours and work out the details."

Reaching in his pocket, he pulled out a twenty-dollar bill and tossed it on the table. "Before I go, there's something else I should tell you. After I finished up in Guadalajara, I took Stacy to Las Brisas in Acapulco so we could do a little brain-storming about the future. Rick Mason was staying there too, in one of the private villas. I imagine he'll tell you all about seeing me and Stacy when he gets back. But I wanted you to hear it from me first."

She would always remember her response. "Are you sure it was Rick? Liz said he took a week off to visit his mother in California."

Nodding emphatically, Louis got to his feet. "Well, I guess this is it," he said, reassembling his face into its customary businessman's mould. And then he added, as if he were concluding a business meeting, "I'm glad we had such a frank exchange."

He looked at her, seeming to search for some way to say goodbye. She thought she saw a sheen of moisture in his eyes before he turned on his heel and strode away.

It was ten at night when she pulled up in her own drive. She had been planning to see Roman but, after parking the car and entering the quiet house, she realized she wasn't ready. A flood of memories, each more poignant than the last, crowded her mind as she warmed a cup of coffee. Staring at the breakfast table, she was absorbed by visions of the past – the boys and Louis cheerfully arguing the virtues of Harleys versus Hondas, racket ball versus squash, the slant six versus the rotary engine, Rossignol versus Volkl skis. During her sons' growing up years, it often seemed as if the males in her home spoke a foreign language, one that was genetically transmitted through the Y chromosome.

Looking out across the now-dark pool, she was drawn even deeper into the past. The image of two young men racing each other in a water-churning freestyle while Louis clocked their prowess, flickered at the back of her eyes like a silent movie. That day they'd come trooping back in the house, each boy claiming victory, smelling of chlorine and sunshine and young manhood, their father's arms proudly circling their still damp shoulders. They had been a unit, bound by ties she thought would never be broken. It seemed incomprehensible that those bonds had been sundered in one brief conversation.

Upstairs, her bedroom vibrated with ghosts. Most of Louis's clothes still hung in the closet, shoes neatly racked, ties a burst of colour against the drabber shades of his suits. The closet smelled of him, and the odour drifted into the bedroom every time she opened the door. She wanted the divorce, had carefully soul-searched her way to that conclusion, and yet the raw wound of decision hurt more with every beat of her heart.

Not until the grandfather clock in the hall struck midnight had the sharpest edges of her loss been dulled. Finally, dry-eyed, she took off her wedding ring for the last time and put it carefully away.

22

APRIL 23, 1989

Liz sat in the breakfast room finishing her coffee and trying to concentrate on the *Arizona Republic*'s business section. The good news was the stock market had gained twenty points yesterday. The bad news, she reminded herself with gallow's humour, was that after this morning she wouldn't have any stocks to worry about. Or a Camelback estate either unless she was very, very lucky next season.

She could hear Rosita moving around in the kitchen, sighing, "Ay, Ay, Ay."

Ay, ay, ay, indeed, Liz thought. It was going to be a long, hard day. She expected to spend part of the morning with her banker, arranging for a second mortgage on the house. Then she would go on to her stockbroker's office to sell the rest of her holdings. By noon she should have sufficient funds coming to cover all the postdated cheques she had written last night. With those tasks complete, she would go to the gallery, tell her staff Rick wouldn't be returning, and allocate some of his responsibilities.

Afterwards she planned to stop by at his apartment, bribing the manager if that was the only way she could get in. With luck – ah, there she went again, hoping for luck although she hadn't had much of that precious commodity lately – she would uncover some clue as to Rick's present whereabouts.

Liz hadn't slept at all and she refused Rosita's offer of breakfast. She was running on pure adrenaline as she left the house. Getting the second mortgage, even with her sterling credit, proved to be a humiliating experience. By the time she left her broker's office after disposing of all her stocks and bonds, often at a loss, her personal fortune was decimated and she was deeply in debt.

Financially, she would be starting over. And a nagging voice at the back of her mind reminded her she wasn't twenty anymore. She couldn't be sure she still had the drive, let alone the desire to rebuild her fortune. There would be no new gallery in New York this year or the next. But, the same voice reminded her, she didn't have Rick to run the one in Scottsdale either.

After briefing her staff she retreated to her office, stopping to pick up Rick's file on her way. Reading it over, she could hardly believe that the Rick Mason described in half a dozen glowing references could be the conniving thief who had pulled off a major art theft.

He had given his mother's name as his next of kin, to be contacted in an emergency. Now, Liz sat at her desk, impatiently punching in the Beverly Hills number. The phone rang several times before someone answered.

"Hello," Liz said. "Is Mrs Mason there?"

"Why do you want to talk to her?"

"This is her son's employer – Liz Kant. I'm trying to reach him."

After a long pause the voice replied, "This is Annabelle Mason. I haven't heard from my son for a couple of months. But if you do get hold of him, tell him I said he's as big a son-of-a-bitch as his father."

Realizing that further conversation with Annabelle Mason would be futile, Liz wasted no time saying goodbye. Next on her agenda was her proposed search of Rick's apartment. She was just getting to her feet when the intercom buzzed.

"Archer Harrison is here to see you," one of the sales girls said. "I told her you didn't want to be disturbed, but she's insistent."

Not another problem, Liz thought wearily. But the Archer Harrison who walked into the office was a far cry from the despondent woman Liz had seen at Maryann's funeral. This Archer had a spring in her step and a determined gleam in her eye.

"I don't mean to be rude," Archer said, refusing to sit down, "but I don't have time for small talk."

"Neither do I," Liz replied gratefully. "What's on your mind?"

"If there's one thing I've learned from the last few months, it's to listen to my intuition." Archer had a far-away look in her eyes and Liz suspected she was thinking of Maryann.

"My intuition tells me I know something that could be very important to you," Archer continued. "My husband just return from Acapulco. While he stayed at Las Brisas . . ." Archer looked askance at Liz. "You do know Las Brisas?"

Liz nodded yes.

"While Louis was there, he saw Rick."

Liz's pulse quickened. "Would you run that by me again?"

"Since you seem to think Rick is in California, I had the feeling his being at Las Brisas was something you'd want to know."

Las Brisas! So that's where the bastard is, Liz exulted. "You're right. It is important. In fact you've just done me an enormous favour. When we both have more time I'll tell you all about it."

Archer made her exit before Liz had the opportunity to thank her properly.

Feeling as if she'd been granted a reprieve, a chance to redeem herself, Liz rushed to her desk and dialled her travel agent, booking a late afternoon flight to Acapulco and a room at Las Brisas. Then she telephoned Hank Begay.

To her relief, he answered on the first ring.

"I have to see you right away," she said. "It's important."

"Is something wrong?"

"Yes. But it's a long story. Make it as fast as you can."

Compelled by the urgency in Liz's voice, Hank broke the speed limit all the way from Pinnacle Peak to Scottsdale. He hurried into Liz's office a bare twenty minutes after she summoned him.

"What's up?" he asked, closing the door.

"Thanks for getting here so quickly. You had better sit down. This is going to take some time."

When he was comfortable, she launched into the story of Rick's theft, starting with the Lundgrens' unexpected appearance at her home the night before and ending with Archer's timely revelation.

Hank resisted the urge to interrupt, to ask for clarification, and just concentrated on what she was saying, trying to sort out the consequences to her and the gallery, to Alan and his future.

"So you see," she concluded, "I need someone to run the gallery while I go to Acapulco."

"You can't deal with Mason by yourself. It's too dangerous," Hank warned, his fists bunching. If he could get his hands on Mason, he'd give the bastard something to think about.

"I'm not afraid," Liz said.

"Have you figured out what you're going to do once you get down there?"

"I haven't had time to think about it."

"Why don't you just go to the police with your story? I'm sure they could have Mason extradited."

"I promised my clients I wouldn't. They want to protect their reputations, and I intend to do everything in my power to protect Alan's."

Hank shook his head. He thought he knew Liz by

now, but she was still capable of surprising him. "After everything that's happened, he still means that much to you?"

"That much – and more," Liz admitted. "No matter what he thinks of me, I never meant to hurt him."

Hank pursed his lips, releasing an audible stream of air through them. "How much does Alan know?"

For the first time, Liz averted her eyes. "Nothing. As far as I'm concerned, he never needs to."

"I'll do whatever you say. But Liz, I wish you'd reconsider going to Mexico."

"I can't. One way or another, I've got to get Rick's confession."

She made it sound as if it were the simplest thing in the world, as if all she had to do was ask Rick nicely. Hank knew it wouldn't happen that way. Rick wasn't going to give Liz a letter exonerating Alan, any more than he'd give back one penny of the stolen money. She was going off on a wild goose chase. But Hank recognized that he was powerless to stop her. Being Liz, she wouldn't be able to live with herself unless she tried. Damn all stubborn, proud people.

"Don't worry about things here. I'll run the gallery while you're gone. When do you want me to start?"

"Now," she said, picking up her bag. "I've got a five o'clock flight to Acapulco, and there a few things I need to do before I leave."

"Then get out of here." He tried for a reassuring smile, although he could barely control his impatience. Like Liz, he had no time to waste.

"I don't know how to thank you."

"Just come back in one piece."

Pausing in mid stride, she turned back and hugged him hard.

"Be careful down there," he admonished. As soon as he heard her retreating footsteps, he hurried to the desk and dialled a Santa Fe number.

356

"What's up?" Alan asked, after they exchanged greetings.

"Sit down, Amigo," Hank replied. "This is going to take a while." Slowly, carefully, measuring each word for its potential impact, he revealed what Liz had told him. "I don't think Liz should go to Acapulco by herself," he concluded.

"If you're so concerned, why didn't you go with her?"

"I offered. But she asked me to stay here and run the gallery."

"Liz made her bed." Alan's voice was cold. "Now she can lie in it."

"I think you'll change your mind after you hear the entire story."

"Don't tell me there's more." Alan couldn't have sounded more sceptical.

"A great deal more." Hank rubbed his forehead thoughtfully. The time had come to break his promise to Liz.

Roman was outside waiting when Archer drove up. The sun, flaring over his shoulder, cast a nimbus around his silver hair. He looked, she thought, like an archangel. But his welcoming kiss was far from saintly.

"Why didn't you want to see me last night?" he asked, finally letting her go. "I hated settling for a phone call."

"I needed to think and as you've just proven, I can't think clearly around you."

"I'm still having a hard time believing Louis was so agreeable when you asked for the divorce. In his shoes, I wouldn't have let you go without one hell of a fight."

"Actually he was quite happy," she replied, following Roman inside.

The house smelled of turpentine, linseed oil, and Mexican food. "You're making lunch?" she asked, suddenly realizing she hadn't eaten since breakfast the previous morning.

"In case you didn't realize it, I've been going half crazy, waiting to see you. I had to do something to keep busy, so I was trying to recreate The Shed's enchiladas."

He stopped in his tracks and their eyes caught. His glance held an arresting blend of anxiety and barely restrained libido. She could see desire in them, the primal male urge to take her to bed and brand her as his own.

"I've been waiting for this day for months," he said, pulling her down on the sofa beside him.

"I haven't been very fair to you, have I?"

"All's fair in love and war," he answered with a wry grin, "and I guess this has been a little bit of both. Up until today I was willing to let you call the shots. Now it's my turn." He paused long enough to take something from his shirt pocket. It was an antique ruby ring. The stone was so deep a red that it seemed the colour of life itself.

"My mother gave this ring to me before she died," he said, holding it out to Archer. "She wanted me to give it to the woman I loved. At the time I was certain I'd never fall in love again so I put it away. I want you to have it."

She knew he was telling her, without actually saying the words, that the ring had never belonged to his wife, that it came untouched by memories of his past.

"Please try it on," he urged.

She shook her head, tears blurring her vision. Somehow she had to make Roman understand the decision she had made in the small hours of the morning. "I wish I could wrap myself up in a neat package, tie it with a ribbon and give myself to you. There is a big part of me that wants to say I'll marry you as soon as my divorce is final. But I can't. Not yet. I went from my father's house to my husband's without taking the time to get to know myself. I won't make that mistake again."

He continued holding the ring in his open palm. "I want you to have it. But you don't have to think of it as an engagement ring." He grinned suddenly. "We're too old for all that nonsense anyway."

Knuckling her wet eyes, she managed to nod her agreement. They were too old to go through the rigmarole of a formal engagement, and hopefully too wise and secure in each other's love to need one no matter how many years might pass before they wed. Extending her left hand, so naked without its accustomed wedding band, she said, "Will you put it on?"

He surprised her by taking her right hand and slipping the ring on her third finger. "There. Now for damn sure it's not an engagement ring. It's whatever you and I want it to be. All we have to do, Darlin', is figure out what that is."

She gave a funny little laugh. Roman never failed to surprise her. It was one of the traits that made her love him so much. "It means you love me enough to give it and I love you enough to wear it," she said. "But, Roman, I want to be as honest as possible. I'm not ready to think about getting married yet and the truth is, I can't guarantee I ever will be. Maybe I grew up a little late but I'm just beginning to discover who I am. I have to try just being me for a while. Am I making any sense?"

Roman had been listening intently, giving her a chance to express herself. It was, he suspected, something Louis had never done. "You're making a lot of sense. I know you need a chance to do some exploring, some growing. All I ask is to be by your side while you do it."

Relief washed over her. It was going to be all right. She wouldn't lose him while she searched for herself. "I've been praying you would understand."

"I do, more than you'll ever know." Before taking her in his arms he looked down at the ruby on her finger, an imprimatur that promised their future. She didn't know it yet but she was his. He'd accepted it as a given the first time he saw her in the coffee shop on Santa Fe. And one day she would accept it too.

When Liz arrived in Acapulco at eight that evening, stars dusted the sky and a light breeze caressed her face.

Ignoring the evening's splendour, she hurried to pick up her luggage. As promised, one of Las Brisas' drivers was waiting for her as she emerged from the airport fifteen minutes later.

It had been a long day, the most trying she had known in a lifetime full of trials. But she suspected the worst still lay ahead. It seemed an eternity since the Lundgrens had arrived on her doorstep, yet it was little more than twenty-four hours ago. As the chauffeured pink jeep wound through the lively Acapulco streets, she leaned back and closed her eyes. She felt incredibly weary, a bone-jelling exhaustion that trembled through her arms and legs, leaving her limp.

And she felt alone. She'd carried her burdens so long, burdens placed on her by her birth, by her own fierce ambition. Her shoulders bowed under them as she slumped in the seat. She had done so many things she regretted. But she couldn't go back and undo them. All she could do, she thought as the driver brought her to Las Brisas' entrance, was go forward.

Squaring her shoulders, she stepped from the jeep and swept into the hotel like a queen. A hundred-dollar bill, slipped to the night clerk while she checked in, produced the number of Rick's villa and the information that he was out for the evening. It also guaranteed that she would be notified as soon as he returned.

By ten she was settled in her own villa, pacing the floor as she waited for the desk clerk to ring her. Through the open window she heard music, laughter. The sweet, seductive odour of night-blooming jasmine scented the air. Acapulco beckoned with all the lazy charm of a place where *mañana* was a way of life.

But she stayed by the phone. Facing Rick was one thing she wouldn't put off. She planned to do it tonight.

23

APRIL 23, 1989

Having made a diligent round of Acapulco's "in" night-spots, Rick returned to his villa after midnight. His brain was inflamed by alcohol, his libido drowned by too many offers of easy sex. All night long he'd been deluged by propositions from attractive, young, single American women – executive secretaries, junior VPs from banks or advertising firms, attorneys, teachers.

They all seemed eager to have the obligatory vacation fling. A few even volunteered the information, as he swayed with them on the dance floor, that they carried their own condoms. His shirt was lipstick-stained from cha-cha'ing, crotch-close, with a series of women whose names and faces blurred in the course of the long evening. He felt like a well-fed man who, when faced with the prospect of eating a six-course banquet, walks away from the table unable to choose a single dish.

Stripping off his shirt, he collapsed into the nearest armchair. This was his fourth evening in Acapulco and it was time to get down to his real reason for being there. Tonight he had been hunting for worthy prey – a woman with money. He had long since realized that wealth and status were a more powerful aphrodisiac than big boobs or a tight cunt. He dreamed of finding some one with "fuck you" money, enough to let him tell people to go to hell without having to worry about the consequences.

Considering his relative youth and his taste for the finer

things, he figured it would take a minimum of ten million dollars to provide sufficient incentive to get him to the altar. But he'd roamed the better hotels and resorts all evening to no avail. Beauty, breeding and money rarely came in a single package. The Liz Kants of the world were few and far between.

Once again, he found himself cursing the lousy karma that had made it impossible to accept her offer of managing the Scottsdale gallery. If only he had delayed a few more days before putting his scam into action, things might have worked out differently. Given enough time, he might have had it all – Liz, the gallery, everything.

Just thinking about it made him want another drink, something potent that would ease him into a dreamless sleep, free of regret. He was on his way to the phone to order room service when he heard a knock at the door. Expecting to find one of the pink-jacketed Las Brisas waiters at his beck and call, he pulled it open – and his heart plummeted in the direction of his crotch. A cold sweat iced his palms.

Liz stood there.

"How did you find me?" he blurted.

She brushed past him. "It was easy."

There was an expression of triumph on her face as she walked into the room. She'd never looked more sure of herself, more beautiful – or more intimidating.

Sweat began to bead his upper lip and his mouth felt dry, as if he'd been chewing cotton balls. Hideously aware of what an over-confident idiot he'd been, he rasped two words. "Louis Harrison?"

She just stood there and stared at him.

"Shit!"

"You're in it up to your eyeballs," she replied, sitting down as if she owned the place, "unless you cooperate with me."

"What the hell do you want?"

"I think that should be obvious."

"If you flew down here to ask me to give the money back, forget it." No way was he going to come out of this without a dime, not after all his hard work.

"Think about it a minute, Rick, and you'll realize you're not in a position to argue. Do you know how many years you'll spend in prison if I report you to the police?" She sounded as confident as a poker player holding a straight flush.

But Rick's fear faded as he realized she had said "if". So she hadn't notified the police yet. Feeling a glimmer of hope, he decided to brazen it out. "I'm not worried, Liz. I worked for you for a long time and I know you better than you realize. Come to think of it, I guess I'd have to say I know you intimately. Calling the police would create a scandal, especially after I told them about us, maybe even hinted you helped me plan the whole thing. That would be the end of you and your precious gallery."

Her eyes flicked away from his. "You don't know me at all, Rick. You never have. I'm prepared to do whatever I must to get what I want. And that includes calling the authorities if you give me no alternative."

"You've got a lot of nerve, coming down here by yourself. Aren't you at all afraid of me?"

"Afraid of you?" Liz laughed dryly. "I don't think violence is your style. You're just a con artist, Rick – not a very good one at that. Besides, there are a number of people who know where I am at this very moment, including one of my Mexican clients who wields a very large stick in this town. If anything happens to me, anything at all, you'll be in a world of trouble. In fact if you even try leaving town before this matter is settled, you'll regret it."

She's bluffing. The certainty came to him as warm and welcome as a well done blow-job. "How did the party go yesterday?" he asked, probing for a weakness in her self-confident façade. "Oooee! I sure wish I could have been there when all those people showed up on your doorstep."

"The evening went very well. You forgot one thing when you planned to ruin me. Those people are my friends."

"I wasn't trying to ruin you. I was just looking out for number one, setting up a nice retirement fund for yours truly."

"I'm not interested in your motives. I came here to strike a deal. In exchange for the money," she paused and examined her perfect manicure, "and a letter clearing Alan Longchase of any part in the theft, I give you my solemn word I will not turn you over to the police."

Rick grinned wolfishly. It was a ridiculous proposal. But now he knew why she was here. To save her precious Indian's reputation. "You're crazy. Why should I do either one?"

"Because the alternative will be very unpleasant."

He had to give her credit. She was one hell of a poker player. He decided to double the stakes. "Be my guest," he said, walking to the phone and holding it out to her.

"Don't push it, Rick."

"Call the police," he taunted, "and I won't just implicate you. I'll tell them we split the money with Longchase."

"That won't save you from going to jail. Be sensible. You can go on with your life and I can go on with mine if you agree to my terms."

"What's that fucking Apache worth to you? A million, two million?"

"You're out of your mind." She stared fixedly out at the patio.

Rick began to smile. "Hell, Liz. You know me well enough to know I won't give you what you want without getting something in return."

She turned to face him, her eyes blazing. "What will it take?"

"First off, you can forget the money."

She nodded tentatively. "I'll take it under consideration. But I want a letter clearing Alan's name, and I won't leave town until I have it."

"What guarantee do I have that you won't take my confession straight to the authorities."

"I give you my word that I won't."

He laughed out loud. "Lady, your word doesn't mean shit to me. But I've got an idea. I've always operated on the theory that anyone can be bought. What's Longchase's good name worth to you?" He didn't give her a chance to answer. "How about going to bed with me for old times' sake? And letting me take a few pictures while we're at it. That way, you show the letter to anyone and I show the pictures."

"You bastard." She erupted from her chair. "You're a miserable excuse for a man."

"You didn't seem to think so a few months ago." He raised his voice in a falsetto mimicry of hers. "Ooh, Rick, you're so gooood. Do it again."

She slapped him – hard.

Now he had her, he thought triumphantly. The ice maiden was melting and he didn't care that fury had started the thaw. He caught her in his arms, pinioning her flailing fists at her side. It was, he realized, the most fun he'd had with a woman since he'd bedded her six months ago. He liked a fighter, and she was a heavy-weight champion when it came to one-on-one combat, in the office or in the sack.

Liz stood still when she realized that her struggles were exciting him.

"I like it better when you fight back," he said.

She pulled free and backed away, seeing the scarlet imprint her hand had made on his cheek. Strangely enough, he looked almost gleeful. Suddenly she realized she wasn't dealing with an adult. Rick was behaving like a hurt, angry child who would carelessly bring the world crashing down around his ears to get his way. His proposition wasn't motivated by sexual desire. He wanted to get even with her for rejecting him. Somehow the knowledge didn't help. In fact it made things worse.

She could have reasoned with an adult. But a hurt child would only respond to his own pain.

"I'll tell you what," he said, stretching lazily. "It's late and I've had a long day. Frankly you look like you could use a little shut-eye. So why don't we both sleep on it. There will be plenty of time *mañana* to strike a bargain. What's the toast they drink to here? *Pesetas, amor,*" he struggled with the unfamiliar Spanish words, "*y tiempo para gustar los.* To money, love and time to enjoy them. Well, Milady, I've got the money and the time. I'm counting on you to supply the *amor.*"

She moved toward the door but he caught her by the arm before she reached it. "Think about it," he said huskily. "We were good together."

She turned to face him. "And you think about this. Unless I get what I want, I'm calling the police."

"No you won't, Liz. You've still got the hots for that fucking Apache, even though he doesn't know you're alive. I don't think you'll do anything to jeopardize his reputation. You might say I'm counting on it." He smiled and blew her a kiss. "*Adios, Señorita.* Sleep well. I want you nice and rested in the morning."

Liz returned to her own villa, furious with herself for the way she'd handled or rather mishandled her meeting with Rick. He hadn't left her any room to manoeuvre. If she wanted that letter she was going to have to accept his proposition. A few hours in his bed, that was all he wanted. It seemed so little. And yet, could she do it? She despised him for suggesting it, and hated herself even more for considering it. But how else could she clear Alan's name? Recalling how she had willingly bedded Rick last October made her skin crawl. Of all her mistakes, it was the worst.

She washed her face and brushed her teeth, pulled a thin, silk gown over her head and went to bed, her mind spinning down a dozen paths as she sought a different solution to her dilemma. Weariness overcame her so quickly that she wasn't even aware of falling asleep, a sleep so profound and deep that she would later recall it as being more like death.

Sometime before dawn an insistent knock tugged her half-awake. She glanced around the dark room, disoriented, her heart pounding. Then it all came back, the disaster that had begun with the Lundgren's arrival on her doorstep. Surely it wasn't morning already. Could that be Rick at the door right now, so sure of himself that he hadn't bothered to wait for sunrise.

"Go away," she shouted, pulling the pillows over her head.

The knock persisted – and persisted.

"Damn you to hell, Rick Mason," she muttered. But she rose from the barely disturbed bed, slipped a peignoir over her shoulders and blinking the sleep from her eyes, opened the door.

Alan Longchase stood in the moonlight. A blood-red leather strap circled his forehead. He wore a breach-clout, leather leggings, beaded moccasins, and a fierce scowl. Two diagonal lines of colour, one red, one white marked his cheekbones. A knife and a braided rope hung from his waist.

Blinking frantically, she whispered, "I must be dreaming."

"Where is Rick Mason?" Alan's voice cracked like a whip.

She looked up at him, her mind racing.

"Where is Mason?" he repeated. "I've come to settle with him."

Her legs felt rubbery and she clung to the door for support. "How did you find me?"

"Hank. Hank told me."

"But he promised," she objected feebly.

"Some promises, Rachel Kantorwitz, are meant to be broken." Alan slipped into the room and shut the door.

The name, Rachel Kantorwitz, riveted Liz. So he knew. She'd been certain he would hate her if he ever learned the truth, despise her for living a lie for so many years. And yet he was here.

He looked at her, his expression unfathomable. "Are you all right?" he asked.

Reaching forward, she touched his arm and felt the solid strength of muscle and bone, the warmth of his flesh. At least he wasn't a dream. She opened her mouth to speak but closed it again. What in the world could she say to bridge the chasm of misunderstanding that divided them? Her eyes grew wider, her mouth dryer, her pulse beat erratically.

"Liz, I know we need to talk – and we will," he said firmly. "But first, I have to deal with Mason. Where is he?"

"In the villa at the top of the hill."

Alan's eyes shone with satisfaction. He moved to leave, but she reached out to stop him. "Give me a minute to dress and I'll go with you."

"No! You've done enough," he commanded. "This is between Mason and me."

Alan had decided how to handle Rick while the jet he'd chartered was taking him to Acapulco. Now he climbed resolutely up the terraced path towards Rick's villa at the pinnacle of the Las Brisas complex.

Leaving Liz behind hadn't been easy. She looked so desirable and vulnerable, fresh from her bed, that the man in him had longed to stay by her side, take her in his arms and hold her for eternity. But his Apache blood demanded a show-down with Rick Mason. Alan couldn't wait to confront Rick and strip him of his power, his manhood. Mason was going to pay dearly for the pain he had caused all of them. Alan knew he would have to control the urge to really hurt him.

A hunter's feral hunger shadowed Alan's eyes as he

slipped over the wall that circled the patio to the rear of Rick's villa. The interior of the building was dark. But moonlight bathed the exterior, revealing a partially-open sliding-glass door. Alan slipped through it and waited, motionless, while his eyes adjusted to shadows. He was in a bedroom. Not eight feet away, Rick sprawled across a king-size bed, his mouth slightly open, sleeping deeply.

Alan moved across the floor, loosening the braided rawhide at his waist.

Rick had been dreaming of running through a green field of money. A smile still cratered his dimples as, half asleep, he tried to turn over and get more comfortable. He must have got twisted in the sheets, he thought, struggling to free himself. Blinking owlishly, he realized the light was on.

What the hell? He remembered turning it off. Still half asleep, he tried to sit up. Shit. It wasn't the bedclothes at all. He was tied hand and foot. Damn Liz. Had she hired a couple goons to try and scare him?

"Wake up, Mason."

Recognition chilled Rick's blood. He knew that voice. Turning his head, he sought its source.

Alan Longchase sat at the foot of the bed. But this was not the beautifully-tuxedoed, civilized Longchase of art show openings. This was fucking Geronimo with a crazed glint in his eyes.

"What the hell are you doing here?" Rick blustered.

The muscles in Alan's jaw stood out in bold relief. "You owe me. I'm here to collect."

Shit, Rick thought, knowing he was in for it. He could deal with Liz. But a wild-eyed, half-naked Apache was another story. "Chill down," Rick implored. "Let's talk."

"There's nothing to talk about."

Rick fought against the bonds, feeling the knotted rawhide bite into his flesh. Damn! Why had he gone to bed buck-naked. "Unless you want to see the inside of a

Mexican jail, you'd better untie me," he threatened, trying to keep his voice steady.

Longchase ignored him. Slipping a knife from the sheath at his waist, he began tossing it from hand to hand as if he had all the time in the world.

For a moment, the flashing blade mesmerized Rick. Christ, the thing looked lethal, a regular pig-sticker.

Without warning, Longchase pivoted and hurled the knife in one lithe movement. With a solid thunk, it landed in the headboard next to Rick's ear. Another inch or two and he would have lost an eye. He opened his mouth to yell.

"Make one sound and you'll be a soprano." Longchase sprang to Rick's side and pulled the knife from the headboard.

Rick bit his lips. He'd always lived by his wits. This wasn't the time to stop. "All right, Longchase, you've made your point," he said. "I'm scared shitless. Does that satisfy you?"

The Indian didn't respond.

"Damn it, Alan," Rick hated the high-pitched sounds he was making, "what the hell do you want from me?"

"All my life, I've tried to live by Anglo rules." The Apache seemed to be speaking to himself. "And what did it get me?" Suddenly, he looked Rick straight in the eye. "You tried to take my woman. When that failed you went after my good name, my power. I've come to take yours."

Rick closed his eyes, a whimper rising in his throat. What the hell did Longchase mean by power? By the time Rick opened his eyes again the tip of the knife was pressed against one of his nipples.

"I could cut you here," Longchase said, "or here," the knife flicked to Rick's belly, "or here." The blade touched his testicles.

"For God's sake, don't do that," Rick sobbed.

"Can you die well, Mason, like an Indian?"

Rick didn't know which terrified him more – the fear

370

that he would shit himself in front of the Indian or that the Indian would castrate him.

"Beg for your life," Longchase whispered. "But softly. If you call out, I'll kill you here and now."

Tears ran down Rick's face. "Please don't cut me," he moaned.

Longchase didn't seem to hear him.

"In the old days," the Indian seemed to be focusing on an inner vision, "punishing you would have been simple. I'd take you into the desert, stake you out and leave you to the animals. Maybe that's still a good idea."

"You're crazy, Man," Rick sobbed, forgetting all about maintaining some semblance of manhood.

Longchase's answering laugh raised the hair on the back of Rick's neck.

"All right. I'm begging you, Man. Put the knife away. I'll do whatever you say. Do you want the money? We can go to the bank in a few hours."

"You Anglos are all alike. All you ever think about is money." Alan moved to Rick's side, placed the point of the knife against Rick's adam's apple and exerted a little upward pressure.

Rick felt his own blood, sticky and warm on his chest. "I swear, I'll do whatever you want. You can have my bank books. I'll sign some blank cheques. You can fill in the amount. I'll write a full confession saying you had nothing to do with the theft. Just don't cut me."

Alan stepped towards Rick. With casual disregard, he slashed the thongs that bound him.

Rick rolled to the side of the bed but then sagged to the floor, his muscles incapable of supporting him.

Alan half dragged, half carried Rick to the desk and propped him in a chair. Then he opened a drawer and took out a pen and a piece of Las Brisas' distinctive stationery.

"Write," he commanded.

Five minutes later, Rick folded his confession and handed it to Alan. "I hope to God you're satisfied."

371

"Not quite. Where are the bank books, the cheques?"

Rick reached for the bottom desk drawer. "In here."

"Sit back." Holding the knife against Rick's chest, Alan opened the drawer. His eyes didn't widen as he read the amount in Rick's Acapulco account, although the number listed was over two million. "Is any of this yours?"

"Two hundred thousand."

"I'll remember. Now sign." Alan put the chequebook down on the desk.

Rick did as he was told. When he had finished, to his dismay, Alan retied his wrists and again pressed the knife against Rick's jugular. "If you make any effort to hang on to the money, I'll hunt you down and kill you."

"I swear man, the money's yours. Just let me go."

Alan seemed to be considering the idea. But then he shook his head from side to side.

"Now what?" Rick sobbed.

"Remember what I said about the old ways, about leaving enemies staked out in the desert?"

Rick nodded dumbly.

"I have decided that the old ways are best," Alan replied, clamping a hand over Rick's mouth and hauling him to his feet.

Liz was frantic. She'd imagined all kinds of catastrophes while Alan was gone. The travelling alarm clock by her bed ticked off the minutes and then the hours as she paced from bedroom to sitting room and back again, expecting the worst.

Alan seemed capable of anything, even murder, when he left. What had he said when she tried to go with him? "You've done enough." What did that mean? Had he come as rescuer or avenger?

She was still pacing when he returned at first light. She met him at the door. "Are you all right?"

"Never better."

372

His words failed to reassure her. A light sweat slicked his chest and the paint on his cheeks had smeared. Bits of brush adhered to his leggings. He looked all savage Apache – except for an incongruous smile. Grinning, he retrieved a bundle of papers from his waistband and handed them over.

"What's this?"

"Read it and see."

She scanned Rick's hand written confession quickly and then opened the bank book. "How did you—"

"Make him give it to me?" Alan interrupted. His smile broadened. "It wasn't very hard. The most important thing to any man, Indian or Anglo, is his pride, his belief in himself and his power. I took those things from Rick. After that, getting the rest was easy."

"Where is Rick now?" she asked, not knowing if she wanted to hear the answer.

"I left him in the desert, tied up."

Liz gasped.

She would never forget Alan's answering chuckle. "He should be able to free himself in a few hours. But I wish I could see him when he walks back into town, stark naked. He's going to have a sunburn in some rather unusual places."

Liz found herself smiling at the ridiculous picture Alan painted. Then, searching his face, she saw it was so full of love that she trembled.

He pulled her into his arms, holding her fast while time slowed and the world became a microcosm with room for only the two of them. His first kiss was a promise, soft and tender, his second raced through her blood, re-awakening her buried desire.

A tingling, effervescent warmth that seemed to begin in the region of her heart coursed through her body to her fingertips and toes. She wanted to give in to her feelings, but she didn't dare. Too often she and Alan had mistaken passion for understanding and kisses for communication.

If they were to have a future, they would have to deal with the past.

"I love you, Alan Longchase," she said, gently pushing him away, "I always have and I always will. But I don't think I ever knew you, at least not the you standing in front of me now. And God knows, I never gave you a chance to know me."

Nodding his agreement, he planted a kiss on her forehead. "We made a mess of things, didn't we?"

Now it was Liz's turn to nod.

"So where do we begin," he asked, guiding her to the sofa.

"With Rachel Kantorwitz," she replied, sitting down beside him. For the next hour Liz spoke of her childhood, working her way through the protective layers she had constructed so carefully over the previous two decades. They came away one by one, painfully, slowly, until her heart, her soul, the inner workings of her mind were laid bare. When she recounted her recent reunion with her dying mother, Liz wept. "So you see," she wiped her eyes, "I was so angry at my father, and so ashamed of myself, that I spent the rest of my life running away from who and what I was. The night you asked me to marry you, I knew I had to tell you the truth. But I was so sure you would reject me if you knew."

Alan reached for her hand and held it tight. "Do you have any idea how frightened I was that night? It took all my courage to propose. When you said no, I was certain you didn't want to marry me because I was an Indian. That was the story of my life before we met."

Liz gave a funny little laugh. "I guess that makes us two of a kind. Is that why you never asked me to meet your family?"

"Partly."

"What's the rest?"

He gave her a crooked smile. "My mother is very

predjudiced against whites. I knew she'd give you a hard time, so I kept putting it off."

"I thought you wanted to keep a part of yourself from me. That was one of my excuses for keeping so much of myself from you. You always seemed so proud of being an Apache, and I was so ashamed of my own past."

"Proud?" His eyes filled with pain. "My father was an alcoholic. We had so little when I was a kid that being dirt poor would have been an improvement. Everything we Longchases have today, we owe to you."

Liz got up and walked to the window. So that was why he had come. Out of gratitude. She wanted and needed so much more.

"What's the matter?" he asked, coming up behind her.

"You don't owe me a thing. I don't want your thanks."

"What *do* you want?" he asked.

For a moment, she almost gave in to the habits of a lifetime. Pride urged her to respond. "Thank you for your help tonight. You can go back to Celia now." Instead, she turned to face him and honestly answered, "I want your love."

He lifted her off her feet, and carried her into the bedroom, his voice husky with need. "You have it – now and forever. I've been wanting to make love to you for hours."

"What are you waiting for?"

Her eyes locked with his and he slid the peignoir from her shoulders. His fingertips traced the curve of her cheek, the line of her neck, leaving fire in their wake.

"God, I want you," he whispered, exposing her breasts to his eyes, lips and tongue.

She reached for him – and the world spun away.

An hour later, Liz emerged from the shower, secure in the knowledge that Alan waited for her on the patio, that from this moment on he would always be there for her as she would for him.

"Breakfast is ready," he called.

"Be out in a minute," she replied.

A pot of fresh-brewed coffee, a bowl of fruit, a platter of pastries and a decanter of juice were on the table when she walked outdoors into a perfect, golden day.

Alan had finished bathing first, and his skin glowed with health. Earlier, a porter had delivered the overnight bag Alan had left in the room he took when he arrived at Las Brisas. Now he wore a pair of tan slacks and a soft cotton shirt. The Apache warrior was gone. But Liz knew she would never forget him.

While Alan poured the coffee, she leaned back, enjoying the beauty of her surroundings for the first time since her own arrival. "I can't believe it's over."

"It isn't," Alan smiled, handing her a cup. "It's just beginning. It's time you and I stopped looking back and started looking ahead. After we eat, I think we ought to go to the bank and see about recovering the money Rick stole."

"Now we're together, money doesn't seem at all important," Liz replied. "But, if you agree, let's use that money to really build an art school on the reservation. And maybe, just maybe, another Alan Longchase will walk through my door someday."

"Lady," he said, "one Alan Longchase is going to be all you can handle. Six months ago, I told you a proper Apache would send an uncle to talk to your father with an offering of horses, when he wanted to get married." He eyed her boldly. "A woman like you should be worth, twenty, maybe twenty-two good horses."

"I'll settle for Odii."

"Then you will marry me?"

"If you still want me after everything that's happened. But, Alan, you're not getting much of a bargain. I can't promise we won't fight again." She smiled. "We seem to be almost as good at that as we are at making love. I'm too old to change. I may have started life as Rachel Kantorwitz, but I'm afraid I've really become Liz Kant."

"Liz Kant is all I've ever known or wanted." His face grew still and solemn. "You aren't getting any prize either. I'm moody as hell. Remember the day we met and you told me how important it would be to paint every day. Sometimes I paint around the clock, and I'm not very good about being interrupted."

"I can deal with that." She smiled impishly. "Considering my present finances, the gallery can use all the work you can turn out. By the way, who is going to be your master dealer?"

"Hank made me promise I'd give the job back to you. All he wants is to move up to Window Rock and marry Eleanor Tsosie."

"Will you sign a new contract?" she teased.

"How about a lifetime agreement?"

She pretended to consider the offer. "I suppose that will have to do."

"Then it's settled," he said, "except for one thing. Have you ever thought about having children?"

"Darling, I'm forty-one years old and I don't exactly see myself changing diapers."

"Other woman your age are having babies," he argued.

"It's more than that. You see, my own childhood was so dreadful. The other kids seemed to take special pleasure in tormenting me because I was different. I wouldn't wish that on anyone else, certainly not my own children."

"I know what you mean. I went through some of the same hell myself." He reached for her hand and she felt his warmth and strength flowing into her. "But our children will be descended from a double line of survivors, people who beat the odds. I can't think of a more remarkable heritage."

The first time she had seen him, so many years before, she remembered wondering what it would take to ignite the fire that smouldered in his eyes. Now she had her answer. It was love – abiding love.

"Come over here and hold me," she said.

He rose in one fluid motion and pulled her into his arms. Before they kissed they stood, beating heart to beating heart. "Forever," Alan said softly. "This time, it's forever."

He pulled her closer, his lips met hers. Liz Kant had finally come home.